The Prisoner of Heaven

Carlos Ruiz Zafón is the author of seven novels, including the international phenomenon *The Shadow of the Wind*, and *The Angel's Game*. His work has been published in more than forty different languages, and honoured with numerous international awards. He divides his time between Barcelona, Spain, and Los Angeles, California.

www.carlosruizzafon.co.uk

Also by Carlos Ruiz Zafón

The Shadow of the Wind
The Angel's Game
The Prince of Mist
The Midnight Palace

The PRISONER *of* HEAVEN

CARLOS RUIZ ZAFÓN

Translated from the Spanish by Lucia Graves

PHOENIX

A PHOENIX PAPERBACK

First published in Great Britain in 2012
by Weidenfeld & Nicolson
This paperback edition published in 2012
by Phoenix,
an imprint of Orion Books Ltd,
Orion House, 5 Upper St Martin's Lane,
London WC2H 9EA

An Hachette UK company

5 7 9 10 8 6 4

First published in Spain as *El Prisionero del Cielo*
by Editorial Planeta, S.A., 2011

A CIP catalogue record for this book
is available from the British Library.

ISBN 978-1-7802-2287-5

Printed and bound in Great Britain by Clays Ltd, St Ives plc

The Orion Publishing Group's policy is to use papers
that are natural, renewable and recyclable products and
made from wood grown in sustainable forests. The logging
and manufacturing processes are expected to conform to
the environmental regulations of the country of origin.

www.orionbooks.co.uk

THE CEMETERY OF FORGOTTEN BOOKS

The Prisoner of Heaven is part of a cycle of novels set in the literary universe of the Cemetery of Forgotten Books of which *The Shadow of the Wind* and *The Angel's Game* are the two first instalments. Although each work within the cycle presents an independent, self-contained tale, they are all connected through characters and storylines, creating thematic and narrative links.

Each individual instalment in the Cemetery of Forgotten Books series can be read in any order, enabling the reader to explore the labyrinth of stories along different paths which, when woven together, lead into the heart of the narrative.

The Prisoner of Heaven

I have always known that one day I would return to these streets to tell the story of the man who lost his soul and his name among the shadows of a Barcelona trapped in a time of ashes and silence. These are pages written in the flames of the city of the damned, words etched in fire on the memory of the one who returned from among the dead with a promise nailed to his heart and a curse upon his head. The curtain rises, the audience falls silent and before the shadow lingering over their destiny descends upon the set, a chorus of pure souls takes the stage with a comedy in their hands and the blessed innocence of those who, believing the third act to be the last, wish to spin a Christmas story – unaware that once the last page is turned, the poison of its words will drag them slowly but inexorably towards the heart of darkness.

Julián Carax
The Prisoner of Heaven
(Éditions de la Lumière, Paris, 1992)

Part One

A Christmas Story

1

Barcelona, December 1957

That year at Christmas time, every morning dawned laced with frost under leaden skies. A bluish hue tinged the city and people walked by, wrapped up to their ears and drawing lines of vapour with their breath in the cold air. Very few stopped to gaze at the shop window of Sempere & Sons; fewer still ventured inside to ask for that lost book that had been waiting for them all their lives and whose sale, poetic fancies aside, would have contributed to shoring up the bookshop's ailing finances.

'I think today will be the day. Today our luck will change,' I proclaimed on the wings of the first coffee of the day, pure optimism in a liquid state.

My father, who had been battling with the ledger since eight o'clock that morning, twiddling his pencil and rubber, looked up from the counter and eyed the procession of elusive clients disappearing down the street.

'May heaven hear you, Daniel, because at this rate, if we don't make up our losses over the Christmas season, we won't even be able to pay the electricity bill in January. We're going to have to do something.'

'Fermín had an idea yesterday,' I offered. 'He thinks it's a brilliant plan that'll save the bookshop from imminent bankruptcy.'

'Lord help us.'

I quoted Fermín, word for word:

'*Perhaps if by chance I was seen arranging the shop window in my underpants, some lady in need of strong literary emotions would be drawn in and inspired to part with a bit of hard cash. According to expert opinion, the future of literature depends on women and as God is my witness the female is yet to be born who can resist the primal allure of this stupendous physique,*' I recited.

I heard my father's pencil fall to the floor behind me and I turned round.

'So saith Fermín,' I added.

I thought my father would smile at Fermín's plea, but when I noticed that he remained silent, I sneaked a glance at him. Not only did Sempere senior not appear to find the suggestion the least bit funny, but he had adopted a pensive expression, as if he were seriously considering it.

'Well, well . . . perhaps Fermín has unexpectedly hit the nail on the head,' he murmured.

I looked at him in disbelief. Maybe the customer drought that had struck in the last few weeks was finally affecting my father's good judgement.

'Don't tell me you're going to allow him to wander around the bookshop in his Y-fronts.'

'No, of course not. It's about the shop window. Now that you've mentioned it, it's given me an idea . . . We may still be in time to save our Christmas after all.'

He disappeared into the back room, then emerged sporting his official winter uniform: the same coat, scarf and hat I remembered him wearing since I was a child. Bea suspected that my father hadn't bought any new clothes since 1942 and everything seemed to indicate that my wife was right. As he slipped on his gloves, my father smiled absently, his eyes twinkling with almost childlike excitement, a look that only momentous tasks managed to bring out in him.

'I'll leave you on your own for a while,' he announced. 'I'm going out to do an errand.'

'May I ask where you're going?'

My father winked at me.

'It's a surprise. You'll see.'

I followed him to the door and saw him set off at a brisk pace towards Puerta del Ángel, one more figure in the grey tide of pedestrians advancing through another long winter of shadows and ashes.

2

Making the most of the fact that I'd been left alone, I decided to turn on the radio and enjoy a bit of music while I reorganised the collections on the shelves to my liking. My father argued that to have the radio on when there were customers in the shop was in bad taste and if I turned it on when Fermín was around, he'd start to hum on the back of any melody, or even worse, given a chance he'd start swaying to what he called 'sensual Caribbean rhythms' and after a few minutes he'd get on my nerves. Taking those practical difficulties into account, I'd come to the conclusion that I should limit my enjoyment of the radio waves to the rare moments when there was nobody else in the shop but me and thousands of books.

That morning, Radio Barcelona was broadcasting a rare recording of a fabulous Louis Armstrong concert – made when the trumpeter and his band had played at the Hotel Windsor Palace on Avenida Diagonal, three Christmases earlier. During the publicity breaks, the presenter insisted on labelling that music as *chass*, with the warning that some of its suggestive syncopations might not be suitable for pious Spanish listeners brought up on the popular *tonadillas* and boleros that ruled the airwaves.

Fermín was in the habit of saying that if Don Isaac Albéniz had been born black, jazz would have been invented in the village of Camprodón, near the Pyrenees. That glorious sound, he said, was one of the precious few true achievements of the twentieth century along with the pointed bras worn by his adored Kim Novak in some of the films we saw at the Fémina Cinema matinees. I wasn't going to argue with that. I let the remainder of the morning drift by between the alchemy of the music and the perfume of books, savouring the satisfaction that comes from a simple task well done.

Fermín had taken the morning off to finalise preparations for his wedding with Bernarda, due to take place at the beginning of February, or so he said. The first time he'd brought up the subject, barely two weeks earlier, we'd all told him he was rushing into it and that too much haste would lead him nowhere fast. My father tried to persuade him to postpone the event for at least two or three months, arguing that weddings were always best in the summer when the weather was good. But Fermín had insisted on sticking to his date, alleging that, being a specimen weathered in the harsh, dry airs of the Extremadura hills, he was prone to break into profuse perspiration during the Mediterranean summer, a semi-tropical affair in his estimation, and didn't deem it appropriate to celebrate his nuptials flashing sweat stains the size of pancakes under his armpits.

I was beginning to think that something odd must be happening to Fermín Romero de Torres – proud standard-bearer of civil resistance against the Holy Mother Church, banks and good manners in that pious 1950s Spain so given to religious services and propaganda newsreels – for him to display such urgency for tying the knot. In his pre-matrimonial zeal he'd even befriended Don Jacobo, the new parish priest at the church of Santa Ana, who was blessed with a relaxed ideology and the manners of a retired boxer. Fermín had infected him with his boundless passion for dominoes and together they staged epic matches at the Bar Admiral on Sundays after mass. Don Jacobo would laugh his head off when my friend asked him, between glasses of fine liqueurs, if he had it from a higher source that nuns actually had thighs, and if that were the case, were they as soft and nibbly as he'd been suspecting since adolescence?

'You'll manage to get that priest excommunicated,' my father scolded him. 'Nuns are not to be looked at, or touched.'

'But the reverend is almost more of a rogue than I am,' Fermín protested. 'If it weren't for the uniform . . .'

I was recalling that conversation and humming to the sound of Maestro Armstrong's trumpet when I heard the soft tinkle of the doorbell and looked up, expecting to see my father returning from his secret mission, or Fermín ready to start the afternoon shift.

'Good morning,' came a deep, broken voice from the doorway.

3

Cast against the light from the street, the silhouette resembled a tree trunk lashed by the wind. The visitor sported a dark, old-fashioned suit and presented a grim figure as he leaned on his walking stick. He took one step forward, limping visibly. The light from the small lamp on the counter revealed a face lined by age and the unmistakable trace of misfortune. The man stared at me for a few moments, sizing me up unhurriedly. He had the cold eyes of a bird of prey, patient and calculating.

'Are you Señor Sempere?'

'I'm Daniel. Señor Sempere is my father, but he's not in right now. Is there anything I can help you with?'

The visitor ignored my question and began to wander around the bookshop examining everything in detail with almost covetous interest. The limp affecting him suggested that the wounds concealed beneath those clothes must have been quite severe.

'Souvenirs from the war,' said the stranger, as if he'd read my thoughts.

I kept my eyes on him, following his inspection tour through the bookshop, suspecting where he was going to drop anchor. Just as I'd imagined, he stopped in front of the ebony and glass cabinet, a relic dating back to the shop's origin in 1888 when Great-grandfather Sempere, then a young man recently arrived from his fortune-seeking adventures in the Americas, had borrowed some money to buy an old glove shop and turn it into a bookshop. That cabinet, crown jewel of the shop, was reserved for the most valuable items.

The visitor drew close enough to the cabinet for his breath to leave a trail on the glass. He pulled out a pair of spectacles, put them on and proceeded to study the contents. His expression made me think of a weasel examining freshly laid eggs in a chicken coop.

'Beautiful piece,' he murmured. 'Looks pricey.'

'A family heirloom. Its value is mostly sentimental,' I replied, feeling uncomfortable at the assessments of that peculiar customer whose gaze seemed bent on costing even the air we were breathing.

After a while he put his spectacles away and spoke in a measured tone.

'I understand that a gentleman, well known for his wit, works for you.'

When I didn't reply immediately, he turned round and threw me a withering look.

'As you can see, I'm on my own. Perhaps, sir, if you would kindly tell me what book you're after, I could try to find you a copy, with pleasure.'

The stranger granted me a smile that was anything but friendly and then nodded.

'I see you have a copy of *The Count of Monte Cristo* in that cabinet.'

He wasn't the first customer to notice the book. I gave him the official sales patter we reserved for such occasions.

'The gentleman has a very good eye. It's a magnificent edition, numbered and with illustrations by Arthur Rackham. It belonged to the private library of an important collector in Madrid. A unique piece, and catalogued.'

The visitor listened without interest, focusing his attention on the consistency of the ebony shelves and making it clear that my words bored him.

'All books look the same to me, but I like the blue on that cover,' he replied in a scornful tone. 'I'll take it.'

Under other circumstances I would have jumped for joy at the thought of being able to sell what was probably the most expensive book in the entire shop, but the thought that it should end up in the hands of that character made my stomach turn. Something told me that if that volume left the bookshop, nobody would ever bother to read even the first paragraph.

'It's a very costly edition. If you like, sir, I can show you other editions of the same work in perfect condition and at much more reasonable prices.'

People with a meagre soul always try to make others feel small too, and the stranger, who could probably conceal his on the head of a pin, gave me his most disdainful look.

'And with blue covers too,' I added.

He ignored the impertinence of my irony.

'No, thank you. This is the one I want. I don't care about the price.'

I agreed reluctantly and walked over to the cabinet. As I pulled out the key and opened the glass door, I could feel the stranger's eyes piercing my back.

'Good things are always under lock and key,' he muttered under his breath.

I took the book and sighed.

'Is the gentleman a collector?'

'I suppose you could call me that. But not of books.'

I turned round with the book in my hand.

'And what do you collect, sir?'

Once again, the stranger ignored my question and stretched a hand out for the book. I had to resist the urge to put the volume back in the cabinet and turn the key. My father would never forgive me if I let such a sale go by when business was so bad.

'The price is three hundred and fifty pesetas,' I said before handing it to him, hoping the figure would make him change his mind.

He nodded without batting an eyelid and pulled out a one-thousand-peseta note from the pocket of a suit that cannot have been worth a *duro*. I wondered whether the note was forged.

'I'm afraid I don't have change for such a large note, sir.'

I would have asked him to wait a moment while I ran down to the nearest bank for change and, at the same time, to make sure it wasn't a fake, but I didn't want to leave him alone in the bookshop.

'Don't worry. It's genuine. Do you know how you can tell?'

The stranger raised the note against the light.

'Look at the watermarks. And these lines. The texture . . .'

'Is the gentleman an expert in forgeries?'

'In this world, everything is a fake, young man. Everything except money.'

He placed the note in my hand and closed my fist over it, patting my knuckles.

'Keep the change for my next visit,' he said. 'On account.'

'It's a lot of money, sir. Six hundred and fifty pesetas . . .'

'Loose change.'

'Let me give you a receipt then.'

'I trust you.'

The stranger examined the book without interest.

'By the way, it's a gift. I'm going to ask you to deliver it in person.'

For a moment, I hesitated.

'We don't normally do deliveries, but in this case we'll be happy to take care of your package, free of charge. May I ask whether the address is in Barcelona itself or . . .?'

'It's right here,' he said.

His icy look seemed to betray years of anger and resentment.

'Would you like to include a dedication, or add a personal note before I wrap the book up, sir?'

The visitor opened the book at the title page with some difficulty. I noticed then that his left hand was artificial, made of painted porcelain. He pulled out a fountain pen and wrote a few words. Then he gave the book back to me and turned to leave. I watched him as he hobbled towards the door.

'Would you be so kind as to give me the name and address where you would like us to deliver the book, sir?' I asked.

'It's all there,' he said, without turning his head.

I opened the book and looked for the page with the inscription the stranger had written out.

For Fermín Romero de Torres,
who came back from among the dead
and holds the key to the future.
13

Then I heard the tinkle of the doorbell and when I looked up, the stranger was gone.

I dashed over to the door and peered out into the street. The visitor was limping away, merging with the silhouettes that moved through the veil of blue mist sweeping up Calle Santa Ana. I was about to call him, but I bit my tongue. The easiest thing would have been to let him go and have done with it, but my instinct and my characteristic lack of prudence got the better of me.

4

I hung the CLOSED sign on the door and locked up, determined to follow the stranger through the crowd. I knew that if my father returned and discovered that I had abandoned my post – on the one occasion when he'd left me alone and bang in the middle of that sales drought – I'd be in serious trouble. But I'd think of a convenient excuse along the way. Better to face my father's temper than be consumed by the anxiety left in me by that sinister character, and not know what was the true intent of his business with Fermín.

A professional bookseller has few opportunities to acquire the fine art of following a suspect in the field without being spotted. Unless a substantial number of his customers are prominent defaulters, such opportunities are only granted to him vicariously by the collection of crime stories and penny dreadfuls on his bookshelves. Clothes maketh not the man, but crime, or its presumption, maketh the detective, especially the amateur sleuth.

While I followed the stranger towards the Ramblas, I recalled the essentials, beginning by leaving a good fifty metres between us, camouflaging myself behind someone larger and always having a quick hideaway ready – a doorway or a shop – in case the subject I was tailing should stop and turn around without warning. When he reached the Ramblas the stranger crossed over to the central boulevard and began to walk down towards the port. The boulevard was festooned with traditional Christmas decorations and more than one shop had decked its window with lights, stars and angels announcing a seasonal bonanza. If the regime's radio said better times were ahead, it must be true.

In those days, Christmas still retained a certain aura of magic and mystery. The powdery light of winter, the hopeful expressions of people who lived among shadows and silences, lent that setting a slight air of promise in which at least children and those who had learned the art of forgetting could still believe.

Perhaps that is why it became increasingly obvious to me that nobody seemed more out of place amid all that Christmas fantasy than the peculiar object of my investigation. He limped slowly, often stopping by one of the bird stalls or flower stands to admire parakeets and roses, as if he'd never before set eyes on one. A couple of times he walked over to the newspaper kiosks that dotted the Ramblas and amused himself glancing at the covers of papers and magazines and idly twirling the postcard carousels. He acted as if he had never been there in his life, like a child or a tourist walking down the Ramblas for the first time – but then children and tourists often display an air of innocence that comes with not knowing one's whereabouts, whereas our man couldn't have looked less innocent even with the blessing of Baby Jesus, whose statue he passed when he reached the Church of Belén.

Then he stopped, apparently entranced by a cockatoo that was eyeballing him from one of the animal stalls opposite the entrance to Calle Puertaferrisa. Approaching the birdcage just as he'd approached the glass cabinet in the bookshop, the stranger started mumbling something to the cockatoo. The bird, a specimen with a large head, the body of a capon and luxurious plumage, survived the stranger's sulphuric breath and applied itself with great relish and concentration to what his visitor was reciting. In case there was any doubt, the bird nodded its head repeatedly and raised its feathery pink crest, visibly excited.

After a few minutes, the stranger, satisfied with his avian exchange, resumed his itinerary. No more than thirty seconds later, as I walked past the bird stall, I noticed that a small hullabaloo had broken out. The shop assistant, plainly embarrassed, was hastily covering the cockatoo's cage with a hood because the bird kept repeating with exemplary elocution the refrain, *Franco, you prick, you can't lift your dick.* I was in no doubt at all about the source of the couplet. The stranger at least displayed a daring sense of humour and audacious political leanings, which in those days were as rare as skirts worn above the knee.

Distracted by the incident, I thought I'd lost sight of him, but soon I glimpsed his hunched figure standing in front of the window of the Bagués jewellery shop. I sidled over to one of the scriveners' booths bordering the entrance to the Palace of La Virreina and observed him carefully. His eyes shone like rubies and the sight of gold and precious stones behind the bulletproof pane seemed to have awoken a lust in him that not even a row of chorus girls from La Criolla in its years of splendour could have aroused.

'A love letter, an application, a request to the distinguished official of your choice, a spontaneous "hope this letter finds you well" for the relatives in the country, young man?'

The scribe whose booth I had adopted as a hiding place was peering out like a father confessor and looked at me expectantly, hoping I'd make use of his services. The poster above the counter read:

OSWALDO DARÍO DE MORTENSSEN

MAN OF LETTERS AND FREE THINKER

Writes love letters, petitions, wills, poems, praises, greetings, pleas, obituaries, hymns, dissertations, applications and all types of compositions in all classic styles and metrics
Ten céntimos per sentence (rhymes are extra)
Special prices for widows, disabled war veterans and minors.

'What say you, young man? A love letter of the sort that makes girls of a courting age wet their petticoats with desire? I'll give you a special price.'

I showed him my wedding ring. Oswaldo, the scribe, shrugged his shoulders, unperturbed.

‘These are modern times,’ he argued. ‘If you knew the number of married men and women who come by my booth . . .’

I read the notice again. There was something familiar about it, which I couldn’t put my finger on.

‘Your name rings a bell . . .’

‘I’ve seen better times. Maybe from back then.’

‘Is it your real name?’

‘*Nom de plume.* An artist’s name needs to match his mission. On my birth certificate I’m Jenaro Rebollo, but with a name like that, who is going to entrust their love letters to me . . .? What do you say to the day’s offer? Are we to prepare a letter of passion and longing?’

‘Some other time.’

The scribe nodded with resignation. He followed my eyes and frowned, intrigued.

‘Watching the lame guy, aren’t you?’ he remarked casually.

‘Do you know him?’ I asked.

‘For about a week now I’ve seen him walk past this place every day and stop right there, by the jeweller’s shop window, where he stares open mouthed as if what was on show were not rings and necklaces but Bella Dorita’s bare derriere,’ he explained.

‘Have you ever spoken to him?’

‘One of my colleagues copied out a letter for him the other day; he’s missing some fingers, you see . . .’

‘Which one of your colleagues was that?’ I asked.

The scribe looked at me doubtfully, fearing the possible loss of a client if he replied.

‘Luisito, the one over there, next to the music store, the one who looks like a seminarist.’

I offered him a few coins in gratitude but he refused them.

‘I make a living with my pen, not with my tongue. There are plenty of the latter already in this courtyard. If you ever find yourself in need of grammatical rescue, you’ll find me here.’

He handed me a card with the same wording as on his poster.

'Monday to Saturday, from eight to eight,' he specified. 'Oswaldo, soldier of the written word, at your service for any epistolary cause.'

I put the card away and thanked him for his help.

'Your bird's flying off.'

I turned and could see that the stranger was moving on again. I hastened after him, following him down the Ramblas as far as the entrance to the Boquería market, where he stopped to gaze at the sight of the stalls and people coming and going, loading or unloading fine delicacies. I saw him limp up to Bar Pinocho and climb on to one of the stools, with difficulty but with aplomb. For the next half-hour the stranger tried to polish off the treats which the youngest in the bar, Juanito, kept serving him, but I had a feeling that he wasn't really up to the challenge. He seemed to be eating more with his eyes, as if when he asked for tapas, which he barely sampled, he was recalling days of healthier appetites. Sometimes the palate does not savour so much as try to remember. Finally, resigned to the vicarious joy of watching others eating and licking their lips, the stranger paid his bill and continued on his voyage until he reached the entrance to Calle Hospital, where the peculiar arrangement of Barcelona's streets had conspired to place one of the great opera houses of the old world next to one of the most squalid red-light districts of the northern hemisphere.

5

At that time of the day the crews of a number of military and merchant ships docked in the port happened to be venturing up the Ramblas to satisfy cravings of various sorts. In view of the demand, the supply had already appeared on the corner: a rota of ladies for rent who looked as if they had clocked up quite a few miles and were ready to offer a very affordable minimum fare. I winced at the sight of tight skirts over varicose veins and purple patches that hurt just to look at them, at wrinkled faces and a general air of last-fare-before-retiring that inspired anything but lust. A sailor must have had to spend many months on the high seas to rise to the bait, I thought, but to my surprise the stranger stopped to flirt with a couple of those ladies of the long-gone springtime, as if he were bantering with the fresh beauties of the finest cabarets.

'Here, ma' love, let me take twenty years off you with my speciality rubdown,' I heard one of them say. She could easily have passed for the grandmother of Oswaldo the scribe.

You'll kill him with a rubdown, I thought. The stranger, with a prudent gesture, declined the invitation.

'Some other day, my darling,' he replied, stepping further into the Raval quarter.

I followed him for a hundred more metres or so, until I saw him stop in front of a narrow, dark doorway, nearly opposite the Hotel Europa. He disappeared into the building and I waited half a minute before going in after him.

Inside, a dark staircase seemed to trail off into the bowels of the building. The building itself looked as if it were listing to port, or perhaps were even on the point of sinking into the catacombs of the Raval district, judging from the stench of damp and a faulty sewerage system. On one side of the hallway stood some sort of porter's lodge where a greasy-looking individual in a sleeveless vest, with a toothpick between his lips and a transistor radio, cast me a look somewhere between inquisitive and plainly hostile.

'You're on your own?' he asked, vaguely intrigued.

It didn´t take a genius to realise I was in the lobby of an establishment that rented out rooms by the hour and that the only discordant note about my visit was the fact that I wasn't holding the hand of one of the cut-price Venuses on patrol round the corner.

'If you like, I'll get a nice girl for you,' he offered, preparing a parcel with a towel, a bar of soap and what I guessed must be a rubber or some other prophylactic device to be used as a last resort.

'Actually, I just wanted to ask you a question,' I began.

The porter rolled his eyes.

'It's twenty pesetas for half an hour and you provide the filly.'

'Tempting. Perhaps some other day. What I wanted to ask you was whether a gentleman has just gone upstairs, a couple of minutes ago. An older man. Not in the best shape. On his own. Filly-less.'

The porter frowned. I realised from his expression that he was instantly downgrading me from potential client to pesky fly.

'I haven't seen anyone. Go on, beat it before I call Tonet.'

I gathered Tonet could not be a very endearing character. I placed my few remaining coins on the counter and gave the porter a conciliatory smile. In a flash, the money vanished as if it were an insect and the porter's hands – with their plastic thimbles – the darting tongue of a chameleon.

'What do you want to know?'

'Does the man I described to you live here?'

'He's been renting a room for a week.'

'Do you know his name?'

'He paid a month in advance, so I didn't ask.'

'Do you know where he comes from, what he does for a living . . .?'

'This isn't a phone-in programme. People come here to fornicate and I don't ask any questions. And this one doesn't even fornicate. So you do the sums.'

I reconsidered the matter.

'All I know is that every now and then he goes out and then comes back. Sometimes he asks me to send up a bottle of wine, bread and a bit of honey. He pays well and doesn't say a word.'

'And you're sure you don't remember any names?'

He shook his head.

'All right. Thanks and I'm sorry I bothered you.'

I was about to leave when the porter's voice called me back.

'Romero,' he said.

'Pardon?'

'I think he said he's called Romero or something like that . . .'

'Romero de Torres?'

'That's it.'

'Fermín Romero de Torres?' I repeated, incredulous.

'That's the one. Wasn't there a bullfighter going by that name before the war?' asked the porter. 'I thought it sounded familiar . . .'

6

I made my way back to the bookshop, more confused than before I left. As I walked past La Virreina Palace, Oswaldo, the scribe, raised a hand in greeting.

'Any luck?' he asked.

I mumbled a negative reply.

'Try Luisito, he might remember something.'

I gave Oswaldo a nod and went over to Luisito's booth. Luisito was cleaning his collection of nibs. When he saw me he smiled and asked me to sit down.

'What's it going to be? Pleasure or business?'

'Your colleague Oswaldo sent me.'

'Our mentor and master,' declared Luisito. 'A great man of letters, unrecognised by the corrupt establishment. And there he is, in the street, working with words at the service of the illiterate.'

'Oswaldo was saying that the other day you served an older man, lame and a bit clapped out, with one hand missing and some fingers of the other . . .'

'I remember him. I always remember one-handed men. Because of Cervantes – he lost a hand in the battle of Lepanto, you know?'

'I know. And could you tell me what business brought this man to you?'

Luisito stirred in his chair, uncomfortable at the turn the conversation was taking.

'Look, this is almost like a confessional. Professional confidentiality is paramount.'

'I understand that. The trouble is, this is a serious matter.'

'How serious?'

‘Sufficiently serious to threaten the well-being of people who are very dear to me.’

‘I see, but . . .’

Luisito craned his neck and tried to catch Oswaldo’s eye at the other end of the courtyard. I saw Oswaldo nod and then Luisito relaxed.

‘The gentleman brought a letter he’d written. He wanted it copied out in good handwriting, because with his hand . . .’

‘And the letter was about . . .?’

‘I barely remember, we write so many letters every day . . .’

‘Make an effort, Luisito. For Cervantes’ sake.’

‘Well, although I may be confusing it with another letter I wrote for some other client, I believe it was something to do with a large sum of money the one-handed gentleman was hoping to receive or recover or something like that. And something about a key.’

‘A key.’

‘Right. He didn’t specify whether this was an Allen key, a piano key or a door key.’

Luisito smiled at me, visibly pleased with his own wit.

‘Do you remember anything else?’

Luisito licked his lips thoughtfully.

‘He said he found the city very changed.’

‘In what way, changed?’

‘I don’t know. Changed. Without dead bodies in the streets.’

‘Dead bodies in the streets? Is that what he said?’

‘If I remember correctly . . .’

7

I thanked Luisito for the information and hurried back, hoping I'd reach the shop before my father returned from his errand and my absence was detected. The CLOSED sign was still on the door. I opened it, unhooked the notice and took my place behind the counter, convinced that not a single customer had come by during the almost forty-five minutes I had been away.

As I wasn't busy, I started to think about what I was going to do with that copy of *The Count of Monte Cristo* and how I was going to broach the subject with Fermín when he arrived. I didn't want to alarm him unnecessarily, but the stranger's visit and my poor attempt at solving what he was up to had left me feeling uneasy. Normally, I would simply have told Fermín what had happened and left it at that, but I knew that on this occasion I had to be tactful. For some time now, Fermín had appeared crestfallen and in a filthy mood. I'd been trying to cheer him up but none of my feeble attempts seemed to make him smile.

'There's no need to clean the books so thoroughly, Fermín,' I would say. 'I've heard that very soon only *noir* will be fashionable.' I was alluding to the way the press was beginning to describe the new novels of crime and punishment that only trickled in occasionally and then in tame translations.

Far from smiling kindly at my poor jokes, Fermín would grab any opportunity to embark on one of his tirades in support of doom and gloom.

'The entire future looks *noir* anyway,' he would declare. 'If there's going to be a flavour in vogue in this age of butchery, it will be the stink of falsehood and crime disguised in a thousand euphemisms.'

Here we go, I thought. The Book of Revelation according to St Fermín Romero de Torres.

'Don't exaggerate, Fermín. You should get more sun and fresh air. The other day I read in the paper that vitamin D increases our faith in fellow humans.'

'Well, I also read in the paper that imported cigarettes make you taller and that banks around the world are deeply committed to eradicating poverty and disease on the planet in less than ten years,' he replied. 'So there you go.'

When Fermín embraced organised pessimism the best option was not to argue with him.

'Do you know, Daniel? Sometimes I think that Darwin made a mistake and that in fact man is descended from the pig, because eight out of every ten members of the human race are swine, and as crooked as a hog's tail.'

'Fermín, I prefer it when you go for the humanist and positive view of things, like the other day when you said that deep down nobody is bad, only frightened.'

'It must have been low blood sugar doing the talking. What rubbish.'

These days, the cheerful Fermín I liked to remember seemed to have beaten a retreat and been replaced by a man consumed by anxieties and stormy moods he did not wish to share. Sometimes, when he thought nobody could see him, he would shrink into a corner, anguish gnawing at his insides. He'd lost some weight, and considering that he was as thin as a rake at the best of times and his body seemed mostly composed of cartilage and attitude, his appearance was becoming worrisome. I'd mentioned it to him once or twice, but he denied there was any problem and dodged the issue with Byzantine excuses.

'It's nothing, Daniel. It's just that I now follow the football league and every time Barça loses my blood pressure plummets. All I need is a bite of Manchego cheese and I'm as strong as an ox again.'

'Really? But you haven't been to a football match in your life.'

'That's what you think. When I was a kid everybody told me I had the legs to be a dancer or a football player.'

'Well, to me you look like a complete wreck, legs and all. Either you're ill or you're just not looking after yourself.'

For an answer he'd show me a couple of biceps the size of sugar almonds and grin as if he were a door-to-door toothpaste seller.

'Feel that! Tempered steel, like the Cid's sword.'

My father attributed Fermín's low form to nerves about the wedding and everything that came with it, from having to fraternise with the clergy to finding the right restaurant or café for the wedding banquet, but I suspected that his melancholy had much deeper roots. I was debating whether to tell Fermín what had happened that morning and show him the book or wait for a better moment, when he dragged himself through the door with a look on his face that would have won top honours at a wake. When he saw me he smiled faintly and offered a military salute.

'Good to see you, Fermín. I was beginning to think you weren't going to come in today.'

'I'd rather be dead than idle. I was held up by Don Federico, the watchmaker. When I walked past his shop he filled me in on some gossip about the fact that someone had seen Señor Sempere walking down Calle Puertaferrisa this morning, looking very dapper and en route to an unknown destination. Don Federico and that hare-brained Merceditas wanted to know whether perhaps he'd taken a mistress – apparently, these days it gives you a certain credibility among the shopkeepers in the district and if the damsel is a cabaret singer, all the more so.'

'And what did you reply?'

'That your father, as an exemplary widower, has reverted to a state of primal virginity, which has baffled the scientific community but earned him a fast-track application for sainthood at the archbishop's office. I don't discuss Señor Sempere's private life with friends or foes because it's nobody's business but his own. And whoever comes to me with such rubbish will get from me no more than a slap in the face and that's that.'

'You're a gentleman of the old school, Fermín.'

'The one who is of the old school is your father, Daniel. Between you and me, and this mustn't go beyond these four walls, it wouldn't be a bad thing if your father let down his hair every now and then. Ever since we started crossing this financial desert he has spent his entire time walled up in the storeroom with that Egyptian Book of the Dead.'

'It's the accounts book,' I corrected him.

'Whatever. In fact, for days now I've been thinking we should take him along to El Molino music hall and then out on the town. Even if our hero is as boring as a paella made of cabbage on that front, I'm sure a head-on collision with an elastic and decidedly buxom lass would shake up the marrow in his bones,' said Fermín.

'Look who's talking. The life and soul of the party. To be honest, you're the one I'm worried about,' I protested. 'For days you've been looking like a cockroach stuffed in a raincoat.'

'Since you mention it, that's an adroit comparison, if I may say so. For the cockroach may not have the swaggering good looks required by the frivolous norms of this daft society we've had the dubious fortune to live in, but both the underrated arthropod and yours truly are characterised by an unmatched instinct for survival, an overwhelming appetite and a leonine libido that won't relent even under extreme radiation levels.'

'It's impossible to argue with you, Fermín.'

'That's because of my natural flair for high dialectics, always ready to strike back at the slightest hint of inanity, dear friend. But your father is a tender, delicate flower and I think the time has come to take action before he turns into a complete fossil.'

'Take what action, Fermín?' my father's voice cut in behind us. 'Don't tell me you're going to set up a tea party with Rociíto.'

We turned round like two schoolboys caught in the act. My father, looking most unlike a tender flower, was watching us severely from the door.

8

'And how on earth do you know about Rociíto?' mumbled Fermín in astonishment.

After savouring the fright he'd given us, my father smiled kindly and gave us a wink.

'I might be turning into a fossil, but my hearing is still pretty good. My hearing and my thinking. That's why I've decided that something had to be done to revitalise our business,' he announced. 'The cabaret outing can wait.'

Only then did we notice that my father was carrying two hefty bags and a large box wrapped in brown paper and tied with thick string.

'Don't tell me you've just robbed the local bank,' I said.

'I try to avoid banks as much as possible: as Fermín says, they're the ones who usually rob us. I've been to the Santa Lucía market.'

Fermín and I looked at each other in bewilderment.

'Aren't you going to help me? This weighs a ton.'

We proceeded to unload the contents of the bags onto the counter while my father unwrapped the box. The bags were packed with small objects, each one protected with more brown paper. Fermín unwrapped one of them and stared at it, perplexed.

'What's that?' I asked.

'I'm inclined to say it's an adult sumpter at a scale of one to one hundred,' Fermín suggested.

'A what?'

'Namely, a donkey or an ass, the delightful hoofed quadruped that with winning charm and zest peoples this uniquely Spanish landscape of ours. Only this is a miniature version, like the model trains they sell in Casa Palau,' Fermín explained.

'It's a clay donkey, a figure for the crib,' my father explained.

'What crib?'

My father opened the cardboard box and pulled out the enormous manger with lights he'd just bought and which, I guessed, he was planning to place in the shop window as a Christmas advertising gimmick. Meanwhile Fermín had already unwrapped a number of oxen, pigs, ducks, as well as three wise old kings riding camels, some palm trees, a St Joseph and a Virgin Mary.

'Succumbing to the tyranny of National-Catholic propaganda and its surreptitious indoctrination techniques through a display of Yuletide figures and tall stories does not sound to me like a solution,' Fermín declared.

'Don't talk rubbish, Fermín,' my father interjected. 'This is a lovely tradition and people like to see nativity scenes during the Christmas season. The bookshop needed some of that colourful, happy spark that Christmas requires. Have a look at all the shops in the area and you'll see how, by comparison, we look like an undertaker's parlour. Go on, help me and we'll set it up in the shop window. And move to the second row all those books on physics and the history of Western philosophy, Fermín. They scare the seasonal customer away.'

'The end is near,' mumbled Fermín.

Between the three of us we managed to position the manger and set the little figures in place. Fermín collaborated unwillingly, frowning and searching for any excuse to express his objection.

'Señor Sempere, with all due respect, may I bring to your attention that this Baby Jesus is thrice the size of his putative father and hardly fits in the cradle?'

'It doesn't matter. They'd sold out of all the smaller ones.'

'Well, I think that next to the Virgin Mary he looks like one of those Japanese fighters with a weight management problem, greased-back hair and swirly underpants tied up like a loincloth over their nether regions.'

'Sumo wrestlers, they're called,' I said.

'The very ones,' Fermín agreed.

My father sighed, shaking his head.

'Besides, look at those eyes. You'd think he was possessed.'

'Come on, Fermín, shut up and switch on the crib lights,' my father ordered, handing him the plug.

By performing one of his balancing acts Fermín managed to slip under the table that held the manger and reach the socket at one end of the counter.

'And there was light,' my father pronounced, gazing enthusiastically at the shining new Sempere & Sons nativity scene.

'Adapt or perish!' he added, pleased with himself.

'Perish,' mumbled Fermín under his breath.

Not a minute had passed after the official lighting-up when a lady, with three children in tow, stopped by the shop window to admire the crib and, after a moment's hesitation, ventured into the shop.

'Good afternoon,' she said. 'Do you have any storybooks about the lives of the saints?'

'Of course,' said my father. 'Allow me to show you the much recommended collection *Little Jesus light of my life,* which I'm sure the children will love. Profusely illustrated and with a foreword by our beloved archbishop. Doesn't get any better.'

'Sounds lovely. The fact is, it's so hard to find books with a positive message these days, the sort that make you feel really good about yourself, instead of pushing all that violence and depravity so in vogue today.'

Fermín rolled his eyes. He was about to open his mouth when I stopped him and dragged him away from the customer.

'I know what you mean, madam,' my father agreed, looking at me out of the corner of his eye, and implying with his expression that I should keep Fermín bound and gagged because we weren't going to lose that sale for anything in the world.

I pushed Fermín into the back room and made sure the curtain was drawn so that my father could tackle the situation unhindered.

'Fermín, I don't know what's up with you. I realise you're not convinced by all this business of nativity scenes, and I respect that, but if an Infant Jesus the size of a steamroller and four clay piglets lift my father's spirits and on top of that pull customers into the bookshop, I'm going to ask you to set the existentialist pulpit aside and look as if you're part of the choir, at least during business hours.'

Fermín sighed and nodded, looking abashed.

'Of course, Daniel,' he said. 'Forgive me. I'd be prepared to walk the road to Santiago dressed up as the tooth fairy if that were to please your father and save the bookshop.'

'All you need to do is tell him you think the crib idea is a good one, and play along with him.'

Fermín nodded.

'Consider it done. I'll apologise to Señor Sempere later for overstepping the mark and as an act of contrition I'll contribute a little nativity figurine to prove that even large department stores can't beat me at Christmas spirit. I have a friend who had to go underground who makes those lovely traditional squatting figurines – the "crappers" – in the image of Franco, so realistic they give you goose pimples.'

'A lambkin or a King Balthazar will do.'

'Your wish is my command, Daniel. Now, if you don't object, I'll go and do something useful and start opening the boxes from the widow Recasen's lot. They've been here for a week gathering dust.'

'Shall I help you?'

'Don't worry. You get on with your stuff.'

I watched him make his way to the stockroom at the far end and put on his blue work overalls.

'Fermín,' I began.

He turned round obligingly. I paused for a moment.

'Something happened today that I need to tell you about.'

'Yes?'

'Actually, I'm not quite sure how to explain this. Someone came in and asked after you.'

'Was she pretty?' asked Fermín, trying to look jolly but unable to hide a flicker of anxiety in his eyes.

'It was a gentleman. In pretty bad shape and rather odd looking, to tell you the truth.'

'Did he leave a name?' asked Fermín.

I shook my head.

'No. But he left this for you.'

Fermín frowned. I handed him the book the stranger had bought a couple of hours before. Fermín took it and stared at the cover without understanding.

'But isn't this the Dumas we had in the glass cabinet at three hundred and fifty?'

I nodded.

'Open it at the first page.'

Fermín did as I asked. When he read the dedication he suddenly went pale and gulped. He closed his eyes for a moment and then looked at me without saying a word, seeming to have aged five years in as many seconds.

'When he left the shop I followed him,' I said. 'For the past week he's been living in a seedy establishment where they rent rooms by the hour, on Calle Hospital, opposite the Hotel Europa, and from what I've been able to find out, he uses a false name – yours, in fact: Fermín Romero de Torres. I've discovered, through one of the scribes in La Virreina, that he had a letter copied out in which he referred to a large amount of money. Does any of this ring a bell?'

Fermín seemed to be curling up, as if every word I spoke were a blow raining down on him.

'Daniel, it's very important that you don't follow this individual or speak to him again. Don't do anything. Keep well away from him. He's very dangerous.'

'Who is this man, Fermín?'

Fermín closed the book and hid it behind a pile of boxes on one of the shelves. He took a quick look in the direction of the shop and once he was sure my father was still busy with the customer and couldn't hear us, he drew closer to me and spoke in a very low voice.

'Please don't tell your father or anyone else about this.'

'Fermín . . .'

'Do me this favour. For the sake of our friendship.'

'But, Fermín . . .'

'Please, Daniel. Not here. Trust me.'

I agreed reluctantly and showed him the one-thousand-peseta note the stranger had paid me with. I didn't have to explain where it had come from.

'That money is cursed, Daniel. Give it to the Sisters of Charity or to some beggar in the street. Or, better still, burn it.'

Without another word he proceeded to remove his overalls and slip on his frayed raincoat and his beret. On that matchstick head of his the beret looked like one of Dali's melting clocks.

'Are you leaving already?'

'Tell your father something unexpected has cropped up. Will you?'

'Of course, but . . .'

'I can't explain this to you now, Daniel.'

He clutched his stomach with one hand as if his insides had got tied in a knot.

'Fermín, if you tell me about it I might be able to help . . .'

Fermín paused for a moment, but then shook his head and walked out into the hallway. I followed him as far as the main door and saw him set off in the rain, just a little man with the entire world on his shoulders, while the night, blacker than ever, stole down over Barcelona.

9

It is a scientifically acknowledged fact that any infant a few months old has an unerring instinct for sensing the exact moment in the early hours when his parents have managed to nod off, so he can raise the tone of his cries, thereby ensuring they don't get more than thirty minutes' sleep at a time.

That night, like almost all others, little Julián awoke around three in the morning and didn't hesitate to announce the fact at the top of his lungs. I opened my eyes and turned over. Next to me, Bea, gleaming in the half-light, slowly stirred, revealing the outline of her body under the sheets, and mumbled something. I resisted my natural impulse to kiss her on the neck and relieve her of that overlong, reinforced nightgown that my father-in-law, probably on purpose, had given her on her birthday. Try as I might, I couldn't get it to disappear in the laundry.

'I'll get up,' I whispered, kissing her on the forehead.

Bea replied by rolling over and covering her head with the pillow. I paused to admire the curve of her back and its enticing descent which no nightdress in the world could have obscured. I'd been married to that wonderful creature for almost two years and was still surprised to wake up by her side, feeling her warmth. I'd started to pull back the sheet and caress her velvety thigh when Bea's hand stuck its nails into my wrist.

'Not now, Daniel. The baby's crying.'

'I knew you were awake.'

'It's hard to get any sleep sharing a house with men who either can't stop crying or can't refrain from fondling your backside – they won't let you string together more than two hours' rest a night.'

'Well, it's your loss.'

I got up and walked down the corridor to Julián's room at the back. Shortly after the wedding we'd moved into the attic apartment in the same building as the bookshop. Don Anacleto, the secondary-school teacher who had lived in it for twenty-five years, had decided to retire and return to his native Segovia to write spicy poems under the shade of the old Roman aqueduct and broaden his understanding of the art of roast suckling pig.

Little Julián welcomed me with loud, shrill crying that threatened to shatter my eardrums. I took him in my arms and after smelling his nappy and confirming that for once there were no nasty surprises, I did what every new father with any sense would do: whisper some silly nonsense and dance about the room with ridiculous little jumps. I was in the middle of doing just that when I realised Bea was staring at me disapprovingly from the doorway.

'Give him to me. You're going to unsettle him even more.'

'He's not complaining,' I protested, handing her the baby.

Bea took him in her arms and murmured a melody in his ear as she gently rocked him. Five seconds later Julián had stopped crying and was giving that enchanted half-smile his mother always managed to elicit from him.

'Go on,' said Bea, softly. 'I'll be along in a second.'

Having been thrown out of the room, my incompetence at handling babies at the crawling stage clearly proven, I went back to our bedroom and lay down, knowing I wouldn't be able to sleep a wink the rest of the night. A while later, Bea appeared round the door and lay down next to me with a sigh.

'I'm dead tired.'

I put my arms around her and we lay there quietly for a few minutes.

'I've been thinking,' said Bea.

Tremble, Daniel, I thought. Bea sat up and then crouched down on the bed facing me.

'When Julián is a bit older and my mother is able to look after him for a few hours a day, I think I'm going to work.'

I nodded.

'Where?'

'In the bookshop.'

I thought it best to keep quiet.

'I think it would do you all good,' she added. 'Your father is getting too old to put in all those hours and, don't be offended, but I think I'm better at dealing with customers than you, not to mention Fermín, who recently seems to scare business away.'

'I won't argue with that.'

'What's the matter with him, anyway? The other day I bumped into Bernarda in the street and she burst out crying. I took her to one of the milk bars on Calle Petritxol and after I'd plied her with cups of hot chocolate and whipped cream she told me that Fermín is behaving really oddly. For some days now, it seems he's been refusing to fill in the parish church papers for the wedding. I have a feeling Fermín isn't getting married. Has he said anything to you?'

'Yes, I've noticed it too,' I lied. 'Perhaps Bernarda is pushing him too hard . . .'

Bea looked at me but didn't say anything.

'What?' I asked finally.

'Bernarda asked me not to tell anyone.'

'Not to tell what?'

Bea fixed her eyes on mine.

'She's late this month.'

'Late? She's got behind with her work?'

Bea looked at me as if I were stupid and then the penny dropped.

'*Bernarda is pregnant?*'

'Don't speak so loudly, you'll wake Julián.'

'Is she pregnant or isn't she?' I repeated, in a tiny voice.

'Looks like it.'

'And does Fermín know?'

‘She hasn’t wanted to tell him yet. She’s scared he’ll make a quick exit.’

‘Fermín would never do that.’

‘All you men would do that, given a chance.’

I was surprised by the harshness of her tone, which she quickly sweetened with an unconvincingly meek smile.

‘How little you know us.’

She sat up in the dark and without saying a word lifted off her nightdress and let it fall to one side of the bed. She let me gaze at her for a few seconds and then, slowly, leaned over me and licked my lips unhurriedly.

‘How little I know you,’ she whispered.

10

The following day the attraction of the illuminated manger was proving its worth and I saw my father smile to himself for the first time in weeks as he entered a few sales in the ledger. From early morning some old customers who hadn't set foot in the bookshop for a while began to drop by, together with new readers who were visiting us for the first time. I let my father deal with them all with his expert hand and enjoyed watching him as he recommended titles, roused their curiosity and guessed at their tastes and interests. It promised to be a good day, the first in many weeks.

'Daniel, we should bring out the collections of illustrated children's classics. The Vértice editions, with the blue spine.'

'I think they're in the basement. Do you have the keys?'

'Bea asked me for them the other day. She wanted to take something down there – something to do with the baby. I don't remember her giving them back to me. Have a look in the drawer.'

'They're not here. I'll run up to the flat to look for them.'

I left my father serving a gentleman who had just come in, looking to buy a history of old Barcelona cafés, and went out through the back room to the staircase in the hallway. The flat Bea and I shared was high up and, apart from the extra light it provided, walking up and down those stairs invigorated both our spirits and our legs. On the way I came across Edelmira, a widow on the third floor who had once been a chorus girl and now made a living by painting Madonnas and saints in her home. Too many years on the stage of the Arnau Theatre had finished off her knees and now she had to hold on to the banisters with both hands to negotiate a simple flight of stairs. In spite of her problems, she always had a smile on her lips and something kind to say.

'How's your beautiful wife, Daniel?'

'Not as beautiful as you, Doña Edelmira. Shall I help you down?'

As usual, Edelmira refused my help and asked me to give her regards to Fermín, who always volunteered slightly flirtatious comments or cheeky propositions when he saw her go by.

When I opened the door of the apartment, it still smelled of Bea's perfume and that mixture of aromas given out by babies and their props. Bea usually got up early and took Julián out for a walk in the shiny new Jané pushchair Fermín had given us, which we all referred to as 'the Mercedes'.

'Bea?' I called out.

It was a small flat and my voice echoed back even before I'd closed the door behind me. Bea had already left. I stepped into the dining room, trying to reconstruct my wife's train of thought and work out where she could have put the basement keys. Bea was far tidier and more methodical than me. I began by looking through the drawers in the dining-room sideboard where she usually kept receipts, unanswered letters and loose change. From there I moved on to side tables, fruit bowls and shelves.

The next stop was the glass cabinet in the kitchen, where Bea usually left notes and reminders. Finally, having had no luck so far, I ended up in the bedroom, standing in front of the bed and looking around me with a critical eye. Bea's clothes took up seventy-five per cent of the wardrobe, drawers and other storage areas in the bedroom. Her line of reasoning was that I always dressed the same, so I could easily make do with a corner of the cupboard. The arrangement of her drawers was far too sophisticated for me. I felt a sudden twinge of guilt as I went through my wife's private belongings, but after rummaging in vain through all the bits of furniture in sight, I still hadn't found the keys.

Let's re-enact the crime scene, I said to myself. I vaguely remembered that Bea had said something about taking down a box with summer clothes. That had been a couple of days ago. If I was right, that day Bea was wearing the grey coat I'd given her on our first wedding anniversary. I smiled at my powers of deduction and opened the wardrobe to search for the coat. There it was. If everything I'd learned reading Conan Doyle and his disciples was correct, my father's keys would be in one of the pockets of that coat. I thrust my hand into the right pocket and felt two coins and a couple of mints, the sort they give you at the chemist. I went on to inspect the other pocket and was pleased to confirm my thesis. My fingers felt the bunch of keys.

And something else.

There was a piece of paper in the pocket. I pulled out the keys and, after a moment's doubt, decided to take out the paper too. It was probably one of those lists of errands Bea would always make to avoid forgetting anything.

When I took a closer look I realised it was an envelope. A letter. It was addressed to her maiden name, Beatriz Aguilar, and the postmark dated it a week earlier. The letter had been sent to the home of Bea's parents, not to the flat in Santa Ana. I turned it over and when I read the name of the sender, the basement keys slipped out of my hand.

Pablo Cascos Buendía

Bewildered, I sat on the bed and stared at the envelope. Pablo Cascos Buendía had been Bea's fiancé when we started going out together. The son of a wealthy family who owned a number of shipyards and industries in El Ferrol, he had always rubbed me up the wrong way, and I could tell the feeling was mutual. At that time, he had been doing his military service as second lieutenant. But ever since Bea had written to him to break off their engagement I hadn't heard any more about him. Until now.

What was a letter from Bea's ex-fiancé, with a recent date stamped on it, doing in her pocket? The envelope was open, but I hesitated for a whole minute before pulling out the letter. Realising this was the first time I had spied behind Bea's back, I was on the point of replacing it and hurrying out of there. My moment of virtue lasted about ten seconds. Any trace of guilt and shame evaporated before I reached the end of the first paragraph.

Dear Beatriz,

I hope you're well and feeling happy in your new life in Barcelona. You haven't replied to any of the letters I've sent you these past months and sometimes I wonder what I've done to make you ignore me. I realise that you're a married woman with a child and that perhaps it's wrong for me to write to you, but I confess that even after all this time I can't forget you, although I've tried and I'm not ashamed to admit that I'm still in love with you.

My life has also taken a new course. A year ago I started to work as head of sales for an important publishing firm. I know how much books mean to you and working among them makes me feel closer to you. My office is in the Madrid branch, although I travel all over Spain for my work.

I never stop thinking about you, about the life we could have shared, the children we might have had together . . . I ask myself every day whether your husband knows how to make you happy and whether you didn't marry him through force of circumstance. I can't believe that the modest life he can offer you is what you want. I know you well. We were colleagues and friends and there haven't been any secrets between us. Do you remember those afternoons we spent together on San Pol beach? Do you remember the plans, the dreams we shared, the promises we made to one another? I've never felt this way about anyone else. Since we broke off our engagement I've been out with a few girls, but now I know that none of them can compare with you. Every time I kiss other lips I think of yours and every time I touch someone else's skin, it's your skin I feel.

In a month's time I'll be travelling to Barcelona to visit our offices there and hold a few meetings with the staff about a future restructuring of the firm. I could easily have solved these matters by letter and telephone. The real reason for my trip is none other than the hope of being able to see you again. I know you'll think I'm mad, but that would be better than thinking I'd forgotten you. I arrive on 20 January and will be staying at the Hotel Ritz on the Gran Vía. Please, I beg you, let's meet, even if only for a while. Let me tell you in person what is in my heart. I've made a reservation in the hotel restaurant for the 21st at 2 o'clock. I'll be there, waiting for you. If you come you'll make me the happiest man in the world and I'll know that my dreams of regaining your love might still come true.

I love you, always,

PABLO

For a couple of seconds I sat there, on the bed I'd shared with Bea just a few hours earlier. I slipped the letter back in the envelope and when I stood up I felt as if I'd just been punched in the stomach. I ran to the bathroom sink and threw up that morning's coffee. I let the cold water run and splashed my face. The eyes of a younger Daniel whose hands were shaking the first time he had caressed Bea gazed back at me from the mirror.

11

When I returned to the bookshop my father shot me a questioning look and glanced at his wristwatch. I knew he must have been wondering where I'd been for the past half-hour, but he didn't say anything. I handed him the keys to the basement, avoiding his eyes.

'But weren't you going to go down to fetch the books?' he asked.

'Of course. Sorry. I'll go right away.'

My father looked at me askance.

'Are you all right, Daniel?'

I nodded, feigning surprise at the question. Before I'd given him a chance to ask me again, I headed off for the basement to collect the boxes he'd asked for. The way down was at the back of the building's entrance hall. A metal door with a padlock, set beneath the first flight of the main staircase, opened on to a spiral stairway descending into the dark and smelling of damp and dead flowers. A small row of light bulbs, flickering anaemically, hung from the ceiling, making the place look like an air-raid shelter. I started down the stairs and, when I reached the basement, groped about for the light switch.

A yellowish bulb lit up above my head, revealing the outline of what was really just a junk room with delusions of grandeur. Rusty old bicycles with no known owner, worthless paintings covered in cobwebs and cardboard boxes piled up on rotting wooden shelves created a tableau that did not invite one to hang around any longer than was strictly necessary. It wasn't until I gazed at the sight before me that I realised how strange it was that Bea should have wanted to come down here instead of asking me to do it. I scanned that maze of household junk and wondered how many more secrets she had hidden there.

When I realised what I was doing I sighed. The words from that letter were seeping into my mind like drops of acid. I made myself promise that I wouldn't start rummaging in boxes, searching for bundles of perfumed envelopes from that creep. I would have broken my promise seconds later had I not heard someone coming down the steps. I raised my head and saw Fermín at the foot of the staircase, staring at the scene with a look of disgust.

'Smells like a corpse and a half here. Are you sure someone hasn't left the embalmed body of Merceditas's mother, among crochet patterns, in one of these boxes?'

'Since you're down here, you can help me take up the boxes my father needs.'

Fermín rolled up his sleeves, ready to get started. I pointed at a couple of boxes with the Vértice label on them and we took one each.

'Daniel, you look even worse than me. Is anything wrong?'

'It must be the basement vapours.'

I left the box on the floor and sat on it.

'May I ask you a question, Fermín?'

Fermín also put his box down and used it as a stool. I looked at him, ready to speak, but unable to pull the words out of my mouth.

'Trouble in the boudoir?' he ventured.

I blushed when I realised how well my friend knew me.

'Something like that.'

'Señora Bea, blessed is she among womenfolk, is not in a mood for battle, or, on the contrary, she is all too willing, and you can barely offer the minimum services? Do bear in mind that when women have a baby, it's as if someone had dropped an atom bomb of hormones into their bloodstream. One of the great mysteries of nature is how they don't go crazy during the twenty seconds that follow the birth. I know all this because obstetrics, after free verse, is one of my hobbies.'

'No, it's not that. At least as far as I know.'

Fermín gave me a puzzled look.

'I must ask you not to tell anyone what I'm about to tell you, Fermín.'

Fermín crossed himself solemnly.

'A short while ago, I accidentally discovered a letter in Bea's coat pocket.'

My pause didn't seem to impress him.

'And?'

'The letter was from her ex-fiancé.'

'Lieutenant Vapid? Hadn't he gone back to El Ferrol to play the lead in a spectacular career as a spoiled brat?'

'That's what I thought. But it seems that in his free time he writes love letters to my wife.'

Fermín jumped up.

'The son-of-a-bitch,' he muttered, even more furious than me.

I pulled the letter out of my pocket and handed it to him. Fermín sniffed the paper before opening it.

'Is it me, or does the swine send letters on perfumed paper?' he asked.

'It wouldn't surprise me. The man's like that. The best part comes afterwards. Read, read . . .'

Fermín read the letter, mumbling to himself and shaking his head.

'Not only is this specimen a disgusting piece of excrement, he's also as cloying as they come. This "kissing other lips" line should be enough to get him jailed for life.'

I put the letter away and looked down at the floor.

'Don't tell me you're suspicious of Señora Bea?' asked Fermín in disbelief.

'No, of course not.'

'You liar.'

I stood up and began to pace around the basement.

'And what would you do if you found a letter like that one in Bernarda's pocket?'

Fermín took his time to consider the matter.

'What I would do is trust the mother of my child.'

'Trust her?'

Fermín nodded.

'Don't take it badly, Daniel, but you have the basic problem of all men who marry a real looker. Señora Bea, who is and always will be a saint as far as I'm concerned, is, in the popular parlance, such a tasty dish you'd want to lick the plate clean. As a result, it's only to be expected that dedicated sleazy types, full-time losers, poolside gigolos and all the half-arsed posers in town should go after her. With or without a husband and child: the simian stuck in a suit we all too kindly call *Homo sapiens* doesn't give a damn about that. You may not have noticed, but I'd bet my silk undies that your saintly wife attracts more flies than a pot of honey in a barn. That cretin is just like one of those scavenger birds, throwing stones to see if he hits something. Trust me, a woman with her head and petticoat both firmly in place can see that type coming from afar.'

'Are you sure?'

'Absolutely. Do you really think that if Doña Beatriz wanted to cheat on you she'd have to wait for a slobbering halfwit to sweet-talk her into it with his reheated boleros? I wouldn't wonder that at least ten suitors put in an appearance every time she goes out, showing off her good looks and her baby. Believe me, I know what I'm talking about.'

'Quite frankly, I'm not sure whether all this is much comfort.'

'Look, what you need to do is put that letter back in the coat pocket where you found it and forget all about it. And don't even think of mentioning the matter to your wife.'

'Is that what you would do?'

'What I'd do is go and find that numbskull and land him such a glorious kick in the balls they'd have to surgically remove them from the back of his neck and all he'd want to do then is join a Carthusian monastery. But that's me.'

I felt the anguish spreading inside me like a drop of oil on clear water.

'I'm not sure you've helped me much, Fermín.'

He shrugged his shoulders, picked up the box, and vanished up the stairs.

We spent the rest of the morning working in the bookshop. After mulling over the business of the letter in my head for a couple of hours, I came to the conclusion that Fermín was right. What I couldn't quite work out was whether he was right about trusting her and keeping quiet, or about going out to get that moron and give him a genital makeover. The calendar on the counter said 20 December. I had a month to decide.

The day's business picked up little by little, with modest but steady sales. Fermín didn't miss a single chance to praise my father for the glorious crib and for his brilliant idea of buying that Baby Jesus reminiscent of a Basque weightlifter.

'Seeing such dazzling salesmanship on display I'll leave the floor to the master and retire to the back room to sort out the collection the widow left with us the other day.'

I took the opportunity to follow Fermín and draw the curtain behind us. Fermín looked at me, slightly alarmed, but I gave him a friendly smile.

'I'll help you if you like.'

'As you wish, Daniel.'

For a few minutes we began to unpack the boxes of books and classify them in piles by genre, condition and size. Fermín didn't open his lips and avoided my eyes.

'Fermín . . .'

'I've already told you not to worry about that business of the letter. Your wife is not a trollop, and if she ever wants to dump you – and pray heaven that will never happen – she'll tell you face to face without the need for soap-opera shenanigans.'

'Got the message, Fermín. But that's not it.'

Fermín looked up, distressed, knowing what was coming.

'I've been thinking that today, after we close, we could go out, grab a bite and have some man-talk, you know, just you and me,' I began. 'To talk about our stuff. About yesterday's visitor. And about whatever it is that's worrying you, which I have an inkling might be connected.'

Fermín left the book he was cleaning on the table. He gazed at me in dismay and sighed.

'I'm in a real mess, Daniel,' he mumbled at last. 'A mess I don't know how to get out of.'

I put my hand on his shoulder. Under the overalls all I could feel was skin and bone.

'Then let me help you. Two heads are always better than one.'

He seemed at a loss.

'Surely we've got out of worse situations, you and I,' I insisted.

He smiled sadly, not too convinced by my forecast.

'You're a good friend, Daniel.'

Not half as good as he deserved, I thought.

12

Back then Fermín still lived in the same old *pensión* on Calle Joaquín Costa, where I had it on good authority that the rest of the lodgers, in secret collaboration with Rociíto and her sisters-in-arms, were preparing a stag night for him that would go down in history. Fermín was already waiting for me by the front door when I went by to pick him up just after nine.

'To be honest, I'm not that hungry,' he announced when he saw me.

'Pity, because I thought we could go down to Can Lluís,' I proposed. 'They're serving chickpea stew and baby lamb chops tonight . . .'

'Well, let's not make hasty decisions here,' Fermín reconsidered. 'A good repast is like a lass in bloom: not to appreciate it is the business of fools.'

With that pearl from the eminent Don Fermín Romero de Torres's stockpile of aphorisms, we ambled down towards what was one of my friend's favourite restaurants in the whole of Barcelona and much of the known world. Can Lluís was located at 49 Calle de la Cera, on the threshold of the Raval quarter. Behind its modest appearance Can Lluís conveyed an intimate atmosphere steeped in the mysteries of old Barcelona, offering exquisite food and impeccable service at prices that even Fermín, or I, could afford. On weekdays, it attracted a bohemian community, in which people from the theatre, literary types and other creatures high and low rubbed shoulders and toasted each other.

When we walked in we spied one of the bookshop's regular customers, Professor Alburquerque, a fine reviewer and local savant who taught at the arts faculty and made Can Lluís his second home. He was enjoying dinner at the bar and leafing through a newspaper.

'Long time no see, Professor,' I said as I walked past him. 'You must pay us a visit some time and replenish your stock. A man can't live on obituaries from *La Vanguardia*.'

'I wish I could. It's those damned dissertations. Having to read the inane babble written by the spoiled rich kids who come through university these days is beginning to give me bouts of dyslexia.'

At that point, one of the waiters served him his pudding, a plump crème caramel wobbling under a surge of burned sugar tears and smelling of the finest vanilla.

'Your lordship will get over it after a couple of spoonfuls of this marvel,' said Fermín. 'Goodness me: it jiggles just like the formidable bust of Doña Margarita Xirgu.'

The learned professor gazed at his pudding in the light of those considerations and agreed, spellbound. We left the wise man enjoying the sugary charms of the famous stage diva and took shelter at a corner table at the back of the dining room, where we were soon served a sumptuous meal. Fermín devoured it with the appetite of a retreating army.

'I thought you weren't hungry,' I let drop.

'Hard muscle burns a lot of calories,' Fermín explained, mopping his plate with the last piece of bread in the basket, although I thought it was just his anxiety doing all the eating.

Pere, the waiter who was serving us, came over to see how everything was going and when he saw Fermín's ravaged plate, he handed him the dessert menu.

'A little dessert to finish off the job, maestro?'

'Come to think of it, I wouldn't say no to a couple of those home-made crème caramels I saw earlier, if possible with a bright red cherry on top of each one,' said Fermín.

Pere assented. He told us that when the owner heard how Fermín had expounded on the consistency and the metaphorical attractions of that recipe, he'd decided to rechristen the crème caramels '*margaritas*'.

'I'm fine with an espresso,' I said.

'The boss says coffee and dessert are on the house,' said Pere.

We raised our wine glasses in the direction of the owner, who was standing behind the bar chatting with Professor Alburquerque.

'Good people,' mumbled Fermín. 'Sometimes one forgets that not everyone in this world is a bastard.'

I was surprised at the bitterness of his tone.

'Why do you say that, Fermín?'

My friend shrugged his shoulders. Shortly after, the crème caramels arrived, swaying temptingly, topped with shiny cherries.

'May I remind you that in a few weeks' time you're getting married and your *margarita* days will be over?' I joked.

'Poor me,' said Fermín. 'I'm afraid I'm all bark and no bite. I'm not the man I used to be.'

'None of us are what we once were.'

Fermín started on the crème caramels, savouring every mouthful.

'I don't know where I've read that deep down we've never been who we think we once were, and we only remember what never happened . . .' said Fermín.

'That's the beginning of a novel by Julián Carax,' I replied.

'True. Where might our friend Carax be? Don't you ever wonder?'

'Every single day.'

Fermín smiled, remembering our past adventures. Then he pointed to my chest and gave me a questioning look.

'Does it still hurt?'

I undid a couple of buttons on my shirt and showed him the scar Inspector Fumero's bullet had left when it went through my chest that faraway day, in the ruins of the Angel of Mist.

'Every now and then.'

'Scars never go away, do they?'

'They come and go, I believe. Fermín: look into my eyes.'

Fermín's evasive eyes looked straight into mine.

'Are you going to tell me what's going on?'

For a couple of seconds Fermín hesitated.

'Did you know that Bernarda is expecting?' he asked.

'No,' I lied. 'Is that what's worrying you?'

Fermín shook his head as he finished up his second crème caramel with the teaspoon, sipping the remains of the syrup.

'She hasn't wanted to tell me yet, poor thing, because she's worried. But she's going to make me the happiest man in the world.'

I looked at him carefully.

'To be honest, right now, you don't exactly look the picture of happiness. Is it because of the wedding? Are you worried about having to go through a church wedding and all that?'

'No, Daniel. I'm actually quite excited about it, even if there are priests involved. I could marry Bernarda every day of the week.'

'Then what?'

'Do you know the first thing they ask you when you want to get married?'

'Your name,' I said, without thinking.

Fermín nodded his head slowly. It hadn't occurred to me to think about that until then. Suddenly I understood the dilemma my good friend was facing.

'Do you remember what I told you years ago, Daniel?'

I remembered it perfectly. During the civil war and thanks to the nefarious dealings of Inspector Fumero who, before joining the fascists, acted as a hired thug for the communists, my friend had landed himself in prison, where he'd been on the verge of losing his mind and his life. When he managed to get out, alive by some sheer miracle, he decided to adopt a new identity and erase his past. He was at death's door when he borrowed a name he saw on an old poster in the Arenas bullring. That is how Fermín Romero de Torres was born, a man who invented his life story day after day.

'That's why you didn't want to fill in those papers in the parish church,' I said. 'Because you can't use the name Fermín Romero de Torres.'

Fermín nodded.

'Look, I'm sure we can find a way of getting you new documentation. Do you remember Lieutenant Palacios, the one who left the police force? He teaches physical education at a school in the Bonanova area, but sometimes he drops by the bookshop. Well, one day, talking about this and that, he told me there was a whole underground market of new identities for people who were returning to Spain after spending years away. He said he knows someone with a workshop near the old Royal Shipyards who has contacts in the police force and for a hundred pesetas can supply people with a new identity card and get it registered in the ministry.'

'I know. His name was Heredia. Quite an artist.'

'Was?'

'He turned up floating in the port a couple of months ago. They said he'd fallen off a pleasure boat while he was sailing towards the breakwater. With his hands tied behind his back. Fascist humour.'

'You knew him?'

'We met now and then.'

'Then you do have documents that certify you are Fermín Romero de Torres . . .'

'Heredia managed to get them for me in 1939, towards the end of the war. It was easier then, Barcelona was a madhouse, and when people realised the ship was sinking they'd even sell you their coat of arms for a couple of *duros*.

'Then why can't you use your name?'

'Because Fermín Romero de Torres died in 1940. Those were bad times, Daniel, far worse than these. He didn't even last a year, poor bastard.'

'He died? Where? How?'

'In the prison of Montjuïc Castle. In cell number thirteen.'

I remembered the dedication the stranger had left for Fermín in the copy of *The Count of Monte Cristo.*

For Fermín Romero de Torres,
who came back from among the dead
and holds the key to the future.

13

'That night I only told you a small part of the story, Daniel.'

'I thought you trusted me.'

'I would trust you with my life. If I only told you part of it, it was to protect you.'

'Protect me? From what?'

Fermín looked down, devastated.

'From the truth, Daniel . . . from the truth.'

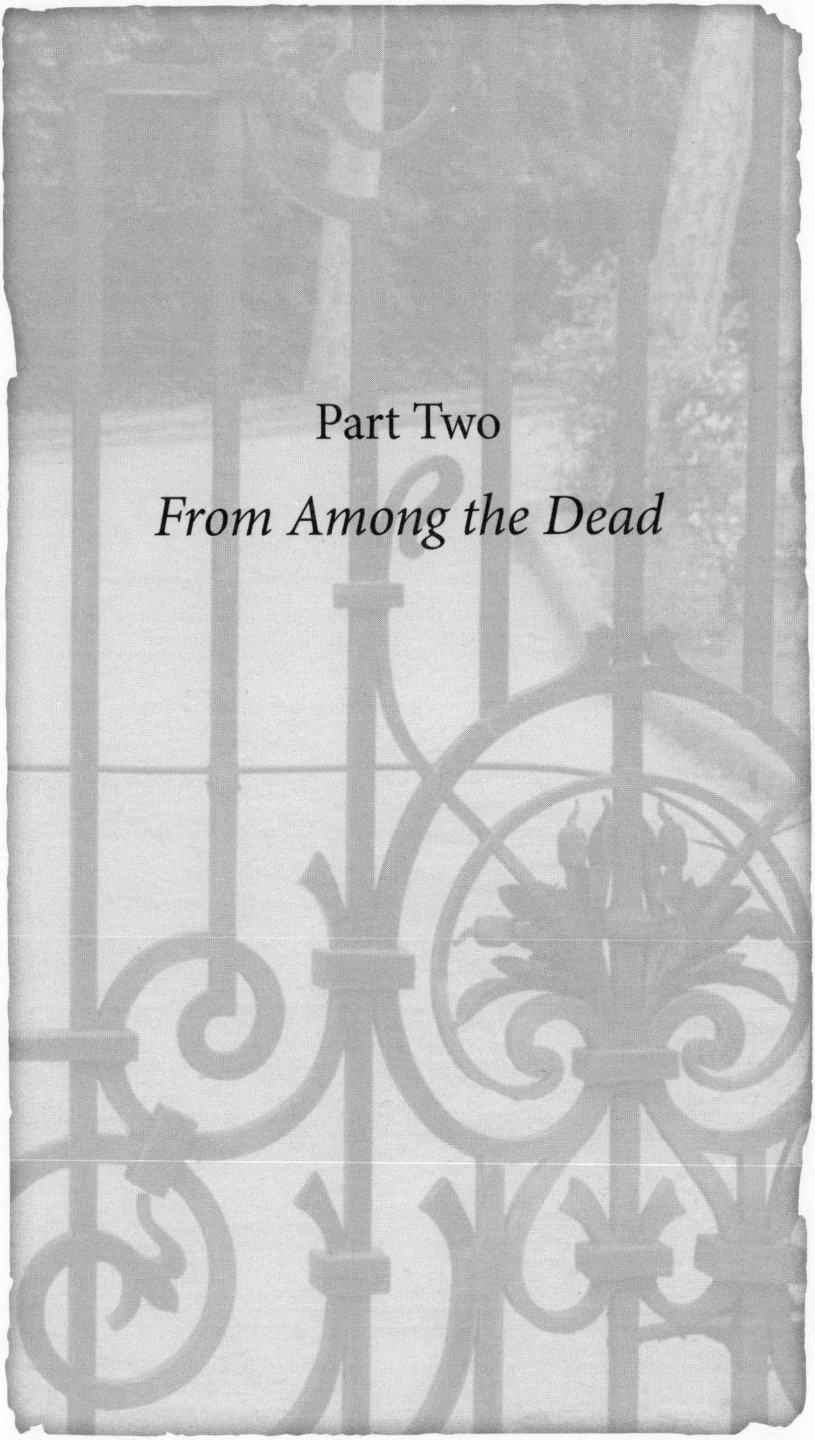

Part Two

From Among the Dead

1

Barcelona, 1939

New prisoners were brought in by night, in cars or black vans that set off from the police station on Vía Layetana and crossed the city silently, nobody noticing or wishing to notice them. The vehicles of the political police drove up the old road scaling the slopes of Montjuïc and more than one prisoner would relate how, the moment they glimpsed the castle on top of the hill silhouetted against black clouds that crept in from the sea, they felt certain they would never get out of that place alive.

The fortress was anchored at the highest point of the rocky mountain, suspended between the sea to the east, Barcelona's carpet of shadows to the north and, to the south, the endless city of the dead – the old Montjuïc Cemetery whose stench rose up among the boulders and filtered through cracks in the stone and through the bars of the cells. In times past, the castle had been used for bombarding the city below, but only a few months after the fall of Barcelona, in January, and the final defeat in April, death came to dwell there in silence and Barcelonians, trapped in the longest night of their history, preferred not to look skywards and recognise the prison's outline crowning the hill.

Upon arrival, prisoners brought in by the political police were assigned a number, usually that of the cell they were going to occupy and where they were likely to die. For most tenants, as some of the jailers liked to refer to them, the journey to the castle was only one-way. On the night tenant number 13 arrived in Montjuïc it was raining hard. Thin veins of black water bled down the stone walls and the air reeked of excavated earth. Two police officers escorted him to a room containing only a metal table and a chair. A naked bulb hung from the ceiling and flickered every time the generator's flow diminished. He stood there waiting in his soaking clothes for almost half an hour, watched by a guard with a rifle.

At last he heard footsteps, the door opened and in came a man who couldn't have been a day over thirty. He wore a freshly ironed wool suit and smelled of eau de cologne. He had none of the martial looks of a professional soldier or police officer: his features were soft and his expression seemed pleasant. To the prisoner he came across as someone affecting the manners of a wealthy young man, giving off a condescending air of superiority in a setting that was beneath him. His most striking feature were his eyes. Blue, penetrating and sharp, alive with greed and suspicion. Only his eyes, behind that veneer of studied elegance and kind demeanour, betrayed his true nature.

Two round lenses augmented them, and his pomaded hair, combed back, lent him a vaguely affected look that didn't match the sinister decor. The man sat down on the chair behind the desk and opened a folder he was carrying. After a quick inspection of its contents, he joined his hands, placed his fingertips under his chin and sat scrutinising the prisoner, who finally spoke up.

'Excuse me, but I think there has been a mistake . . .'

The blow on the prisoner's stomach with the rifle butt knocked the wind out of him and he fell, curled up into a ball.

'You only speak when the governor asks you a question,' the guard told him.

'On your feet,' commanded the governor in a quavering voice, still unused to giving orders.

The prisoner managed to stand up and face the governor's uncomfortable gaze.

'Name?'

'Fermín Romero de Torres.'

The prisoner noticed disdain and indifference in those blue eyes.

'What sort of name is that? Do you think I'm a fool? Come on: name, the real one.'

The prisoner, a small, frail man, held out his papers for the governor. The guard snatched them from him and took them over to the table. The governor had a quick look at them, then clicked his tongue and smiled.

'Another Heredia job . . .' he murmured before throwing the documents into the wastepaper basket. 'These papers are no good. Are you going to tell me your name or do we have to get serious?'

Tenant number 13 tried to utter a few words, but his lips trembled and all he managed to do was stammer something incomprehensible.

'Don't be afraid, my good man, nobody's going to bite you. What have you been told? There are plenty of fucking reds out there who like to spread slanders around, but here, if people collaborate, they get treated well, like Spaniards. Come on, clothes off.'

The new tenant seemed to hesitate for a moment. The governor looked down, as if the whole situation was making him feel uncomfortable and only the prisoner's stubbornness was keeping him there. A second later, the guard dealt him another blow with the rifle butt, this time in the kidneys, and knocked him down again.

'You heard the governor. Strip down. We don't have all night.'

Tenant number 13 managed to get up on his knees and remove his dirty, bloodstained clothes. Once he was completely naked, the guard stuck the rifle barrel under a shoulder and forced him to stand up. The governor looked up from the desk and grimaced with disgust when he saw the burns covering his torso, buttocks and much of his thighs.

'It looks like our champion is an old acquaintance of Fumero's,' the guard remarked.

'Keep your mouth shut,' ordered the governor without much conviction.

He looked at the prisoner with impatience and realised he was crying.

'Come on, stop crying and tell me your name.'

The prisoner whispered his name again.

'Fermín Romero de Torres . . .'

The governor sighed wearily.

'Look, I'm beginning to lose my patience. I want to help you and I don't really feel like having to call Inspector Fumero and tell him you're here . . .'

The prisoner started to whimper like a wounded dog and was shaking so violently that the governor, who clearly found the scene distasteful and wanted to put an end to the matter as soon as possible, exchanged a glance with the guard and, without saying a word, wrote the name the prisoner had given him in the register, swearing under his breath.

'Bloody war,' he muttered to himself when they took the prisoner to his cell, dragging him naked through the flooded tunnels.

2

The cell was a dark, damp rectangle. Cold air blew in through a small hole drilled in the rock. The walls were covered with crudely etched marks and messages left by previous tenants. Some had written their names, a date, or left some other proof of their existence. One of them had busied himself scratching crucifixes in the dark, but heaven did not seem to have noticed them. The iron bars securing the cell were rusty and left a film of brown on one's hands.

Huddled up on the ramshackle bunk, Fermín tried to cover his nakedness with a bit of ragged cloth which, he imagined, served as blanket, mattress and pillow. The half-light was tinged with a coppery hue, like the breath of a dying candle. After a while, his eyes became accustomed to the gloom and his ears sharpened, allowing him to pick up the sound of slight movements through a litany of dripping leaks and echoes carried by the draught that seeped in from outside.

Fermín had been sitting there for half an hour when he noticed a shape in the dark, at the other end of the cell. He stood up and stepped slowly towards it: it was a dirty canvas bag. The cold and the damp had started to get into his bones and, although the smell from that bundle, spattered with dark stains, did not augur well, Fermín thought that perhaps it contained the prisoner's uniform nobody had bothered to give him and, with a bit of luck, a blanket to protect him from the bitter cold. He knelt down and untied the knot closing one end of the bag.

When he drew the canvas aside, the dim light from the oil lamps flickering in the corridor revealed what at first he took to be the face of a doll, one of those dummies tailors place in their shop windows to show off their suits. The stench and his nausea made him realise it was no dummy. Covering his nose and mouth with one hand, he pulled the rest of the canvas to one side, then stepped backwards until he collided with the wall of the cell.

The corpse seemed to be that of an adult anywhere between forty and seventy-five years of age, who couldn't have weighed more than fifty kilos. A tangle of white hair and a beard covered much of his face and skeletal torso. His bony hands, with long, twisted nails, looked like the claws of a bird. His eyes were open, the corneas shrivelled up like overripe fruit. His mouth was open too, with his tongue, black and swollen, wedged between rotten teeth.

'Take his clothes off before they come and fetch him,' came a voice from the cell on the other side of the corridor. 'You won't get anything else to wear until next month.'

Fermín peered into the shadows and spied two shining eyes observing him from the bunk in the other cell.

'Don't be afraid, the poor soul can't hurt anyone any more,' the voice assured him.

Fermín nodded and walked over to the sack again, wondering how he was going to carry out the operation.

'My sincerest apologies,' he mumbled to the deceased. 'May God rest your soul.'

'He was an atheist,' the voice from the opposite cell informed him.

Fermín gave another nod and decided to skip the formalities. The cold permeating the cell was so intense it cut through one's bones and any courtesy seemed redundant. Holding his breath, he set to work. The clothes smelled the same as the dead man. Rigor mortis had begun to spread through the body and the task of undressing the corpse turned out to be much harder than he'd anticipated. Once the deceased's best clothes had been plucked off, Fermín covered him again with the sack and closed it with a reef knot that even the great Houdini would have been unable to tackle. At last, dressed in a ragged and foul-smelling prison uniform, Fermín huddled up again on the bed, wondering how many prisoners had worn it before him.

'Much appreciated,' he said finally.

'You're very welcome,' said the voice on the other side of the corridor.

'Fermín Romero de Torres, at your service.'

'David Martín.'

Fermín frowned. The name sounded familiar. For five long minutes he shuffled through distant memories and echoes from the past and then, suddenly, it came to him. He remembered whole afternoons spent in a corner of the library on Calle del Carmen, devouring a series of books with racy covers and titles.

'Martín the author? Of *City of the Damned*?'

A sigh in the shadows.

'Nobody appreciates pen names any more.'

'Please excuse my indiscretion. It's just that I had an almost scholarly devotion to your work. That's why I know you were the person writing the novels of the immortal Ignatius B. Samson . . .'

'At your service.'

'Well, Señor Martín, it's an honour to meet you, even if it is in these wretched circumstances, because I've been a great admirer of yours for years and . . .'

'Are you two lovebirds going to shut up? Some people here are trying to sleep,' roared a bitter voice that seemed to come from the next-door cell.

'There goes old Sourpuss,' a second voice cut in, coming from further down the corridor. 'Pay no attention to him, Martín. If you fall asleep here you just get eaten alive by bedbugs, starting with your privates. Go on, Martín, why don't you tell us a story? One about Chloé . . .'

'Sure, so you can jerk off like a monkey,' answered the hostile voice.

'Fermín, my friend,' Martín announced from his cell. 'Let me introduce you to Number Twelve, who finds something wrong in everything, and I mean *everything*, and Number Fifteen, insomniac, educated and the cell block's official ideologue. The rest don't speak much, especially Number Fourteen.'

'I speak when I have something to say,' snapped a deep, icy voice Fermín assumed must belong to Number 14. 'If we all followed suit, we'd get some peace at night.'

Fermín took in this peculiar community.

'Good evening, everyone. My name is Fermín Romero de Torres and it's a pleasure to make all your acquaintances.'

'The pleasure is entirely yours,' said Number 15.

'Welcome, and I hope your stay is brief,' offered Number 14.

Fermín glanced again at the sack housing the corpse and gulped.

'That was Lucio, the former Number Thirteen,' Martín explained. 'We don't know anything about him because the poor fellow was mute. A bullet blew off his larynx at the battle of the Ebro.'

'A shame he was the only one,' remarked Number 15.

'What did he die of?' asked Fermín.

'In this place one just dies from being here,' answered Number 12. 'It doesn't take much more.'

3

Routine helped. Once a day, for an hour, the inmates from the first two cell blocks were taken to the yard within the moat to get a bit of sun, rain, or whatever the weather brought with it. The menu consisted of a half-full bowl of some cold, greasy, greyish gruel of indeterminate provenance and rancid taste which, after a few days, and with hunger cramps in one's stomach, eventually became odourless and thus easier to get down. It was doled out halfway through the afternoon and in time prisoners came to look forward to its arrival.

Once a month prisoners handed in their dirty clothes and were given another set which had supposedly been plunged into boiling water for a minute, although the bugs didn't seem to have noticed it. On Sundays inmates were advised to attend mass. Nobody dared miss it, because the priest took a roll call and if there was any name missing he'd write it down. Two absences meant a week of fasting. Three, a month's holiday in one of the solitary confinement cells in the tower.

The cell blocks, courtyard and any other areas through which the prisoners moved were heavily guarded. A body of sentries armed with rifles and guns patrolled the prison and, when the inmates were out of their cells, it was impossible for them to look in any direction and not see at least a dozen of those guards, alert, their weapons at the ready. They were joined by the less threatening jailers, none of whom looked like soldiers; the general feeling among the prisoners was that they were a bunch of unfortunate souls who had been unable to find a better job in those hard times.

Every block of cells had a jailer assigned to it. Armed with a bundle of keys, he worked twelve-hour shifts sitting on a chair at the end of the corridor. Most of the jailers avoided fraternising with the prisoners and didn't give them a word or a look beyond what was strictly necessary. The only one who seemed to be an exception was a poor devil nicknamed Bebo, who had lost an eye in an air raid when he worked as a nightwatchman in a factory in Pueblo Seco.

It was rumoured that Bebo had a twin brother jailed in Valencia and perhaps this was why he showed some kindness towards the prisoners. When nobody was watching, he would occasionally slip them some drinking water, a bit of dry bread or whatever he could scrounge from the hoard the guards amassed out of packages sent by the prisoners' families. Bebo liked to drag his chair near David Martín's cell and listen to the stories the writer sometimes told the other inmates. In that particular hell, Bebo was the closest thing to an angel.

Normally, after Sunday mass, the governor addressed a few edifying words to the prisoners. All they knew about him was that his name was Mauricio Valls and that before the war he'd been an aspiring writer who worked as secretary and errand-boy for a well-known local author, a long-standing rival of the ill-fated Don Pedro Vidal. In his spare time Valls penned bad translations of Greek and Latin classics and, with the help of a couple of kindred souls, edited a cultural pamphlet with high pretensions and low circulation. They also organised literary gatherings in which a whole battalion of like-minded luminaries deplored the state of things, forecasting that if one day they were able to call the shots, the world would rise to Olympian heights.

His life seemed destined for the bitter, grey existence of mediocrities whom God, in his infinite cruelty, has endowed with delusions of grandeur and a boundless ambition far exceeding their talents. The war, however, had recast his destiny as it had that of so many others, and his luck had changed when, in a situation somewhere between chance and fortune-hunting, Mauricio

Valls, until then enamoured only of his own prodigious talent and exquisite refinement, wedded the daughter of a tycoon whose far-reaching enterprises supported much of General Franco's budget and his troops.

The bride, eight years his senior, had been confined to a wheelchair since the age of thirteen, consumed by a congenital illness that mercilessly devoured her muscles and her life. No man had ever looked into her eyes or held her hand to tell her she was beautiful and ask what her name was. Mauricio, who like all untalented men of letters was, deep down, as practical as he was conceited, was the first and last to do so, and a year later the couple married in Seville, with General Queipo de Llano and other luminaries of the state apparatus in attendance.

'Valls, you'll go far,' Serrano Súñer himself predicted during a private audience in Madrid to which Valls had gone to plead for the post of director of the National Library.

'Spain is living through difficult moments and every well-born Spaniard must put his shoulder to the wheel and help contain the hordes of Marxists attempting to corrupt our spiritual resolve,' the Caudillo's brother-in-law announced, looking resplendent in his pantomime-admiral's uniform.

'You can count on me, Your Excellency,' Valls offered. 'For whatever is needed.'

'Whatever is needed' turned out to be the post of director, not of the wondrous National Library in Madrid as he would have wished, but of a prison with a dismal reputation, perched on a clifftop overlooking the city of Barcelona. The list of close friends and protégés requiring plum posts was exceedingly lengthy and Valls, despite all his endeavours, only made the bottom third of the queue.

'Be patient, Valls. Your efforts will be rewarded.'

That is how Mauricio Valls learned his first lesson in the complex national art of elbowing ahead after any change of regime: thousands of supporters had joined the ranks and the competition was fierce.

4

That, at least, was the story. This unconfirmed catalogue of suspicions, accusations and third-hand rumours reached the ears of the prisoners – and of whoever would listen – thanks to the shady machinations of the previous governor. He had been unceremoniously removed from office after only two weeks in charge and was poisoned with resentment against that upstart Valls, who had robbed him of the post he'd been fighting for throughout the entire war. As luck would have it, the outgoing governor had no family connections and carried with him the fateful precedent of having been caught, when inebriated, uttering humorous asides about the Generalissimo of all Spains and his remarkable likeness to Dopey. Before being installed as deputy governor of a Ceuta prison he had put all his efforts into badmouthing Don Mauricio Valls to the four winds.

What was uncontested was that nobody could refer to Valls by any name other than 'the governor'. The official version, which he himself put about and authorised, was that he, Don Mauricio, was a man of letters, of recognised achievement and cultured intellect, blessed with a fine erudition acquired during the years he'd studied in Paris. Beyond his temporary position in the penitentiary sector of the regime, his future and his mission lay in educating the ordinary people of a decimated Spain, teaching them how to think with the help of a select circle of sympathisers.

His lectures often included lengthy quotes from his own writings, poems or educational articles which he published regularly in the national press on literature, philosophy and the much needed renaissance of thought in the Western world. If the prisoners applauded enthusiastically at the end of these masterly sessions, the governor would make a magnanimous gesture and order the jailers to give out cigarettes, candles or some other luxury confiscated from the batch of donations and parcels sent to the prisoners by their families. The more desirable items had been previously expropriated by the guards, who took them home or sometimes even sold them to the inmates. It was better than nothing.

Those who died from natural or loosely attributed causes – on average between five and ten a week – were collected at midnight, except at weekends or on religious holidays, when the body would remain in the cell until the Monday or the next working day, usually keeping a new tenant company. When prisoners called out to announce that one of their companions had passed away, a jailer would walk over, check the body for pulse or breath and then put it into one of the canvas sacks used for this purpose. Once the sack had been tied, it remained in the cell until the undertakers from the neighbouring Montjuïc Cemetery came by to collect it. Nobody knew what they did with them and when the prisoners asked Bebo about it, he refused to answer, lowering his eyes.

Once a fortnight a summary trial took place and those condemned were shot at dawn. Sometimes, owing to the bad state of the rifles or the ammunition, the execution squad didn't manage to pierce a vital organ and the agonised cries from the wounded who had fallen into the moat rang out for hours. Occasionally an explosion was heard and the shouts would suddenly cease. The theory circulating among the prisoners was that one of the officers finished them off with a grenade, but nobody was sure whether that was strictly accurate.

Another rumour making the rounds was that on Friday mornings the governor received visits in his office from wives, daughters, fiancées, or even aunts and grandmothers of the prisoners. Having removed his wedding ring, which he hid in the top drawer of his desk, he listened to their requests, considered their pleas, offered a handkerchief for their tears and accepted gifts and favours of another kind, after promising them better diets and treatment for their loved ones, or the review of dubious sentences, which regrettably were never addressed.

On selected occasions, Mauricio Valls served them teacakes and a glass of muscatel, and if, despite the hard times and poor nutrition, they were still attractive enough to pinch he would read them some of his writings and confess that his marriage to an ailing spouse was a trial of sanctity imposed upon his manhood. He'd then go on about how much he deplored his job as a jailer and how he considered it humiliating for a man of such high culture and refinement to be confined to that shameful post, when his natural destiny was to be a part of the country's higher echelons.

The advice from the more experienced prisoners was not to mention, and if possible not even think about, the governor. Most of them preferred to talk about the families they had left behind and the life they remembered. Some had photographs of girlfriends or wives which they treasured and would defend with their lives if anyone tried to snatch them away. More than one prisoner had told Fermín that the first three months were the worst. Afterwards, once you lost all hope, time began to go faster and the senseless days deadened your soul.

5

On Sundays, after mass and the governor's speech, some of the prisoners would gather in a sunny corner of the courtyard to share a cigarette or two and listen to the stories David Martín would tell them, when his mind was clear. Fermín, who knew them all because he'd read the entire *City of the Damned* series, would join the group and let his imagination fly. But often Martín didn't seem to be fit enough even to tell them the time of day, so the others would leave him alone while he wandered around talking to himself. Fermín observed him closely, following him at times, because there was something about that poor devil that broke his heart. Using all his cunning and wily tricks, Fermín would try to obtain cigarettes for him, or even a few lumps of sugar, which Martín loved.

'You're a good man, Fermín. Try not to let it show,' the writer would tell him.

Martín always carried an old photograph on him, which he liked to gaze at for long spells. It showed a man dressed in white, holding the hand of a girl of about eight. They were both watching the sunset from the end of a wooden jetty that stretched out over a beach, like a gangway suspended over crystalline waters. Usually, when Fermín asked him about the photograph, Martín didn't reply. He would just smile, before putting the picture back in his pocket.

'Who is the girl in the photograph, Señor Martín?'

'I'm not sure, Fermín. Sometimes my memory lets me down. Doesn't that happen to you?'

'Of course. It happens to everyone.'

It was rumoured that Martín was not altogether in his right mind, but soon after Fermín started to befriend him he realised that the poor man was far worse than the rest of the prisoners assumed. There were moments when he proved more lucid than anyone, but often he didn't seem to understand where he was and he spoke about people and places that obviously existed only in his imagination or memory.

Often Fermín would wake up in the early hours and hear Martín talking in his cell. If he drew stealthily up to the bars and listened carefully, he could hear him clearly arguing with someone he called 'Señor Corelli' who, judging by the words he exchanged with him, appeared to be a notoriously sinister character.

On one of those nights Fermín lit the remains of his last candle and raised it in the direction of the opposite cell. He wanted to make sure Martín really was alone and that both voices, his own and the other voice belonging to the person called Corelli, were coming from the same lips. Martín was walking in circles round his cell, and when their eyes met, Fermín realised that his prison mate couldn't see him. He was behaving as if those walls didn't exist and his conversation with that strange man was taking place far from there.

'Pay no attention to him,' murmured Number 12 from the shadows. 'He does that every night. He's off his trolley. Lucky him.'

The following morning, when Fermín asked him about the man called Corelli and his midnight conversations, Martín looked at him in surprise and gave him a puzzled smile. On another occasion, when Fermín was so cold he couldn't sleep, he walked over to the bars again and listened to Martín talking to one of his invisible friends. That night Fermín dared to interrupt him.

'Martín? It's me. Fermín, your neighbour across the landing. Are you all right?'

Martín walked over to the bars of his cell and Fermín could see his face was covered in tears.

'Señor Martín? Who is Isabella? You were talking about her a moment ago.'

Martín stared at him.

'Isabella is the only good thing remaining in this shitty world,' he replied after a while, with unusual bitterness. 'If it weren't for her, we might as well set fire to the whole thing and let it burn until even the ashes have blown away.'

'I'm sorry, Martín. I didn't mean to bother you.'

Martín withdrew into the shadows. The following day he was found shivering in a pool of his own blood. Seeing that Bebo had fallen asleep in his chair, he'd managed to slit his wrists by scratching them against the stone. When they took him away on a stretcher he was so pale Fermín thought he would never see him again.

'Don't worry about your friend, Fermín,' said Number 15. 'If that was anyone else, he'd go straight into the canvas sack, but the governor won't let Martín die. Nobody knows why.'

David Martín's cell was empty for five weeks. When Bebo brought him back, carrying him like a child, dressed in white pyjamas, Martín's arms were bandaged up to his elbows. He didn't remember anyone and spent the first night talking to himself and laughing. Bebo placed his chair facing Martín's bars and kept a close eye on him all night, handing him sugar lumps he'd stolen from the officers' room and hidden in his pockets.

'Señor Martín, please don't speak like that. God will punish you,' the jailer whispered to him between one sugar lump and the next.

In the real world, Number 12 had been Dr Román Sanahuja, head of General Medicine at Barcelona's Hospital Clínico, an honourable man, cured of ideological delusions, whose conscience and refusal to denounce his friends had sent him to the castle. As a rule, no prisoner's line of work was recognised within those walls. Unless such a line could reel in some benefit for the governor. In Dr Sanahuja's case, his usefulness was soon established.

'Unfortunately I don't have adequate medical resources at my disposal,' the governor had explained to him. 'Quite frankly, the regime has other worries and doesn't give a toss if you all rot in your cells from gangrene. After much battling I've got them to supply me with a badly equipped medicine cabinet and a washed-up quack who wouldn't even be accepted as a janitor in a veterinary clinic, I'm sure. But that's what there is. I know for a fact that before succumbing to the error of neutrality, you were a doctor of some renown. For reasons that are not of your concern, I have a vested interest in ensuring our mutual friend David Martín does not leave us prematurely. If you agree to collaborate and help keep him in reasonably good health, considering the circumstances, I can assure you I will make your stay in this place more agreeable and will personally see that your case is re-examined with a view to shortening your sentence.'

Dr Sanahuja nodded.

'It has come to my notice that some of the prisoners regard Martín as being rather soft in the head, as you would say. Is that so?' asked the governor.

'I'm not a psychiatrist, but in my humble opinion, I believe Martín is clearly unbalanced.'

The governor weighed up that remark.

'And, according to your expert medical opinion, how long would you say he could last?' he asked. 'Alive, I mean.'

'I don't know. Conditions in this prison are unhealthy and . . .'

The governor cut him off with a bored expression.

'And sane? How long do you think Martín can remain in possession of his mental faculties?'

'Not long, I think.'

'I see.'

The governor offered him a cigarette, which the doctor refused.

'You like him, don't you?'

'I hardly know him,' replied the doctor. 'He seems a decent enough man.'

The governor smiled.

'And an execrable writer. Possibly the worst this country has ever had.'

'You're the recognised authority on all matters literary, Governor. I know nothing about the subject.'

The governor gave him an icy look.

'I've sent men into solitary confinement for three months for less impertinent remarks. Few survive, and those who do come back in a worse state than your friend Martín. Don't make the fatal mistake of assuming that your qualifications grant you any privileges. Your records say you have a wife and three daughters out there. Your luck, as well as that of your family, depends on how useful you make yourself to me. Am I getting this across clearly?'

Dr Sanahuja swallowed hard.

'Yes, Governor.'

'Thank you, *Doctor*.'

From time to time, the governor would ask Sanahuja to take a look at Martín. It was no secret that the governor didn't trust the resident prison doctor, a dishonest charlatan who seemed to have forgotten the notion of preventive care from signing so many death certificates. The governor dismissed him shortly afterwards.

'How would you describe the patient's general state, Doctor?'

'Weak.'

'I see. What about his demons, so to speak? Is he still talking to himself and imagining things?'

'There's no noticeable change in that regard.'

'I'll take that as a yes. I read an excellent article in the *ABC* by my good friend Sebastián Jurado, in which he talks about schizophrenia, the poets' illness.'

'I'm not qualified to make such a diagnosis.'

'But you are, I hope, qualified to keep him alive, aren't you?'

'I'm doing my best with what I've got.'

'Your best may not be good enough. Consider the plight of your daughters. So young and vulnerable. So unprotected and with all those callous swine and reds still hiding out there.'

As the months went by, Dr Sanahuja became quite fond of Martín and one day, while sharing cigarette stubs, he told Fermín what he knew about the man whom some, because of his ravings and his status as the prison's resident lunatic, had jokingly nicknamed 'the Prisoner of Heaven'.

6

'Truth be told, I think that by the time they brought David Martín here he'd already been ill for some time. Have you ever heard of schizophrenia, Fermín? It's one of the governor's favourite new words.'

'It's what we civilians like to refer to as "being off one's rocker".'

'It's no joke, Fermín. It's a very serious illness. Not my speciality, but I've seen a few cases and the patients often hear voices, or they see and remember people and events that have never taken place . . . The mind slowly deteriorates and the patient can no longer distinguish between reality and fiction.'

'Like seventy per cent of Spaniards . . . And do you think poor Martín suffers from this illness, Doctor?'

'I'm not sure. As I said, I'm not a specialist, but I'd say he shows some of the most common symptoms.'

'Perhaps in this case his illness is a blessing . . .'

'It's never a blessing, Fermín.'

'And does he know that he is, shall we say, affected?'

'Madmen always think it's the others who are mad.'

'That's what I was saying about seventy per cent of Spaniards . . .'

A guard was watching them from the top of a sentry box, as if he were trying to read their lips.

'Lower your voice or we'll get into trouble.'

The doctor signalled to Fermín to turn around and walk towards the other end of the courtyard.

'In times like these, even walls have ears,' said the doctor.

'All we need now is for the walls to grow half a brain between the ears and we might get out of this mess,' answered Fermín.

'Do you know what Martín said to me the first time I was told by the governor to give him a medical examination?

'*"Doctor, I think I've discovered the only way of getting out of this prison."*

'*"How?"*

'*"Dead."*

'*"Can't you think of a more practical way?"*

'*"Have you read* The Count of Monte Cristo, *Doctor?"*

'*"As a kid. I barely remember it."*

'*"Well, reread it. It's all there."*

'I didn't want to tell him the governor had ordered all books by Dumas to be removed from the prison library, together with anything by Dickens, Galdós and many other authors whose works he considered rubbish for entertaining the uncultured masses. He replaced them with a collection of some of his own unpublished novels and short stories, together with books by friends of his, bound in leather by Valentí, a prisoner with a graphic arts background. Once Valentí had handed in his work, the governor let him die of exposure, forcing him to spend five nights out in the yard, in the rain, in the middle of January, just because he'd joked about the elegance of the governor's prose. Valentí managed to leave this place through Martín's method: dead.

'After I'd been here for some time, listening to conversations among the jailers, I realised that David Martín had come to the prison at the request of the governor himself. He was being held at La Modelo Prison, accused of a string of crimes which I don't think anyone really believed he'd committed. Among other things, they said he'd killed his mentor and best friend in a fit of jealousy – a wealthy man called Pedro Vidal, a writer like him – as well as Vidal's wife, Cristina. People also said he'd cold-bloodedly murdered a number of policemen and someone else, I can't remember who. These days they accuse so many people of so many things, you just don't know what to make of it. I find it hard to believe that Martín is a murderer, but it's also true that during the war years I saw so many people on either side remove their mask and show who they really were, that anything seems possible. Everyone casts the stone and then points a finger at his neighbour.'

'If I were to tell you . . .' remarked Fermín.

'The fact is that the father of this Vidal character is a powerful industrialist, stinking rich. They say he was one of the key bankers on the national side. Why is it that all wars are won by bankers? Anyway, this magnate, Vidal, personally asked the Ministry of Justice to find Martín and make sure he rotted in prison because of what he'd done to his son and his daughter-in-law. Apparently, Martín had fled the country and been on the run for almost three years when they found him near the border. He couldn't have been in his right mind to return to Spain where they were waiting to crucify him – at least, that's what I think. And to make matters worse, this happened during the final days of the war, when thousands of people were crossing over in the opposite direction.'

'Sometimes one just gets tired of fleeing,' said Fermín. 'The world's very small when you don't have anywhere to go.'

'I suppose that's what Martín must have thought. I don't know how he managed to cross the border, but some Puigcerdà locals notified the Civil Guards after they'd seen him wandering around the town for days, dressed in rags and talking to himself. Then some shepherds said they'd seen him on the Bolvir road, a couple of kilometres from Puigcerdà, near a large old house called La Torre del Remei, which in wartime had been turned into a hospital for wounded soldiers. It was run by a group of women who probably felt sorry for Martín and, taking him for a soldier, offered him shelter and food. When the Civil Guards got there he'd already left, but that night they caught him walking over the frozen lake, trying to make a hole in the ice with a stone. At first they thought he was trying to commit suicide, so they took him to Villa San Antonio, the sanatorium. Apparently one of the doctors there recognised him – don't ask me how – and as soon as his name reached the military headquarters he was transferred to Barcelona.'

'The lion's den.'

'You can say that again. It seems the trial barely lasted two days. The list of accusations against him was endless and although there was hardly any evidence or proof of any sort to sustain them, for some strange reason the public prosecutor managed to produce a good number of witnesses. Dozens of people filed through court, showing such zealous hatred for Martín that even the judge was surprised – no doubt they had all been given handouts by the elder Vidal. Among them were old colleagues of Martín's from the years when he worked for a minor newspaper called *The Voice of Industry.* Coffee-shop intellectuals, poor devils and envious pricks of all sorts came out of the woodwork to swear that Martín was guilty of everything he was accused of, and more. You know how things work here. On the judge's orders, and Vidal senior's advice, all his works were confiscated and burned, being considered subversive material, immoral and contrary to decent behaviour. When Martín declared in the trial that the only decent behaviour he defended was reading, and anything else was the reader's business, the judge added another ten years to the sentence he'd already given him. It seems that instead of keeping his mouth shut during the trial Martín replied to everything he was asked without mincing his words, and ended up digging his own grave.'

'Everything can be forgiven in this world, save telling the truth.'

'The fact is, he was given a life sentence. *The Voice of Industry*, owned by Vidal senior, published a long piece listing all his crimes, and to cap it all, an editorial. Guess who signed it.'

'Our illustrious prison governor, Don Mauricio Valls.'

'The very one. He described him as "the worst writer in history" and was delighted that his books had been destroyed because they were "an affront to humanity and good taste".'

'That's exactly what they said about the Palau de la Música auditorium,' Fermín pointed out. 'We're so fortunate in this country to be blessed with the very cream of the international intellectual community. Unamuno was right when he said: let others do the inventing, we'll provide the opinions.'

'Innocent or not, after witnessing his public humiliation and the burning of every single page he'd ever written, Martín ended up in a cell in La Modelo Prison, where he probably would have died in a matter of weeks if it hadn't been for the fact that our governor, who had been following the case with great interest and for some strange reason was obsessed with Martín, was given access to his file and then asked for his transfer to this place. Martín told me that the day he arrived here, Valls had him brought into his office and fired off one of his lectures.

'"*Martín, you're a convicted criminal and probably a fanatical subversive, but something binds us together. We're both men of letters and although you spent your failed career writing rubbish for the ignorant masses who lack all intellectual guidance, I think you may be able to help me and thus redeem your errors. I have a collection of novels and poems I've been working on for the past few years. They're of an extraordinarily high literary standard. So much so, I very much fear that in this illiterate country there could be no more than three hundred readers capable of understanding and appreciating their worth. That is why I've been thinking that perhaps, because of the way you have prostituted your writings, and your closeness to the common man who reads potboilers in trams, you might help me make some small changes that will draw my work nearer to the lamentable levels of Spanish readers. If you agree to collaborate, I can assure you that I'll make your existence far more pleasant. I could even get your case reopened. Your little friend . . . What's her name? Ah, yes, Isabella. A beauty, if you will allow me the comment. Anyhow, your girlfriend came to see me and told me she's hired a young lawyer, someone called Brians, and has managed to raise enough money for your defence. Let's not kid ourselves: we both know there were no grounds for your case and you were sentenced thanks to dubious witnesses. You seem to make enemies with incredible ease, even among people I'm sure you don't even know exist. Don't make the mistake of making another enemy of me, Martín. I'm not one of those poor devils. Here, between these walls, to put it plainly, I am God.*"

'I don't know whether Martín accepted the governor's proposal or not, but I have a feeling he did, because he's still alive and clearly our particular God is still interested in keeping it that way, at least for the moment. He's even provided Martín with paper and the writing tools he has in his cell, I suppose so that he can rewrite our governor's great works and enable him to enter the Hall of Fame, achieving the literary glory he so craves. Personally, I don't know what to think. My impression is that poor Martín is in no fit state to rewrite even his own name. He seems to spend most of his time trapped in a sort of purgatory he's been building in his own head, where remorse and pain are eating him alive. Although my field is general medicine and I'm not qualified to give a diagnosis . . .'

7

The good doctor's story kindled Fermín's interest. True to his unconditional support of lost causes, he decided to do a little investigation on his own, hoping to discover more about Martín and, at the same time, perfect the idea of the escape *via mortis*, in the style of Monsieur Alexandre Dumas. The more he turned the matter over in his mind, the more he thought that, at least in this particular, the Prisoner of Heaven was not as nuts as they all made him out to be. Whenever they were allowed out into the yard, Fermín would contrive to go up to Martín and engage in conversation with him.

'Fermín, you and I are beginning to look like a couple. Every time I turn around, there you are.'

'I'm sorry, Señor Martín, it's just that I'm intrigued about something.'

'And what is it, exactly, that intrigues you so, pray tell?'

'Well, to put it bluntly, I can't for the life of me fathom how a decent fellow like you has consented to help that conceited, repugnant meatball of a governor in his rapacious attempts to pass himself off as chief literary lion.'

'Direct, aren't you? There don't seem to be any secrets in this place.'

'It's just that I have a natural flair for the art of detection and the finer investigative pursuits.'

'In which case you surely must also have surmised that I'm not a decent fellow, but a criminal.'

'That seems to have been the judge's estimation.'

'Backed up by an army and a half of witnesses who testified under oath.'

'Incidentally, all on a crook's payroll and chronically constipated with envy and petty chicanery, if I may say so.'

'You may, but it hardly changes anything. Tell me, Fermín, is there anything about me you don't know?'

'Heaps of things. But the one issue that really sticks in my gullet is why you are in business with that self-absorbed dunce. People like him are the gangrene of this country.'

'There are people like him everywhere, Fermín. Nobody holds the patent.'

'But only here do we take them seriously.'

'Perhaps, but don't judge him so hastily. In this whole farce, the governor is a far more complex character than it would appear. This self-absorbed dunce, as you so generously call him, is, for starters, a very powerful man.'

'God, according to him.'

'Within this particular purgatory, that may not be too far off the mark.'

Fermín screwed up his nose. He didn't like what he was hearing. It almost sounded as if Martín had been sipping the wine of his own downfall.

'Has he threatened you? Is that it? What more can he do to you?'

'To me? Nothing, except make me laugh. But to others, outside this place, he can do a lot of harm.'

Fermín kept quiet for a long while.

'You must forgive me, Señor Martín. I didn't mean to offend you. I hadn't thought of that.'

'You don't offend me, Fermín. On the contrary. I think you hold a far too generous view of my circumstances. Your trust says much more about yourself than about me.'

'It's that young miss, isn't it? Isabella.'

'It's a missus.'

'I didn't know you were married.'

'I'm not. Isabella isn't my wife. Or my lover, if that's what you're thinking.'

Fermín kept silent. He didn't want to doubt Martín's words, but just hearing him talk about that girl – whether she was single or married – he was quite convinced that she was the person poor Martín loved most in the world, probably the only thing that kept him alive in that well of misery. And the saddest thing was that he didn't even seem to realise it.

'Isabella and her husband run a bookshop, a place that has always held a very special meaning for me, ever since I was a child. The governor told me that if I didn't do what he was asking, he'd make sure they were accused of selling subversive material. They'd have their business seized and then they'd be sent to prison and their son, who isn't even three years old, would be taken from them.'

'That fucking son-of-a-bitch,' Fermín muttered.

'No, Fermín,' said Martín. 'This isn't your war. It's mine. It's what I deserve for having done what I've done.'

'You haven't done anything, Martín.'

'You don't know me well enough, Fermín. Not that you need to. What you must concentrate on is getting out of here.'

'Glad you bring that up, since that's the other thing I wanted to ask you. I hear you're developing an experimental method for getting out of this chamber pot. If you need a skinny guinea pig – but one that is bursting with enthusiasm – consider me at your service.'

Martín observed him thoughtfully.

'Have you read Dumas?'

'From cover to cover.'

'You look the type. If that's the case, you'll have an inkling of what's coming. Listen well.'

8

Fermín had been in captivity for six months when a series of circumstances substantially changed the course of his life. The first of these was that during that period, when the regime still believed that Hitler, Mussolini and Co. were going to win the war and that Europe would soon parade the same colours as the Generalissimo's underpants, an unhindered wave of thugs, informers and newly appointed commissars drove up the number of imprisoned, arrested, prosecuted or 'disappeared' citizens to an all-time high.

The country's jails couldn't cope with the influx. The military authorities had instructed the Montjuïc prison management to double or even treble their intake and thus absorb part of the torrent of convicts flooding that defeated, miserable Barcelona of 1940. To that effect, in his flowery Sunday speech, the governor informed the prisoners that from then on they would share their cells. Dr Sanahuja was moved into Martín's cell, presumably to keep an eye on him and protect him from his suicidal fits. Fermín had to share cell 13 with his grumpy old next-door neighbour, Number 14. All the prisoners in the block were coupled together in order to make room for the new arrivals who were driven up every night in vans from La Modelo or the Campo de la Bota prisons.

'Don't pull that face. I like it even less than you do,' Number 14 informed his new companion when he moved in.

'Let me warn you that unbridled hostility gives me insidious bouts of gas,' Fermín threatened. 'So drop the Buffalo Bill act. Make an effort to behave and try to piss facing the wall and without splashing, or one of these days you'll wake up sprouting mushrooms.'

Ex-Number 14 spent five days without speaking to Fermín. Finally, surrendering in the face of the sulphuric flatulence Fermín offered him in the middle of the night, he switched strategy.

'I did warn you,' said Fermín.

'All right. I give in. My name is Sebastián Salgado, a trade unionist by profession. Let's shake hands and be friends, but, please, I beg you, stop farting like that, because I'm beginning to hallucinate and in my dreams I see Comrade Joseph Stalin doing the charleston.'

Fermín shook Salgado's hand and noticed that he was missing his little finger and his ring finger.

'Fermín Romero de Torres, pleased to make your acquaintance at last. Member of the secret service in the Caribbean sector of the Catalan Government, now in the clandestine reserve. But my true vocation is bibliographer and lover of literature.'

Salgado looked at his new comrade-in-arms and rolled his eyes.

'And they say Martín is mad.'

'A madman is one who considers himself sane and thinks that fools don't belong in his rank.'

Salgado nodded, defeated.

The second circumstance occurred a few days later, when a couple of guards turned up at dusk to fetch him. Bebo opened their cell, trying to hide his concern.

'You, Skinny Arse, get up,' one of the guards muttered.

For a moment Salgado thought his prayers had been answered and Fermín was being taken away to be shot.

'Be brave, Fermín.' He smiled encouragingly. 'Off to die for God and country, what could be more beautiful?'

The two guards grabbed Fermín, shackled his hands and feet, and dragged him away among the anguished looks of the entire block and Salgado's roars of laughter.

'You're not farting your way out of this one, that's for sure,' laughed his companion.

9

Fermín was led through a maze of tunnels until they reached a long corridor with a heavy wooden door visible at one end. He felt queasy, convinced that his miserable life was now over and that Inspector Fumero would be waiting behind that door with a welding torch and the night off. To his surprise, when he reached the door one of the guards removed his shackles while the other one rapped gently.

'Come in,' answered a familiar voice.

That is how Fermín found himself in the governor's office, a room luxuriously decorated with fancy furniture and carpets presumably stolen from some ritzy mansion in the Bonanova area. The scene was rounded off with a Spanish flag – eagle, coat of arms and inscription – a portrait of the Caudillo with more retouching than a publicity shot of Marlene Dietrich, and the governor himself, Don Mauricio Valls, smiling behind his desk, enjoying an imported cigarette and a glass of brandy.

'Sit down. Don't be afraid,' he invited.

Fermín noticed a tray next to him, with a plateful of actual red meat grilled to perfection, sautéed fresh peas and steaming mashed potatoes that smelled of hot butter and spices.

'It's not a mirage,' said the governor softly. 'It's your dinner. I hope you brought an appetite.'

Fermín, who hadn't seen anything like it since 1936, threw himself on the food before the vision evaporated. The governor watched him wolf it down with a mild expression of disgust and disdain behind his fixed smile, smoking and smoothing his slicked-back hair every other minute. When Fermín had licked his plate clean as a mirror, Valls told the guards to leave. On his own, the governor seemed far more sinister than with an armed escort.

'Fermín, isn't it?' he asked casually.

Fermín nodded.

'You'll wonder why I've summoned you.'

Fermín shrank in his chair.

'Nothing that need worry you. On the contrary. I've made you come because I want to improve your living conditions and, who knows, perhaps review your sentence: we both know that the charges brought against you didn't hold water. That's the problem with times like ours, a lot of things get stirred up and sometimes it's the innocent who suffer. Such is the price of our national renaissance. Over and above such considerations, I want you to understand that I'm on your side. I'm a bit of a prisoner here myself. I'm sure we both want to get out as soon as possible and I thought we could help one another. Cigarette?'

Fermín accepted timidly.

'If you don't mind, I'll save it for later.'

'Of course. As you please. Here, have the whole packet.'

Fermín slid it into his pocket. The governor leaned over the table, smiling. There's a snake just like that in the zoo, thought Fermín, but that one only eats mice.

'So, how do you like your new cellmate?'

'Salgado? A true humanitarian.'

'I don't know whether you're aware that before we put him inside, this swine was an assassin for hire working for the communists.'

Fermín shook his head.

'He told me he was a trade unionist.'

Valls laughed softly.

'In May 1938, all on his own, he slipped into the home of the Vilajoana family on Paseo de la Bonanova and did away with them all, including their five children, the four maids and the eighty-six-year-old grandmother. Do you know who the Vilajoanas were?'

'Well, actually . . .'

'Jewellers. At the time of the crime there were jewels and cash in the house to the value of sixty-five thousand pesetas. Do you know where this money is now?'

'I don't know.'

'You don't know, and nobody knows. The only person who knows is Comrade Salgado, who decided not to hand it over to the proletariat but to hide it, so he could live in grand style after the war. Which is something he'll never do because we'll keep him here until he sings like a canary or until your friend Fumero slices what's left of him into little cutlets.'

Fermín nodded, putting two and two together.

'I'd noticed he is missing a couple of fingers on his left hand and he walks in a funny way.'

'One of these days you must ask him to pull his trousers down and you'll see he's also missing some other key equipment he's lost along the way because of his stubborn refusal to cooperate.'

Fermín gulped.

'I want you to know that I find such atrocities repugnant. That's one of the two reasons why you're here, and why I've ordered Salgado to be moved to your cell. Because I believe that when people talk they get to understand one another. I want you to discover where he's hidden the stash from the Vilajoanas, and from all the other thefts and crimes he committed in the last few years, and I want you to tell me.'

Fermín felt his heart fall to the ground.

'And the other reason?'

'The second reason is that I've noticed that you have recently become pals with David Martín. Which is fine by me. Friendship is a virtue that ennobles humans and helps rehabilitate prisoners. I'm not sure if you know that Martín is a writer of sorts.'

'I've heard something.'

The governor threw him an icy glance but kept up his friendly smile.

'Martín isn't a bad person, really, but he's mistaken about a lot of things. One of them is this naïve notion that he has to protect the weak and the innocent and such.'

'How extravagant of him.'

'Indeed. That's why I thought that perhaps it would be good if you keep close to him, with your eyes and ears well open, and tell me what he tells you, what he thinks and feels . . . I'm sure there must be something he's mentioned to you that has caught your attention.'

'Come to think of it, Governor, he's recently been complaining quite a lot about a spot in his groin where his underpants rub against him.'

The governor sighed and muttered something under his breath, visibly tired from having to feign so much politeness with such an undesirable specimen.

'Look here, you imbecile, we can do this the easy way or the hard way. I'm trying to be reasonable, but all I have to do is to pick up the phone and your friend Fumero will be here in half an hour. I've been told that lately, as well as the welding torch, he keeps a cabinetmaker's toolbox in one of the basement cells with which he works wonders. Am I making myself clear?'

Fermín clasped his hands to hide his trembling.

'Beautifully. Forgive me, Governor. I hadn't eaten beef for so long that the protein must have gone straight to my head. It won't happen again.'

The governor resumed his smile and continued as if nothing had happened.

'In particular, I'm interested in finding out whether he's ever mentioned a cemetery of forgotten books, or dead books, or something along those lines. Think carefully before you answer. Has Martín ever talked to you about such a place?'

Fermín shook his head.

'I swear, sir, I've never in my life heard Señor Martín, or anyone else, mention that place . . .'

The governor winked at him.

'I believe you. And that's why I know that if he does mention it, you'll tell me. And if he doesn't, you'll bring up the subject and find out where it is.'

Fermín nodded repeatedly.

'And one more thing. If Martín talks to you about a job I've asked him to do for me, convince him that in his own best interests, and in particular those of a certain young lady he holds in very high esteem, as well as the husband and child of the latter, he'd better get cracking and write his best work.'

'Do you mean Señora Isabella?' Fermín asked.

'Ah, I see he's mentioned her to you . . . You should see her,' said the governor while he wiped his glasses with a handkerchief. 'Young, really young, with that firm schoolgirl flesh . . . You don't know how often she's been sitting here, right where you are now, pleading for that poor wretch Martín. I won't tell you what she's offered me because I'm a gentleman but, between you and me, the devotion this girl feels for Martín is very telling. If I had to make a bet, I'd say that kid, Daniel, isn't her husband's but Martín's. He might have abysmal taste when it comes to literature but an exquisite eye for sluts.'

The governor stopped when he noticed that the prisoner was giving him an impenetrable look which he didn't appreciate.

'What are you staring at?' he challenged him.

He banged the table with his knuckles and instantly the door behind Fermín opened. The two guards grabbed him by his arms, hauling him up from his chair until his feet were dangling in the air.

'Remember what I've told you,' said the governor. 'In four weeks' time I want you in that chair again. If you bring me results, I can assure you your stay here will change for the better. If not, I'll book you into the basement cell with Fumero and his toys. Are we clear?'

'Crystal.'

Then, with a bored expression, the governor signalled to his men to take the prisoner away and downed his glass of brandy, sick and tired of having to talk to those uncultured yokels, day in, day out.

10

Barcelona, 1957

'Daniel, you've gone pale,' murmured Fermín, rousing me from my trance.

The dining room in Can Lluís, the streets we had walked down to get there, had all disappeared. All I could see before me was that office in Montjuïc Castle and the face of that man talking about my mother with words and insinuations that seared my very soul. At the same time, something cold and sharp moved inside me, an anger I had never known before. For a split second what I most yearned for in the world was to have that son-of-a-bitch before me so I could wring his neck and watch him until the veins in his eyes burst.

'Daniel . . .'

I closed my eyes and took a deep breath. When I opened them again I was back in Can Lluís, and Fermín Romero de Torres was looking at me, completely vanquished.

'Forgive me, Daniel,' he said.

My mouth was dry. I poured myself a glass of water and drank it down, waiting for words to come to my lips.

'There's nothing to forgive, Fermín. Nothing of what you've told me is your fault.'

'For a start, it's my fault for having to tell you,' he said, in such a soft voice it was barely audible.

I saw him lower his eyes, as if he didn't dare look me in the face. He seemed so overcome with pain from remembering that episode and having to reveal the truth to me that I felt ashamed of my own bitterness.

'Fermín, look at me.'

Fermín managed to look at me out of the corner of his eye and I smiled at him.

'I want you to know that I'm grateful to you for having told me the truth and that I understand why you preferred not to tell me anything about this years ago.'

Fermín nodded weakly but something in his eyes made me realise that my words were no comfort to him at all. On the contrary. We sat in silence for a few moments.

'There's more, isn't there?' I asked at last.

Fermín nodded.

'And what follows is worse?'

Fermín nodded again.

'Much worse.'

I looked away and smiled at Professor Alburquerque, who was now leaving, not without raising a hand in farewell.

'Well then, why don't we ask for another bottle of water and you tell me the rest?'

'Better if it's wine,' Fermín considered. 'The strong stuff.'

11

Barcelona, 1940

A week after the meeting between Fermín and the prison governor, a couple of individuals nobody in the cell block had ever set eyes on before – though they reeked of the political branch from a mile off – handcuffed Salgado and took him away without saying a word.

'Bebo, do you know where they're taking him?' asked Number 19.

The jailer shook his head, but the look in his eyes suggested that he'd heard something and preferred not to discuss the matter. With nothing else to talk about, Salgado's absence immediately became a subject for debate and speculation among the prisoners, who came up with all sorts of theories.

'That guy was a mole, put in here by the Nacionales *to get information out of us with that yarn about having been locked up because he was a trade unionist.'*

'Sure, that's why they pulled two fingers off him and goodness knows what else, to make it all sound more convincing.'

'I bet he's dining in the Amaya with his pals as we speak, stuffing himself with hake Basque-style, and laughing at us all.'

'What I think is that he's confessed whatever it was they wanted him to confess and they've chucked him ten kilometres out at sea with a stone tied round his neck.'

'He did look like a spook. Thank God I didn't open my mouth. The lot of you will be in a stew.'

'You never know, we might even be sent off to jail.'

For lack of other amusements, the discussions rumbled on until, two days later, the same men who had taken him away brought him back. The first thing all the inmates noticed was that Salgado couldn't stand up and was being dragged along like a bundle. The second thing was that he was as pale as a corpse and drenched in cold sweat. The prisoner had returned half naked and covered in a brownish scab that looked like a mixture of dry blood and excrement. They dropped him on the cell floor as if he were a sack of manure and left without saying a word.

Fermín took him in his arms and laid him down on the bunk. He started to wash him slowly with a few shreds of cloth he tore off his own shirt and a bit of water Bebo brought him on the quiet. Salgado was conscious and breathed with difficulty, but his eyes shone with an inner fire. Where, two days earlier, he'd had a left hand, he now had a throbbing stump of purplish flesh cauterised with tar. While Fermín cleaned his face, Salgado smiled at him with his few remaining teeth.

'Why don't you tell those butchers once and for all what they want to know, Salgado? It's only money. I don't know how much you've hidden, but it's not worth this.'

'Like hell!' he muttered with what little breath he had left. 'That money is mine.'

'It belongs to all those you murdered and robbed, if you don't mind the observation.'

'I didn't rob anyone. They'd robbed the people before that. And if I executed them it was to deliver the justice the people were demanding.'

'Sure. Thank God you came along, the Mediterranean Robin Hood, to right all wrongs and avenge the plight of the common folk.'

'That money is my future,' spat Salgado.

With the damp cloth, Fermín wiped Salgado's cold forehead, lined with scratches.

'One mustn't dream of one's future; one must earn it. And you have no future, Salgado. Neither you, nor a country that keeps producing beasts like you and the governor, and then looks the other way. Between us all we've destroyed the future and all that awaits us is shit like the shit you're dripping with now and that I'm sick of cleaning off you.'

Salgado emitted a sort of rasping whimper, which Fermín took to be laughter.

'Keep your sermons to yourself, Fermín. Don't pretend you're a hero now.'

'No, there are enough heroes. What I am is a coward. Exactly that,' said Fermín. 'But at least I know it and admit it.'

Fermín went on cleaning him as best he could, silently, and then covered him with the piece of blanket they shared – teeming with nits and stinking of urine. He sat next to the thief until Salgado closed his eyes and fell into a sleep from which Fermín didn't think he was ever going to wake.

'Tell me he's already dead,' came Number 15's voice.

'Bets accepted,' Number 17 added. 'A cigarette that he'll kick the bucket.'

'Go to sleep, or to hell, all of you,' said Fermín.

He curled up at the other end of the cell and tried to nod off, but soon realised he wasn't going to sleep that night. After a while he stuck his head between the bars and let his arms hang over the metal shaft fixed across them. On the other side of the corridor, from the shadows of the cell opposite his, two eyes, gleaming in the light of a cigarette, were watching him.

'You haven't told me what Valls wanted you for the other day,' said Martín.

'You can imagine.'

'Any request out of the ordinary?'

'He wants me to worm out of you something about a cemetery of books, or something like that.'

'Interesting,' said Martín.

'Fascinating.'

'Did he tell you why he was interested in the subject?'

'Quite frankly, Señor Martín, our relationship isn't that close. The governor merely threatens me with mutilation of various sorts unless I carry out his orders within four weeks and I merely say "yes, sir".'

'Don't worry, Fermín. In four weeks' time you'll be out of here.'

'Oh, sure, on a beach in the Caribbean, with two well-fed mulatto girls massaging my feet no less.'

'Have faith.'

Fermín let out a despondent sigh. The cards of his future were being dealt out among lunatics, thugs and dying men.

12

That Sunday, after the speech in the yard, the governor cast Fermín a questioning look, rounding it off with a smile that turned his stomach. As soon as the guards allowed the prisoners to fall out, Fermín edged over towards Martín.

'Brilliant speech,' Martín remarked.

'Historic. Every time that man speaks, the history of Western thought undergoes a Copernican revolution.'

'Sarcasm doesn't suit you, Fermín. It goes against your natural tenderness.'

'Go to hell.'

'I'm on my way. Cigarette?'

'I don't smoke.'

'They say it helps you die faster.'

'Bring it on then.'

He didn't manage to get beyond the first puff. Martín took the cigarette from his fingers and gave him a few pats on the back while Fermín seemed to be coughing up even the memories of his first communion.

'I don't know how you can swallow that. It tastes of singed dogs.'

'It's the best you can get here. Apparently they're made from cigarette stubs picked up in the corridors of the Monumental bull-ring.'

'The bouquet suggests it's more likely from the urinals.'

'Take a deep breath, Fermín. Feeling better?'

Fermín nodded.

'Are you going to tell me something about that cemetery so that I have a bit of offal to throw at the head swine? It doesn't have to be true. Any nonsense you can come up with will do.'

Martín smiled as he exhaled the fetid smoke through his teeth.

'How's your cellmate, Salgado, the defender of the poor?'

'Here's a story for you. I thought I'd reached a certain age and had seen it all in this circus of a world. But, early this morning, when it looked like Salgado had given up the ghost, I hear him get up and walk over to my bunk like a vampire.'

'He does have something of the vampire,' agreed Martín.

'Anyway, he comes over and stands there staring at me. I pretend to be asleep and when Salgado takes the bait, I see him scurry off to a corner and with the only hand he has left he starts to poke around in what medical science refers to as the rectum or final section of the large intestine,' Fermín continued.

'What did you say?'

'You heard it. Good old Salgado, still convalescing from his most recent session of medieval amputation, decides to celebrate being back on his feet by exploring that long-underrated area of human anatomy where Mother Nature has decreed the sun doesn't shine. I can't believe my eyes and don't even dare breathe. A minute goes by and Salgado looks as if he has two or three fingers, all the ones he has left, stuck in there in search of the philosopher's stone or some very deep piles. All of which is accompanied by a low, hushed moaning which I'm not going to bother to reproduce.'

'I'm dumbfounded,' said Martín.

'Then brace yourself for the grand finale. After a minute or two of prospective digging, he lets out a Saint John of the Cross-type sigh and the miracle happens. When he removes his fingers from anal territory he pulls out something shiny that even from the corner where I'm lying I can certify is no standard faecal arrangement, pardon my French.'

'So what was it, then?'

'A key. Not a spanner, just one of those small keys, the sort used for briefcases or a locker in the gym.'

'What then?'

'Then he takes the key, polishes it with a bit of spit – because I imagine it must have smelled of roses – and then goes over to the wall where, after making sure I'm still asleep, a fact that I confirm through finely rendered snores, like those of a Saint Bernard puppy, he proceeds to hide the key by inserting it in a crack between stones which he then covers with filth and, I dare say, some collateral resulting from his explorations in his nether parts.'

For a while Martín and Fermín looked at one another without speaking.

'Are you thinking what I'm thinking?' asked Fermín.

Martín nodded.

'How much do you reckon the old crap shooter must have hidden in his little nest of greed?' asked Fermín.

'Enough to believe that it's worth his while to lose fingers, hands, part of his testicular mass and God knows what else to keep its whereabouts secret,' Martín guessed.

'And what do I do now? Before I let a snake like the governor snatch Salgado's little treasure – to fund hardback editions of his collected works and buy himself a seat in the Royal Academy of Language – I'd rather swallow that key, or, if necessary, even introduce it into the ignoble part of my own digestive tract.'

'Don't do anything for the time being,' Martín advised. 'Make sure the key is still there and await my instructions. I'm putting the finishing touches to your escape.'

'No offence, Señor Martín, since I'm extremely grateful for your counsel and moral support, but you're getting me to put my head and some other esteemed appendages on the block with this idea of yours, and considering the general consensus that you're as mad as a hatter, it troubles me to think I'm placing my life in your hands.'

'None taken, but, if you don't trust a novelist, who are you going to trust?'

Fermín watched Martín walk off down the yard wrapped in his portable cloud of cigarette-stub smoke.

'Holy mother of God,' he murmured to the wind.

13

The macabre betting syndicate organised by Number 17 continued to thrive for a few more days during which Salgado sometimes looked as if he were about to expire and then, just as suddenly, would get up, drag himself to the bars of the cell and declaim at the top of his voice the stanza: 'You-fucking-bastards-you're-not-getting-a-penny-out-of-me-you-fucking-sons-of-bitches' and variations on the theme, until he screamed himself hoarse and collapsed exhausted on the floor, from where Fermín had to lift him and take him back to the bed.

'Is old Cockroach succumbing, Fermín?' asked Number 17 every time he heard him slump to the floor.

Fermín no longer bothered giving medical updates on his cellmate. If it happened, they'd soon see the canvas sack passing by.

'Look here, Salgado, if you're going to die, do so once and for all, and if you plan to live, I beg you to do it silently because I'm fed up to the back teeth with your foaming-at-the-mouth recitals,' Fermín told him, tucking him up with a piece of dirty canvas. In Bebo's absence, he'd managed to obtain it from one of the jailers after winning him over with a foolproof strategy for seducing young girls – by overcoming their resistance with carefully measured doses of whipped cream and sponge fingers.

'Don't give me that charitable crap. I know what you're up to. You're no better than this pack of vultures willing to bet their underpants that I'm going to croak,' Salgado replied. He seemed ready to keep up his foul mood to the very end.

'I'm not one to argue with a man in his death throes but I'm letting you know that I haven't bet a single *real* in this gambling den, and if I ever wanted to give myself over to vice it wouldn't be betting on the life of a human being. Although you're as much a human being as I'm a glow-worm,' Fermín pronounced.

'Don't think for a minute that all that talk of yours is going to distract me,' Salgado snapped back maliciously. 'I know perfectly well what you and your bosom friend Martín are plotting with all that *Count of Monte Cristo* business.'

'I don't know what you're babbling about, Salgado. Sleep for a bit, or for a year, since nobody's going to miss you anyhow.'

'If you think you're getting out of this place you're as mad as he is.'

Fermín felt a cold sweat on his back. Salgado bared his smashed teeth in a smile.

'I knew it,' he said.

Swearing under his breath, Fermín curled up in his corner, as far away as he could get from Salgado. The peace only lasted a minute.

'My silence has a price,' Salgado announced.

'I should have let you die when they brought you back,' murmured Fermín.

'As proof of my gratitude I'm prepared to give you a discount,' said Salgado. 'All I ask of you is to do me one last favour and I'll keep your secret.'

'How do I know it's the last?'

'Because you're going to get caught, just like everyone else who's tried to leg it out of here, and after they've riled you for a few days you'll be garrotted in the yard, as an edifying sight for the rest of us. And then I won't be able to ask you for anything else. What do you say? A small favour and my complete cooperation. I give you my word of honour.'

'Your word of honour? Man, why didn't you say so before? That changes everything.'

'Come closer . . .'

Fermín hesitated for a moment, but told himself he had nothing to lose.

'I know that son-of-a-bitch Valls has put you up to it, to find out where I've hidden the money,' he said. 'Don't bother to deny it.'

Fermín shrugged his shoulders.

'I want you to tell him,' Salgado instructed Fermín.

'Whatever you say, Salgado. Where is the money?'

'Tell the governor that he must go alone, in person. If anyone goes with him he won't get a *duro* out of it. Tell him he must go to the old Vilardell factory in Pueblo Nuevo, behind the graveyard. At midnight. Not before, and not after.'

'Sounds like an episode from *The Phantom*, Salgado, one of the bad ones . . .'

'Listen carefully. Tell him he must go into the factory and find the old guards' lodge, next to the textile mill. When he gets there he must knock on the door, and when they ask him who's there, he must say: "Durruti lives".'

Fermín chuckled.

'It's the most idiotic thing I've heard since the governor's last speech.'

'You just tell him what I've told you.'

'And how do you know I won't go there myself? If I follow your cheap melodrama and passwords I could take the money.'

Avarice shone in Salgado's eyes.

'Don't tell me: because I'll be dead,' Fermín completed.

Salgado's reptilian smile spilled over his lips. Fermín studied those eyes, eaten away by his thirst for revenge. He realised then what Salgado was after.

'It's a trap, isn't it?'

Salgado didn't reply.

'What if Valls survives? Haven't you stopped to think what they'll do to you?'

'Nothing they haven't done to me already.'

'I'd say you've got balls, if it wasn't for the fact that you only have a bit of one left. And if this move of yours doesn't pan out, you won't even have that much,' Fermín suggested.

'That's my problem,' retorted Salgado. 'So what's it to be, Monte Cristo? Is it a deal?'

Salgado offered him his one remaining hand. Fermín stared at it for a few moments before shaking it reluctantly.

14

Fermín had to wait for the traditional Sunday lecture after mass and the brief period in the yard to go over to Martín and confide in him what Salgado had asked him to do.

'It won't interfere with the plan,' Martín assured him. 'Do what he's asking you to do. We can't risk a tip-off at this point.'

Fermín, who for days had been hovering between feelings of nausea and a racing heart, dried the cold sweat dripping down his forehead.

'Martín, it's not that I don't trust you, but if this plan you're preparing is so good, why don't you use it to get out of here yourself?'

Martín nodded, as if he'd been expecting that question for days.

'Because I deserve to be here, and even if I didn't, there's nowhere left for me outside these walls. I have nowhere to go.'

'You have Isabella . . .'

'Isabella is married to a man who is ten times better than me. All I would achieve by getting out of here would be to make her miserable.'

'But she's doing everything possible to get you out . . .'

Martín shook his head.

'You must promise me one thing, Fermín. It's all I'm going to ask you to do in exchange for helping you escape.'

This is the month for requests, thought Fermín, nodding readily.

'Whatever you say.'

'If you manage to leave this place I want you, if you can, to take care of her. From a distance, without her knowing, without her even knowing you exist. I want you to take care of her and of her son, Daniel. Will you do that for me, Fermín?'

'Of course.'

Martín smiled sadly.

'You're a good man, Fermín.'

'That's the second time you've told me, and every time it sounds worse to me.'

Martín pulled out one of his stinking cigarettes and lit it.

'We don't have much time. Brians, the lawyer Isabella hired to act on my case, was here yesterday. I made the mistake of telling him what Valls wants me to do.'

'The business about rewriting that garbage of his . . .'

'Exactly. I asked him not to say anything to Isabella, but I know him, and sooner or later he will, and Isabella, whom I know even better, will fly into a rage and come here to threaten Valls with broadcasting his secret from the rooftops.'

'Can't you stop her?'

'Trying to stop Isabella is like trying to stop a cargo train: a fool's errand.'

'The more you talk about her the more I'd like to meet her. I like women with spirit . . .'

'Fermín, let me remind you of your promise.'

Fermín put his hand on his heart and nodded solemnly. Martín continued.

'As I was saying, when this happens, Valls might do something stupid. He's driven by vanity, envy and greed. When he feels he's been cornered he'll make a false move. I don't know what, but I'm sure he'll try to do something. It's important that by then you're already out of here.'

'As you know, I'm not too keen on this place . . .'

'You don't understand. We've got to speed up the plan.'

'When to?'

Martín watched him at length through the curtain of smoke rising from his lips.

'To tonight.'

Fermín tried to swallow, but his mouth felt as if it were full of dust.

'But I don't even know what the plan is yet . . .'

'Listen carefully.'

15

That afternoon, before returning to his cell, Fermín approached one of the two guards who had escorted him to Valls's office.

'Tell the governor I need to talk to him.'

'What about?'

'Tell him I have the results he was waiting for. He'll know what I mean.'

Before an hour had passed, the guard and his colleague were at the door of cell number 13 to fetch Fermín. Salgado watched the whole thing eagerly from the bunk as he massaged his stump. Fermín winked at him and set off, escorted by the guards.

The governor received him with an effusive smile and a plateful of delicious pastries from Casa Escribá.

'Fermín, dear friend, what a pleasure to see you here again, ready for an intelligent and productive conversation. Do sit down, please. And enjoy this fine selection of sweets brought to me by the wife of one of the prisoners.'

Fermín, who for days hadn't been able to swallow so much as a birdseed, picked up a ring-shaped pastry so as not to disobey Valls, and held it in his hand as if he were holding an amulet. Valls poured himself a glass of brandy and dropped into his ample general's armchair.

'So? I understand you have good news for me,' the governor said, inviting Fermín to talk.

Fermín nodded.

'In the belles-lettres department, I can assure Your Honour that Martín is more than persuaded and motivated to carry out the polishing and ironing task he was requested to do. Moreover, he remarked that the material you supplied him with, sir, is of such a high quality and so fine, that he thinks it will pose no difficulties. All he needs to do is dot a few i's and cross a few t's in your work of genius to produce a masterpiece worthy of the great Paracelsus.'

Valls paused to absorb Fermín's barrage of words, but nodded politely without removing his frozen smile.

'There's no need for you to sweeten it for me, Fermín. It's enough for me to know that Martín will do what he has to do. We're both aware that he doesn't like the task he's been assigned, but I'm glad he's seeing reason at last and understands that making things possible benefits us all. And now, about the other two points . . .'

'I was coming to that, sir. Concerning the burial ground of the lost volumes . . .'

'The Cemetery of Forgotten Books,' Valls corrected him. 'Have you been able to extract its location from Martín?'

Fermín nodded with utter conviction.

'From what I've been able to gather, the aforementioned ossuary is hidden behind a labyrinth of tunnels and chambers, beneath the Borne market.'

Valls weighed up that revelation, visibly surprised.

'And the entrance?'

'I wasn't able to get that far, sir. I imagine that it must be through some trapdoor camouflaged behind the uninviting paraphernalia and stench of some of the wholesale vegetable stalls. Martín didn't want to talk about it and I thought that if I pressed him too much he might dig his heels in.'

Valls nodded slowly.

'You did the right thing. Go on.'

'And finally, in reference to Your Excellency's last request, taking advantage of the death throes and moral agonies of that despicable Salgado, I was able to persuade him, in his delirium, to confess where he'd hidden the copious booty from his criminal activities in the service of Freemasonry and Marxism.'

'So, you think he's going to die?'

'Any moment now. I think he's already commended himself to Saint Leon Trotsky and is awaiting his last breath to rise into the politburo of posterity.'

'I told those animals they wouldn't extract anything out of him by force,' Valls muttered under his breath.

'Technically, I believe they extracted a gonad or a limb, but I agree with you, sir, that with vermin like Salgado the only possible method is applied psychology.'

'So then? Where did he hide the money?'

Fermín leaned forward and adopted a confidential tone.

'It's complicated to explain.'

'Don't beat about the bush or I'll send you down to the basement to have your vocal cords refreshed.'

Fermín then proceeded to sell Valls that outlandish plot he'd obtained from Salgado's lips. The governor listened incredulously.

'Fermín, let me warn you that if you're lying you'll be deeply sorry. What they've done to Salgado won't even be a foretaste of what they'll do to you.'

'I can assure Your Lordship that I'm repeating, word for word, what Salgado told me. If you like I'll swear on the irrefutable portrait of Franco that lies on your desk.'

Valls looked him straight in the eye. Fermín held his gaze without blinking, just as Martín had taught him to do. Finally, having procured the information he was looking for, the governor removed his smile as well as the plate of pastries. Without any pretence at cordiality, he snapped his fingers and the two guards came in to lead Fermín back to his cell.

This time Valls didn't even bother to threaten Fermín. As they dragged him down the corridor, Fermín saw the governor's secretary walking past them and stopping outside Valls's office.

'Governor, Sanahuja, the doctor in Martín's cell . . .'

'Yes. What?'

'He says Martín has fainted and thinks it might be something serious. He asks for permission to go to the medicine cabinet and get a few things . . .'

Valls stood up in a fury.

''So what are you waiting for? Go on. Take him there and let him have whatever he needs.'

16

Following the governor's orders, a jailer was left posted in front of Martín's cell while Dr Sanahuja treated him. The jailer was a young man of about twenty who was new to the shift. The night shift was supposed to be covered by Bebo, but instead that novice had inexplicably turned up, looking incapable even of sorting out his bunch of keys and more nervous than any of the prisoners. At about nine o'clock the doctor, noticeably tired, walked over to the bars of his cell and spoke to him.

'I need more clean gauze and some antiseptic.'

'I can't abandon my post.'

'And I can't abandon a patient. Please. Gauze and antiseptic.'

The jailer stirred nervously.

'The governor doesn't like it when his instructions are not followed word for word.'

'He'll like it even less if anything happens to Martín because you've ignored me.'

The young jailer assessed the situation.

'Listen, boss,' argued the doctor. 'We're unlikely to walk through the walls or swallow the iron bars . . .'

The jailer swore and rushed off to the medicine cabinet, while Sanahuja stood by the bars of his cell and waited. Salgado had been asleep for a couple of hours, breathing with difficulty. Fermín tiptoed up to the front of his cell and exchanged glances with the doctor. Sanahuja then threw him a parcel, the size of a pack of cards, wrapped in a shred of material and tied with a piece of string. Fermín caught it in the air and quickly retreated to the shadows at the far end of his cell. When the jailer returned with what

Sanahuja had asked him for, he peered through the bars, inspecting Salgado's silhouette on the bunk.

'He's on his last legs,' said Fermín. 'I don't think he'll last till tomorrow.'

'You keep him alive until six. I don't want him to screw things up for me. Let him die during someone else's shift.'

'I'll do what is humanly possible, boss,' replied Fermín.

17

That night, while Fermín unwrapped the parcel Dr Sanahuja had tossed him from the other side of the corridor, a black Studebaker was driving the governor down the road from Montjuïc towards the dark streets bordering the port. Jaime, the chauffeur, was taking great care to avoid potholes and any jolts that might inconvenience his passenger or interrupt the flow of his thoughts. The new governor was not like the previous one. The previous governor would strike up conversations with him in the car and once in a while he had sat in the front, next to him. Governor Valls never addressed Jaime except to give him an order and rarely caught his eye, unless he'd made a mistake, or driven over a stone, or taken a bend too fast. Then his eyes would smoulder in the rear-view mirror and his face would adopt a sour expression. Governor Valls did not let him turn on the radio because, he said, all the programmes were an insult to his intelligence. Nor did he let Jaime display photographs of his wife and daughter on the dashboard.

Luckily, at that time of night there was no traffic and the route didn't throw up any unwelcome surprises. In just a few minutes the car had passed the old Royal Shipyards, skirted the monument to Columbus and started up the Ramblas. Two minutes later they had reached the Café de la Ópera and stopped. The Liceo audience, on the other side of the street, had already gone in for the evening performance and the Ramblas were almost deserted. The chauffeur got out and, after making sure there was nobody in the way, opened the door for Mauricio Valls. The governor stepped out, looking at the boulevard with indifference, then straightened his tie and brushed off his shoulder pads.

'Wait here,' he said to the driver.

When the governor entered the café, it was almost empty. The clock behind the bar said five minutes to ten. The governor responded to the waiter's greeting with a nod and sat down at a table at the far end. He calmly slipped off his gloves and pulled out his silver cigarette case, the one his father-in-law had given him on his first wedding anniversary. He lit a cigarette and gazed at the old café. The waiter came over with a tray and wiped the table with a damp cloth that smelled of bleach. The governor threw him a look of disdain which the waiter ignored.

'What will the gentleman have?'

'Two camomile teas.'

'In the same cup?'

'No. In separate cups.'

'Is the gentleman expecting someone?'

'Obviously.'

'Very good. Can I get you anything else?'

'Honey.'

'Yes, sir.'

The waiter left unhurriedly, while the governor made some contemptuous remark under his breath. A radio on the counter was murmuring a phone-in programme for lonely hearts, interspersed with publicity from Bella Aurora cosmetics, whose daily use guaranteed perpetual youth and sparkling beauty. Four tables away an elderly man seemed to have fallen asleep with a newspaper in his hands. The rest of the tables were empty. The two steaming cups arrived five minutes later. At a snail's pace, the waiter placed them on the table, followed by a jar of honey.

'Will that be all, sir?'

Valls nodded. He didn't move until the waiter had returned to the bar. Then he proceeded to pull a small bottle out of his pocket. He unscrewed the top, while casting a quick glance at the other customer who still seemed knocked out by his newspaper. The waiter stood behind the bar, with his back to the room, methodically drying glasses with a white cloth.

Valls took the bottle and emptied its contents into the cup on the other side of the table. Then he added a generous dollop of honey and began to stir the camomile with the teaspoon until the honey had dissolved completely. On the radio someone was reading an anguished letter from a faithful listener from Betanzos whose husband, apparently annoyed because she'd burned his All Soul's Day stew, had taken to going to the bar to listen to the football with his friends, was hardly ever home and hadn't gone to mass since that day. She was recommended prayer, patience and to make use of her feminine wiles, but only within the strict limits of the Christian family. Valls checked the clock again. It was a quarter past ten.

18

At twenty past ten, Isabella Sempere walked in through the door. She wore a simple coat, no make-up, and her hair was tied up. Valls saw her and raised a hand. Isabella paused for a moment to look at him blankly, then slowly walked over to the table. Valls stood up and held out his hand with a friendly smile. Isabella ignored the gesture and sat down.

'I've taken the liberty of ordering two camomile teas. It's the best thing to have on such a chilly evening.'

Isabella nodded absently, avoiding Valls's eyes. The governor studied her closely. As every time she had come to see him, Señora Sempere had made herself look as plain as possible in an attempt to hide her beauty. Valls examined the shape of her lips, her throbbing neck and the swell of her breasts under her coat.

'I'm listening,' said Isabella.

'Above all, let me thank you for agreeing to meet me at such short notice. I received your note this afternoon and thought it would be a good idea to discuss the matter away from the office and the prison.'

Isabella responded with another nod. Valls had a sip of his camomile and licked his lips.

'Excellent. The best in all Barcelona. Taste it.'

Isabella ignored his invitation.

'As you will understand, we can't be discreet enough. May I ask you whether you've told anyone you were coming here tonight?'

Isabella shook her head.

'Your husband, perchance?'

'My husband is stocktaking in the bookshop. He won't get home until the early hours of the morning. Nobody knows I'm here.'

'Shall I get you something else? If you don't feel like a camomile tea . . .'

Isabella shook her head and held the cup in her hands.

'It's fine.'

Valls smiled serenely.

'As I was saying, I got your letter. I quite understand your indignation and wanted to tell you that it's all due to a misunderstanding.'

'You're blackmailing a poor, mentally ill person, your prisoner, by getting him to write a book with which to promote yourself. I don't think I misunderstood anything up to that point.'

Valls slid a hand towards Isabella.

'Isabella . . . May I call you that?'

'Don't touch me, please.'

Valls pulled his hand away, putting on a conciliatory smile.

'All right, but let's talk calmly.'

'There's nothing to talk about. If you don't leave David in peace, I'll take your story and your fraud to Madrid or wherever is required. Everyone will know what sort of a person and what sort of a literary figure you are. Nothing and nobody is going to stop me.'

Isabella's eyes brimmed with tears and the cup of camomile shook in her hands.

'Please, Isabella. Drink a little. It will do you good.'

Isabella drank a couple of sips.

'Like this, with a bit of honey, is how it tastes best,' Valls added.

Isabella took two or three more sips.

'I must say, I do admire you, Isabella,' said Valls. 'Few people would have the courage and the composure to defend a poor wretch like Martín . . . someone whom everyone has abandoned and betrayed. Everyone but you.'

Isabella glanced nervously at the clock above the bar. It was ten thirty-five. She took a couple more sips of camomile and then finished it off.

'You must be very fond of him,' Valls ventured. 'Sometimes I wonder whether, given a bit of time, when you get to know me a bit better and see what I'm really like, you'll become just as fond of me as you are of him.'

She looked at him coldly for a long while, the empty cup in her hands.

'You make me feel sick, Valls. You and all the filth like you.'

Valls smiled warmly.

'I know, Isabella. But it's the filth like me that always rules in this country and the people like you who are always left in the shadow. It makes no difference which side is holding the reins.'

'Not this time. This time your superiors will know what you're doing.'

'What makes you think they'll care, or that they don't do the same or much worse? After all, I'm only an amateur.'

Valls smiled and pulled a folded sheet of paper out of his jacket pocket.

'Isabella, I want you to know I'm not the sort of person you think I am. And to prove it, here is the order for freeing David Martín, effective tomorrow.'

Valls showed her the document. Isabella examined it in disbelief. Valls pulled out his pen and, without further ado, signed it.

''There you are. David Martín is, technically, a free man. Thanks to you, Isabella. Thanks to you . . .'

When Isabella looked at him again her eyes had glazed over. Valls noticed how her pupils were slowly dilating and a film of perspiration appeared over her upper lip.

'Are you all right? You look pale . . .'

Isabella staggered to her feet and held on to the chair.

'Are you feeling dizzy, Isabella? Can I take you somewhere?'

Isabella retreated a few steps and bumped into the waiter as she made her way to the door. Valls remained seated, sipping his camomile tea until the clock said ten forty-five. Then he left a few coins on the table and slowly walked towards the exit. The car was waiting for him on the pavement. The chauffeur stood next to it, holding the door open for him.

'Would the governor like to go home or back to the castle?'

'Home. But first we're going to make a stop in Pueblo Nuevo, in the old Vilardell factory,' he ordered.

On his way to pick up the promised bounty, Mauricio Valls, the illustrious future of Spanish letters, gazed at the procession of black, deserted streets in that accursed Barcelona he so detested, and shed a few tears for Isabella, and for what might have been.

19

When Salgado awoke from his stupor and opened his eyes, the first thing he noticed was that there was someone standing motionless at the foot of his bunk, watching him. He felt a slight panic and for a moment thought he was still in the basement room. A flickering light from the oil lamps in the corridor outlined familiar contours.

'Fermín, is that you?' he asked.

The figure in the shadows nodded and Salgado breathed deeply.

'My mouth is dry. Is there any water left?'

Slowly, Fermín drew closer. He had something in his hand: a cloth and a small glass bottle.

Salgado saw Fermín pour the liquid from the bottle on to the cloth.

'What's that, Fermín?'

Fermín didn't reply. His face showed no expression. He leaned over Salgado and looked him in the eye.

'Fermín, no . . .'

Before Salgado was able to utter another syllable, Fermín placed the cloth over his mouth and nose and pressed hard, holding Salgado's head down on the bed. Salgado tossed about with what little strength he had left, while Fermín kept the cloth over his face. Salgado looked at him, terror-stricken. Seconds later he lost consciousness. Fermín didn't lift the cloth. He counted five more seconds and only then did he remove it. Sitting on the bunk with his back to Salgado, he waited a few minutes. Then, just as Martín had told him to do, he walked over to the door of the cell.

'Jailer!' he called.

He heard the new boy's footsteps approaching down the corridor.

In Martín's plan it was supposed to be Bebo doing the night shift, not that moron.

'What's the matter now?' asked the jailer.

'It's Salgado. He's had it.'

The jailer shook his head with exasperation.

'Fucking hell. Now what?'

'Bring the sack.'

The jailer cursed his bad luck.

'If you like, I'll put him in, boss,' Fermín offered.

The jailer nodded with just a hint of gratitude.

'If you bring the sack now, you can go and notify them while I put him in. That way they'll come and collect him before midnight,' Fermín added.

The jailer nodded again and went off in search of the canvas sack. Fermín stood by the door of his cell. On the other side of the corridor, Martín and Sanahuja watched him in silence.

Ten minutes later, the jailer returned holding the sack by one end, unable to hide the nausea caused by the stench of rotten flesh it gave off. Fermín moved away to the far end of the cell without waiting to be told. The jailer opened the cell door and threw the sack inside.

'Let them know now, boss. That way they'll take the bacon away before midnight – or we'll have to keep him here until tomorrow night.'

'Are you sure you can manage to put him in on your own?'

'Don't worry, boss, I've had plenty of practice.'

The jailer nodded again, not entirely convinced.

'Let's hope we're in luck and it works out, because his stump is starting to ooze and I can't begin to tell you what that's going to smell like . . .'

'Shit,' said the jailer, scuttling off.

As soon as he heard him reach the end of the corridor, Fermín began to undress Salgado. Then he removed his own clothes and got into the thief's stinking rags. Finally, Fermín put his own clothes on Salgado and placed him on the bed, lying on his side with his face to the wall, and pulled the blanket over him, so that it half-covered his face. Then he grabbed the canvas sack and got inside it. He was about to close it when he remembered something.

Hurriedly, he got out again and went over to the wall. With his nails, he scratched the space between two stones where he'd seen Salgado hide the key, until the tip began to show. He tried to pull it out with his fingers, but the key kept slipping and remained stuck between the stones.

'Hurry up,' Martín hissed from the other side of the corridor.

Fermín gripped the key with his nails and pulled hard. The nail of his ring finger was ripped off and for a few seconds he was blinded with pain. Fermín muffled a scream and sucked his finger. The taste of his own blood, salty and metallic, filled his mouth. When he opened his eyes again he noticed that about a centimetre of the key was protruding from the wall. This time he was able to pull it out easily.

He slipped into the sack again and tied the knot from the inside, as best he could, leaving an opening of about a hand's breadth. Holding back the retching he felt rising up his throat, he lay on the floor and tightened the strings until only a small gap was left, the size of a fist. He held his nose shut with his fingers. It was preferable to breathe in his own filth than to smell that rotting stench. Now, all that remained for him to do was wait, he told himself.

20

The streets of Pueblo Nuevo were buried in a thick, humid fog that slithered up from the citadel of shacks on the Somorrostro beach. The governor's Studebaker advanced slowly through veils of mist, past shadowy canyons formed by factories, warehouses and dark, crumbling outbuildings. In front of them, the car's headlights carved out two tunnels of light. Soon the silhouette of the old Vilardell textile mill peered through the fog. Chimneys and crests of abandoned pavilions and workshops were outlined at the far end of the street. The large entrance was guarded by a spiked gate; behind it, just visible, was a spread of tangled undergrowth out of which rose the skeletons of burned lorries and wrecked wagons. The chauffeur stopped in front of the entrance to the old factory.

'Leave the engine running,' ordered the governor.

The beams from the headlights pierced the blackness beyond the gate, revealing the ruinous state of the plant, bombed during the war and abandoned like so many other buildings all over the city.

On one side, a few huts were boarded up with wooden planks. Next to these, facing a garage that looked as if it had gone up in flames, stood what Valls supposed must be the former home of the security guards. The reddish glow of a candle, or an oil lamp, licked the edges of one of the closed windows. The governor took in the scene unhurriedly from the back seat of the car. After a few minutes' wait, he leaned forward and spoke to the chauffeur.

'Jaime, do you see that house on the left-hand side, opposite the garage?'

It was the first time the governor had addressed him by his first name. Something in that sudden warm and polite tone made the driver prefer his usual cold treatment.

'The lodge, you mean?'

'Exactly. I want you to walk over there and knock on the door.'

'You want me to go in there? Into the factory?'

The governor sighed with impatience.

'Not into the factory. Listen carefully. You see the house, don't you?'

'Yes, sir.'

'Very good. Well, you walk to the gate, you slip in through the gap between the bars, and you go over to the lodge and knock on the door. Everything clear so far?'

The chauffeur nodded with little enthusiasm.

'Right. Once you've knocked, someone will open the door, and then you say to him: "Durruti lives".'

'Durruti?'

'Don't interrupt. You just repeat what I've told you. They'll give you something. Probably a case or a bundle. You bring it back here and that's it. Simple, no?'

The chauffeur had gone pale and kept looking into the rear-view mirror, as if he expected someone or something to spring out from the shadows at any moment.

'Calm down, Jaime. Nothing's going to happen. I'm asking you to do this as a personal favour. Tell me, are you married?'

'I got married three years ago, sir.'

'Ah, that's good. And do you have any children?'

'We have a beautiful two-year-old girl, and my wife is expecting, sir.'

'Congratulations. Family is what matters most, Jaime. You're a good Spaniard. If you'll accept, as an advance christening present, and as proof of my gratitude for your excellent work, I'll give you a hundred pesetas. And if you do this small favour for me I'll recommend you for a promotion. How would you like an office job in the Council? I have good friends there and they tell me they're looking for men with character to pull the country out of the black hole the reds have left it in.'

The chauffeur smiled weakly at the mention of money and good prospects.

'Won't it be dangerous or . . .?'

'Jaime, it's me, the governor. Would I ask you to do something dangerous or illegal?'

The chauffeur looked at him but didn't say anything. Valls smiled at him.

'Repeat what it is you have to do, come on.'

'I go up to the door of the house and knock. When they open the door, I say: "Long live Durruti".'

'Durruti lives.'

'That's it. Durruti lives. They give me a case and I bring it back.'

'And we go home. That simple.'

The chauffeur nodded and, after a moment's hesitation, got out of the car and walked up to the gate. Valls watched his silhouette pass through the beams from the headlights and reach the entrance. There the chauffeur turned for a second to look at the car.

'Go on, you idiot, go in,' murmured Valls.

The chauffeur slipped in between the bars and, picking his way through rubble and weeds, slowly approached the door of the lodge. The governor pulled out the revolver he kept in the inside pocket of his coat and cocked the hammer. The chauffeur reached the door and stopped there. Valls saw him knock twice then wait. Almost a minute went by and nothing happened.

'One more time,' muttered Valls to himself.

The chauffeur was now looking towards the car, as if he didn't know what to do next. Suddenly, a pale yellowish light filled the space where, just a second before, there had been a closed door. Valls saw the chauffeur uttering the password. He turned one more time to look at the car, smiling. The shot, fired at point-blank range, shattered his temple and went clean through his skull. A mist of blood emerged from the other side and the body, already dead, stood for a moment wrapped in a halo of gunpowder before collapsing to the ground like a broken doll.

Valls stepped hurriedly out of the back seat of the Studebaker and took the wheel. Holding his revolver against the dashboard and pointing it towards the factory entrance with his left hand, he put the car into reverse and pressed down on the accelerator. The car reversed into the darkness, bumping over potholes and puddles that peppered the road. As he drove backwards he was able to see the glare of a few shots hitting the gate, but none of them reached the car. Only when he'd reversed some two hundred metres did he turn the Studebaker around. Then, accelerating fully, he drove away from that place, biting his lips with rage.

21

Tied up inside the sack, Fermín could only hear their voices approaching the cell.

'Hey, we've been lucky,' cried the novice jailer.

'Fermín has fallen asleep,' said Dr Sanahuja from his cell.

'Some have it easy,' said the jailer. 'There it is, you can take it away.'

Fermín heard footsteps around him and felt a sudden jerk when one of the two gravediggers firmly retied the knot. Then they picked up the sack between them and, without any care, dragged him along the stone corridor like a dead weight. Fermín didn't dare move a single muscle.

The knocks he received from steps, corners and doors stabbed him without mercy. He put a fist in his mouth and bit it to stop himself from screaming. After what seemed like a long roundabout route Fermín noticed a sudden drop in the temperature and the absence of the claustrophobic echo that resounded throughout the castle. They were outdoors. He was hauled for a few metres over a paved surface spattered with puddles that soaked the canvas. The cold air soon pierced the sack.

Finally, he felt he was being lifted and thrown into space. He landed on what seemed to be a hard wooden surface, then heard footsteps moving away. Fermín took a deep breath. The inside of the sack was damp and reeked of excrement, putrid flesh and diesel. Fermín heard a lorry engine start and after a jolt, the vehicle began to move. Soon the downward pull of a slope made the sack roll forward and Fermín deduced that the lorry was trundling down the same road that had brought him to the prison months before. He remembered how the climb up the mountain had been long and full of bends. After a short while, however, he noticed that the vehicle was turning and heading in a new direction, along flat, rough, unpaved ground. They had left the main road and Fermín was sure they were advancing further into the mountain instead of driving down towards the city. Something had gone wrong.

Only then did it occur to him that perhaps Martín had not worked everything out, that he'd missed a key detail. After all, nobody knew for certain what they did with the prisoners' dead bodies. Martín may not have stopped to consider that perhaps they got rid of them by throwing them into a furnace. He imagined Salgado, waking up from his heavy chloroform-induced sleep, laughing and saying that Fermín Romero de Torres, or whatever the hell he was called, before burning in Hell, had burned in Life.

The journey continued for a few minutes. Then, as the vehicle began to slow down, Fermín noticed it for the first time. Never in his life had he smelled anything so revolting. His heart shrank and as an indescribable stench brought on waves of nausea, he wished he'd never listened to that madman, Martín, and had remained in his cell.

22

When the governor arrived at Montjuïc Castle, he stepped out of the car and rushed into his office. His secretary was ensconced behind his small desk near the door, typing the day's correspondence with two fingers.

'Leave that and get that son-of-a-bitch Salgado brought here at once,' he ordered.

The secretary looked at him, disconcerted, wondering whether he should open his mouth.

'Don't just sit there like a halfwit. Get moving.'

The secretary stood up, looking flustered, avoiding the governor's furious eyes.

'Salgado has died, Governor. Just tonight . . .'

Valls closed his eyes and took a deep breath.

'Governor . . . sir . . .'

Without bothering to explain, Valls ran off and didn't stop until he reached cell number 13. When he saw him, the young jailer snapped out of his drowsiness and gave him a military salute.

'Your Excellency, what . . .'

'Open up. Quick.'

The jailer opened the cell and Valls charged in. He walked over to the bunk and, grabbing the shoulder of the body lying on it, pulled hard. Salgado was left face up. Valls leaned over him and smelled his breath. He then turned towards the jailer, who was looking at him terror-stricken.

'Where's the body?'

'The men from the undertaker's took it . . .'

Valls slapped him so hard he knocked him over. Two guards

had turned up in the corridor, waiting for instructions from the governor.

'I want him alive,' he told them.

The two guards nodded and left at a brisk pace. Valls stayed there, leaning against the bars of the cell shared by Martín and Dr Sanahuja. The jailer, who had got to his feet and hardly dared breathe, thought he saw the governor laughing.

'Your idea, Martín, I suppose?' Valls asked at last.

The governor bowed lightly and, as he walked away down the corridor, slowly clapped his hands.

23

Fermín could feel the lorry slowing down and negotiating the last obstacles along the dirt track. After a couple of minutes of potholes and groans from the lorry, the engine stopped. The stench wafting in through the canvas was indescribable. The two gravediggers walked round to the rear of the lorry and Fermín heard the click of the metal bar that locked the back panel. Suddenly, a strong pull on the sack flung him into the void.

He hit the ground on his side, a dull pain spreading through his shoulder. Before he could react, the two gravediggers lifted the sack from the stony ground and, holding one end each, carried it uphill until they stopped a few metres further on. They dropped the sack again and then Fermín heard one of them kneel down and start to untie the knot. He could hear the other man's footsteps as he moved away and picked up a metal object. Fermín tried to take in some air but that miasma burned his throat. He shut his eyes and felt the cold breeze on his face. The gravedigger grabbed the sack by the closed end and tugged hard. Fermín's body rolled over stones and puddles.

'Come on, let's count to three,' said one of them.

Four hands gripped him by his ankles and wrists. Fermín struggled to hold his breath.

'Hey, listen, isn't he sweating?'

'How the fuck can a stiff be sweating, you jerk? It must be the puddles. Come on, one two and . . .'

Three. Fermín felt himself swing in the air. A moment later he was flying and had abandoned himself to his fate. He opened his eyes in mid-flight and all he managed to see before the impact was that he was plunging into a ditch dug into the mountainside. In the moonlight he could only glimpse something pale covering the ground. Fermín was convinced that what he was seeing were stones and, calmly, in the half-second he took to fall, decided he didn't mind dying.

But the landing was gentle. Fermín's body had fallen on something soft and damp. Five metres further up, one of the gravediggers was holding a spade which he emptied into the air. A whitish powder spread like a shiny mist that caressed his skin and, a second later, began to devour it like acid. The two gravediggers walked away and Fermín stood up to discover he was in an open grave packed with rotting bodies and covered in quicklime. He tried to shake off the fiery dust and scrambled over the bodies until he reached the wall of earth. He climbed up the wall, digging his hands into the earth and ignoring the pain. When he reached the top, he managed to drag himself to a puddle of dirty water and wash off the lime. He stood up and saw the lights of the lorry disappearing into the night. Turning around for a moment to look behind him, Fermín stared at the open grave spreading at his feet like an ocean of tangled corpses. He felt sick and he fell on his knees, vomiting bile and blood over his hands. Panic and the stench of death almost stopped his breathing. Then he heard a rumbling sound in the distance. He looked up and saw the headlights of two cars approaching. He ran to the side of the hill and reached a small esplanade from where he had a view of the sea at the foot of the mountain and the lighthouse of the port at the end of the breakwater.

High above him, Montjuïc Castle rose among black clouds that swept across the sky and masked the moon. The sound of cars was getting closer. Without thinking twice, Fermín threw himself down the slope, falling and rolling through tree trunks, stones and brambles that hit him and tore his skin off in shreds. He no longer felt pain, or fear, or tiredness when he reached the road, from where he set off running towards the warehouses in the port. He ran without stopping or breathing, losing all sense of time, unaware of the injuries that covered his body.

24

Dawn was spilling over the horizon when he reached the boundless labyrinth of shacks blanketing the beach of the Somorrostro. An early mist crept up from the sea, snaking between the rooftops. Fermín wandered through the alleyways and tunnels of the city of the poor until he collapsed between two piles of rubble. He was found by two ragged children, dragging wooden boxes, who stopped to stare at the skeletal figure that seemed to be bleeding from every pore.

Fermín smiled at them and made the victory sign with two fingers. The children looked at one another. One of them said something Fermín couldn't hear. He then abandoned himself to exhaustion and with his eyes half open was aware of being lifted from the ground by four people and then being laid down on a camp bed near a fire. He felt the warmth on his skin and slowly recovered the feeling in his feet, hands and arms. The pain came later, like a slow but unstoppable tide. Around him, hushed voices of women murmured blurred words. They removed the few rags that still clung to him. Cloths soaked in warm water and camphor caressed his naked, broken body with infinite gentleness.

He opened his eyes a fraction when he felt the hand of an old woman on his forehead, her weary, wise gaze fixed on him.

'Where have you come from?' asked that woman whom Fermín, in his delirium, mistook for his mother.

'From among the dead, Mother,' he whispered. 'I've come back from among the dead.'

Part Three

Reborn

1

Barcelona, 1940

The incident at the old Vilardell factory never made the papers. It didn't suit anyone to let the story come out. What took place there would only be remembered by those present. That very night, when Mauricio Valls returned to the castle to discover that prisoner number 13 had escaped, he informed Inspector Fumero of the political police division about a tip-off from one of the prisoners. Before sunrise, Fumero and his men were already posted in their positions.

The inspector left two of his men guarding the perimeter and concentrated the rest at the main entrance, from which, as Valls had already explained, one could see the guards' lodge. The body of Jaime Montoya, the prison governor's heroic chauffeur who had volunteered to enter the premises alone and investigate a prisoner's claim regarding the existence of subversive elements, was still lying there among the rubble. Shortly before daybreak, Fumero ordered his men to enter the old factory. They surrounded the lodge and when its occupants, two men and a young woman, became aware of their presence, only a minor incident occurred: the woman, who carried a firearm, shot one of the policemen in the arm. It was just a scratch. Apart from that slip, Fumero and his men had overpowered the rebels within thirty seconds.

The inspector then ordered his men to round them all up into the lodge and drag the body of the dead driver inside too. Fumero didn't ask for names or documents. He had the rebels disrobed and bound hand and foot with wire to some rusty metal chairs lying in a corner. Once the rebels had been tied down, Fumero told his men to leave him alone with them and post themselves by the door of the lodge and by the factory gates to await his instructions. On his own with the prisoners, he closed the door and sat down facing them.

'I haven't slept all night and I'm tired. I want to go home. You tell me where the money and the jewels you're hiding for Salgado are and nothing will happen here, all right?'

The prisoners stared at him with a mixture of bewilderment and terror.

'We don't know anything about jewels or about anyone called Salgado,' said the older man.

Fumero nodded somewhat wearily. His eyes moved unhurriedly over the three prisoners, as if he were able to read their thoughts and was bored by them. After a few moments' uncertainty, he chose the woman and drew his chair closer until he was barely half a metre away from her. The woman was trembling.

'Leave her alone, you son-of-a-bitch,' spat the other, younger man. 'If you touch her I swear I'll kill you.'

Fumero smiled wistfully.

'Your girlfriend is very pretty.'

Navas, the officer posted by the door of the lodge, could feel the cold sweat soaking his clothes. He ignored the shrieks coming from inside. When his colleagues threw him a furtive glance from the factory gates, he shook his head.

Nobody exchanged a single word. Fumero had been in the lodge for about half an hour when finally the door opened behind Navas. He stepped aside and avoided looking directly at the damp marks on the inspector's black clothes. Fumero walked slowly towards the gates while Navas, after a brief look inside the lodge, closed the door, trying not to vomit. At a signal from Fumero, two of the men came over carrying cans of petrol and doused the walls of the lodge and the surrounding area. They didn't stay behind to watch it go up in flames.

Fumero was waiting for them sitting in the passenger seat when they returned to the car. They drove off in silence as a column of smoke and flames rose above the ruins of the old factory, leaving a trail of ashes spreading in the wind. Fumero lowered the car window and stretched out his hand into the cold, humid air. He had blood on his fingers. Navas drove with his eyes fixed ahead, but all he could see was the pleading look of that young woman, still alive, before he closed the door. Aware that Fumero was watching him, he gripped the wheel tight to hide his trembling.

From the pavement, a group of ragged children watched the car drive by. One of them, making the shape of a gun with his fingers, pretended to be firing at them. Fumero smiled and replied with the same gesture. Seconds later, the car disappeared into the narrow streets surrounding the jungle of chimneys and warehouses, as if it had never been there.

2

Fermín spent seven days in the hut, delirious. No damp cloth managed to calm his fever; no ointment was able to ease the pain which, they said, was consuming him. The old women of the place, who took it in turns to look after him and give him tonics in the hope of keeping him alive, said that the stranger had a demon inside him, the demon of remorse, and that his soul wanted to flee to the end of the tunnel and rest in a dark void.

On the seventh day, the man whom everyone addressed as Armando and whose authority in the shanty town was second only to God's went over to the hut and sat down next to the sick man. He examined his wounds, lifted his eyelids with his fingers and read the secrets written in his dilated pupils. The old women who nursed him had gathered in a circle behind Armando, waiting in respectful silence. After a while Armando nodded to himself and left the hut. A couple of young men who were waiting by the door followed him as far as the line of surf where the waves broke on the water's edge, and listened carefully to his instructions. Armando watched them leave and stayed on, sitting on the wreck of a trawler that had been washed up by the storm and lay there, halfway between the beach and purgatory.

He lit a small cigar, enjoying it in the dawn breeze. While he smoked and considered what he should do, Armando pulled out a page from *La Vanguardia* he'd been keeping in his pocket for days. There, buried among advertisements for girdles and publicity for the latest shows in the Paralelo district, was a brief news story about the escape of a prisoner from Montjuïc Castle. The item had the stale taste of an official communiqué. The only licence the journalist had allowed himself was a closing remark declaring that never before had anyone succeeded in escaping from that unassailable fortress.

Armando looked up and gazed at the mountain of Montjuïc, rising to the south. The castle, with its crenellated towers outlined in the mist, presided over Barcelona. Armando smiled bitterly. He set fire to the article with the embers from his cigar and watched it turn to ashes in the breeze. As always, newspapers avoided the truth as if their life depended on it, and perhaps with good reason. Everything about that story smelled of half-truths and unspoken details. Among them the claim that nobody had ever been able to escape from Montjuïc Prison. Although in this case, he thought, the news item was probably right, because he, the man they called Armando, only existed in the invisible world of the poor and the untouchables. There are times and places where not to be anyone is more honourable than to be someone.

3

The days dragged. Once a day, Armando stopped by the hut to ask after the dying man. The man's fever made timid attempts at receding and the tangle of bruises, cuts and wounds covering his body seemed to be slowly healing beneath the ointments. He spent most of the day asleep or murmuring incomprehensible words between sleeplessness and slumber.

'Will he live?' Armando sometimes asked.

'He hasn't made up his mind yet,' replied the old woman whom that poor soul had mistaken for his mother.

Days crystallised into weeks and it soon became evident that nobody was going to come and ask after the stranger: nobody asks for what they'd rather ignore. Normally the police and the Civil Guard didn't enter the Somorrostro. A law of silence made it plain that the city and the world ended at the gates of the shanty town, and both sides were keen to maintain the invisible frontier. Armando knew that many on the other side secretly or openly prayed for a storm that would obliterate the city of the poor, but until that day came, they all preferred to look elsewhere, with their backs to the sea and to the people who barely survived between the water's edge and the jungle of factories of Pueblo Nuevo. Even so, Armando had his doubts. The story he divined behind the outsider they had taken in could well lead to a breach of that law of silence.

A few weeks later, a couple of young policemen turned up asking whether anyone had seen a man who looked like the stranger. Armando remained vigilant for days, but when nobody else came by to look for the man he concluded that no one wanted to find him. Perhaps he had died and didn't even know it.

A month and a half after his arrival, the wounds on his body began to heal. When the man opened his eyes and asked where he was, they helped him sit up to sip a bowl of broth, but they didn't tell him anything.

'You must rest.'

'Am I alive?' he asked.

Nobody confirmed whether he was or wasn't. He spent much of the day asleep, or overcome by a weariness that never left him. Every time he closed his eyes and gave himself up to exhaustion, he travelled to the same place. In his dream, which recurred night after night, he scaled the walls of a bottomless mass grave strewn with corpses. When he reached the top and turned to look behind him, he saw the flood of ghostly bodies stirring like an eddy of eels. The dead bodies opened their eyes and climbed the walls, following him. They trailed him over the mountain and returned to the streets of Barcelona, looking for their old dwelling places, knocking on the doors of those they had once loved. Some went in search of their murderers and combed the city, thirsty for revenge, but most of them only wanted to return to their homes, to their beds, and embrace the children, wives and lovers they had left behind. Yet nobody would open the door to them. Nobody would hold their hands or wanted to kiss their lips. The dying man, bathed in sweat, woke up in the dark every night with the deafening cries of the dead in his soul.

A stranger often visited him. He smelled of tobacco and eau de cologne, two substances that were hard to come by in those days. He sat on a chair by his side, looking at him with impenetrable eyes. His hair was black as tar and his features sharp. When he noticed that the patient was awake, he smiled at him.

'Are you God or the devil?' the dying man once asked him.

The stranger shrugged and thought about it.

'A bit of both,' he answered at last.

'In principle, I'm an atheist,' the patient informed him. 'Although in fact I have a lot of faith.'

'Like so many. Rest now, my friend. Heaven can wait. And hell is too small for you.'

4

Between visits from the strange gentleman with the jet-black hair, the convalescent would let himself be fed, washed and dressed in clean clothes that proved too big for him. When he was finally able to stand up and take a few steps on his own, they led him down to the edge of the sea where he bathed his feet and felt the Mediterranean light caressing his skin. One day he spent the entire morning watching a group of ragged children with dirty faces playing in the sand, and he thought perhaps he would like to live, at least a little longer. As time went by, memories and anger began rising to the surface, and with them both the wish to return to the city and the fear of doing so.

Legs, arms, and other parts began to function more or less as he remembered. He recovered the rare pleasure of peeing into the wind with no burning sensations or shameful mishaps and told himself that a man who could urinate standing up and without help was a man in a fit state to face his responsibilities. That same night, in the early hours, he rose quietly and walked through the citadel's narrow alleyways as far as the boundary marked by the railway tracks. On the other side stood the forest of chimneys and the cemetery's skyline of angels and mausoleums. Further in the distance, in a tableau of lights that spread up the hillsides, lay Barcelona. He heard footsteps behind him and when he turned round he was met by the serene gaze of the man with the jet-black hair.

'You've been reborn,' he said.

'Well, let's hope this time around things turn out better. I've had a pretty bad time so far . . .'

The man with the jet-black hair smiled.

'Allow me to introduce myself. I'm Armando, the Gypsy.'

Fermín shook his hand.

'Fermín Romero de Torres, not a Gypsy, but still of relatively good coinage.'

'Fermín, my friend: I get the impression that you're considering going back to those people.'

'You can't make a leopard change its spots,' Fermín proclaimed. 'I've left a few things unfinished.'

Armando nodded.

'I understand. But not yet, dear friend,' he said. 'Have patience. Stay with us for a time.'

The fear of what awaited him on his return and the generosity of those people kept him there until one Sunday morning, when he borrowed a newspaper some children had found in the bin of a refreshment stall on La Barceloneta beach. It was hard to tell how long the newspaper had been lying among the rubbish, but it was dated three months after the night of his escape. He combed the pages searching for a hint, a sign or some mention, but there was nothing. That afternoon, when he'd already made up his mind to return to Barcelona at nightfall, Armando approached Fermín and told him that one of his men had gone over to the *pensión* where he used to live.

'Fermín, you'd better not go round there to fetch your things.'

'How did you know my address?'

Armando smiled, avoiding the question.

'The police told them you'd died. A notice of your death appeared in the papers weeks ago. I didn't say anything because I realise that to read about one's own passing when one is convalescing doesn't help.'

'What did I die of?'

'Natural causes. You fell down a ravine when you were trying to flee from the law.'

'So, I'm dead?'

'As dead as the polka.'

Fermín weighed up the implications of his new status.

'And what do I do now? Where do I go? I can't stay here for ever, taking advantage of your kindness and putting you all in danger.'

Armando sat down next to him and lit one of the cigarettes he himself rolled. It smelled of eucalyptus.

'Fermín, you can do what you want, because you don't exist. I'd almost suggest that you stay here, because you're now one of us, people who have no name and are not documented anywhere. We're ghosts. Invisible. But I know you must return and resolve whatever you've left behind out there. Unfortunately, once you leave this place I can't offer you my protection.'

'You've already done enough for me.'

Armando patted Fermín's shoulder and handed him a folded sheet of paper he carried in his pocket.

'Leave the city for a while. Let a year go by and, when you return, begin here,' he said, moving away.

Fermín unfolded the sheet of paper and read:

FERNANDO BRIANS

LAWYER

Calle de Caspe, 12

Attic Floor, room 1

Barcelona. Telephone 564375

'How can I repay you for everything you've done for me?'

'One day, when you've sorted out your business, come by and ask for me. We'll go and see Carmen Amaya dance and you can tell me how you managed to escape from up there. I'm curious,' said Armando.

Fermín looked into those black eyes and nodded slowly.

'What cell were you in, Armando?'

'Cell thirteen.'

'Were those crosses on the wall yours?'

'Unlike you, Fermín, I *am* a believer, but I've lost my faith.'

That afternoon nobody said goodbye to Fermín or tried to stop him leaving. He set off, one more invisible person, towards the streets of a Barcelona that smelled of electricity. In the distance the towers of the Sagrada Familia seemed stranded in a blanket of red clouds that threatened a storm of biblical proportions, and he went on walking. His feet took him to the bus depot on Calle Trafalgar. There was some money in the pockets of the coat Armando had given him, and he bought a ticket for the longest trip available. He spent the night on the bus, driving through deserted roads under the rain. The following day he did the same, until, after three days on trains, on foot and on midnight buses, he reached a place where the streets had no name and the houses had no number and where nothing or no one could remember him.

He had a hundred jobs and no friends. He made money, which he spent. He read books that spoke of a world in which he no longer believed. He started to write a letter that he never knew how to end, battling with reminiscences and remorse. More than once he walked up to a bridge or a precipice and gazed calmly at the chasm below. At the last moment the memory of that promise would always return, and the look in the eyes of the Prisoner of Heaven. After a year, Fermín left the room he had rented above a café and, with no baggage other than a copy of *City of the Damned* he'd found in a flea market – possibly the only book of Martín's that hadn't been burned and which Fermín had read a dozen times – he walked two kilometres to the train station and bought the ticket that had been waiting for him all those months.

'One way to Barcelona, please.'

The ticket-office clerk issued the ticket and gave it to him with a disdainful look.

'Rather you than me,' he said. 'With all those goddam Catalan dogs.'

5

Barcelona, 1941

It was starting to get dark when Fermín stepped off the train in the Estación de Francia. A cloud of steam and soot belched out by the engine stole along the platform, masking the passengers' feet as they descended after the long journey. Fermín joined the silent procession towards the exit, among people in threadbare clothes, dragging suitcases held together with straps, people aged well before their time carrying all their belongings in a bundle, children with empty eyes and emptier pockets.

A pair of Civil Guards patrolled the entrance. Fermín saw how they followed the passengers with their eyes and stopped some of them at random to ask for documentation. He kept walking in a straight line towards one of them. When he was only about a dozen metres away, he noticed that the Civil Guard was watching him. In Martín's novel, the book that had kept Fermín company all those months, one of the characters swore that the best way of disarming the authorities was to speak to them first before they addressed you. So before the officer was able to point him out, Fermín walked straight up to the man and said in a calm voice:

'Good evening, chief. Would you be so kind as to tell me where I can find the Hotel Porvenir? I believe it's in Plaza Palacio, but I hardly know the city.'

The Civil Guard examined him silently, somewhat disconcerted. His colleague had moved closer, covering his right side.

'You'll have to ask someone when you get out,' he said in a rather unfriendly tone.

Fermín nodded politely.

'That's what I'll do. I'm sorry to have bothered you.'

He was about to continue walking towards the entrance hall when the other officer took hold of his arm.

'Plaza Palacio is on the left as you go out. Opposite the Military Headquarters.'

'Most obliged. Have a good evening.'

The Civil Guard let go of him and Fermín walked away slowly, pacing himself, until he reached the entrance hall and then the street.

A scarlet sky curved over Barcelona. The city looked dark, entwined with sharp, black silhouettes. A half-empty tram hauled itself along, shedding a flickering light on the cobblestones. Fermín waited for it to go by before crossing to the other side. As he stepped over the shining rails he gazed into the distance, where the sides of Paseo Colón seemed to converge and the hill and castle of Montjuïc loomed above the city. He looked down again and set off up Calle Comercio towards the Borne market. The streets were deserted and a cold breeze blew though the alleyways. He had nowhere to go.

He remembered Martín telling him that years ago he'd lived in that area, in a large old house buried in the shadowy canyon of Calle Flassaders, next to the old Mauri chocolate factory. Fermín headed off in that direction but when he arrived he realised that the building in question had been shelled during the war. The authorities hadn't bothered to remove the rubble, so the neighbours had piled it up out of the way, presumably to make room for them to walk along the street, which was narrower than the corridors of some homes in the smarter parts of town.

Fermín looked around him. A dim glow of bulbs and candles drifted down from the balconies. He moved further into the ruins, jumping over debris, broken gargoyles and beams twisted into improbable knots, looking for a space among the wreckage. At last he lay down under a stone that still had number 30 engraved on it, David Martín's former address. Covering himself with his coat and the old newspapers he wore under his clothes, he curled up into a ball, closed his eyes and tried to get to sleep.

Half an hour went by and the chill was starting to seep into his bones. A humid wind licked the ruins, searching for holes and cracks. Fermín opened his eyes and stood up. He was trying to find a more sheltered place when he noticed a figure watching him from the street. Fermín froze. The figure took a few steps towards him.

'Who goes there?' asked the figure.

The figure advanced a little further and the far-off light of a street lamp revealed the profile of a tall, well-built man dressed in black. Fermín noticed the collar: a priest. He raised both hands in a gesture of peace.

'I was leaving, Father. Please, don't call the police.'

The priest looked him up and down. His eyes seemed harsh and he had the air of someone who had spent half his life lifting sacks in the port instead of chalices.

'Are you hungry?' he asked.

Fermín, who would have eaten any of those rough stones if someone had sprinkled a few drops of olive oil over them, shook his head.

'I've just had dinner at the Siete Puertas and I've stuffed myself silly with lobster stew,' he said.

The priest gave him a hint of a smile. He turned round and started walking.

'Come on,' he ordered.

6

Father Valera lived on the top floor of a building at the end of Paseo del Borne, overlooking the market rooftops. Fermín quickly polished off three bowlfuls of thin soup and a few bits of stale bread, together with a glass of watered-down wine the priest placed in front of him, while he eyed him with curiosity.

'Aren't you having dinner, Father?'

'I don't usually eat dinner. You enjoy it. I see your hunger goes all the way back to 1936.'

While Fermín slurped his soup with its garnish of bread, he let his eyes roam around the dining room. Next to him, a glass cabinet displayed a collection of plates and glasses, various figures of saints and what looked like a modest set of silver cutlery.

'I've also read *Les Misérables*, so don't even think of it,' warned the priest.

Fermín nodded, ashamed.

'What's your name?'

'Fermín Romero de Torres, at your service, *Monsignore*.'

'Are they after you, Fermín?'

'Depends how you look at it. It's a complicated matter.'

'It's none of my business if you don't want to tell me. But with clothes like those you can't wander around out there. You'll end up in jail before you even reach Vía Layetana. They're stopping a lot of people who have been lying low for a while. You must be very careful.'

'As soon as I gain access to some monetary funds that I've had in deep storage, I thought I'd drop by El Dique Flotante and come out looking my usual dapper self.'

'No doubt. But for the time being, humour me. Stand up a moment, will you?'

Fermín put down the spoon and stood up. The priest examined him carefully.

'Ramón was twice your size, but I think some of the clothes from when he was young would fit you.'

'Ramón?'

'My brother. He was killed down there, in the street, by the front door, in May 1938. They were looking for me, but he confronted them. He was a fine musician. He played in the municipal band. Principal trumpet.'

'I'm so sorry, Father.'

The priest shrugged his shoulders.

'More or less everyone has lost someone, whatever side they belong to.'

'I don't belong to any side,' Fermín replied. 'What's more, I think flags are nothing but painted rags that represent rancid emotions. Just seeing someone wrapped up in one of them, spewing out hymns, badges and speeches, gives me the runs. I've always thought that anyone who needs to join a herd so badly must be a bit of a sheep himself.'

'You must have a very hard time in this country.'

'You have no idea. But I always tell myself that having direct access to *serrano* ham makes up for everything. And anyhow, it's the same the world over.'

'That's true. Tell me, Fermín. How long since you last tasted real *serrano* ham?'

'March sixth 1934. Los Caracoles on Calle Escudellers. Another life.'

The priest smiled.

'You can stay here for tonight, Fermín, but tomorrow you'll have to find some other place. People talk. I can give you a bit of money for a *pensión*, but don't forget they all ask for identity cards and register their lodgers' names with the police.'

'That goes without saying, Father. Tomorrow, before sunrise, I'll vanish faster than goodwill. And I won't accept a single *céntimo* from you. I've already taken enough advantage of your . . .'

The priest put a hand up and shook his head.

'Let's see how some of Ramón's things look on you,' he said, rising from the table.

Father Valera insisted on providing Fermín with a pair of slightly worn shoes, a modest but clean wool suit, a couple of changes of underwear and a few personal toiletries which he put in a suitcase. A shining trumpet was displayed on one of the shelves, next to a number of photographs of two smiling, good-looking young men, in what looked like the annual *fiestas* of the Gracia district. One had to look closely to realise that one of them was Father Valera, who now looked thirty years older.

'I have no hot water. And they don't fill the tank till the morning, so either you wait, or you use the water jug.'

While Fermín washed himself as best he could, Father Valera prepared a pot of coffee with some sort of chicory mixed with other substances that looked vaguely suspicious. There was no sugar but that cup of dirty water was warm and the company was pleasant.

'Anyone would say we're in Colombia, enjoying the finest selection of coffee beans,' said Fermín.

'You're a peculiar fellow, Fermín. Can I ask you something personal?'

'Will the secrecy of the confessional cover it?'

'Let's say it will.'

'Fire away.'

'Have you killed anyone? During the war, I mean.'

'No,' replied Fermín.

'I have.'

Fermín went rigid, his cup half empty. The priest lowered his eyes.

'I've never told anyone.'

'It remains bound by the secrecy of the confessional,' Fermín assured him.

The priest rubbed his eyes and sighed. Fermín wondered how long this man had lived there alone, harbouring that secret and the memory of his dead brother.

'You must have had your reasons, Father.'

The priest shook his head.

'God has abandoned this country,' he said.

'Don't worry then. As soon as he sees what's brewing north of the Pyrenees, he'll come back with his tail between his legs.'

The priest kept quiet for a long time. They finished off the ersatz coffee and Fermín, to cheer up the poor priest, who seemed to look gloomier with every passing minute, poured himself a second cup.

'Do you really like it?'

Fermín nodded.

'Would you like me to hear your confession?' the priest suddenly asked him. 'I'm not joking now.'

'Don't be offended, Father, but I don't really believe in that sort of thing . . .'

'But perhaps God believes in you.'

'I doubt it.'

'You don't have to believe in God to confess. It's something between you and your conscience. What is there to lose?'

During the next couple of hours Fermín told Father Valera everything he'd kept to himself since he fled from the castle over a year ago. The priest listened to him attentively, nodding every now and then. At last, when Fermín felt he had said it all and the stone slab that had been suffocating him for months without him realising had been lifted, Father Valera pulled out a flask of liqueur from a drawer and, without asking, poured what was left of it into a glass and handed it to Fermín.

'I was hoping for absolution, Father, not a reward of a swig of cognac.'

'It comes to the same thing. Besides, I'm no longer in a position to forgive or to judge anyone, Fermín. But I think you needed to get all that off your chest. What are you going to do now?'

Fermín shrugged.

'If I've returned, and I'm risking my neck by doing so, it's because of the promise I made to Martín. I must find the lawyer and then Señora Isabella and that boy, Daniel, and protect them.'

'How?'

'I don't know. I'll think of something. Any suggestions?'

'But you don't even know them. They're just strangers that a man you met in prison told you about . . .'

'I know. When you put it that way it sounds crazy, doesn't it?'

The priest was looking at him as if he could see through his words.

'Might it not be that you've seen so much misery and so much evil among men that you want to do something good, even if it's madness?'

'And why not?'

Valera smiled. The priest took the glass with the untouched drink from Fermín's hands and knocked it back.

'I knew God believed in you.'

7

The following day, Fermín tiptoed out of the flat so as not to disturb Father Valera, who had fallen asleep on the sofa with a book of poems by Machado in his hand and was snoring like a fighting bull. Before leaving he kissed him on the forehead and left the silverware – which the priest had wrapped in a napkin and slipped into his suitcase – on the dining-room table. Then he set off down the stairs with clean clothes and a clean conscience, determined to stay alive, at least for a few more days.

That day the sun was strong and a fresh breeze swept over the city. The sky looked bright and steely, casting long shadows as people walked by. Fermín spent the morning strolling through streets he remembered, stopping in front of shop windows and sitting on benches to watch pretty girls go by – and they all looked pretty to him. Around noon he walked over to a café at the entrance to Calle Escudellers, near the Los Caracoles restaurant of such happy memories. The café itself was notorious among those with fearless and undemanding palates for offering the cheapest sandwiches in town. The trick, said experts, was not to ask about the ingredients.

Sporting his smart new clothes and an armour of newspapers packed beneath them to lend him some bulk, a hint of muscles and low-cost warmth, Fermín sat at the bar, checked the list of delicacies within reach of modest pockets and began negotiating with the waiter.

'I have a question, young man. In today's special, peasant's bread with *mortadella* and cold cuts from Cornellá, does the bread come with fresh tomato?'

'Just arrived from our market garden in El Prat, behind the sulphuric acid plants.'

'A premium bouquet. And tell me, my good man, does this establishment extend credit to suitable individuals?'

The waiter lost his cheerful expression and withdrew behind the bar, hanging his rag over his shoulder with a hostile gesture.

'Not even to God almighty.'

'I see. And would you consider making an exception in the case of a decorated disabled war hero?'

'Scram or we'll call the police.'

In light of the stringent policies being enforced, Fermín beat a hasty retreat, searching for a quiet corner where he could reconsider his plans. He'd just settled on the steps of the building next door when a young girl, who couldn't have been a day older than seventeen but already possessed the curves of a budding starlet, walked past him and fell flat on her face.

Fermín stood up to help her and had only just taken hold of her arm when he heard a voice that made the words from the hostile waiter who had sent him on his way sound like heavenly music.

'Look here, you goddam slut, don't give me this crap or I'll slice your face up and dump you in the street, which is already filled with unemployed cut-up whores.'

The author of such a notable speech turned out to be a sallow-skinned pimp with a questionable eye for fashion. Despite the fact that the man was twice Fermín's size, and was holding what appeared to be a sharp object, or at least a fairly pointy one, Fermín, who was beginning to be fed up to his back teeth with bullies, stood between the girl and her aggressor.

'And who the fuck are you, you loser? Go on, beat it before I cut your face up.'

Fermín felt the girl grip his arms in fear. She smelled of a particular mixture of sweet cinnamon and refried calamari. A quick glance was enough for Fermín to realise that the situation was unlikely to be resolved through diplomacy, so he decided to move into action. After a lightning assessment of his opponent he concluded that the grand total of his body mass was mainly flab, and that when it came to actual muscle, or grey matter, he was not packing a lethal punch.

'Don't talk to me in that way, even less to the young lady.'

The pimp looked at him in astonishment, as if he hadn't taken in the words. A second later, the individual, who was expecting anything from this wimp except a fight, got the surprise of his life when a suitcase slammed into his soft parts and sent him to the ground clutching his privates. This was followed by four or five knocks in strategic places inflicted with the leather corners of the case that left him, at least for a short while, notably lacking in any mood to fight back.

A group of passers-by who had witnessed the incident began to applaud and, when Fermín turned to check whether the girl was all right, he was welcomed by her adoring look, laced with undying gratitude and tenderness.

'Fermín Romero de Torres, at your service, miss.'

The girl stood on her toes and kissed his cheek.

'I'm Rociíto.'

The specimen at his feet was gasping and struggling to get up. Before the balance of the contest stopped favouring him, Fermín decided to distance himself from the scene of the confrontation.

'We'd better make haste and shove off,' he announced. 'Now we've lost the initiative, the battle will go against us . . .'

Rociíto took his arm and guided him through the twisted web of narrow streets that led to Plaza Real. Once they were in the sunlight and in the open, Fermín stopped for a second to recover his breath. Rociíto noticed that Fermín was becoming increasingly pale. He looked unwell. She guessed that the emotions induced by the skirmish, or perhaps plain old hunger, had caused a drop in her brave champion's blood pressure. She walked him to the terrace of the Hostal Dos Mundos, where Fermín collapsed into one of the chairs.

Rociíto, who might have been seventeen but had a clinical eye that many an experienced doctor would have coveted, proceeded to ask for a selection of tapas with which to revive him. When Fermín saw the feast arriving, he was alarmed.

'Rociíto, I don't have a *céntimo* on me . . .'

'It's on me,' she cut in proudly. 'Gotta take care of my man and keep 'im well nourished.'

Rociíto kept stuffing him with small *chorizos*, bread and spicy potatoes, all washed down with a monumental pitcher of beer. Fermín slowly revived and recovered his lively colouring to the girl's visible satisfaction.

'For dessert, if you like, I can serve you up a house special that will knock you sideways,' offered the young woman, licking her lips.

'Listen, kid, shouldn't you be at school right now, with the nuns?'

Rociíto laughed at his joke.

'You rogue, you've sure got a mouth!'

As the feast went on, Fermín realised that, if it depended on the girl, he had before him a promising career as a procurer. But matters of greater importance claimed his attention.

'How old are you, Rociíto?'

'Eighteen and a half, Señorito Fermín.'

'You look older.'

'It's me tits. Got them when I was thirteen. A joy to look at, aren't they, even though I shouldn't say so.'

Fermín, who hadn't laid eyes on such a conspiracy of curves since his longed-for days in Havana, tried to recover his common sense.

'Rociíto,' he began, 'I can't take care of you . . .'

'I know, Señorito Fermín. Don't think me stupid. I know you're not the sort of man to live off a woman. I might be young, but I know how to see 'em coming . . .'

'You must tell me where I can send you a proper refund for this handsome banquet. Right now you catch me at a rather delicate financial moment . . .'

Rociíto shook her head.

'I've a room here, in the *hostal.* I share it with Lali, but she's out all day because she works the merchant ships . . . Why don't you come up, señorito, and I'll give you a massage?'

'Rociíto . . .'

'It's on the house . . .'

Fermín gazed at her with a touch of melancholy.

'You have sad eyes, Señorito Fermín. Let little Rociíto cheer you up, even if it's just for a while. What harm can there be in that?'

Fermín looked down in embarrassment.

'How long is it since you've been with a real woman?'

'I can't even remember.'

Rociíto offered him a hand and, pulling him behind her, took him up to a tiny room with just enough space for a ramshackle bed and a sink. A small balcony looked out on the square. The girl drew the curtain and in a flash removed the floral-print dress she was wearing next to her bare skin. Fermín gazed at that miracle of nature and let himself be embraced by a heart almost as old as his own.

'We don't need to do anything, if you don't want, all right?'

Rociíto laid him down on the bed and stretched out next to him. She held him tight and stroked his head.

'Shhh, shhh,' she whispered.

With his face buried in that eighteen-year-old bosom, Fermín burst into tears.

When evening fell and Rociíto had to begin her shift, Fermín pulled out the piece of paper Armando had given him a year ago, with the address of Brians, the lawyer, and decided to pay him a visit. Rociíto insisted on lending him some loose change, enough to take a tram or two and have a coffee. She made him swear, time and time again, that he would come back to see her, even if it was just to take her to the cinema or to mass: she had a particular devotion for Our Lady of Carmen and she loved ceremonies, especially if there was singing involved. Rociíto went down the stairs with him and when they said goodbye she gave him a kiss on the lips and a nip on the bum.

'Gorgeous,' she said as she watched him leave under the arches of the square.

As Fermín crossed Plaza de Cataluña, a ribbon of clouds was beginning to swirl in the sky. The flocks of pigeons that usually flew over the square had taken shelter in the trees and waited impatiently. People could smell the electricity in the air as they hurried towards the entrances of the metro. An unpleasant wind had started to blow, dragging a tide of dry leaves along the ground. Fermín quickened his pace and by the time he reached Calle Caspe, the rain was bucketing down.

8

Brians was a young man with the air of a bohemian student who looked as if he survived on salty crackers and coffee, which is what his office smelled of. That, and dusty paper. The lawyer's workplace was a small, cramped room at the end of a dark corridor, perched on the attic floor of the same building that housed the great Tivoli Theatre. Fermín found him still there at eight-thirty in the evening. He opened the door in his shirtsleeves and acknowledged his visitor with a nod and sigh.

'Fermín, I suppose. Martín spoke to me about you. I was beginning to wonder when you'd be coming by.'

'I've been away for a while.'

'Of course. Come in, please.'

Fermín followed him into the cubicle.

'What a night, eh?' said the lawyer. He sounded nervous.

'It's only water.'

Fermín looked around him and noticed only one chair. Brians offered it to him and sat on a pile of volumes on criminal and civil law.

'I'm still waiting for the furniture.'

Fermín could see there wasn't even room for a pencil sharpener in that place, but thought it best not to open his mouth. On the table was a plate with a grilled-meat sandwich and a beer. A paper napkin informed him that the sumptuous dinner came from the café on the ground floor.

'I was about to eat. I'll be happy to share it with you.'

'No, no, go ahead, you young ones need to grow and besides, I've had my dinner.'

'Can't I offer you anything? Coffee?'

'If you have a Sugus . . .'

Brians rummaged in a drawer that held just about everything except Sugus sweets.

'A liquorice lozenge?'

'I'm fine, thanks.'

'Then, if you don't mind . . .'

Brians gave the sandwich a hearty bite, munching with gusto. Fermín wondered which of them looked more famished. Next to the desk, the door to an adjoining room stood ajar. Fermín caught a glimpse of an unmade folding bed, a coat stand with crumpled shirts and a pile of books.

'Do you live here?' asked Fermín.

Clearly the lawyer Isabella had been able to afford for Martín was not a high flyer. Brians followed Fermín's eyes and gave him a modest smile.

'This is, temporarily, my office and my home, yes,' Brians replied, leaning over to close his bedroom door.

'You must think I don't look much like a lawyer. You're not the only one. So does my father.'

'Pay no attention. My father was always fond of telling us we were nothing but a useless lot of imbeciles who would end up lifting rocks at a quarry, if we were lucky. And look at me now, as cool as they come. Succeeding in life when your family believes in you and supports you, what's the merit in that?'

Brians nodded reluctantly.

'If you look at it that way . . . Truth be told, I only established myself on my own a short time ago. Before that I used to work for a well-known lawyer's practice just round the corner, on Paseo de Gracia. But we fell out over a number of things. It hasn't been easy since then.'

'Don't tell me. Valls?'

Brians nodded, finishing off his beer in three gulps.

'From the moment I accepted Señor Martín's case, Valls didn't stop until he'd got almost all my clients to leave me and I was laid off. The few who followed me are the ones who don't have a *céntimo* and can't pay my fees.'

'And Señora Isabella?'

A shadow fell over the lawyer's face. He left the beer glass on the desk and looked hesitantly at Fermín.

'Don't you know?'

'Know what?'

'Isabella Sempere is dead.'

9

The storm pounded over the city. Fermín held a cup of coffee in his hands while Brians, standing by the open window, watched the rain lash the roofs of the Ensanche district and recounted Isabella's last days.

'She fell ill suddenly, without any explanation. If you'd known her . . . Isabella was young, full of life. She had an iron constitution and had survived the hardships of war. It all happened overnight. The night you managed to escape from the castle, Isabella came home late. When her husband found her, she was kneeling down in the bathroom, sweating and with palpitations. She said she wasn't feeling well. They called the doctor, but before he arrived she started having convulsions and throwing up blood. The doctor said it was food poisoning and told her to follow a strict diet for a few days, but by the morning she was worse. Señor Sempere wrapped her up in blankets and a neighbour who was a taxi driver drove them to the Hospital del Mar. She'd broken out in dark blotches, like ulcers, and her hair was coming out in handfuls. In the hospital they waited a couple of hours but in the end the doctors refused to see her because someone in the waiting room, a patient who hadn't been seen yet, said he knew Sempere and accused him of being a communist or some such nonsense. I suppose he did it to jump the queue. A nurse gave them a syrup which, she said, would help Isabella clean out her stomach, but Isabella couldn't swallow anything. Sempere didn't know what to do. He took her home and started to call one doctor after another. Nobody knew what was wrong with her. A medical assistant who was a regular customer at the bookshop knew someone who worked at the Hospital Clínico. Sempere took Isabella there.'

'In the Clínico Sempere was told it might be cholera and he must take her home, because there was an outbreak and the hospital was overflowing. A number of people in the area had already died. Every day Isabella was worse. She was delirious. Her husband did everything he could. He moved heaven and earth, but after a few days she was so weak he couldn't even take her to the hospital. She died a week after falling ill, in the flat on Calle Santa Ana, above the bookshop . . .'

A long silence reigned between them, punctuated only by the splattering rain and the echo of thunder moving away as the wind abated.

'It wasn't until a month later that I heard she'd been seen one night in the Café de la Ópera, opposite the Liceo. She was sitting with Mauricio Valls. Ignoring my advice, Isabella had threatened him with exposing his plan to use Martín to rewrite some crap of his with which he expected to become famous and be showered with medals. I went there to find out more. The waiter remembered that Valls had arrived before her in a car and that he'd asked for two camomile teas and honey.'

Fermín weighed up the young lawyer's words.

'And you believe Valls poisoned her?'

'I can't prove it, but the more I think about it, the more obvious it seems to me. It had to be Valls.'

Fermín stared at the floor.

'Does Señor Martín know?'

Brians shook his head.

'No. After your escape, Valls ordered Martín to be held in a solitary confinement cell in one of the towers.'

'What about Doctor Sanahuja? Didn't they put them together?'

Brians gave a dejected sigh.

'Sanahuja was court-martialled for treason shortly after your escape. He was shot a week later.'

Another long silence flooded the room. Fermín stood up and began to walk around in circles, looking agitated.

'And why has nobody looked for me? After all, I'm the cause of all this . . .'

'You don't exist. To avoid loss of face before his superiors and the end of a promising career working for the regime, Valls summoned the patrol he'd sent out to search for you and made them swear that they'd gunned you down while you were trying to escape along the slopes of Montjuïc, and they'd flung your body into the common grave.'

Fermín tasted the anger on his lips.

'Well, look here, I've half a mind to go up to the offices of the Military Government right now and invite them to kiss my resurrected arse. I'd like to see how Valls explains my return from the grave.'

'Don't talk nonsense. You wouldn't solve anything by doing that. You'd simply be taken up to Carretera de las Aguas and shot in the back of the head. That worm isn't worth it.'

Fermín nodded in assent, but the feelings of shame and guilt were gnawing at his insides.

'What about Martín? What will happen to him?'

Brians shrugged.

'What I know is confidential. It can't go beyond these four walls. There's a jailer in the castle, a guy called Bebo, who owes me more than a couple of favours. They were going to kill a brother of his but I managed to get his sentence commuted to ten years in a Valencia prison. Bebo is a decent guy and tells me everything he sees and hears in the castle. Valls won't allow me to see Martín, but through Bebo I've found out that he's alive and that Valls keeps him locked up in the tower and watched round the clock. He's given him pen and paper. Bebo says Martín is writing.'

'Writing what?'

'Goodness knows. Valls believes, or so Bebo tells me, that Martín is working on the book he asked him to write, based on his notes. But Martín, who, as you and I know, is not quite in his right mind, seems to be writing something else. Sometimes he reads out loud what he's written, or he stands up and starts walking round the cell, reciting bits of dialogue or whole sentences. Bebo does the night shift by his cell and whenever he can he slips him cigarettes and sugar lumps, which is all he eats. Did Martín ever talk to you about something called *The Angel's Game*?'

Fermín shook his head.

'Is that the title of the book he's working on?'

'That's what Bebo believes. From what he's been able to piece together from what Martín tells him and what he overhears him saying to himself, it sounds like some sort of autobiography or confession . . . If you want my opinion Martín has realised he's losing his mind, so he's trying to write down what he remembers before it's too late. It's as if he were writing himself a letter to find out who he is . . .'

'And what will happen when Valls discovers that he hasn't followed his orders?'

Brians gave him a mournful look.

10

Round about midnight it stopped raining. From the lawyer's attic Barcelona looked lugubrious beneath a sky of low clouds that swept over the rooftops.

'Do you have anywhere to go, Fermín?' asked Brians.

'I have a tempting offer to start a career as a gigolo and bodyguard and move in with a wench who is a bit flighty but has a good heart and spectacular bodywork. But I don't see myself playing the role of a kept man even at the feet of the Venus of Jerez.'

'I don't like the thought of you living on the streets, Fermín. It's dangerous. You can stay here as long as you like.'

Fermín looked around him.

'I know this isn't the Hotel Colón, but I have a camp bed in the back there, I don't snore and, quite frankly, I could use the company.'

'Don't you have a girlfriend?'

'My fiancée was the daughter of the founding partner in the firm from which Valls and company managed to get me fired.'

'You're paying dearly for this Martín business. A vow of poverty and chastity.'

Brians smiled.

'Give me a lost cause and you'll make me happy.'

'That makes two of us. All right then, I'll take you up on your generous offer. But only if you allow me to help and contribute. I can clean, tidy up, type, cook and offer you advice as well as investigative and security services. And if, in a moment of weakness, you find yourself in a tight spot and need to unwind a bit, I'm sure that through my friend Rociíto I can provide you with professional services that will leave you as good as new: when you're young and tender you have to watch out for a build-up of seminal fluids going to your head, or you could make matters worse.'

Brians shook his hand.

'That's a deal. I hereby hire you as assistant articled clerk for Brians & Brians, defenders of the insolvent.'

'As my name is Fermín, I swear that before the week is over I will have found you a customer of the sort who pays up front and in cash.'

That is how Fermín Romero de Torres moved temporarily into Brians's minuscule office, where he began by rearranging, cleaning and updating all his files, folders and open cases. Within a couple of days the practice looked as if it had trebled in size thanks to Fermín, who had left the place as clean as a pin. Fermín spent most of the day closeted in the office, but he devoted a couple of hours to sundry expeditions from which he returned with handfuls of flowers he nicked from the lobby of the Tivoli Theatre, a bit of coffee – which he obtained by buttering up a waitress from the bar on the ground floor – and fine foods from the Quílez grocers, which he charged to the account of the legal firm that had fired Brians, having first introduced himself as their new errand boy.

'Fermín, this ham is fabulous, where did you get it?'

'Try the Manchego, it's out of this world.'

He spent the mornings going through all Brians's cases and copying his notes out neatly. In the afternoons he would pick up the telephone and, working his way through the directory, plunge into a search for solvent clients. When he sniffed a possibility, he would then round off the phone call with a visit to the prospect's address. Out of a total of fifty cold calls to businesses, professionals and private citizens in the district, ten turned into visits and three into new clients for Brians.

The first of these was a widow who had entered into a dispute with an insurance company because they'd refused to make the payment due on the death of her husband, arguing that the cardiac arrest he had suffered after a huge dish of red-hot spicy prawns at the Siete Puertas restaurant was in fact a case of suicide, not covered by the policy. The second was a taxidermist to whom a retired bullfighter had taken the five-hundred-kilo Miura bull with which he'd ended his career in the rings. Once the bull was stuffed, the bullfighter had refused to pay for it and take it home. He said that the glass eyes the taxidermist had given it made it look as if it were possessed by malevolent forces from the other side, and he'd rushed out of the shop claiming Gypsy sorcery had brought on an irritable colon emergency. And the third client was a tailor from Ronda San Pedro who had had five perfectly healthy molars extracted by a dentist with no qualifications but plenty of gall. They were small cases, but all the clients had paid a deposit and signed a contract.

'Fermín, I'm going to put you on the payroll.'

'I won't hear of it. Consider my services strictly pro bono.'

Fermín refused to accept any emolument for his good offices, except occasional small loans with which on Sunday afternoons he took Rociíto to the cinema, to dance at La Paloma or to the funfair at the top of the Tibidabo mountain. Romance was in the air, and Fermín was slowly reclaiming his old self. Once, in the funfair's hall of mirrors, Rociíto gave him a love bite on the neck that smarted for a whole week. On another occasion, taking advantage of the fact that they were the only passengers on the full-sized aeroplane replica that gyrated, suspended from a crane, between Barcelona and the blue heavens, Fermín recovered full command of his manhood after a long absence from the scenarios of rushed love.

Not long after that, one lazy afternoon when Fermín was savouring Rociíto's splendid attributes on the top of the big wheel, it occurred to him that those times, against all expectations, were turning out to be good times. Then he felt afraid, because he knew they couldn't last long and those stolen drops of happiness and peace would evaporate sooner than the youthful bloom of Rocií-to's flesh and eyes.

11

That same night Fermín sat in the office waiting for Brians to return from his rounds of courts, offices, practices, prisons and the thousand and one audiences with the high and mighty he had to endure to obtain information. It was almost eleven when he heard the young lawyer's footsteps approaching down the corridor. He opened the door for him and Brians came in dragging his feet and his soul, looking more crestfallen than ever. He collapsed in a corner and put his hands over his head.

'What's happened, Brians?'

'I've just come from the castle.'

'Bad news?'

'Worse. Valls refused to see me. They made me wait for four hours and then they told me to leave. They've withdrawn my visitor's licence and my permit for entering the premises.'

'Did they let you see Martín?'

Brians shook his head.

'He wasn't there.'

Fermín looked at him without understanding. Brians didn't speak for a few moments, searching for the right words.

'When I was leaving Bebo followed me and told me what he knew. It happened two weeks ago. Martín had been writing like a man possessed, day and night, barely sleeping. Valls suspected something was up and instructed Bebo to confiscate the pages Martín had written so far. Three guards were needed to hold him down and pull the manuscript from him. He'd written over five hundred pages in under two months.

'Bebo handed them to Valls, and when Valls started to read, it seems he flew into a rage.'

'It wasn't what he was expecting, I take it . . .'

Brians shook his head.

'Valls spent all night reading and the following morning went up to the tower, escorted by four of his men. He had Martín shackled hand and foot and then stepped into the cell. Bebo was listening through a chink in the cell door and heard part of the conversation. Valls was furious. He told him he was very disappointed in him. He'd handed him the seeds of a masterpiece and Martín, ungratefully, instead of following his instructions, had embarked on that rubbish that made no sense whatsoever. "This isn't the book I was expecting from you, Martín," Valls kept repeating.'

'And what did Martín say?'

'Nothing. He ignored him. As if he weren't there. Which made Valls all the more furious. Bebo heard Valls slap and punch Martín, but Martín didn't utter a sound. When Valls grew tired of hitting and insulting him and getting no response at all, Bebo says that Valls pulled out a letter he had in his pocket, a letter Señor Sempere had written to Martín months before which had been confiscated. In this letter there was a note Isabella had written to Martín on her deathbed . . .'

'Son-of-a-bitch . . .'

'Valls left him there, locked up with that letter, because he knew that nothing would hurt him more than to know Isabella had died . . . Bebo says that when Valls left and Martín read the letter he started to scream, and he screamed all night, banging on the walls and the iron door with his hands and with his head . . .'

Brians looked up and Fermín knelt down in front of him and put a hand on his shoulder.

'Are you all right, Brians?'

'I'm his lawyer,' he said in a shaky voice. 'I'm supposed to protect him and get him out of there . . .'

'You've done everything you could, Brians. And Martín knows that.'

Brians dissented, murmuring to himself.

'And that's not the end of it,' he said. 'Bebo told me that since Valls didn't allow him any more paper, Martín started writing on the back of the pages the governor had thrown in his face. And as he had no ink, he would cut his hands and arms and use his own blood . . .

'Bebo tried to talk to him, to calm him . . . He no longer accepted the cigarettes or the sugar lumps he liked so much . . . He didn't even acknowledge Bebo's presence. Bebo thinks that when he heard about Isabella's death he lost his sanity altogether and moved into the hell he'd created in his mind . . . At night he shouted so loud everyone could hear him. Rumours began to circulate among visitors, prisoners and the prison staff. Valls was getting nervous. Finally, he ordered two of his gunmen to take Martín away one night . . .'

Fermín gulped.

'Where to?'

'Bebo isn't sure. From what he was able to hear, he thinks he was taken to an old house next to Güell Park . . . it seems that during the war a number of men were killed in that place and then buried in the garden . . . When the gunmen returned they told Valls that everything had been taken care of, but Bebo told me that on that very night he heard them talking among themselves and they seemed rattled. Something had happened in the house. It seems there was someone else there.'

'Someone?'

Brians shrugged his shoulders.

'So then David Martín is alive?'

'I don't know, Fermín. Nobody knows.'

12

Barcelona, 1957

Fermín was speaking in a feeble voice and looked disconsolate. Conjuring up those memories seemed to have left him lifeless. I poured him one last glass of wine and watched him dry his tears with his hands. I handed him a napkin but he ignored it. The rest of the Can Lluís clientele had gone home some time ago, and I imagined that it must be past midnight, but nobody had wanted to disturb us and they'd left us alone in the dining room. Fermín looked at me exhausted, as if having revealed the secrets he'd kept for so many years had robbed him of his will to live.

'Fermín . . .'

'I know what you're going to ask me. The answer is no.'

'Fermín, is David Martín my father?'

Fermín looked at me severely.

'Your father is Señor Sempere, Daniel. You must never be in any doubt about that. Never.'

I nodded. Fermín remained anchored in his chair, looking absent, staring into space.

'What about you, Fermín? What happened to you?'

Fermín took a while to reply, as if that part of the story were completely unimportant.

'I went back to the streets. I couldn't stay there, with Brians. Nor could I stay with Rociíto. Nor with anyone else . . .'

Fermín broke off his account, and I took up the thread of the narrative for him.

'You returned to the streets, a beggar without a name, with nobody and nothing in the world, a man whom everyone thought was mad and who would have wished to die, had it not been for a promise he had made . . .'

'I'd promised Martín I'd take care of Isabella and her son . . . of you. But I was a coward, Daniel. I was in hiding for so long, I was so frightened of returning, that when I did your mother was no longer there . . .'

'And is that why I found you that night in Plaza Real? It wasn't a coincidence? How long had you been following me?'

'Months. Years.'

I imagined him following me as a child, when I went to school, when I played in Ciudadela Park, when I stopped with my father in front of that shop window to gaze at the pen I believed blindly had belonged to Victor Hugo, when I sat in Plaza Real to read to Clara and caress her with my eyes thinking nobody could see me. A beggar, a shadow, a figure nobody noticed and all eyes avoided. Fermín, my protector and friend.

'And why didn't you tell me the truth years later?'

'At first I wanted to, but then I realised that it would do you more harm than good. Nothing could change the past. I decided to hide the truth because I thought it best for you to be more like your father and less like me.'

We fell into a long silence during which we eyed each other furtively, not knowing what to say.

'Where's Valls?' I asked at last.

'Don't even think of it,' Fermín cut in.

'Where is he now?' I asked again. 'If you don't tell me I'll find out myself.'

'And what will you do? Will you turn up at his house, ready to kill him?'

'Why not?'

Fermín laughed bitterly.

'Because you have a wife and a son, because you have a life ahead of you and people who love you and whom you love. Because you have it all, Daniel.'

'All except my mother.'

'Revenge won't give you back your mother, Daniel.'

'That's easy to say. Nobody murdered yours . . .'

Fermín was about to say something, but he bit his tongue.

'Why do you think your father never told you about the war, Daniel? Do you think he doesn't imagine what happened?'

'If that's so, why did he keep quiet? Why didn't he do anything?'

'Because of you, Daniel. Because of you. Your father, like so many people who had to live through those years, swallowed everything and kept quiet. They just had to lump it. You pass them in the street every day and don't even see them. They've rotted away all these years with that pain inside them so that you, and others like you, could live. Don't you dare judge your father. You have no right to.'

I felt as if my best friend had slapped me.

'Don't be angry with me, Fermín . . .'

Fermín shook his head.

'I'm not angry.'

'I'm just trying to take all this in, Fermín. Let me ask you a question. Just one.'

'About Valls? No.'

'Just one question, Fermín. I swear. If you don't want to, you don't have to reply.'

Fermín nodded reluctantly.

'Is this Mauricio Valls the same Valls I think he is?' I asked.

Fermín nodded.

'The very one. The one who was Minister of Culture until about four or five years ago. The one who appeared in the papers every other day. The great Mauricio Valls. Author, editor, thinker and messiah of the national intellectual class. *That* Valls,' said Fermín.

I realised I'd seen that man's photograph in the papers dozens of times, that I'd heard his name being mentioned and had seen it printed on the spines of some of the books we had in the shop.

Until that night, the name Mauricio Valls was just one more in that dim parade of dignitaries one barely notices but which always seems to be there. Until that night, if anyone had asked me who Mauricio Valls was, I would have said he was only vaguely familiar to me, a public figure of those blighted years to whom I'd never paid much attention. Until that night it would never have crossed my mind to imagine that one day that name, that face, would thereafter be the name and the face of the man who murdered my mother.

'But . . .' I protested.

'No buts. You said one more question and I've answered it already.'

'Fermín, you can't leave me like this . . .'

'Listen carefully, Daniel.'

Fermín looked me in the eye and gripped my wrist.

'I swear that, when the moment is right, I myself will help you find that son-of-a-bitch, if it's the last thing I do in my life. Then we'll settle our scores with him. But not now. Not like this.'

I looked at him doubtfully.

'Promise me you won't do anything stupid, Daniel. Promise you'll wait for the right moment.'

I looked down.

'You can't ask me that, Fermín.'

'I can and I must.'

At last I nodded and Fermín let go of my arm.

13

When I finally got home it was almost two in the morning. I was about to walk through the front door of the building when I noticed there was light inside the shop, a faint glow coming from behind the back-room curtain. I stepped in through the side door in the hallway and found my father sitting at his desk, enjoying the first cigarette I'd seen him smoke in years. In front of him, on the table, lay an open envelope and the pages of a letter. I pulled a chair over and sat down facing him. My father stared at me, sunk in an impenetrable silence.

'I didn't know you smoked,' I ventured.

He simply shrugged.

'Good news?' I asked, pointing at the letter.

My father handed it to me.

'It's from your Aunt Laura, the one who lives in Naples.'

'I have an aunt in Naples?'

'She's your mother's sister, the one who went to live in Italy with her mother's side of the family the year you were born.'

I nodded absently. I didn't remember her. Her name belonged among the strangers who came to my mother's funeral all those years ago, and whom I'd never seen again.

'She says she has a daughter who is coming to study in Barcelona and wants to know whether she can stay here for a while. Her name is Sofía.'

'It's the first time I've ever heard her mentioned,' I said.

'That makes two of us.'

The thought of my father sharing his flat with a teenager who was a perfect stranger seemed unlikely.

'What are you going to say to her?'

'I don't know. I'll have to say something.'

We continued sitting there quietly for almost a minute, gazing at one another without daring to speak about the matter that really filled our minds – not the visit of an unknown cousin.

'I suppose you were out with Fermín,' my father said at last, putting out his cigarette.

I nodded.

'We had dinner at Can Lluís. Fermín finished everything, down to the napkins. I saw Professor Alburquerque there when we arrived and told him to drop by the bookshop.'

The sound of my own voice reciting banalities had an accusatory echo. My father observed me tensely.

'Did Fermín tell you what's been the matter with him lately?'

'I think it's nerves, because of the wedding and all that stuff that doesn't agree with him.'

'And that's it?'

A good liar knows that the most efficient lie is always a truth that has had a key piece removed from it.

'Well, he told me about the old days, about when he was in prison and all that.'

'Then he must have told you about Brians, the lawyer. What did he say?'

I wasn't sure what my father knew or suspected, so I decided to tread carefully.

'He told me he was imprisoned in Montjuïc Castle and that he managed to escape with the help of a man called David Martín. Apparently you knew him.'

My father was silent for a while.

'Nobody has dared to say this to my face, but I know there are people who at the time believed, and still believe, that you mother was in love with Martín,' he said with such a sad smile that I knew he considered himself one of them.

My father had a tendency to grin the way some people do when they're trying to hold back their tears.

'Your mother was a good woman. A good wife. I wouldn't like you to think strange things about her because of what Fermín may have told you. He didn't know her. I did.'

'Fermín didn't insinuate anything,' I lied. 'Just that Mum and Martín were bound by a strong friendship and that she tried to help him get out of the prison by hiring that lawyer, Brians.'

'I suppose he will also have spoken to you about that man, Valls . . .'

I hesitated for a second before nodding. My father saw the consternation in my eyes and shook his head.

'Your mother died of cholera, Daniel. Brians – I'll never know why – insists on accusing that man, just a bureaucrat with delusions of grandeur, of a crime for which he has no evidence or proof.'

I didn't say anything.

'You must get that idea out of your head. I want you to promise you're not even going to think about this.'

I sat there with my mouth shut, wondering whether my father was really as naïve as he appeared to be or whether the pain of her loss had blinded him and pushed him towards the convenient cowardice of survivors. I recalled Fermín's words and told myself that neither I nor anyone else had any right to judge him.

'Promise you won't do anything stupid, and you won't look for this man,' he insisted.

I nodded without conviction. He grabbed my arm.

'Swear you won't. For the sake of your mother's memory.'

I felt a pain gripping my face and realised I was gnashing my teeth so strongly they were in danger of cracking. I looked away but my father wouldn't let go of me. I stared into his eyes, and until the last second, thought I might be able to lie to him.

'I swear on my mother's memory that I won't do anything while you live.'

'That is not what I asked you.'

'It's all I can give you.'

My father dropped his head between his hands and took a deep breath.

'The night your mother died, upstairs, in the flat . . .'

'I remember it clearly.'

'You were five.'

'I was four.'

'That night Isabella asked me never to tell you what had happened. She thought it was better that way.'

It was the first time I'd heard him refer to my mother by her name.

'I know, Dad.'

He looked into my eyes.

'Forgive me,' he whispered.

I held my father's gaze. Sometimes he seemed to grow a little older just by looking at me and remembering. I stood up and hugged him quietly. He held me tight and when he burst into tears the anger and the pain he'd buried in his soul all those years gushed out like blood. I knew then, without being able to explain clearly why, that slowly, inexorably, my father had begun to die.

Part Four

Suspicion

1

Barcelona, 1957

The first glint of daybreak found me in the doorway of little Julián's bedroom. For once he was sound asleep, far from everything and everyone, with a smile on his lips. I heard Bea's footsteps approaching and felt her hands on my back.

'How long have you been standing here?' she asked.

'A while.'

'What are you doing?'

'I'm looking at him.'

Bea walked up to Julián's cot and leaned over to kiss his forehead.

'What time did you come in last night?'

I didn't reply.

'How is Fermín?'

'Not too bad.'

'And you?' I tried to smile. 'Do you want to talk about it?' she insisted.

'Some other day.'

'I thought there were no secrets between us,' said Bea.

'So did I.'

She looked at me in surprise.

'What do you mean, Daniel?'

'Nothing. I don't mean anything. I'm very tired. Shall we go back to bed?'

Bea took my hand and led me to the bedroom.

We lay down on the bed and I embraced her.

'I dreamed about your mother tonight,' said Bea. 'About Isabella.'

The rain began to pelt against the windowpanes.

'I was a little girl, and she was holding my hand. We were in a large and very old house, with huge rooms and a grand piano, and a glass-covered balcony that looked on to a garden with a pond. There was a little boy by the pond. He looked just like Julián, but I knew that it was really you, don't ask me why. Isabella knelt down by my side and asked me whether I could see you. You were playing by the water with a paper boat. I said I could. Then she told me to look after you. To look after you for ever because she had to go far away.'

We lay there without speaking for a long time, listening to the patter of the rain.

'What did Fermín tell you last night?'

'The truth,' I replied. 'He told me the truth.'

As I tried to reconstruct Fermín's story Bea listened in silence. At first I felt anger swelling up inside me again, but as I advanced through the story I was overwhelmed by sadness and despair. It was all new to me and I still didn't know how I was going to be able to live with the secrets and implications of what Fermín had revealed to me. Those events had taken place almost twenty years before, and the passage of time had turned me into a mere spectator in a play where the course of my fate had been determined.

When I finished talking, I noticed the anxious look in Bea's eyes. It wasn't hard to guess what she was thinking.

'I've promised my father that during his lifetime I won't look for that man, Valls, or do anything else,' I added, to reassure her.

'During *his* lifetime? And what happens afterwards? Haven't you thought about us? About Julián?'

'Of course I have. And you must not worry,' I lied. 'After talking to my father I've understood that all this happened a long time ago and there's nothing we can do to change it.'

Bea seemed rather unconvinced.

'It's the truth . . .' I lied again.

She held my gaze for a few moments, but those were the words she wanted to hear and she finally surrendered to the temptation of believing them.

2

That afternoon, with the rain still lashing the flooded, deserted streets, the grim figure of Sebastián Salgado appeared outside the bookshop. He was observing us with his unmistakable predatory air through the shop window, the lights from the nativity scene illuminating his ravaged face. His suit – the same old suit he'd worn on his first visit – was soaking wet. I went over to the door and opened it for him.

'Lovely manger,' he said.

'Aren't you coming in?'

I held the door open and Salgado limped in. After a few steps he stopped, leaning on his walking stick. Fermín eyed him suspiciously from the counter. Salgado smiled.

'It's been a long time,' he intoned.

'I thought you were dead,' replied Fermín.

'I thought you were dead, too, as did everyone else. That's what they told us. That you'd been caught trying to escape and they'd shot you.'

'Fat chance.'

'To be honest, I always hoped you'd managed to slip away. You know: the devil looks after his own and all that . . .'

'You move me to tears, Salgado. When did you get out?'

'About a month ago.'

'Don't tell me you were let out for good behaviour,' said Fermín.

'I think they got tired of waiting for me to die. Do you know I was granted a pardon? I've got it on a sheet of paper, signed by General Franco himself.'

'You must have had it framed, I'm sure.'

'I've put it in a place of honour: above the toilet, in case I ever run out of tissue.'

Salgado took a few more steps towards the counter and pointed to a chair in a corner.

'Do you mind if I sit down? I'm still not used to walking more than ten metres in a straight line and I get tired very easily.'

'It's all yours,' I offered.

He fell into the chair and took a deep breath as he rubbed his knee. Fermín looked at him like someone who has spied a rat climbing out of a toilet.

'Funny, isn't it, to think that the one person everyone thought would be the first to kick the bucket turns out to be the last . . . Do you know what has kept me alive all these years, Fermín?'

'If I didn't know you so well I'd say it was the Mediterranean diet and the fresh sea air.'

Salgado gave an attempt at a laugh that sounded like a hoarse cough or his bronchial tubes on the verge of collapse.

'You never change, Fermín. That's why we got along so famously back then. What times those were. But I don't want to bore the young man here with memories of the good old days. This generation isn't interested in our stuff. They're into the charleston, or whatever they call it these days. Shall we talk business?'

'I'm listening.'

'You're the one who must do the talking, Fermín. I've already said all I had to say. Are you going to give me what you owe me? Or are we going to have to kick up a fuss you'd do better to avoid?'

Fermín remained impassive for a few moments, leaving us in an uncomfortable silence. Salgado was staring straight at him with venom in his eyes. Fermín gave me a look I didn't quite understand and sighed dejectedly.

'You win, Salgado.'

He pulled a small object out of his pocket and handed it to him. A key. *The key*. Salgado's eyes lit up like those of a child. He got to his feet and slowly approached Fermín, accepting the key with his remaining hand, trembling with emotion.

'If you're planning to reintroduce it into restricted areas of your anatomy, I beg you to step into the bathroom for the sake of decorum. This is a family venue, open to the general public,' Fermín warned him.

Salgado, who seemed to have recovered the bloom of first youth, broke into a smile of boundless satisfaction.

'Come to think of it, you've actually done me a huge favour keeping it for me all these years,' he declared.

'That's what friends are for,' answered Fermín. 'God bless, and don't hesitate never to come back here again.'

Salgado smiled and winked at us. He walked towards the door, already lost in thought. Before stepping into the street he turned round for a moment and raised a hand in a conciliatory farewell.

'I wish you luck and a long life, Fermín. And rest assured, your secret is safe with me.'

We watched him leave in the rain, an old man anyone might have thought was at death's door but who, I was sure, didn't feel the cold raindrops lashing at him then, or even the years of imprisonment and hardships he carried in his blood. I glanced at Fermín, who seemed nailed to the ground, looking pale and confused at the sight of his old cellmate.

'Are we going to let him go just like that?' I asked.

'Have you a better plan?'

3

After the proverbial minute's wait, we hurried down the street armed with dark raincoats and an umbrella the size of a parasol that Fermín had bought in one of the bazaars in the port – intending to use it both winter and summer for his escapades to La Barceloneta beach with Bernarda.

'Fermín, with this thing we stick out like a sore thumb,' I warned him.

'Don't worry. I'm sure the only thing that swine can see are gold doubloons raining down from heaven,' replied Fermín.

Salgado was some hundred metres ahead of us, hobbling briskly under the rain along Calle Condal. We narrowed the gap a little, just in time to see him about to climb on to a tram going up Vía Layetana. We sprinted forward, closing the umbrella as we ran, and by some miracle managed to leap on to the tram's running board. In the best tradition of those days we made the journey hanging from the back. Salgado had found a seat in the front, offered to him by a Good Samaritan, who couldn't have known who he was dealing with.

'That's what happens when people reach old age,' said Fermín. 'Nobody remembers they've been bastards too.'

The tram rumbled along Calle Trafalgar until it reached the Arco de Triunfo. We peered inside and saw that Salgado was still glued to his seat. The ticket collector, a man with a bushy moustache, scowled at us.

'Don't think that because you're hanging out there I'm going to give you a discount. I've had an eye on you ever since you jumped on board.'

'Nobody cares about social realism any more,' murmured Fermín. 'What a country.'

We handed him a few coins and he gave us our tickets. We were beginning to think Salgado must have fallen asleep when, as the tram turned into the road leading to the Estación del Norte, he stood up and pulled the chain to request a stop. The driver was now slowing down, so we jumped off opposite the palatial art nouveau headquarters of the Hydroelectric Company and followed the tram on foot to the stop. We saw Salgado step down, assisted by two passengers, and then head off towards the train station.

'Are you thinking what I'm thinking?' I asked.

Fermín nodded. We followed Salgado to the station's grand entrance hall, camouflaging ourselves – or perhaps making our presence painfully obvious – behind Fermín's oversized umbrella. Once inside, Salgado approached a row of metal lockers lined up along one of the walls like miniature niches in a cemetery. We sat on a bench in the shadows of the hall. Salgado was standing in front of the countless lockers, staring at them, utterly absorbed.

'Do you think he's forgotten where he hid the booty?' I asked.

'Of course he hasn't. He's been waiting twenty years for this moment. He's simply savouring it.'

'If you say so . . . But he's forgotten, if you ask me.'

We remained there, watching and waiting.

'Fermín, you never really told me where you hid the key when you escaped from the castle . . .'

Fermín threw me a hostile glance.

'Forget it,' I conceded.

The wait continued a few minutes longer.

'Perhaps he has an accomplice . . .' I said, 'and he's waiting for him.'

'Salgado isn't the sharing sort.'

'Perhaps there's someone else who . . .'

'Shhh,' Fermín hushed me, pointing at Salgado, who had moved at last.

The old man walked over to one of the lockers and placed his hand on the metal door. He pulled out the key, inserted it in the lock, opened the door and looked inside. At that precise moment a pair of Civil Guards doing their rounds turned into the entrance hall from the station platforms and walked over to where Salgado was standing, trying to pull something out of the locker.

'Oh dear, oh dear . . .' I murmured.

Salgado turned and greeted the two officers. They exchanged a few words and one of them pulled a case out of the locker and left it on the floor by Salgado's feet. The thief thanked them effusively for their help and the Civil Guards touched their three-cornered hats and continued on their beat.

'God bless Spain,' murmured Fermín.

Salgado grabbed the case and dragged it along to another bench, at the opposite end from where we were sitting.

'He's not going to open it here, is he?' I asked.

'He has to make sure it's all there,' replied Fermín. 'That nasty piece of work has put up with years of misery to recover his treasure.'

Salgado looked around him a few times to make sure there was nobody nearby, and finally decided to take action. We saw him open the suitcase just a few centimetres and peer inside.

He remained like that for almost a minute, motionless. Fermín and I looked at one another without understanding. Suddenly Salgado closed the suitcase and got up, then walked off towards the exit, leaving the suitcase behind him in front of the open locker.

'But what's he doing?' I asked.

Fermín stood up and signalled to me.

'You get the suitcase, and I'll follow him . . .'

Without giving me time to reply, Fermín hastened towards the exit. I hurried over to the place where Salgado had abandoned the case. A smart alec, who was reading a newspaper on a nearby bench, had also set eyes on it and, looking both ways first to check that nobody was watching, got up and was preparing to swoop on it like a bird of prey. I quickened my pace. The stranger was about to grab the case when, by the miracle of a split second, I managed to snatch it from him.

'That suitcase isn't yours,' I said.

The individual fixed me with a hostile look and clutched the handle.

'Shall I call the Civil Guards?' I asked.

Looking flustered, the scamp let go of the case and moved swiftly away in the direction of the platforms. I took it over to the bench and, after making sure no one was looking, opened it.

It was empty. Salgado's treasure was gone.

Only then did I hear shouts and turned my head to discover that some incident had occurred outside the station. I got to my feet and looked through the glass doors. The two Civil Guards were pushing their way through a circle of bystanders that had congregated in the rain. When the crowd parted, I saw Fermín kneeling on the ground, holding Salgado in his arms. The old man's eyes were staring into space.

A woman came into the station, a hand clamped over her mouth.

'What happened?' I asked.

'A poor old man, he just keeled over . . .' she said.

I went outside and walked across to the knot of people observing the scene. I could see Fermín looking up and exchanging a few words with the Civil Guards. One of them was nodding. Fermín then took off his raincoat and spread it over Salgado's corpse, covering his face. By the time I arrived there, a three-fingered hand was peeping out from under the garment. On the palm, shining in the rain, was the key. I protected Fermín with the umbrella and put a hand on his shoulder. We slowly moved away.

'Are you all right, Fermín?'

My good friend shrugged.

'Let's go home,' he managed to say.

4

As we left the station behind us I took off my raincoat and put it over Fermín's shoulders. He'd abandoned his on Salgado's body. I didn't think my friend was in a fit state to take a long walk, so I hailed a taxi. I opened the door for him and, once he was seated, closed it and got in on the other side.

'The suitcase was empty,' I said. 'Someone played a dirty trick on Salgado.'

'It takes a thief to catch a thief . . .'

'Who do you think it was?'

'Perhaps the same person who said I had his key and told him where he could find me,' Fermín murmured.

'Valls?'

Fermín gave a dispirited sigh.

'I don't know, Daniel. I no longer know what to think.'

I noticed the taxi driver looking at us in the mirror, waiting.

'We're going to the entrance to Plaza Real, on Calle Fernando,' I said.

'Aren't we going back to the bookshop?' asked Fermín, who didn't have enough fight left in him even to argue about a taxi ride.

'I am. But you're going to Don Gustavo's, to spend the rest of the day with Bernarda.'

We made the journey in silence, staring out at Barcelona, a blur in the rain. When we reached the arches on Calle Fernando, where years before I'd first met Fermín, I paid the fare and we got out. I walked Fermín as far as Don Gustavo's front door and gave him a hug.

'Take care of yourself, Fermín. And eat something, or Bernarda will get a bone sticking into her on the wedding night.'

'Don't worry. When I set my mind to it, I can put on more weight than an opera singer. As soon as I go up to the flat I'll gorge myself with those almond cakes Don Gustavo buys in Casa Quílez and by tomorrow I'll look like stuffed turkey.'

'I hope so. Give my best to the bride.'

'I will, although with things the way they are on the legal front and with all that red tape, I can see myself living in sin.'

'None of that. Remember what you once told me? That destiny doesn't do home visits, that you have to go for it yourself?'

'I must confess I took that sentence from one of Carax's books. I liked the sound of it.'

'Well, I believed it and still do. That's why I'm telling you that your destiny is to marry Bernarda on the arranged date with all your papers in order – with priests, rice and your name and surnames.'

My friend looked at me sceptically.

'As my name is Daniel, you're getting married with all due pomp and ceremony,' I promised Fermín. He looked so dejected I thought nothing would manage to revive his spirits: not a packet of Sugus, not even a good movie at the Fémina Cinema with Kim Novak sporting one of her glorious brassieres that defied gravity.

'If you say so, Daniel . . .'

'You've given me back the truth,' I said. 'I'm going to give you back your name.'

5

That afternoon, when I returned to the bookshop, I set in motion my plan for rescuing Fermín's identity. The first step consisted in making a few phone calls from the back room and establishing a course of action. The second required gathering the right team of recognised experts.

The following day turned out to be pleasant and sunny. Around noon I walked over to the library on Calle del Carmen, where I'd arranged to meet Professor Alburquerque, convinced that whatever he didn't know, nobody knew.

I found him under the tall arches of the main reading room, surrounded by piles of books and papers, concentrating, pen in hand. I sat down opposite him, on the other side of the table, and let him get on with his work. It took him almost a minute to become aware of my presence. When he looked up he stared at me in surprise.

'That must be really good stuff,' I ventured.

'I'm working on a series of articles on Barcelona's accursed writers,' he explained. 'Do you remember someone called Julián Carax, an author you recommended a few months ago in the bookshop?'

'Of course,' I replied.

'Well, I've been looking into him and his story is truly extraordinary. Did you know that for years a diabolical character went around the world searching for Carax's books and burning them?'

'You don't say,' I said, feigning surprise.

'It's a very odd case. I'll let you read it when I've finished.'

'You should write a book on the subject,' I proposed. 'A secret history of Barcelona seen through its accursed writers, those forbidden in the official version.'

The professor considered the idea, intrigued.

'It had occurred to me, I must say, but I have so much work what with my newspaper articles and the university . . .'

'If you don't write it, nobody will . . .'

'Yes, well, maybe I'll take the plunge and get on with it. I don't know where I'll find the time, but . . .'

'Sempere & Sons can offer you its full catalogue and any assistance you may need.'

'I'll bear it in mind. So? Shall we go for lunch?'

Professor Alburquerque called it a day and we set off for Casa Leopoldo where we sat down with a glass of wine and some sublime *serrano* ham tapas, to wait for two plates of bull's-tail stew, the day's special.

'How's our good friend Fermín? A couple of weeks ago, when I saw him in Can Lluís, he looked very downcast.'

'Oddly enough, he's the person I wanted to talk to you about. It's a rather delicate matter and I must ask you to keep it between ourselves.'

'But of course. What can I do?'

I proceeded to outline the problem as concisely as I could, without touching upon thorny or unnecessary details. The professor sensed that there was plenty more to the story than I was telling him, but he displayed his customary discretion.

'Let's see if I've understood,' he said. 'Fermín cannot make use of his identity because, officially, he was pronounced dead almost twenty years ago and therefore, in the eyes of the state, he doesn't exist.'

'Correct.'

'But, from what you tell me, I gather that this identity that was cancelled was also fictitious, an invention of Fermín himself during the war, to save his skin.'

'Correct.'

'That's where I get lost. Help me, Daniel. If Fermín thought up a false identity once, why can't he make up another one now to get married with?'

'For two reasons, Professor. The first is purely practical and that is, whether he uses his name or another invented one, currently Fermín does not possess any legal identity. Therefore, whatever identity he decides to use must be created from scratch.'

'But he wants to continue being Fermín, I suppose.'

'Exactly. And that is the second reason, which is not practical but spiritual, so to speak, and far more important. Fermín wants to continue being Fermín because that is the person Bernarda has fallen in love with, the man who is our friend, the one we all know and the one *he* wants to be. The person he used to be hasn't existed for years. It's a skin he sloughed off. Not even I, who am probably his best friend, know what name he was given when he was christened. For me, and for all those who love him, and especially for himself, he is Fermín Romero de Torres. And when you think of it, if it's a question of creating a new identity for him, why not create his present one?'

Professor Alburquerque finally nodded in assent.

'Correct,' he pronounced.

'So, do you think this is feasible, Professor?'

'Well, it's a quixotic mission if ever there was one,' considered the professor. 'How to endow the gaunt knight Don Fermín de la Mancha with lineage, greyhound and a sheaf of false documents with which to pair him off with his beautiful Bernarda del Toboso in the eyes of God and the register office?'

'I've been thinking about it and consulting legal books,' I said. 'In this country, a person's identity begins with a birth certificate, which, when you stop to consider, is a very simple document.'

The professor raised his eyebrows.

'What you're suggesting is delicate. Not to say a serious crime.'

'Unprecedented in fact, at least in the judicial annals. I've verified it.'

'Have you? Please continue, this is getting better.'

'Let's suppose that someone, hypothetically speaking, had access to the offices of the Civil Registry and could, to put it bluntly, *plant* a birth certificate in the archives . . . Wouldn't that provide sufficient grounds to establish a person's identity?'

The professor shook his head.

'Perhaps for a newborn child. But if we're speaking, hypothetically, of an adult, we'd have to create an entire documentary history. And even if you had access, hypothetically, to the archives, where would you get hold of those documents?'

'Let's say I was able to create a series of credible facsimiles. Would you think it possible then?'

The professor considered the matter carefully.

'The main risk would be that someone uncovers the fraud and wants to bring it to light. Bearing in mind that in this case the so-called accuser who could have spilled the beans regarding documental irregularities is deceased, the problem would boil down to a), being able to gain access to the archives and introduce a file into the system with a fictitious but plausible identity and b), generating the whole string of documents required to establish that identity. I'm talking about papers of all shapes and sizes, and all sorts of certificates including certificates of baptism from parish churches, identity cards . . .'

'With regard to point a), I understand that you're writing a series of articles on the marvels of the Spanish legal system, commissioned by the Council for a report on that institution. I've been looking into it a little and discovered that during the war, a number of archives in the Civil Registry were bombed. That means that hundreds, even thousands, of identities must have been reconstructed any old how. I'm no expert, but I imagine that this would open a gap or two which someone well informed, well connected and with a plan could take advantage of . . .'

The professor looked at me out of the corner of his eye.

'I see you've been doing some serious research, Daniel.'

'Forgive me, Professor, but Fermín's happiness is worth that and much more.'

'And it does you credit. But it could also earn whoever attempted to do such a thing a heavy sentence if he was caught red handed.'

'That's why I thought that if someone, hypothetically, had access to one of those reconstructed archives in the Civil Registry, he could take a helper along with him who would, so to speak, assume the more risky part of the operation.'

'If that were the case, the hypothetical helper would have to be able to guarantee the facilitator a twenty per cent lifelong discount on the price of any book bought at Sempere & Sons. Plus an invitation to the wedding of the newborn.'

'That's a done deal. And I'd even raise that to twenty-five per cent. Although, come to think of it, I know someone who, hypothetically, would be prepared to collaborate pro bono, just for the pleasure of scoring a goal against a rotten, corrupt regime, receiving nothing in exchange.'

'I'm an academic, Daniel. Emotional blackmail doesn't work with me.'

'For Fermín, then.'

'That's another matter. Let's go into the technicalities.'

I pulled out the one-thousand-peseta note Salgado had given me and showed it to him.

'This is my budget for running costs and issuance of documents,' I remarked.

'I see you're sparing no expense. But you'd do better to put that money aside for other endeavours that will be required by this noble deed. My services come free of charge,' replied the professor. 'The bit that worries me most, dear assistant, is the much needed documentary trail. Forget all the new public works and prayer books: the new centurions of the regime have also doubled the already colossal structure of the state bureaucracy, worthy of the worst nightmares of our friend Franz Kafka. As I say, a case like this will require generating all kinds of letters, applications, petitions and other documents that must look credible and have the consistency, tone and smell that are characteristic of a dusty, dog-eared and unquestionable file . . .'

'We're covered on that front,' I said.

'I'm going to have to be given the list of accomplices in this conspiracy, to make sure you're not bluffing.'

I went on to explain the rest of my plan.

'It could work,' he concluded.

As soon as the main dish arrived, we wrapped up the matter and the conversation took a different direction. Although I'd been holding back during the entire meal, by the time coffee was served, I could no longer restrain myself. Feigning a certain indifference, I asked innocently:

'By the way, Professor, the other day a customer was chatting to me about something in the bookshop and the name Mauricio Valls cropped up – the one who was Minister of Culture and all those things. What do you know about him?'

The professor raised an eyebrow.

'About Valls? What everyone knows, I suppose.'

'I'm sure you know much more than everyone, Professor. Much more.'

'Well, actually, I hadn't heard that name for a while, but until not long ago Mauricio Valls was a real big shot. As you say, he was our famous new Minister of Culture for a few years, head of a number of institutions and organisations, a man well placed in the regime and of great prestige in those circles, patron to many, golden boy of all the cultural pages in the Spanish press . . . As I say, a big shot.'

I smiled weakly, pretending to be pleasantly surprised.

'And he isn't any longer?'

'Quite frankly, I'd say he disappeared off the map a while ago, or at least from the public scene. I'm not sure whether he was given some embassy or some post in an international institution, you know how these things work. But in fact I've lost track of him lately . . . I know he set up a publishing house with a number of partners some years ago. The business does very well – it doesn't stop bringing out new books. In fact, once a month I receive an invite for the launch of one of their titles . . .'

'And does Valls go to these events?'

'He used to, years ago. We always joked about the fact that he spoke more about himself than about the book or the author he was presenting. But that was some time ago. I haven't seen him for years. May I ask why this interest, Daniel? I didn't think of you as someone keen on our literature's small vanity fair.'

'I'm just curious.'

'I see.'

While Professor Alburquerque paid the bill, he looked at me askance.

'Why is it that I always think you're not even telling me a quarter of the story?'

'One day I'll tell you the rest, Professor. I promise.'

'You'd better, because cities have no memory and they need someone like me, a sage with his feet on the ground, to keep it alive.'

'This is the deal: you help me solve Fermín's problem and in exchange, one day I'll tell you things that Barcelona would rather forget. For your secret history.'

The professor held out his hand and I shook it.

'I'll take your word for it. Now, returning to the subject of Fermín and the documents we're going to have to pull out of a hat . . .'

'I think I have the right man for the job.'

6

Oswaldo Darío de Mortenssen, prince of Barcelona scribes and an old acquaintance of mine, was enjoying a break after his lunch, in his booth next to La Virreina Palace, sipping a double espresso with a dash of cognac and smoking a cigar. When he saw me approaching he raised a hand in greeting.

'The prodigal son returns. Have you changed your mind? Shall we get going on that love letter that will give you access to the forbidden zips and buttons of the desired young lady?'

I showed him my wedding ring again and he nodded, remembering.

'I'm sorry. Force of habit. You're one of the old guard. What can I do for you?'

'The other day I remembered why your name sounded familiar to me, Don Oswaldo. I work in a bookshop and I found a novel of yours from 1933, *The Riders of Twilight.*'

That sparked a host of memories. Oswaldo smiled nostalgically.

'What times those were . . . Barrido and Escobillas, my publishers, ripped me off to the last *céntimo*, the swines. May they roast for ever in hell. Still, the pleasure of writing it – nobody can take that away from me.'

'If I bring it along one day, will you sign it for me?'

'Of course. It was my swansong. The world wasn't ready for a western set in the Ebro delta, with bandits on canoes instead of horses, and mosquitoes the size of watermelons.'

'You're the Zane Grey of the Spanish coast.'

'I wish. What can I do for you, young man?'

'Lend me your talent and cunning for an equally worthy venture.'

'I'm all ears.'

'I need you to help me invent a documentary past for a friend, so he can marry the woman he loves without legal impediments.'

'A good man?'

'The best I know.'

'If that's the case, it's a deal. My favourite scenes were always weddings and christenings.'

'We'll need official applications, reports, petitions, certificates – the whole shooting match.'

'That won't be a problem. We'll delegate part of the logistics to Luisito, whom you already know. He's completely trustworthy and a master in twelve different calligraphies.'

I pulled out the one-thousand-peseta note the professor had refused and handed it to him. Oswaldo put it away swiftly, his eyes as big as saucers.

'And they say you can't make a living from writing in Spain,' he said.

'Will that cover the working expenses?'

'Amply. When I've got it all organised I'll let you know what the whole operation adds up to, but off the top of my head I'd guess that three or four hundred will get us there.'

'I leave that to your discretion, Oswaldo. My friend Professor Alburquerque . . .'

'Fine writer . . .' Oswaldo cut in.

'And an even better gentleman. As I say, my friend, the professor, will drop by and give you a list of the documents required, and all the details. If there's anything you need, you'll find me at the Sempere & Sons bookshop.'

His face lit up when he heard the name.

'Ah, the sanctuary. As a young man I used to go round every Saturday and those encounters with Señor Sempere opened my eyes.'

'That would have been my grandfather.'

'I haven't been there for years. My finances are tight and I've taken to borrowing books from libraries.'

'Well, do pay us the honour of returning to the bookshop, Don Oswaldo. Consider it your home and we can always sort something out with prices.'

'I will.'

He put out a hand and I shook it.

'It's a pleasure to do business with the Semperes.'

'May it be the first of many such occasions.'

'What happened to the lame man whose eyes twinkled at the sight of gold?'

'Turned out that all that glittered wasn't gold,' I said.

'A sign of our times . . .'

7

Barcelona, 1958

That month of January came wrapped in bright icy skies that blew powdery snow over the city's rooftops. The sun shone every day, casting sharp angles of light and shadow on the façades of a crystalline Barcelona. Double-decker buses drove by with the top tier empty and passing trams left a halo of steam on the tracks.

Christmas lights glowed in garlands of blue fire all over the old town and carols bearing sugary wishes of goodwill and peace trickled out of a thousand and one loudspeakers by shop doors. The Yuletide message was so pervasive that a policeman guarding the nativity scene set up by the town hall in Plaza San Jaime turned a blind eye when someone had the bright idea of placing a Catalan beret on the Infant Jesus – ignoring the demands of a group of pious old women who expected him to haul the man off with a slap to police headquarters. In the end, someone from the archbishop's office reported the incident and three nuns turned up to restore order.

Christmas sales had picked up and a seasonal star in the shape of black numbers in the accounts of Sempere & Sons guaranteed that we would at least be able to cope with the electricity and heating bills. With a bit of luck, we might even enjoy a proper hot meal once a day. My father seemed to have recovered his spirits and decreed that this year we wouldn't wait so long before decorating the bookshop.

'We're going to have that crib hanging around for a long time,' grumbled Fermín with little or no enthusiasm.

After 6 January, the feast of the Three Kings, my father instructed us to wrap up the nativity scene carefully and take it down to the basement for storage until the following Christmas.

'With care,' warned my father. 'I don't want to be told that the boxes slipped accidentally, Fermín.'

'With the utmost care, Señor Sempere. I'll vouch for the integrity of the crib with my life, and that includes all the farm animals dotted round the swaddled Messiah.'

Once we had made room for the boxes containing all the Christmas decorations, I paused for a moment to have a quick look round the basement and its forgotten corners. The last time we'd been there, the conversation had covered matters that neither Fermín nor I had brought up again, but they still lay heavily on my mind at least. Fermín seemed to read my thoughts and he shook his head.

'Don't tell me you're still thinking about that idiot's letter.'

'Every now and then.'

'You won't have said anything to Doña Beatriz, I hope.'

'No. I put the letter back in her coat pocket and didn't say a word.'

'What about her? Didn't she mention that she'd received a letter from Don Juan Tenorio?'

I shook my head. Fermín screwed up his nose, as if to say that it wasn't a good sign.

'Have you decided what you're going to do?'

'What about?'

'Don't act innocent, Daniel. Are you or are you not going to follow your wife to her potential tryst with that old boyfriend at the Ritz and cause a little stir?'

'You're presupposing that she'll be going there,' I protested.

'Aren't you?'

I looked down, upset with myself.

'What kind of a husband doesn't trust his wife?' I asked.

'Would you like me to give you a list of names and surnames, or will statistics do?'

'I trust Bea. She wouldn't cheat on me. She isn't like that. If she had anything to say to me, she'd say it to my face, without lying.'

'Then you don't have anything to worry about, do you?'

Something in Fermín's tone made me think that my suspicions and insecurities had disappointed him. Although he was never going to admit it, I was sure it saddened him to think I devoted my time to unworthy thoughts and to doubting the sincerity of a woman I didn't deserve.

'You must think I'm a fool.'

Fermín shook his head.

'No. I think you're a fortunate man, at least when it comes to love. And like most people who are so fortunate, you don't realise it.'

A knock on the door at the top of the stairs interrupted us.

'Unless you've discovered oil down there, will you please come back up right away, there's work to do,' called my father.

Fermín sighed.

'Since he's got out of the red he's become a tyrant,' he said.

The days crawled by. Fermín had at last agreed to delegate the preparations for the wedding and the banquet to my father and Don Gustavo, who had taken on the role of parental authorities. As best man, I advised the presiding committee, but mine was a merely honorary title since Bea acted as chief executive and artistic director and coordinated all those involved with an iron fist.

'Fermín, I have orders from Bea to take you along to Casa Pantaleoni to try on your suit.'

'A striped prisoner's suit is all I'm going to wear . . .'

I'd given him my word that when the time came his name would be in order and his friend the parish priest would be able to intone those words: 'Do you, Fermín, take Bernarda to be your lawful wedded wife?' without us all ending up in the police station. But as the date drew closer Fermín was being eaten up by anxiety. Bernarda survived the suspense by means of prayers and egg-yolk flans, although, once her pregnancy had been confirmed by a trustworthy, discreet doctor, she spent much of her day fighting nausea and dizziness. Everything seemed to indicate that Fermín's firstborn was going to be a handful.

Those were days of apparent and deceptive calm, but beneath the surface I'd succumbed to a dark, murky current that was slowly dragging me into the depths of a new and irresistible emotion: hatred.

In my spare time, without telling anyone where I was going, I would slip out and walk over to the nearby Ateneo Library on Calle Canuda, where I tracked every step of Mauricio Valls's life in the newspaper room. What for years I'd regarded as an indistinct and uninteresting figure took on a painful clarity and precision that increased with every passing day. My investigation allowed me to reconstruct Valls's public career during the last fifteen years, piece by piece. A lot of water had flowed under the bridge since his early days with the regime. With time and good contacts, if one were to believe what the papers said (something Fermín compared to believing that orange squash was obtained by squeezing fresh oranges from Valencia), Don Mauricio Valls had seen his wishes come true and become a shining star in Spain's literary and artistic firmament.

His ascent had been nothing short of spectacular. From 1944 onwards he landed posts and official appointments of growing importance in the country's cultural and academic institutions. His articles, talks and publications multiplied. Any self-respecting award ceremony, conference or cultural event required the participation and presence of Don Mauricio. In 1947, with a couple of business partners, he created Ediciones Ariadna, a publishing company with offices in Madrid and Barcelona mostly devoted to his self-promotion, which the press spared no effort in canonising as the 'most prestigious editorial brand' in Spanish literature.

By 1948, the same papers began to refer regularly to Mauricio

Valls as 'the most brilliant and well-respected intellectual in the New Spain'. The country's self-appointed intelligentsia and those who aspired to join the club seemed to be conducting a passionate romance with Don Mauricio. Journalists covering the cultural pages went out of their way to extol Valls, seeking his favour and, with luck, the publication by Ediciones Ariadna of some manuscript they'd been keeping in a drawer, so that they could become part of the official scene and taste at least a few sweet crumbs falling from his table.

Valls had learned the rules of the game and controlled the board better than anyone. At the start of the fifties, his fame and influence had already extended beyond official circles and were beginning to seep into so-called civil society and its members. Mauricio's slogans had been fashioned into a canon of revealed truths adopted by the same three or four thousand Spaniards who saw themselves as the chosen few and who made it a matter of pride to parrot the gospel like diligent pupils while looking down at the low-brow masses.

En route to the top, Valls had gathered around him a clique of like-minded characters who ate out of his hand and were gradually placed at the head of institutions and in positions of power. If anyone dared question Valls's words or his worth, such an individual would be mercilessly crucified by the press. After being ridiculed in malicious terms, the poor wretch would end up as a pariah, a beggar to whom all doors were slammed shut and whose only alternatives were obscurity or exile.

I spent endless hours reading every word as well as between the lines, comparing different versions of the story, cataloguing dates and making lists of successes and potential skeletons in cupboards. In other circumstances, if the purpose of my study had been purely anthropological, I would have taken my hat off to Don Mauricio and his masterly moves. Nobody could deny that he'd learned to read the heart and soul of his fellow citizens and pull the strings that moved their desires, hopes and dreams. He knew the game inside out, and nobody played it better.

If I was left with anything after endless days submerged in the official version of Valls's life, it was the belief that the building blocks of a new Spain were being set in place and that Don Mauricio's meteoric ascent to the altars of power exemplified a rising trend that, in all probability, would outlast the dictatorship and put down deep and immovable roots throughout the entire country for decades to come.

In 1952 Valls reached the summit of his career when he was named Minister of Culture for a three-year period, a position on which he capitalised to consolidate his authority and place his lackeys in the last few posts he had not yet managed to control. His public projection took on a golden monotony: his words were quoted as the source of all wisdom. His presence on jury panels, tribunals and all sorts of formal audiences was constant, while his arsenal of diplomas, laurels and medals continued to grow.

And then, suddenly, something strange happened.

I wasn't aware of it at first. The litany of praise and news flashes continued relentlessly, but after 1956, I spotted a detail buried among all those reports which was in stark contrast to everything published prior to that date. The tone and content of the articles were unchanged, but by reading each one of them and comparing them, I noticed something.

Don Mauricio Valls had never again appeared in public.

His name, his prestige, his reputation and his power were still going from strength to strength. There was just one piece missing: his person. After 1956 there were no photographs, no mention of his attendance nor any direct references to his participation in official functions.

The last cutting confirming Mauricio Valls's presence was dated 2 November 1956, when he received an award for the year's most distinguished achievements in publishing. The solemn ceremony, held in Madrid's Círculo de Bellas Artes, was attended by the highest authorities and the cream of society. The text of the news report followed the usual, predictable lines of the genre, in other words a short item couched in flattering tones. The most interesting thing about it was the accompanying photograph, the last published picture of Valls, taken shortly before his sixtieth birthday. Elegantly dressed in a well-cut suit, he was smiling modestly as he received a standing ovation from the audience. Some of the usual crowd at that type of event appeared next to Valls and, behind him, slightly off-camera, their expression serious and impenetrable, stood two individuals ensconced behind dark glasses, dressed in black, who didn't seem to be part of the ceremony. They looked severe and disconnected from the whole farce. Vigilant.

Nobody had photographed Don Mauricio or seen him in public after that night in the Círculo de Bellas Artes. However hard I tried, I didn't find a single appearance. Tired of pursuing avenues that seemed to lead nowhere, I went back to the beginning and pieced his story together, until I got to know it as if it were my own. I sniffed his trail in the hope of finding a clue, some sign that might tell me where he was. Where was that man who smiled in photographs and paraded his vanity through endless pages with an entourage of flatterers, hungry for favours?

My hatred grew during those solitary afternoons in the old Ateneo library, where not so long ago I'd devoted my cares to nobler causes, like the smooth skin of my first impossible love, the blind Clara, or the mysteries of Julián Carax and his novel *The Shadow of the Wind*. The harder it became to follow Valls's trail, the more I refused to admit that he had the right to disappear and erase his name from history. From my history. I needed to know what had happened to him. I needed to look him in the eye, even if it was just to remind him that someone, a single person in the entire universe, knew who he really was and what he had done.

8

One afternoon, tired of chasing ghosts, I cancelled my session at the newspaper library and went out for a stroll with Bea and Julián through a clean, sunny Barcelona I had almost forgotten. We walked from home to Ciudadela Park. I sat on a bench and watched Julián play with his mother on the lawn. As I gazed at them I reminded myself of Fermín's words. A fortunate man, that was me, Daniel Sempere. A fortunate man who had allowed blind resentment to grow inside him until he felt sick at the very thought of himself.

I watched Julián devote himself to one of his grand passions: crawling about on all fours until he was filthy. Bea kept a close eye on him. Every now and then he would pause and turn towards me. Suddenly, a gust of air lifted Bea's skirt and Julián burst out laughing. I clapped and Bea gave me a disapproving look. I searched my son's eyes: soon, I thought, they'll begin to look at me as if I were the wisest man in the world, the bearer of all answers. I decided never to mention the name of Mauricio Valls again or pursue his shadow.

Bea came over and sat down beside me. Julián crawled after her as far as the bench. When he reached my feet I picked him up and he set about cleaning his hands on the lapels of my jacket.

'Just back from the dry cleaner's,' said Bea.

I shrugged, resigned. Bea leaned over and took my hand.

'Nice legs,' I said.

'I don't see what's so amusing. Your son will pick that up from you. Thank goodness there was nobody around.'

'There was a little old grandad hiding behind a newspaper over there. I think he's collapsed with tachycardia.'

Julián decided that the word 'tachycardia' was the funniest thing he'd heard in his life and we spent a good part of the journey home singing 'ta-chy-car-dia' while Bea walked a few steps in front of us, fuming.

That night, 20 January, Bea put Julián to bed and then fell asleep on the sofa next to me, while I reread, for the third time, one of David Martín's old novels. It was the copy Fermín had found during his months of exile, after his escape from the prison, and had kept all those years. I liked savouring every turn of phrase and dissecting the architecture of every sentence. I thought that if I could decode the music of his prose I might discover something about that man whom I'd never known and whom everyone assured me was not my father. But that night I couldn't do it. Before reaching the end of a single paragraph, my thoughts would fly from the page and all I could see in front of me was that letter from Pablo Cascos Buendía, arranging to meet my wife the following day at the Ritz, at two o'clock in the afternoon.

At last I closed the book and gazed at Bea, sleeping by my side, sensing that she held a thousand times more secrets than David Martín's stories about the sinister city of the damned. It was after midnight when Bea opened her eyes and caught me scrutinising her. She smiled at me, but a flicker of anxiety crossed her face.

'What's on your mind?' she asked.

'I was thinking about how lucky I am,' I said.

Bea stared at me, unconvinced.

'You say that as if you didn't believe it.'

I stood up and put out a hand to her.

'Let's go to bed,' I invited.

She took my hand and followed me down the corridor to the bedroom. I lay down on the bed and looked at her in silence.

'You've been acting strangely, Daniel. What's wrong? Have I said something?'

I shook my head and gave her a smile as innocent as a white

lie. Bea slowly began to undress. When she removed her clothes she never turned round, or hid in the bathroom or behind a door, as the official marriage-guidance booklets advised. I watched her calmly, reading the lines of her body. Bea's eyes were fixed on mine. She slipped on that nightdress I detested and got into bed, turning her back on me.

'Goodnight,' she said, her voice tense and, to someone who knew her well, annoyed.

'Goodnight,' I whispered.

Listening to her breathing I knew that it took her over half an hour to fall asleep, but in the end she was too exhausted to dwell on my peculiar behaviour. As I lay by her side, I wondered whether I should wake her to beg her forgiveness or simply kiss her. I did nothing. I remained there, motionless, gazing at the curve of her back and feeling that dark force inside me whispering that in a few hours Bea would go to meet her ex-fiancé and those lips and that skin would belong to another, as his corny letter seemed to insinuate.

When I awoke, Bea had left. I hadn't managed to get to sleep until daybreak and when the church bells struck nine o'clock I woke up with a start and got dressed in the first clothes I found. Outside, a cold Monday awaited me, sprinkled with snowflakes that drifted in the air and settled on passers-by like glass spiders hanging from invisible threads. When I walked into the bookshop, my father was standing on the stool he climbed on to every morning to change the date on the calendar. 21 January.

'Oversleeping is not acceptable when you're over twelve,' he said. 'It was your turn to open up today.'

'Sorry. Bad night. It won't happen again.'

I spent a couple of hours trying to occupy my mind and my hands with menial tasks in the bookshop but all I could do was think of that damned letter that I kept reciting to myself. Halfway through the morning Fermín came over to me surreptitiously and offered me a Sugus sweet.

'Today's the day, isn't it?'

'Shut up, Fermín,' I shot back at him, so brusquely that my father raised his eyebrows.

I took refuge in the back room and heard them murmuring. I sat at my father's desk and stared at the clock. It was one twenty in the afternoon. I tried to let the minutes go by but the hands of the clock seemed unwilling to move. When I returned to the shop Fermín and my father gave me a worried look.

'Daniel, you might like to take the rest of the day off,' said my father, 'Fermín and I will manage on our own.'

'Thanks. I think I will. I've hardly slept and I'm not feeling very well.'

I didn't have the courage to look at Fermín as I slipped out through the back room. I walked up the five flights of stairs with leaden feet. When I opened the front door of the apartment I heard water running in the bathroom. I dragged myself to the bedroom and stopped in the doorway. Bea was sitting on the edge of the bed. She hadn't seen me or heard me come in. I watched her as she slipped on her silk stockings and got dressed with her eyes fixed on the mirror. She didn't notice my presence for a couple of minutes.

'I didn't know you were there,' she said halfway between surprise and irritation.

'Are you going out?'

She nodded as she put on scarlet lipstick.

'Where are you going?'

'I have a couple of errands to do.'

'You're looking very pretty.'

'I don't like going out looking a mess,' she replied.

I regarded her as she applied her eyeshadow. *'A fortunate man,'* said the sarcastic voice.

'What errands?' I asked.

Bea turned to look at me.

'What?'

'I was asking you what errands you have to do.'

'A few things. This and that.'

'And Julián?'

'My mother came to fetch him. She's taken him out for a walk.'

'I see.'

Bea came closer and, putting aside her irritation, gave me a worried look.

'Daniel, what's the matter with you?'

'I didn't sleep a wink last night.'

'Why don't you take a nap? It will do you good.'

'Good idea,' I agreed.

Smiling wanly, Bea took me round to my side of the bed. She helped me lie down, covered me with the bedspread and gave me a kiss on the forehead.

'I'll be late,' she said.

I watched her leave.

'Bea . . .'

She stopped halfway down the corridor and turned round.

'Do you love me?' I asked.

'Of course I love you. Don't be silly.'

I heard the door close and then Bea's feline footsteps in her stiletto heels going down the stairs. I picked up the phone and waited for the operator to speak.

'The Ritz Hotel, please.'

The line took a few seconds to connect.

'*Ritz Hotel, good afternoon, how can I help you?*'

'Could you check whether you have someone staying at the hotel, please?'

'*May I have the name of the guest?*'

'Cascos. Pablo Cascos Buendía. I think he must have arrived yesterday . . .'

'*Just a minute please . . .*'

A long minute's wait, hushed voices, echoes down the line.

'*Sir . . .*'

'Yes?'

'*I can't see any reservation in that name, sir . . .*'

I felt enormously relieved.

'Could the reservation have been made under a company name?'

'*I'll just check.*'

This time the wait was shorter.

'*Yes, you were right. Señor Cascos Buendía. Here it is, Continental Suite. The reservation was made by the Ariadna publishing company.*'

'What did you say?'

'*I was saying, sir, that Señor Cascos Buendía's booking is in the name of Ediciones Ariadna. Would you like me to put you through to his room?*'

The phone slipped out of my hands. Ariadna was the publishing firm Mauricio Valls had started up years ago.

Cascos worked for Valls.

I slammed down the phone and went out into the street following my wife, my heart poisoned with suspicion.

9

There was no trace of Bea among the crowd filing past Puerta del Ángel towards Plaza de Cataluña. I assumed that was the way my wife would have chosen to go to the Ritz, but with Bea you never knew. She liked trying out different routes between destinations. After a while I gave up and guessed she must have taken a taxi – a bit more in keeping with the stylish clothes she'd chosen for the occasion.

It took me fifteen minutes to get to the hotel. Although it can't have been more than ten degrees Centigrade I was perspiring and short of breath. The doorman eyed me suspiciously, but he opened the door and allowed me in with the merest hint of a bow. The layout of the lobby puzzled me: it looked like the setting for a spy story or a decadent romantic saga. My limited experience of luxury hotels had not prepared me to work out what was what. I noticed a counter, behind which stood a conscientious receptionist observing me with a mixture of curiosity and alarm. I walked over to him with a smile that failed to impress him.

'The restaurant, please?'

The receptionist examined me with polite scepticism.

'Do you have a reservation, sir?'

'I have a meeting with a hotel guest.'

The receptionist smiled coldly and nodded.

'You'll find the restaurant at the end of that corridor, sir.'

'Much obliged.'

I made my way there with my heart in my mouth. I had no idea what I was going to say or do when I came face to face with Bea and that man. I was met by the head waiter who stopped me in my tracks. His expression, behind a stiff smile, betrayed scant approval of my attire.

'Do you have a reservation, sir?' he asked.

I shoved him aside and walked into the dining hall. Most tables were empty. An elderly couple with a mummified air and nineteenth-century manners interrupted their solemn soup-sipping to stare at me in disgust. A few more tables were occupied by what seemed to be dull businessmen accompanied by one or two incongruously attractive ladies, most likely to be billed as corporate expenses. There was no sign of Cascos or Bea.

The head waiter was approaching, flanked by two assistants. I turned round to face him and smiled politely.

'Didn't Señor Cascos Buendía have a reservation for two o'clock?' I asked.

'Señor Cascos asked to have his meal taken up to his suite,' the head waiter informed me.

I checked my watch. It was twenty past two. I made my way to the corridor with the lifts. One of the doormen had his eye on me but before he could reach me I'd already slipped into one of the lifts. I pressed the button for one of the upper floors forgetting that I had no idea where the Continental Suite was.

'Start at the top,' I told myself.

I got out of the lift on the seventh floor and began to wander down grand corridors, all of them deserted. After a while I came across a door leading to the fire-escape stairs and walked down to the floor below. I went from door to door, looking unsuccessfully for the Continental Suite. It was two thirty by my watch. On the fifth floor I came across a maid dragging a trolley filled with feather dusters, bars of soap and towels and asked her where the suite was. She gave me a worried look, but I must have frightened her enough for her to point upwards.

'Eighth floor.'

I preferred to avoid the lifts in case the hotel staff were looking for me. Three flights of stairs and a long corridor later I reached the doors of the Continental Suite dripping with sweat. I stood there for a second to catch my breath, trying to imagine what was going on behind the thick wooden door and wondering whether I still had enough common sense to walk away. I thought I could see someone observing me from the other end of the corridor and feared it might be one of the doormen, but when I looked closer the figure disappeared round the corner. It must have been another hotel guest, I imagined. Finally I rang the doorbell.

10

I heard footsteps. The image of Bea doing up her blouse flashed through my mind. A turn of the doorknob. I clenched my fists. A guy with slicked-back hair, wearing a white bathrobe and five-star hotel slippers, opened the door. Some years had passed, but one never forgets faces one wholeheartedly detests.

'Sempere?' he asked incredulously.

The punch landed between his upper lip and his nose. I felt his flesh and cartilage tearing under my fist. Cascos put his hands to his face and staggered, blood spouting through his fingers. I pushed him hard against the wall and stepped into the room. I heard Cascos tumble to the floor behind me. The bed was made and a steaming plate of food lay on a table facing the terrace with a privileged view of the Gran Vía. Only one place had been set. I turned and confronted Cascos, who was trying to get up by holding on to a chair.

'Where is she?'

Cascos's face was deformed with pain, blood dripping down on to his chest. I could see I'd cut his lip open and almost certainly broken his nose. I noticed a sharp burning sensation on my knuckles and when I looked at my hand I saw I'd grazed my skin when I smashed his face in. I felt no remorse whatsoever.

'She didn't come. Happy?' spat Cascos.

'Since when do you devote your time to writing to my wife?'

I thought he was laughing and before he could utter another word I hurled myself against him again and dealt him a second punch with all my pent-up anger. The blow loosened his teeth and left my hand feeling numb. Cascos groaned in agony and collapsed into the chair he had been leaning on. When he saw me bending over him he covered his face with his arms. I sank my hands into his neck and pressed my fingers into his flesh as if I were trying to rip out his throat.

'What have you got to do with Valls?'

Cascos stared at me with a terrified expression, convinced that I was going to kill him then and there. He mumbled something unintelligible. Saliva and blood dripped from his mouth on to my hands.

'Mauricio Valls. What have you got to do with him?'

My face was so close to his I could see my reflection in his pupils. The capillaries in his eyes were starting to burst and a web of black lines opened up towards the iris. Realising I was choking him, I let go of him abruptly. Cascos made a rasping sound as he took in air and felt his neck. I sat down on the bed opposite him. My hands were trembling and covered in blood. I went into the bathroom and washed them. I splashed my face and hair with cold water and when I saw my reflection in the mirror I barely recognised myself. I'd been on the point of killing a man.

11

When I returned to the room, Cascos was still slumped on the chair, panting. I filled a glass with water and handed it to him. Seeing me approach again he moved to one side, expecting another blow.

'Here,' I said.

He opened his eyes and when he saw the glass he seemed uncertain for a moment or two.

'Here,' I repeated. 'It's only water.'

He accepted the glass with a trembling hand and took it to his lips. I noticed that I'd broken some of his teeth. Cascos groaned and his eyes filled with tears from the pain when the cold water touched the dental pulp exposed beneath the enamel. We remained silent for over a minute.

'Shall I call a doctor?' I asked at last.

He looked up and shook his head.

'Go away before I call the police.'

'Tell me what you have to do with Mauricio Valls and I'll go.'

I looked at him coldly.

'He's . . . he's one of the partners of the publishing house where I work.'

'Did he ask you to write that letter?'

Cascos hesitated. I stood up and took a step towards him. I grabbed his hair and pulled hard.

'Don't hit me again,' he pleaded.

'Did Valls ask you to write that letter?'

Cascos was avoiding my eyes.

'It wasn't him,' he managed to say.

'Who, then?'

'One of his secretaries, Armero.'

'Who?'

'Paco Armero. He's an employee at the firm. He told me to renew contact with Beatriz. He said that if I did there would be something for me. A reward.'

'Why did you have to renew contact with Bea?'

'I don't know.'

I made as if to hit him again.

'I don't know,' whimpered Cascos. 'It's the truth.'

'And that's why you asked her to meet you here?'

'I still love Beatriz.'

'Pretty way of showing it. Where is Valls?'

'I don't know.'

'How can you not know where your boss is?'

'Because I don't know him. OK? I've never seen him. I've never spoken to him.'

'Explain.'

'I started working for Ariadna a year and a half ago, in the Madrid office. In all this time I've never seen him. Nobody has.'

He stood up slowly and walked over to the telephone. I didn't stop him. He picked up the receiver, his eyes poisoned with hatred.

'I'm going to call the police . . .'

'That won't be necessary,' came a voice from the hallway.

I turned to discover Fermín, in what I imagined must be one of my father's suits, holding up a card vaguely resembling some kind of police badge.

'Inspector Fermín Romero de Torres. Police. Someone has reported a disturbance. Which of you two can sum up what has taken place here?'

I don't know who was more disconcerted, Cascos or me. Fermín took advantage of the situation to gently pull the receiver away from Cascos's hand.

'Allow me,' he said, brushing him to one side. 'I'll call headquarters.'

He pretended to dial a number and smiled at us.

'Give me headquarters, please. Yes, thank you.'

He waited a few seconds.

'Yes, Mari Pili, it's me, Romero de Torres. Put me through to Palacios. Yes, I'll wait.'

While Fermín pretended to wait and covered the receiver with his hand, he gestured to Cascos.

'Have you banged your head on the bathroom door or is there anything you wish to declare?'

'This savage attacked me and tried to kill me. I want to press charges immediately. I want to see him behind bars before the end of the day.'

Fermín gave me an officious look and nodded.

'Indeed. We have a dungeon that's just the ticket, rats and all.'

He pretended to hear something on the telephone and signalled to Cascos to be quiet.

'Yes, Palacios. At the Ritz. Yes. It's a 424. One person wounded. Mostly facial. It depends. I'd say a real mess. Fine. I'll proceed immediately to the suspect's summary arrest.'

He put down the phone.

'All sorted.'

Fermín came over to me and, grabbing my arm with authority, motioned for me to keep quiet.

'Don't say a word. Anything you say now will be used against you and all your criminal associates till justice is served.'

Doubled up with pain and confused by Fermín's peculiar display of procedural methods, Cascos stared at the scene in disbelief.

'Aren't you going to handcuff him?'

'This being a posh establishment, we'll put the shackles on him in the police car. Standard procedure, sir.'

Cascos, who was still bleeding and was probably seeing double, barred our way with little conviction.

'Are you sure you're a policeman?'

'Elite corps. I'll get room service to bring you up a tartar steak right away so you can treat your injuries with a soothing mask. Works wonders for bags under the eyes and close-up bruising, take it from a pro. My esteemed colleagues will swing by later to take your statement and prepare the official charges to make sure this rascal receives an airtight conviction for hard labour in a high-security Moroccan prison,' he recited, moving Cascos's arm out of the way and pushing me as fast as he could towards the exit.

12

We hailed a taxi outside the hotel door and travelled along Gran Vía in silence for a while.

'Jesus, Mary and Joseph!' Fermín finally burst out. 'Are you mad? I look at you and I don't know who you are . . . What were you trying to do? Kill that imbecile?'

'He works for Mauricio Valls,' was my only answer.

Fermín rolled his eyes.

'Daniel, this obsession of yours is beginning to get out of hand. I wish I hadn't told you all that . . . Are you all right? Let's have a look at your hand . . .'

I showed him my fist.

'For God's sake.'

'How did you know . . .?'

'Because I know you as if I'd given birth to you, even if there are days when I almost regret I do,' he said furiously.

'I don't know what came over me . . .'

'Well, I know exactly what came over you. And I don't like it. I don't like it one bit. That's not the Daniel I know. And it's not the Daniel I want for a friend.'

My hand was hurting, but to know I'd disappointed Fermín hurt far more.

'Fermín, please don't get angry with me.'

'Oh, excuse me! Maybe you just want me to hand you a medal . . .'

For a while we didn't speak, each looking out on his side of the street.

'Thank God you came,' I said at last.

'Did you think I was going to leave you on your own?'

'You won't tell Bea, will you?'

'Sure, and then I'll write a letter to the editor of *La Vanguardia* setting out your exploits so everybody can rejoice in your bravery.'

'I don't know what I was thinking . . .'

He looked severely at me, but finally relaxed his expression and patted my hand. I swallowed my pain.

'Let's not go on about it. I suppose I would have done the same.'

I gazed at Barcelona marching past the windows.

'What was the card?'

'What?'

'The police ID card you showed . . . What was it?'

'The parish priest's Barcelona football club card. Expired.'

'You were right, Fermín. I've been a fool to suspect Bea.'

'I'm always right. I was born like that.'

I had to bow to the evidence and keep my mouth shut. I'd already said enough stupid things for one day. Fermín had gone very quiet and seemed preoccupied. It troubled me to think I'd caused him such disappointment that he didn't know what to say to me.

'What's on your mind, Fermín?'

He turned, looking concerned.

'I was thinking about that man.'

'Cascos?'

'No. Valls. About what that idiot said earlier. About its significance.'

'What do you mean?'

Fermín's face was grim.

'I mean that what worried me before was that you wanted to find Valls.'

'And now it doesn't?'

'There's something that worries me more, Daniel.'

'What?'

'That he may be the one looking for you.'

We stared at each other.

'Have you any idea why?' I asked.

Fermín, who always had a reply for everything, slowly shook his head and looked away.

We spent the rest of the journey in silence. When I got home I went straight up to the flat, took a long hot shower and swallowed four aspirins. Then I lowered the blinds and, hugging a pillow that smelled of Bea, fell asleep like the idiot I was, wondering where she was – that woman for whom I didn't mind having made such a huge fool of myself.

13

'I look like a hedgehog,' declared Bernarda, staring at her hundredfold image reflected in the mirrored room of Modas Santa Eulalia.

Kneeling down at her feet, two seamstresses went on marking the bridal dress with dozens of pins, watched closely by Bea, who walked in circles round Bernarda inspecting every pleat and every seam as if her life depended on it. Bernarda, standing with arms outstretched in the hexagonal fitting room, hardly dared breathe, but her eyes were riveted on the different angles of her figure, as she searched for signs of swelling around her belly.

'Are you sure it's not noticeable, Señora Bea?'

'Not a bit. Flat as a pancake. Where you should be, of course.'

'Oh, I don't know, I don't know . . .'

Bernarda's ordeal and the seamstresses' efforts to adjust and tailor continued for another half-hour. When there didn't seem to be any pins left in the world with which to skewer poor Bernarda, the firm's star couturier and creator of the dress drew the curtain aside and made an appearance. After a quick survey and a few corrections on the lining of the skirt, he gave his approval and snapped his fingers at his assistants, ordering them to make themselves scarce.

'Not even Balenciaga could have made you look so beautiful,' he concluded happily.

Bea smiled and nodded.

The couturier, a slender gentleman with affected manners and theatrical gestures who went simply by the name of Evaristo, kissed Bernarda on the cheek.

'You're the best model in the world. The most patient and long-suffering. It has been hard work, but well worth it.'

'And do you think, sir, that I'll be able to breathe in this dress?'

'My darling, you're marrying an Iberian macho buck in the Holy Mother Church. Your breathing days are over, believe me. Anyhow, a wedding dress is like a diving bell: it's not ideal for breathing, the fun begins when they take it off you.'

Bernarda crossed herself at the couturier's insinuations.

'What I'm going to ask you to do now is remove the dress with the greatest care. The seams are loose and with all those pins I wouldn't like to see you walking up to the altar looking like a colander,' said Evaristo.

'I'll help her,' said Bea.

Casting a meaningful look at Bea, Evaristo inspected her from head to toe.

'And when am I going to be able to dress and undress *you*, my love?' he asked, flouncing off through the curtain.

'What a look the rascal gave you!' said Bernarda. 'I didn't think he was into female company, if you get my meaning.'

'I think Evaristo keeps all sorts of company, Bernarda.'

'Is that possible?' she asked.

'Come on, let's try to get you out of this without dropping a single pin.'

While Bea freed Bernarda from her captivity, the maid swore under her breath.

Ever since she'd found out the price of that dress, which her employer, Don Gustavo, had insisted on paying out of his own pocket, Bernarda had been in a terrible state.

'Don Gustavo should never have spent such a bundle. He insisted that it had to be here, the most expensive shop in Barcelona I'm sure, and on hiring this guy Evaristo, who is a half-nephew of his or something like that. Apparently Evaristo says that any fabric that isn't from Casa Gratacós gives one a rash. And they're so pricey!'

'Don't look a gift horse in the mouth . . . Besides, Don Gustavo is thrilled that you'll be getting married in style. He's like that. You're the daughter he never had.'

'I'm his maid, and I would have been quite happy wearing my mother's wedding dress, with a couple of alterations, and Fermín doesn't care. Every time I show him a new dress all he wants to do is take it off me . . . And look what that's led to, may God forgive me,' said Bernarda patting her belly.

'Bernarda, I was also pregnant when I got married and I'm sure God has far more pressing things to worry about.'

'That's what my Fermín says, but I don't know . . .'

'You listen to Fermín and don't worry about anything.'

In her slip, and exhausted after standing for two hours in high heels with her arms stretched out, Bernarda fell into an armchair and sighed.

'Poor thing, he's lost so much weight, he's as thin as a rake. I'm really worried about him.'

'You'll see how he gets better from now on. Men are like that. They're like geraniums. When they look as if they're ready to be tossed into the bin they revive.'

'I don't know, Señora Bea. Fermín seems very depressed to me. He tells me he wants to get married, but I have my doubts.'

'Come on, he's crazy about you, Bernarda.'

Bernarda shrugged.

'Look, I'm not as stupid as I seem. Since I was thirteen all I've done is clean houses and I may not understand a lot of things, but I know that my Fermín has seen the world and he's had his share of adventures. He never tells me anything about his life before we met, but I know he's had other women and he's been round the block a few times.'

'And he's ended up choosing you out of them all. So there.'

'I know. But you know what I'm afraid of, Señora Bea? That I'm not good enough for him. When I see him looking at me spell-bound and he tells me he wants us to grow old together and all that sweet-talk he comes up with, I always think that one morning he'll wake up and look at me and he'll say: "Where on earth did I find this dimwit?"'

'I think you're wrong, Bernarda, Fermín will never think that. He has you on a pedestal.'

'Well, that's not a good thing either. I've seen a lot of gentlemen, the sort who put their wives on pedestals as if they were the Virgin Mary, who then run after the first pretty young thing they see passing by, like dogs after a bitch on heat. You wouldn't believe the times I've seen that with these little eyes God gave me.'

'But Fermín isn't like that, Bernarda. Fermín is one of the good ones. One of the few. Men are like chestnuts they sell in the street: they're all hot and they all smell good when you buy them, but when you take them out of the paper cone you realise that most of them are rotten inside.'

'You're not saying that because of Señor Daniel, are you?'

Bea took a while to reply.

'No. Of course not.'

Bernarda glanced at her.

'Everything all right at home, Señora Bea?'

Bea fiddled with a pleat on the shoulder strap of Bernarda's slip.

'Yes, Bernarda. The trouble is that I think we've both gone and got ourselves husbands who have a secret or two.'

Bernarda nodded.

'Sometimes they're like children.'

'Men. What do you expect?'

'But the thing is, I like them,' said Bernarda. 'And I know that's a sin.'

Bea laughed.

'And how do you like them. Like Evaristo?'

'No, good heavens, no. If he keeps looking at himself in the mirror he'll wear it out! A man who takes longer than me to get smartened up gives me the creeps. I like them a bit rougher, I'm afraid. I know my Fermín isn't exactly what you'd call handsome.

But he is to me – handsome and good. And very manly. In the end, I think that's what matters, that he's truly a good person and that he's real. That he's someone you can hold on to on a cold winter's night and who knows how to make you feel warm inside.'

Bea smiled in assent.

'Amen. Although a birdie told me the one you liked was Cary Grant.'

Bernarda blushed.

'Don't you? Not to marry, of course. I'd say he fell in love the first time he looked at himself in the mirror. But between you and me, and may God forgive me, I wouldn't say no to a good squeeze from him . . .'

'What would Fermín say if he heard you, Bernarda?'

'What he always says. "After all, we're all going to get eaten up by worms in the end . . ."'

Part Five

The Name of the Hero

1

Barcelona, 1958

Many years later, the twenty-three guests gathered there to celebrate the occasion would look back and remember the historic eve of the day when Fermín Romero de Torres abandoned his bachelorhood.

'It's the end of an era,' proclaimed Professor Alburquerque, raising his glass of champagne in a toast, voicing better than anyone what we were all feeling.

Fermín's stag night, an event whose effects on the global female population Gustavo Barceló compared to the death of Rudolf Valentino, took place on a clear February night of 1958. The venue was the magnificent dance hall of La Paloma, where the groom had in the past performed some heart-rending tangos, attaining moments that would now enter the secret dossier of a distinguished career at the service of the eternal female. My father, who for once in his life had been persuaded to leave home, had secured the services of a semi-professional dance band, La Habana del Baix Llobregat, who agreed to play for a knockdown price a selection of Fermín's favourite fare: mambos, *guarachas* and *sones montunos* that transported the groom to his faraway days of intrigue and international glamour in the great gaming salons of a forgotten Cuba. Everyone, to a greater or lesser degree, let their hair down, throwing themselves on to the dance floor to shake a leg in Fermín's honour.

Barceló had convinced my father that the glasses of vodka he kept handing him were mineral water with a few drops of anisette, and soon we were all able to witness an unprecedented sight: Señor Sempere dancing cheek-to-cheek with one of the easy ladies brought along by Rociíto – the true life and soul of the party – to brighten up the event.

'Dear God,' I murmured as I watched my father with that veteran madam of the night, swaying his hips and bumping his backside against hers in time to the beat.

Barceló circulated among the guests, handing out cigars and the little cards he'd had printed to commemorate the occasion, at a firm specialising in mementoes for first communions, christenings and funerals. The fine paper card depicted a caricature of Fermín dressed up as an angel, his hands together as in prayer, with the following message:

FERMÍN ROMERO DE TORRES

19??–1958

The great lover retires

1958–19??

The paterfamilias arises

For the first time in ages, Fermín was happy and calm. Half an hour before the start of the bash I'd taken him along to Can Lluís, where Professor Alburquerque certified that he'd been at the Civil Registry that very morning, armed with the entire dossier of documents and papers masterfully produced by Oswaldo Darío de Mortenssen and his assistant, Luisito.

'Dear Fermín,' the professor announced. 'Allow me to welcome you officially to the world of the living. With our friends from Can Lluís as witnesses, Don Daniel Sempere and I hereby present you with a brand-new you, which comes with this fresh and legitimate identity card.'

An emotional Fermín examined his new documentation.

'How did you manage such a miracle?'

'We'll spare you the technicalities,' said the professor. 'What really matters is that when you have a true friend who is ready to take the risk and move heaven and earth so that you can get married with everything in order and start bringing offspring into the world to continue the Romero de Torres line, almost anything is possible, Fermín.'

Fermín looked at me with tears in his eyes and hugged me so tight I thought I was going to suffocate. I'm not ashamed to admit that it was one of the happiest moments in my life.

2

Half an hour of music, drinks and naughty dancing had gone by when I took a breather and walked over to the bar to ask for something non-alcoholic. I didn't think I could swallow another drop of rum and lemon, the evening's official beverage. The waiter served me a glass of cold sparkling water and I leaned my back against the bar to take in the fun. I hadn't noticed that Rociíto was standing at the other end. She was holding a glass of champagne, watching the party she had organised with a melancholy expression. From what Fermín had told me, I worked out that Rociíto must be close to her thirty-fifth birthday, but almost twenty years in the profession had taken their toll and even in the multicoloured half-light the crowned queen of Calle Escudellers appeared older.

I went up to her and smiled.

'Rociíto, you're looking more beautiful than ever,' I lied.

She was wearing her smartest clothes and her hair showed the stunning handiwork of the best hairdresser in the Raval, but what really struck me was how sad she looked that night.

'Are you all right, Rociíto?'

'Look at 'im, poor thing. All skin and bone and he's still in the mood for dancing. He always was a great dancer.'

Her eyes were glued to Fermín and I knew that she would always see in him the champion who had saved her from that small-time pimp. After her twenty years of working the streets, he was probably one of the few worthwhile men she'd met.

'Don Daniel, I didn't want to say anything to Fermín, but I won't be going to the wedding tomorrow.'

'What are you saying, Rociíto? Fermín had saved you a place of honour . . .'

Rociíto lowered her eyes.

'I know, but I can't be there.'

'Why?' I asked, although I could guess what the reply would be.

'Because it would make me really sad and I want Señorito Fermín to be happy with his missus.'

Rociíto had started to cry. I didn't know what to say, so I hugged her.

'I've always loved him, you know? Ever since we met. I know I'm not the right woman for him. I know he sees me as . . . well, he sees me as Rociíto.'

'Fermín loves you very much, you must never forget that.'

The woman moved away and dried her tears in embarrassment. She smiled and shrugged her shoulders.

'Forgive me. You see, I'm so stupid: soon as I drink a couple of drops I don't even know what I'm saying.'

'That's all right.'

I offered her my glass of water and she accepted it.

'One day you realise your youth has passed you by and the train's left, if you see what I mean.'

'There's always another train. Always.'

Rociíto nodded.

'That's why I'm not going to the wedding, Don Daniel. Some months ago I met this gentleman from Reus. He's a good man. A widower. A good father. Owns a scrapyard and whenever he's in Barcelona he comes to see me. He's asked me to marry him. We're not kidding ourselves, not him or me, you know? Growing old on your own is very hard, and I know I don't have the figure to be on the street any more. Jaumet, the man from Reus, he's asked me to go on a journey with him. His children have already left home and he's been working all his life. He says he wants to see a bit of the world before it's too late, and he's asked me to go with him. As his wife, not a tart you use and then chuck out. The boat leaves tomorrow morning early. Jaumet says a captain can marry a couple on the high seas and if not, we'll look for a priest in any old port.'

'Does Fermín know?'

As if he'd heard us from afar, Fermín stopped bopping about on the dance floor and looked at us. He stretched his arms out towards Rociíto and gave her that silly look of someone in urgent need of a kiss and a cuddle that had always served him so well. Rociíto laughed, muttering under her breath, and before joining the love of her life on the dance floor for a last bolero, she turned to me and said:

'Take good care of him, Daniel. There's only one Fermín.'

The band had stopped playing and the dance floor opened up to receive Rociíto. Fermín took her hands. The lamps in La Paloma were slowly dimmed and from among the shadows the beam from a spotlight cast a hazy circle of light at the couple's feet. The others drew aside and the orchestra gently struck up the slow rhythms of the saddest bolero ever written. Fermín put his arm round Rociíto's waist. Looking into each other's eyes, far from the world, the lovers of that Barcelona that would never return danced close together for the last time. When the music died away Fermín kissed her on the lips and Rociíto, bathed in tears, stroked his cheek, then walked slowly towards the exit without saying goodbye.

3

The orchestra came to the rescue with a *guaracha* and Oswaldo Darío de Mortenssen, who from writing so many love letters had become an encyclopedia of sad tales, encouraged everyone to return to the dance floor and pretend they hadn't noticed anything. Looking somewhat crestfallen, Fermín walked over to the bar and sat on a stool next to me.

'Everything all right, Fermín?'

He nodded weakly.

'I think a bit of fresh air would do me good, Daniel.'

'Wait here for me, I'll get our coats.'

We were walking down Calle Tallers towards the Ramblas when, about fifty metres ahead of us, we glimpsed a familiar-looking figure, moving along slowly.

'Hey, Daniel. Isn't that your father?'

'The very one. And he's soused.'

'The last thing I ever expected to see in this world,' said Fermín.

'If you didn't expect it, imagine me!'

We quickened our pace until we caught up with him and when he saw us, my father smiled, glassy-eyed.

'What's the time?' he asked.

'Very late.'

'That's just what I thought. Hey Fermín, what a great party. And what girls. There were some bums in there worth going to war for.'

I rolled my eyes. Fermín took my father's arm and guided his steps.

'Señor Sempere, I never thought I'd have to say this, but you're suffering from alcohol poisoning and you'd better not say anything that you might later regret.'

My father nodded, suddenly embarrassed.

'It's that devil, Barceló. I don't know what he's given me, and as I'm not used to drinking . . .'

'Never mind. Just take a glass of bicarbonate of soda and sleep it off. Tomorrow morning you'll be as fresh as a daisy and no damage done.'

'I think I'm going to be sick.'

Between us, we held him upright while the poor man threw up everything he'd drunk. I held his sweat-drenched forehead with my hand and when we were sure there was nothing left inside him, not even his first plate of baby food, we settled him for a moment on the steps of someone's front door.

'Take a deep, slow breath, Señor Sempere.'

My father nodded with his eyes shut. Fermín and I exchanged glances.

'Listen, weren't you going to get married soon?'

'Tomorrow afternoon.'

'Hey, congratulations!'

'Thank you, Señor Sempere. So, what do you say? Do you think we can make it home bit by bit?'

My father nodded.

'There's a brave man, we're almost there.'

A cool, dry wind helped clear my father's head. By the time we walked up Calle Santa Ana ten minutes later, he'd sized up the situation and the poor man was mortified with embarrassment. He'd probably never been drunk before in his life.

'Please, not a word about this to anyone,' he pleaded.

We were about twenty metres away from the bookshop when I noticed someone sitting in the main doorway of the building. The large street lamp from Casa Jorba, on the corner with Puerta del Ángel, outlined the silhouette of a young girl clutching a suitcase on her knees. When she saw us she stood up.

'We have company,' murmured Fermín.

My father saw her first. I noticed something strange in his expression, a tense calm that gripped him as if he'd suddenly recovered his sobriety. He advanced towards the girl but suddenly stood petrified.

'Isabella?' I heard him say.

Fearing the drink was still clouding his judgement and that he might collapse then and there, in the middle of the street, I took a few steps forward. Then I saw her.

4

She can't have been more than seventeen. As she emerged into the light cast by the street lamp, she smiled timidly at us, lifting a hand as if in greeting.

'I'm Sofía,' she said, with a light accent.

My father stared at her in astonishment, as if he'd seen a ghost. I gulped, feeling a shiver run through my body. That girl was the spitting image of my mother: she had the same face that appeared in the set of photographs my father kept in his desk.

'I'm Sofía,' the girl repeated, looking uncomfortable. 'Your niece. From Naples . . .'

'Sofía,' stammered my father. 'Ah, Sofía.'

Thank God Fermín was there to take hold of the situation. After bringing me to my senses with a slap on the wrist, he explained that Señor Sempere was feeling a little under the weather.

'You see, we're just back from a wine-tasting event and it only takes a glass of Vichy water to put the poor man in a trance. Pay no attention to him, *signorina,* he doesn't usually look so plastered.'

We found the urgent telegram sent by Aunt Laura, the girl's mother, announcing her arrival. It had been slipped under the door while we were out.

Up in the flat, Fermín settled my father on the sofa and ordered me to prepare a pot of strong coffee. In the meantime, he engaged in conversation with the girl, asking her about her trip and bringing up all manner of banalities while my father slowly came back to life.

With her delightful accent and her vivacious air, Sofía told us she'd arrived at the Estación de Francia that night at half past ten. From the station she had taken a taxi to Plaza de Cataluña.

When she discovered there was no one at home she'd sheltered in a nearby bar until they closed. Then she'd sat down to wait in the doorway, trusting that someone would turn up sooner or later. My father remembered the letter from her mother telling him that Sofía was coming to Barcelona, but he hadn't imagined it was going to be so soon.

'I'm very sorry you had to wait in the street,' he said. 'Normally, I never go out, but tonight was Fermín's bachelor party and . . .'

Delighted with the piece of news, Sofía jumped up and congratulated Fermín with a peck on the cheek. And although he had now retired from active duty, Fermín couldn't restrain himself and invited her to the wedding on the spot.

We'd been chatting away for about half an hour when Bea, who was returning from Bernarda's own hen party, heard voices on her way up the stairs and rang the doorbell. When she stepped into the dining room and saw Sofía she went pale and glanced at me.

'This is my cousin Sofía, from Naples,' I announced. 'She's come to Barcelona to study and she's going to stay here for a while . . .'

Bea tried to conceal her alarm and greeted her with absolute normality.

'This is my wife, Beatriz.'

'Bea, please. Nobody calls me Beatriz.'

Time and coffee slowly softened the impact of Sofía's arrival and after a bit, Bea suggested that the poor soul must be exhausted and had better get some sleep. Tomorrow would be another day, she said, even if it was a wedding day. It was decided that Sofía would move into the room that had been my bedroom when I was a child and, after making sure my father wasn't going to fall into a coma again, Fermín packed him off to bed too. Bea told Sofía she would lend her one of her dresses for the ceremony and when Fermín, whose breath smelled of champagne from two metres off, was on the point of making some inappropriate remark on the similarities and differences between their shapes and sizes, I gave him a jab in the ribs with my elbow to shut him up.

*

A photograph of my parents on their wedding day observed us from a shelf.

The three of us sat there, in the dining room, gaping at it in disbelief.

'Like two peas in a pod,' murmured Fermín.

Bea looked at me out of the corner of her eye, trying to read my thoughts. She took my hand with a cheerful expression, ready to change the subject.

'So tell me, how was the celebration?'

'Dignified and restrained. How was the ladies' party?'

'Ours was anything but that.'

Fermín threw me a serious look.

'I told you that when it comes to such matters women are far more loutish than us.'

Bea gave us a quizzical smile.

'Who are you calling loutish, Fermín?'

'Forgive this unpardonable slip, Doña Beatriz. It's the bubbly in my bloodstream that's making me talk nonsense. I swear to God that you're a model of virtue and decorum and this humble servant of yours would rather be struck dumb and spend the rest of his days in a Carthusian cell in silent penitence than insinuate that you possess the remotest hint of loutishness.'

'No such luck,' I remarked.

'We'd better not discuss this any further,' Bea cut in, looking at us as if we were both eleven years old. 'And now I suppose you're going to take your customary pre-wedding walk down to the breakwater,' she said.

Fermín and I looked at one another.

'Go on. Off you go. And you'd better make it to the church on time tomorrow . . .'

5

The only place we found open at that time of night was El Xampanyet, on Calle Montcada. They must have felt sorry for us because they let us stay for a bit, while they cleaned up, and when they closed, hearing that Fermín was hours away from becoming a married man, the owner expressed his condolences and presented us with a bottle of house medicine.

'Be brave, and may God be with you,' he pronounced.

We wandered through the narrow streets of the Ribera quarter, putting the world to rights, as we usually did, until the sky took on a purple hue and we knew the time had come for the groom and his best man – in other words, me – to head for the breakwater. There we would sit once again to greet the dawn facing the greatest mirage in the universe: the reflection of Barcelona awakening in the harbour waters.

We sat there with our legs dangling over the jetty to share the bottle we'd been given at El Xampanyet. Between one gulp and the next, we gazed silently at the city, tracing the flight of a flock of seagulls over the dome of La Mercé Church and watching them draw an arc between the towers of the Post Office building. In the distance, crowning the mountain of Montjuïc, the castle loomed darkly, a ghostly bird of prey scrutinising the city at its feet, expectant.

The silence was broken by a ship's horn. On the other side of the National Dock a large cruiser was weighing anchor. Pulling away from the pier it set sail with a surge of the propellers, leaving a wide wake behind it on the waters of the port. Dozens of passengers came out to wave from the stern. I wondered whether Rociíto was among them, next to her mature, handsome scrap merchant from Reus. Fermín watched the ship, deep in thought.

'Do you think Rociíto will be happy, Daniel?'

'What about you, Fermín? Will you be happy?'

We saw the cruiser move into the distance and the figures grow smaller until they became invisible.

'Fermín, there's one thing that intrigues me. Why didn't you want anyone to give you wedding presents?'

'I don't like to put people in a tight spot. And besides, what were we going to do with sets of glasses, teaspoons with the Spanish shield and all that kind of stuff people give at weddings?'

'Well, I was looking forward to giving you a present.'

'You've already given me the biggest present anyone could give me, Daniel.'

'That doesn't count. I'm talking about a present for personal use and enjoyment.'

Fermín looked intrigued.

'Don't tell me it's a porcelain Madonna or a figurine of Saint Teresa. Bernarda has such an ample collection already that I don't know where we're going to find room to sit down.'

'Don't worry. It's not an object.'

'Don't tell me it's money . . .'

'As you know, I don't have a *céntimo*, unfortunately. The one with the funds is my father-in-law and he doesn't splash it about.'

'These new Francoists are as tight as two coats of paint.'

'My father-in-law is a good man, Fermín. Don't have a go at him.'

'Let's draw a line under the matter, but don't change the subject now you've put the sweet in my mouth. What present?'

'Guess.'

'A batch of Sugus sweets.'

'Cold, cold . . .'

Fermín arched his eyebrows, dying with curiosity. Suddenly, his eyes lit up.

'No . . . It was about time.'

I nodded.

'There's a time for everything. Now, listen carefully. You mustn't tell anyone what you're about to see today, Fermín. No one . . .'

'Not even Bernarda?'

6

The first light of the day spilled like liquid copper over the cornices of Rambla de Santa Mónica. It was a Sunday morning and the streets were quiet and deserted. When we entered the narrow alleyway of Calle Arco del Teatro, the ghostly beam of light penetrating from the Ramblas dimmed and by the time we reached the large wooden door we had become submerged in a city of shadows.

I climbed the steps and rapped with the knocker a few times. The echo trailed off inside, like ripples on a pond. Fermín, who had assumed a respectful silence and looked like a boy on his first day of school, turned to me anxiously.

'Isn't it rather early to call?' he asked. 'I hope the chief doesn't get annoyed . . .'

'This isn't a department store. There are no opening times,' I reassured him. 'And here the chief is called Isaac. Don't speak unless he asks you something first.'

Fermín nodded compliantly.

'Not a peep.'

A couple of minutes later I heard the dance of cogs, pulleys and levers operating the lock and I stepped down again. The door opened just a fraction and the vulturine face of Isaac Montfort, the keeper, peered round with its usual steely look. The keeper's eyes alighted first on me and, after a quick glance at Fermín, proceeded to X-ray, catalogue and examine him from head to toe.

'This must be the illustrious Fermín Romero de Torres,' he murmured.

'At your service, and God's and . . .'

I silenced Fermín with a nudge and smiled at the severe keeper.

'Good morning, Isaac.'

'A good morning, Sempere, will be one when you don't call at dawn, or while I'm in the toilet, or on a religious holiday,' replied Isaac. 'Come on, in with you.'

The keeper opened the door a bit further and we slid through. When the door closed behind us, Isaac retrieved his oil lamp from the floor and Fermín was able to observe the elaborate movements of the lock as it folded back upon itself like the insides of the biggest clock in the world.

'A burglar could age like a good Camembert trying to prise this one open,' he let slip.

I threw him a warning glance and he quickly put a finger to his lips.

'Collection or delivery?' asked Isaac.

'Well, you see, I've been meaning to bring Fermín here for ages so he could get to know the place first-hand. I've often talked to him about it. He's my best friend and he's getting married today, at noon,' I explained.

'Gracious,' said Isaac. 'Poor thing. Are you sure you wouldn't like me to offer you nuptial asylum here?'

'Fermín is quite convinced about getting married, Isaac.'

The keeper looked Fermín up and down. Fermín smiled apologetically.

'What courage.'

Isaac guided us along the wide corridor to the entrance of the gallery leading into the large hall. I let Fermín walk ahead of me so that he could discover with his own eyes a vision that no words could describe.

His tiny figure was engulfed by the great beam of light pouring down from the glass dome in the ceiling. Brightness fell in a vaporous cascade over the sprawling labyrinth of corridors, tunnels, staircases, arches and vaults that seemed to spring from the floor like the trunk of an endless tree of books and branched heavenwards displaying an impossible geometry. Fermín stepped on to a gangway extending like a bridge into the base of the structure. He gazed at the sight open mouthed. I drew up to him and put a hand on his shoulder.

'Welcome to the Cemetery of Forgotten Books, Fermín.'

7

In my experience, whenever someone discovered that place, their reaction was always one of bewitchment and amazement. The beauty and the mystery of the premises reduced the visitor to a silent, dream-like contemplation. Naturally, Fermín had to be different. He spent the first half-hour hypnotised, wandering like a man possessed through every nook and cranny of the large jigsaw formed by the winding labyrinth. He stopped to rap his knuckles against flying buttresses and columns, as if he doubted their solidity. He stood at different angles and perspectives, forming a spyglass with his hands and trying to decipher the logic of the construction. He walked through the spiral of libraries with his large nose almost touching the infinite rows of spines running along endless pathways, making a mental note of titles and cataloguing whatever he discovered on his way. I followed a few steps behind him, with a mixture of alarm and anxiety.

I was beginning to suspect that Isaac was going to kick us out of there when I bumped into the keeper on one of the bridges suspended between book-lined vaults. To my surprise, not only did he show no sign of irritation but he was smiling good-humouredly as he watched Fermín's progress during his first exploration of the Cemetery of Forgotten Books.

'Your friend is a rather peculiar specimen,' Isaac reckoned.

'You haven't scratched the surface yet.'

'Don't worry about him, leave him alone. He'll come down from his cloud eventually.'

'What if he gets lost?'

'He seems to be on the ball. He'll work it out.'

I wasn't so sure, but I didn't want to contradict Isaac. I walked with him to the room that doubled as his office and accepted the cup of coffee he was offering me.

'Have you explained the rules to your friend?'

'Fermín and rules are incompatible notions. But I have summed up the basics and he replied with a convincing: "But of course, who do you take me for?"'

While Isaac filled my cup again he caught me gazing at a photograph of his daughter Nuria hanging above his desk.

'It will soon be two years since she left us,' he said with a sadness that cut through the air.

I looked down, distressed. A hundred years could go by and the death of Nuria Montfort would still be on my mind, as would the certainty that if I'd never met her she might still be alive. Isaac caressed the photograph with his eyes.

'I'm getting old, Sempere. It's about time someone took my post.'

I was about to protest at such a suggestion when Fermín walked in with his face all flushed, and panting as if he'd just run a marathon.

'So?' asked Isaac. 'What do you think?'

'Glorious. Although it doesn't appear to have a toilet. At least not that I noticed.'

'I hope you didn't pee in some corner.'

'I made a superhuman effort to hold it in and make it back here.'

'It's that door on the left. You'll have to pull the chain twice, the first time it never works.'

While Fermín relieved himself, Isaac poured out a cup of coffee which awaited him steaming hot when he returned.

'I have a few questions I'd like to ask you, Don Isaac.'

'Fermín, I don't think . . .' I pleaded.

'It's fine. Go ahead, ask.'

'The first lot is related to the history of the premises. The second one concerns technical and architectural works. And the third is basically bibliographic . . .'

Isaac laughed. It was the first time I'd ever heard him laugh and I didn't know whether to take it as a sign from heaven or the presage of some imminent disaster.

'First you'll have to choose the book you want to save,' Isaac proposed.

'I've had my eye on a few, but even if it's just for sentimental reasons, I've selected this one, if that's all right.'

He pulled a book out of his pocket. It was bound in red leather, with the title embossed in gold letters and an engraving of a skull on the title page.

'Well I never: *City of the Damned, episode thirteen: Daphne and the impossible staircase*, by David Martín,' Isaac read.

'An old friend,' Fermín explained.

'You don't say. Strangely enough, there was a time when I'd often see him around here,' said Isaac.

'That must have been before the war,' I remarked.

'No, no . . . I saw him some time later.'

Fermín and I looked at one another. I wondered whether Isaac had been right and he was beginning to get too old for the job.

'I don't wish to contradict you, chief, but that's impossible,' said Fermín.

'Impossible? You'll have to make yourself a bit clearer . . .'

'David Martín fled the country before the war,' I explained. 'At the start of 1939, towards the end of the conflict, he came back, crossing over the Pyrenees, and was arrested in Puigcerdà a few days later. He was held in prison until well into 1941, when he was most probably murdered.'

Isaac was staring at us in disbelief.

'You must believe him, chief,' Fermín assured him. 'Our sources are reliable.'

'I can assure you that David Martín sat in that same chair you're sitting in, Sempere, and we chatted for a while.'

'Are you quite sure, Isaac?'

'I've never been more certain of anything in all my life,' replied the keeper. 'I remember because I hadn't seen him for years. He was in a bad way and looked ill.'

'Can you remember the date when he came?'

'Perfectly. It was the last night of 1941. New Year's Eve. That was the last time I saw him.'

Fermín and I were lost in our calculations.

'That means that what that jailer, Bebo, told Brians, was true,' I said. 'The night Valls ordered him to be taken to the old mansion near Güell Park to be killed . . . Bebo said he later overheard the gunmen saying that something had happened there, that there was someone else in the house . . . Maybe someone prevented Martín from being killed . . .' I speculated.

Isaac was listening to these musings with concern.

'What are you talking about? Who wanted to murder Martín?'

'It's a long story,' said Fermín. 'With tons of footnotes.'

'Well, I hope to hear it one day . . .'

'Did you think Martín was in his right mind, Isaac?' I asked.

Isaac shrugged.

'One never knew with Martín . . . That man had a tormented soul. When he left I asked him to let me walk him as far as the train, but he told me there was a car waiting for him outside.'

'A car?'

'A Mercedes-Benz, no less. Belonging to someone he called the Boss and who, from what he said, was waiting for him by the front door. But when I went out with him there was no car, no boss, there was nothing at all . . .'

'Don't take this the wrong way, chief, but what with it being New Year's Eve, and with the festive spirit of the occasion, couldn't it be that you'd overdone it on the bubbly and, dazed by Christmas carols and the high sugar content of Jijona nougat, you might have imagined all this?' asked Fermín.

'As far as the bubbly is concerned, I only drink fizzy lemonade, and the strongest thing I have here is a bottle of hydrogen peroxide,' Isaac specified. He didn't seem offended.

'Forgive me for doubting you. It was a mere formality.'

'I understand. But believe me when I say that unless whoever came that night was a ghost, and I don't think he was because one of his ears was bleeding and his hands were shaking with fever – and besides, he polished off all the sugar lumps I had in my kitchen cupboard – Martín was as alive as you or me.'

'And he didn't say what he was coming here for, after so long?'

Isaac nodded.

'He said he'd come to leave something with me and that, when he could, he'd come back for it. Either he'd come or he'd send someone . . .'

'And what did he leave with you?'

'A parcel wrapped in paper and bits of string. I don't know what was inside.'

I swallowed hard.

'Do you still have it?'

8

The parcel, pulled out from the back of a cupboard, lay on Isaac's desk. When my fingers brushed the paper, the fine layer of dust covering it rose in a cloud of particles that caught the glow of the oil lamp Isaac held on my left. On my right, Fermín unsheathed his paperknife and handed it to me. The three of us looked at one another.

'God's will be done,' said Fermín.

I slipped the knife under the string binding the parcel and cut it. With the greatest care I removed the wrapping until the content became visible. It was a manuscript. The pages were soiled, covered in stains of wax and blood. The first page bore a title written in diabolical handwriting.

The Angel's Game
By David Martín

'It's the book he wrote while he was imprisoned in the tower,' I murmured, 'Bebo must have saved it.'

'There's something underneath . . .' said Fermín.

The corner of a piece of parchment peeped out from beneath the manuscript. I gave it a tug and retrieved an envelope. It was sealed with red wax, stamped with the figure of an angel. On the front of the envelope was a single word, written in red ink:

Daniel

A cold sensation rose up my arms. Isaac, who was witnessing the scene with a mixture of astonishment and consternation, crept out of the room, followed by Fermín.

'Daniel,' Fermín called out gently. 'We're leaving you alone so you can open the envelope calmly and in private . . .'

I heard their footsteps as they slowly walked away and was only able to catch the start of their conversation.

'Listen, chief, with so many emotions I forgot to mention that earlier, when I came in, I couldn't help overhearing you say that you were thinking of retiring and that there might be an opening soon for the position . . .'

'That's right. I've been here too long. Why?'

'Well, you see, I know we've only just met, so to speak, but I might be interested . . .'

The voices of Isaac and Fermín melted into the echoing labyrinth of the Cemetery of Forgotten Books. Left on my own, I sat in the keeper's armchair and removed the sealing wax. The envelope contained a folded sheet of ochre-coloured paper. I opened it and began to read.

Barcelona, 31 December 1941

Dear Daniel,

I write these words in the hope and conviction that one day you'll discover this place, the Cemetery of Forgotten Books, a place that changed my life as I'm sure it will change yours. This same hope leads me to believe that perhaps then, when I'm no longer here, someone will talk to you about me and the friendship that linked me to your mother. I know that if you ever read these words you'll be overwhelmed by questions and doubts. You'll find some of the answers in this manuscript, where I have tried to portray my story as I remember it, knowing that my days of lucidity are numbered and that often I can only recall what never took place.

I also know that when you receive this letter, time will have started to wipe out the traces of those events. I know you will harbour suspicions and that if you discover the truth about your mother's final days you will share my anger and my thirst for revenge. They say it's for the wise and the righteous to forgive, but I know I'll never be able to do so. My soul is already condemned and has no hope of salvation. I know I will devote every drop of breath left in me to try to avenge the death of Isabella. But that is my destiny, not yours.

Your mother would not have wished for you a life like mine, at any price. Your mother would have wished you to have a full life, devoid of hatred and resentment. For her sake, I beg you to read this story and once you have read it, destroy it. Forget everything you might have heard about a past that no longer exists, clean your heart of anger and live the life your mother wanted to give you, always looking ahead.

And if one day, kneeling at her graveside, you feel the fire of anger trying to take hold of you, remember that in my story, as in yours, there was an angel who holds all the answers.

Your friend,

DAVID MARTÍN

Over and over again I read the words David Martín was sending me through time, words that seemed to me suffused with repentance and madness, words I didn't fully understand. I held the letter in my hand for a few more moments and then placed it in the flame of the oil lamp and watched it burn.

I found Fermín and Isaac standing at the foot of the labyrinth, chatting like old friends. When they saw me their voices hushed and they looked at me expectantly.

'Whatever that letter said only concerns you, Daniel. You don't have to tell us anything.'

I nodded. The echo of church bells resounded faintly through the walls. Isaac looked at us and checked his watch.

'Listen, weren't you two going to a wedding today?'

9

The bride was dressed in white, and though she wore no dazzling jewellery or ornaments, in the eyes of her groom no woman, in all of history, had ever looked more beautiful than Bernarda did on that early February day, when the sun lit up the square outside the Church of Santa Ana. Don Gustavo Barceló – who must surely have bought all the flowers in Barcelona, for they flooded the entrance to the church – cried like a baby and the priest, the groom's friend, surprised us all with a lucid sermon that brought tears even to Bea's eyes, who was no soft touch.

I almost dropped the rings, but all was forgotten when the priest, once the preliminaries were over, invited Fermín to kiss the bride. Just then, I turned my head for a second and thought I saw a figure in the back row of the church, a stranger who was looking at me and smiling. I couldn't say why, but for a moment I was certain that the unknown man was none other than the Prisoner of Heaven. But when I looked again, he was no longer there. Next to me Fermín held Bernarda tight and smacked a kiss right on her lips that unleashed an ovation captained by the priest.

When I saw my friend kissing the woman he loved it occurred to me that this moment, this instant stolen from time and from God, was worth all the days of misery that had brought us to this place and the many others that were doubtless waiting for us on our return to life. And that everything that was decent and clean and pure in this world and everything for which it was worth living and breathing was in those lips, in those hands and in the look of that fortunate couple who, I knew, would be together for the rest of their lives.

Epilogue

1960

A young man, already showing a few grey hairs, walks in the noon sun amongst the gravestones of the cemetery, beneath a sky melting over the blue of the sea.

In his arms he carries a child who barely understands his words but who smiles when their eyes meet. Together they approach a modest grave, set apart on a balcony overlooking the Mediterranean. The man kneels down in front of the grave and, holding his son, lets him stroke the letters engraved on the stone.

ISABELLA SEMPERE

1917–1939

The man remains there for a while, in silence, his eyelids pressed together to hold his tears.

His son's voice brings him back to the present and when he opens his eyes again he sees that the boy is pointing at a small figure peeping through the petals of some dried flowers, in the shadow of a glass vase at the foot of the tomb. He is certain that it wasn't there the last time he visited the grave. His hand searches among the flowers and picks up a plaster statuette, so small it fits in his fist. An angel. The words he thought he'd forgotten flare up in his memory like an old wound.

And if one day, kneeling at her graveside, you feel the fire of anger trying to take hold of you, remember that in my story, as in yours, there was an angel who holds all the answers . . .

The child tries to clutch the angel figure resting in his father's hand and when he touches it with his fingers he accidentally pushes it. The angel falls on the marble and breaks. And that is when the man sees it. A tiny piece of paper hidden inside the plaster. The paper is fine, almost transparent. He unrolls it and instantly recognises the handwriting:

Mauricio Valls
El Pinar
Calle de Manuel Arnús
Barcelona

The sea breeze rises through the gravestones and the breath of a curse caresses his face. He puts the piece of paper in his pocket. Shortly afterwards, he places a white rose on the tombstone and then retraces his steps, carrying the boy in his arms, towards the avenue of cypress trees where the mother of his son is waiting. All three melt into an embrace and when she looks into his eyes she discovers something that was not in them a few moments ago. Something turbulent and dark that frightens her.

'Are you all right, Daniel?'

He looks at her for a long time and smiles.

'I love you,' he says, and kisses her, knowing that the story, his story, has not ended.

It has only just begun.

THE END

ATHENIAN DEMOCRACY

ATHENIAN DEMOCRACY

By A. H. M. JONES

Late Professor of Ancient History in the University of Cambridge

BASIL BLACKWELL

OXFORD

1978

0 631 17890 2

First published in paperback 1977
Reprinted 1978

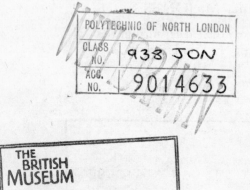

Printed in Great Britain at
The Camelot Press Ltd, Southampton
and bound by
The Kemp Hall Bindery, Oxford

PREFACE

THE reprinting of collections of already published articles is in principle to be reprobated, but in this case there are extenuating circumstances. All the papers here collected deal with the same theme and are closely interlocked. Two, 'The Economic Basis of the Athenian Democracy' and 'The Athenian Democracy and its Critics', are out of print and very difficult to obtain. The fifth, 'How did the Athenian Democracy work'? (based on a course of lectures given at Cambridge in 1956), and the appendix on 'The Citizen Population of Athens during the Peloponnesian War' (expanded from a paper read to the Cambridge Philological Society in 1953), are here presented for the first time.

I have to thank the editors of *Past and Present*, the *Cambridge Historical Journal* and the *Economic History Review*, and the Syndics of the Cambridge University Press, for permission to republish the first, third, fourth and second articles respectively, and Sir Basil Blackwell for undertaking the publication.

I owe a debt of gratitude to various friends who have offered me criticisms and suggestions, including Mr. M. I. Finley, Mr. Guy Griffith, Mr. D. M. Lewis and Mr. Russell Meiggs. My special thanks are due to Mr. Geoffrey de Ste Croix, whose vigilant care has corrected many errors, and whose forthright arguments have sometimes caused me to alter my views.

I have reprinted the articles almost as they stood, only correcting some errors of fact, and making the references uniform and eliminating some redundant notes. There is as a result some overlapping and repetition, but it would have been difficult to remove this without recasting the whole, and I hope that readers will bear with it charitably.

A. H. M. JONES

Jesus College
CAMBRIDGE
June 1957

CONTENTS

I

THE ECONOMIC BASIS OF THE ATHENIAN DEMOCRACY

The Economic Basis of the Athenian Democracy[1]

PRIMA FACIE the Athenian Democracy would seem to have been a perfectly designed machine for expressing and putting into effect the will of the people. The majority of the magistrates were annually chosen by lot from all qualified candidates who put in their names, so that every citizen had a chance to take his turn in the administration. In the fifth century the military officers, of whom the most important were the ten generals, were elected by the assembly. In the fourth, when finance became a difficult problem, a few high financial officers were also elected. This was an inevitable concession to aristocratic principles: for the Greeks considered popular election to be aristocratic rather than democratic, since the ordinary voter will prefer a known to an unknown name—and in point of fact the generals usually tended to be men of wealth and family, though a professional soldier or two were usually members of the board in the fourth century. But the assembly, of which all adult male citizens were members, kept a strict control over the generals, who received precise instructions and departed from them at their peril. The assembly was in a very real sense a sovereign body, holding forty regular meetings a year and extraordinary sessions as required, and not merely settling general questions of policy, but making detailed decisions in every sphere of government—foreign affairs, military operations, finance.

The administrative lynch-pin of the constitution was the council of five hundred, annually chosen by lot from all the demes (wards or parishes) of Athens and Attica in proportion to their size, and thus forming a fair sample of the people as a whole. It had two main functions, to supervise and co-ordinate the activities of the magistrates, and to prepare the agenda of the assembly. No motion might be put to the assembly unless the question had been placed on the order paper by the council and duly advertised; snap divisions were thus precluded. On uncontroversial issues the council usually produced a draft motion, which could however be freely debated and amended in the assembly by any citizen; in this way much formal business was cleared away. On controversial issues the council normally—and naturally in view of its composition—forebore to express an opinion, and merely put the question before the people, leaving it to any citizen to draft the motion during the actual debate. The presidents of the council and the assembly were chosen daily by lot from the council to preclude any undue influence from the chair.

Finally, as ultimate guardians of the constitution, there were the popular law courts. Juries were empanelled by lot for each case from a body of 6,000 citizens annually chosen by lot, and decided not only private cases but political issues. These juries as a regular routine judged any charges of peculation or malfeasance brought against magistrates on laying down their office; they decided the fate of any citizen accused of treason or of 'deceiving the people' by his speeches in the assembly; they could quash any motion voted in the assembly as being contrary to the laws, and punish its author. Political trials were frequent in Athens, and in the fourth century in particular the indictment for an illegal motion was constantly employed for political purposes, often on very technical grounds. The result was that the popular juries—in such cases sometimes thousands strong—tended to become a Supreme Court.

In general all citizens who were not expressly disqualified for some offence, such as an unpaid debt to the treasury, had equal political rights: in particular all could speak and vote in the assembly. For membership of the council and of the juries and probably for all magistracies there was an age qualification of 30 years. For offices, or at any rate some of them, there were also qualifications of property: but these were mostly moderate and, by the late fourth century, at any rate, and probably by the fifth, were in practice ignored.[2] To make the system work truly democratically it was further necessary that every citizen, however poor, should be able to afford the time for exercising his political rights, and from the time of Pericles pay was provided for this purpose.[3] Magistrates were paid at varying rates according to the nature of their duties;[4] members of the council received 5 obols a day by the fourth century—the rate may have been lower in the fifth;[5] and members of the juries were given a subsistence allowance of 2 obols, raised in 425 B.C. to 3.[6] Finally from the beginning of the fourth century citizens who attended the assembly—or rather the quorum who arrived first, for a limited sum of money was allocated to each assembly—were paid a subsistence allowance of 1, then 2, then 3 obols.[7] Later the rate was more liberal, 1 drachma for ordinary days, 1½ for the ten standing meetings when the agenda was heavier.[8]

Two charges have been brought against the Athenian democracy, one both by ancient and by modern critics, the other in recent times only. The first is that the pay, which was an essential part of the system, was provided by the tribute paid by Athens' allies in the Delian League, and that the democracy was therefore parasitic on the empire: the second, that Athenians only had the leisure to perform their political functions because they were supported by slaves—the democracy was in fact parasitic on slavery.

To the first charge there is a very simple answer, that the democracy continued to function in the fourth century when Athens had lost her empire; the Second Athenian League, which lasted effectively only from 377 to 357, was never a paying proposition, the contributions of the allies by no means covering the cost of military and naval operations. And not only did the democracy continue to function, but a new and important form of pay, that for attendance in the assembly, was introduced early in the century. This being so it is hardly worth while to go into the financial figures, particularly as there must be many gaps in our calculations. The magistrates numbered about 350 in the later fourth century, and, if they received on an average 1 drachma a day, the annual bill would be 21 talents.[9] The council, if all the members were paid for every day of the year, would have cost rather under 26 talents a year, but if councillors, like jurors, were paid for actual attendance, the bill would be considerably less, since sessions were not held every day and many members did not attend regularly.[10] Assembly pay cannot be calculated as we do not know how large the quorum was. The major item was the 6,000 jurors for whom Aristophanes[11] budgets 150 talents a year, presumably by the simple method of multiplying 3 obols by 6,000 jurors by 300 court days (the courts did not sit on the forty or more assembly days[12] nor on the numerous festivals).[13] This is a theoretical maximum, for the whole 6,000 were not empanelled in juries on every court day—Aristophanes' jurors rise at dead of night to queue for their tickets.[14] As against this, the internal revenue of Athens, apart from imperial receipts, can be inferred to have been in the range of 400 talents a year in the fifth century.[15] Since other peace-time expenditure was minimal, pay was thus amply covered by internal income at this period. In the fourth century the revenue dropped considerably; Demosthenes indeed stated that earlier in the century it amounted to only 130 talents.[16] He is perhaps thinking of the regular income from taxes and rents, excluding receipts from fines, confiscations and court fees, which were a considerable proportion of the whole.[17] Even so, we know that in the first half of the fourth century it was at times a tight squeeze.[18] By 340, however, the regular revenue had risen to 400 talents again, and things were easy.[19]

That Athens profited financially from her empire is of course true. But these profits were not necessary to keep the democracy working. They enabled Athens to be a great power and to support a much larger citizen population at higher standards of living. One oligarchic critic emphasises the casual profits incidental on Athens' position as an imperial city; the imperial litigation which brought in more court fees, the increased cus-

full civil (as opposed to political) rights, except that they could not own land—hence their concentration on industry and commerce—and were subject to all the duties of citizens, including military and naval service and taxation at a slightly higher scale. They were a contented class, and many demonstrated their loyalty to their adoptive city by generous gifts at times of crisis.[46]

What of slaves? Here it will be as well to clear up another misconception. It is often stated, mainly on the authority of Plato and Aristotle, that 'the Greeks' considered manual work degrading. Now it is true that gentlemen like Plato and Aristotle despised workers and justified their contempt by asserting that manual work deformed the body and the soul. But that this was the attitude of the average poor Greek there is no evidence. An anecdote recorded by Xenophon[47] probably gives a better insight into his point of view. Eutherus, who has lost his overseas estates as a result of the war, has been reduced to earning his living by manual labour. Socrates asks what he will do when his bodily strength fails and suggests that he find a job as a rich man's bailiff. Eutherus is horrified at the suggestion—'I could not endure to be a slave . . . I absolutely refuse to be at any man's beck and call'. What the Athenian thete objected to was not hard work—incidentally his main military duty in the fifth century was rowing in the galleys, a task in most later civilisations considered fit only for infidel slaves or convicts—but being another man's servant. He would work as an independent craftsman or at a pinch as a casual labourer,[48] but he would not take even a black-coated job as a regular employee; we find that such highly responsible posts as the manager of a bank or the foreman overseer of a mine are filled by slaves or freedmen of the owner.[49]

Is it true, as we are still too often told, that the average Athenian, in the intervals between listening to a play of Sophocles and serving as a magistrate, councillor or juror, lounged in the market place, discussing politics and philosophy, while slaves toiled to support him? Contemporary critics of the democracy did not think so. Plato's Socrates, analysing the people in a democracy, divides them into the drones, that is the active politicians and their cliques of supporters, and the mass of the people 'who support themselves by their labour and do not care about politics, owning very little property; this is the largest and most powerful element in a democracy when it is assembled'.[50] Xenophon's Socrates, rebuking Charmides for his shyness at addressing the assembly, asks if he is afraid 'of the fullers among them or the shoemakers or the carpenters or the smiths or the peasants or the merchants or the shopkeepers: for the assembly is composed of all of them'.[51] Aristotle, analysing the people (that is the mass of poor citizens) in different cities, classifies them as craftsmen, shopkeepers, seamen of various kinds—fishermen, ferrymen, sailors on merchantmen or warships—and casual day labourers and those who have little property so that they can enjoy no leisure.[52]

Slaves were employed in many capacities—as domestic servants, as clerks and agents in commerce and banking, in agriculture, and in industry and mining. All well-to-do Athenian families had several servants, and no doubt wealthy men kept large households of a dozen or more—precise figures are lacking—but the domestic servant probably did not go very far down the social scale. A man for whom Lysias wrote a little speech does indeed roundly assert that everyone has slaves; but he is trying to convince the jury that it is contrary to public policy to encourage slaves to inform against their masters.[53] In comedy domestic slaves appear when dramatically convenient, even in the poorest households,[54] but this evidence is suspect: comedy was written after all by well-to-do authors, and slaves provided a variety of stock comic turns. It has been argued that because in the fifth century every hoplite took with him an attendant to carry his food and kit, and was allowed a drachma a day by the State on his account (in addition to his own drachma[55]), every hoplite must have owned an able-bodied male slave. Those hoplites who owned suitable slaves certainly used them for this purpose,[56] but there is no evidence that every hoplite's attendant was his own slave. The high rate of the State allowance, on the contrary, is only explicable on the assumption that many hoplites would have to hire a man for the purpose, and Thucydides' inclusion of the baggage carriers with the light-armed among the Athenian casualties at Delium implies that they were citizens.[57] More significant than these uncertain inferences is a remark by Demosthenes, who, castigating the harshness with which Androtion and Timocrates collected the arrears of war tax, pictures them 'removing doors and seizing blankets and distraining on a servant girl, if anyone employed one'.[58] Now the payers of war tax can be estimated to have numbered only about 6,000 out of a population of 21,000.[59] If not all of them had a domestic servant, one may hazard that under a quarter of the population enjoyed that luxury.

Commerce and banking need not detain us, as the numbers were small. In agriculture, too we hear little of slaves. The property of large landowners did not normally consist of a single great estate, but of several farms scattered over Attica.[60] Some of these farms were let to free tenants, Athenian or metic;[61] one at least—the home farm—would be worked by a minimum staff of slaves, supplemented by hired labour;[62] for it was uneconomic in a seasonal trade like agriculture to maintain all the year round enough slaves to cope with peak demands. The hired labour was sometimes supplied by slave gangs, leased from a contractor to do a particular job, such as to get in the harvest or the vintage;[63] but it often consisted of free persons—in one of his private speeches Demosthenes remarks that many citizen women were driven by poverty to work in the harvest.[64] Shepherds seem normally to have been slaves,[65] but the politician Phrynichus is alleged to have been one in his poverty-stricken youth.[66] How far down the scale of wealth the use of agricultural slaves went it is difficult to say, but the greater part of Attica was probably occupied by peasant farmers too poor to afford them. Of the 6,000 citizens who paid war tax, a large number were, as Demosthenes puts it, 'farmers who stinted themselves, but owing to the maintenance of their children and domestic expenses and other public demands fell into arrears with their war tax'.[67] These were the men who sometimes could not afford a single domestic servant, and certainly did not maintain a farm hand; they would fall into the class which Aristotle described as using the labour of their wives and children through lack of slaves.[68] Below them were the remaining 3,000 of the hoplite class who did not qualify for war tax, and will have owned property to the value of between 25 and 20 minae.[69] These were quite poor men; Demosthenes introducing a poor hoplite witness apologises to the jury—'he is poor, it is true, but not a rascal'[70]—and the wealthy Mantitheus, when his deme mustered for a call-up, found that many of his fellow demesmen were embarrassed for journey money, and distributed 30 drachmae to each.[71] A farm worth 20 minae would, on the basis of the single land price recorded, comprise about 5 acres, and would bring in if let only about 160 drachmae a year in rent, not enough to feed, let alone clothe, a single man; it can only have supported a family if worked by family labour.[72]

In industry, and particularly mining, slaves were employed on a larger scale. The wealthy Nicias in the fifth century is said to have owned 1,000 slaves, whom he let out to a mining contractor at 1 obol a day, the contractor feeding and clothing them and replacing casualties; two rich contemporaries are said to have owned 600 and 300 respectively whom they exploited in a similar way.[73] In the fourth century another mine concessionaire owned thirty slaves,[74] which was probably a more usual number. Well-to-do Athenians also normally invested a small proportion of their wealth in slave craftsmen, who either worked together in a factory, or independently, paying their owner a fixed sum and keeping for themselves whatever they earned beyond it. The largest factory of which we hear, the shield factory of the brothers Lysias and Polemarchus, numbered nearly 120 men;[75] but this is quite exceptional, and is due to the fact that the owners were metics, who could not invest in land, and that the thirty years of the Peloponnesian war had naturally led to a boom in armaments. In the fourth century Pasion the banker also ran a shield factory as a side-line; it brought in a net revenue of a talent a year, and must have contained over sixty men; Pasion again was a metic, until he was rewarded with the citizenship for his public services,[76] and he was the richest man in Athens of the time—he had before he died acquired land to the value of 20 talents besides his bank and factory. Demosthenes' father was also exceptional in owning two factories, thirty-two knife makers and twenty bed makers, with a capital value of nearly 6½ talents (4 talents in slaves and 2½ talents in raw materials in stock) out of a total fortune of 14 talents, the rest of which was in cash and investments with the exception of his house and furniture.[77] We hear of some others in the fifth century whose wealth was entirely invested in slaves; Isocrates' father rose to affluence from the profits of a group of flute-makers,[78] and Xenophon makes Socrates cite five contemporaries, including a miller, a baker and cloakmaker, who lived comfortably on the earnings of their slaves.[79] More usually rich Athenians seem to have distributed their capital between land, house property, some cash investments and a dozen or so slave craftsmen. Socrates, asking a high-class prostitute where her money came from, suggests (ironically) land, house property or craftsmen as typical sources of income.[80] Timarchus inherited, besides land and houses, nine or ten shoemakers, who paid him 2 obols a day each:[81] Leocrates owned bronzesmiths to the value of 35 minae (about a dozen, that is [82]): Ciron, besides an estate worth a talent, and two houses, owned a few rent-paying slaves, valued with three domestic slaves and the furniture at 13 minae:[83] Euctemon possessed a farm, a house, a baths, and a brothel and wineshop and some craftsmen.[84]

These facts and figures concern the well-to-do families who could afford to pay a professional speech writer to compose a plea in their mutual litigation about their inheritances, and who normally belonged to the 1,200 richest families enrolled on the trierarchic register. How far humbler folk owned industrial slaves it is very difficult to say. Xenophon in one passage speaks of those who could buying slaves as fellow workers,[85] which might suggest that a craftsman sometimes bought a man and trained him as an apprentice; and a poor cripple, pleading for his public assistance of 1 obol a day, complains that he is getting old and his children are too young to support him (a rather unlikely conjunction of pleas) and that he is too poor to buy a slave to carry on his work.[86] This may suggest that a craftsman who bought a slave and trained him was looking forward to retiring on his earnings. But, as Aristophanes recognised, the greater part of the work in industry as in agriculture was done by poor citizens. Addressing them Poverty declared in the *Plutus*: 'If wealth should gain his sight again and distribute himself equally, no one would practise a craft or skill. And when you have lost both of these, who will work as a smith or a shipwright or a tailor or a wheelwright or a shoemaker or a bricklayer or a launderer or a tanner or plough the land or harvest the crops, if you can live in idleness and neglect all this work?'

We have no reliable evidence for the total number of slaves in Attica at any time. For the late fourth century we have two figures, which, if we could rely on them, would be startling. The Byzantine lexicon of Suidas[87] cites Hypereides (probably in connection with his proposal to free the slaves after the battle of Chaeronea in 338 B.C.) as speaking of 'more than 150,000 from the silver mines and over the rest of the country.' Athenaeus,[88] who wrote at the end of the second century A.D., quotes Ctesicles, a chronicler of unknown date, as stating that at the census held by Demetrius of Phaleron (317–07) 400,000 slaves were registered. These are, as Beloch[89] has convincingly demonstrated, quite impossible figures, and must have been corrupted in the course of their transmission to the late sources in which we read them. To turn to more reliable if less explicit evidence, according to Thucydides more than 20,000 slaves, mainly skilled men, escaped during the ten years' occupation of Deceleia by the Spartans;[90] these would probably be in the main miners and agricultural slaves, but would include many city workers, since the sixteen miles of city walls cannot have been so completely patrolled as to prevent escapes.

Xenophon declares that the mines could provide employment for many more than 10,000, as those—if any—who remembered what the slave tax used to fetch before the Deceleian war could testify (he was writing sixty years later).[91] But whatever their numbers their distribution is fairly clear. They were owned in the main by the 1,200 richest families and in decreasing numbers by the next 3,000 or so. It is unlikely that any slaves were owned by two-thirds to three-quarters of the citizen population. The great majority of the citizens earned their living by the work of their hands, as peasant farmers, craftsmen, shopkeepers, seamen and labourers; so contemporary witnesses state, and so the detailed evidence, so far as it goes, suggests. In only one occupation was slave labour predominant, in mining, and even here, contrary to common belief, some citizens worked. Xenophon, advocating that the State acquire a large body of slaves to be leased to the citizens for use in the mines, suggests that not only will existing contractors add to their manpower but that 'there are many of those who are themselves in the mines who are growing old, and many others, both Athenians and aliens, who would not or could not work with their hands, but would gladly make their living by supervising'.[92] In one of the Demosthenic speeches we meet a man who boasts 'In earlier times I made a lot of money from the silver mines, working and toiling myself with my own hands': he had struck lucky and was now one of the 300 richest men in Athens.[93]

That the poorer citizens lived on State pay for political services is, even for the fourth century, when the system was most fully developed, demonstrably false. A man could only be a councillor two years in his life, and could hold none of the magistracies chosen by lot for more than one annual tenure.[94] He could by attending the assembly—and getting there in time to qualify for pay—earn a drachma on thirty days and 1½ drachmae on ten days in the year. On some festivals—the number varied according to the state of the exchequer—he could draw his theoric payment of 2 obols.[95] On other days, if lucky enough to be successful in the annual ballot for the 6,000 jurors, he could queue in hopes of being empanelled on a jury and earning 3 obols, just enough to feed himself. At this rate a bachelor without dependants could barely with consistent good luck scrape a living; for a man with a family it was quite impossible.

The majority of the citizens were then workers who earned their own livings and whose political pay served only to compensate them in some measure for loss of working time. Agricultural and industrial slaves in the main merely added to the wealth of a relatively small rentier class, whose principal source of income was land; this same class employed most of the domestic slaves. It only remains to ask how far the Athenian State drew its revenue, directly or indirectly, from slaves. The State owned a certain number of slaves. Most famous are the 1,200 Scythian archers who policed the assembly and the law courts and enforced the orders of the magistrates.[96] There were a number of others ranging from the workers in the mint to the city gaoler and the public slave *par excellence* who had custody of the public records and accounts. Athens thus ran her police force and her rudimentary civil service in part by slave labour—the clerks of the magistrates were mostly salaried citizens.[97] There was apparently a tax on slaves, known only from the mention in Xenophon cited above,[98] but it can hardly have been an important item in the revenue to receive so little notice. The mines, which were mainly exploited by slave labour, also brought in revenue to the State, but less than might have been expected seeing that concessionaires sometimes made large fortunes. The mines flourished in the fifth century, from their first serious exploitation in 483 till the Spartan occupation of Deceleia in 413. They then went through a prolonged bad period till the 330s, when they were again in full swing. We have no figures for the fifth century. In the fourth we have a full record of one year's concessions (367-6), when the sums paid totalled 3,690 drachmae, and a partial record of a later year—probably 342-1—when the revenue came to about 3 talents.[99] There was probably a royalty payment of one twenty-fourth in addition to the prices paid for concessions.[100] It is somewhat mysterious where the 400 talents of Athenian revenue came from, but a negligible proportion of it arose even indirectly from slave labour.

The charge brought by fifth-century oligarchic critics (and thoughtlessly repeated by many modern writers), that the Athenian democracy depended for its political pay on the tribute of the subject allies, was brought to the test of fact when Athens lost her empire in 404 B.C., and was proved to be a calumny when the democracy continued to pay the citizens for their political functions out of domestic revenues. The modern charge that the Athenian democracy was dependent on slave labour was never brought to the test, since the Athenians never freed all their slaves. This is not surprising, for slavery was an established institution, which most people accepted without question as 'according to nature,' and to abolish it would have meant a wholesale disregard of the rights of property, which the Athenians throughout their history were careful to respect. It is more surprising that on some occasions of crisis motions for a partial or wholesale freeing of slaves were carried. In 406 all male slaves of military age were freed and granted the citizenship to man the ships which won the battle of Arginusae.[101] After the expulsion of the Thirty in 403, Thrasybulus, the left-wing leader of the restored democracy, carried a measure, later quashed as illegal by the moderate leader Archinus, to free and enfranchise all slaves who had fought for the democracy.[102] In 338, after the defeat of Chaeronea, the left-wing politician Hypereides proposed and carried a motion to free all (able-bodied male) slaves to resist the Macedonians; this motion was again quashed as illegal by a conservative politician.[103]

These facts suggest that there was no bitterness between the mass of the citizens and the slaves, but rather a sense of fellow-feeling. This was a point which shocked contemporary Athenian oligarchs. The 'Old Oligarch' speaks bitterly of the insolence of slaves at Athens, and complains that it is illegal to strike them—the reason, he explains, is that the people are indistinguishable in dress and general appearance from slaves, and it would be easy to strike a citizen by mistake.[104] The moderate oligarch Theramenes is careful to assure his colleagues among the Thirty that he is not one of 'those who think there would not be a good democracy until slaves and those who through poverty would sell the city for a drachma participate in it'.[105] Plato mocks at the excess of freedom in the democracy, in which 'men and women who have been sold are no less free than their purchasers'.[106]

Though the Athenians treated their slaves with a humanity which was exceptional according to the standards of the time, they never abolished slavery, and the charge that Athenian democracy was dependent on their labour was never brought to the test of fact. But had Hypereides' motion been allowed to stand, and extended to slaves of all ages and both sexes, it would not seem, on the basis of the evidence cited earlier in this article, that its effects would have been catastrophic. All wealthy and well-to-do citizens (or rather their wives and unmarried daughters) would have been incommoded by having to do their own housework. A very small number of wealthy or comfortably off men who had invested all their money in mining and industrial slaves would have been reduced to penury, and a larger number, but still a small minority, would have lost the proportion of their income which derived from industrial slaves, and would have had to let their farms instead of cultivating them by slave labour. A number of craftsmen would have lost their apprentices and journeymen. But the great majority of Athenians who owned no slaves but cultivated their own little farms or worked on their own as craftsmen, shopkeepers or labourers would have been unaffected.

II

THE ATHENS OF DEMOSTHENES

The Athens of Demosthenes

DEMOSTHENES' aims and policy have often been discussed, but his biographers have rarely paid much attention to the Athenians to whom he spoke. We are left with the general impression that, in contrast with the patriotic orator, they were an idle, cowardly, pleasure-loving crew, who would not fight or pay their taxes, but preferred to draw their dole at home, paying—or rather failing to pay—mercenaries to fight their battles. Is this estimate just? It is the picture which appears to emerge from Demosthenes' speeches, which, with those of contemporary orators, afford almost all the evidence available. This evidence I propose to examine afresh.

'Pay war tax' (*εἰσφέρετε*) and 'serve yourselves in the army' (*αὐτοὶ στρατεύεσθε*) are the two key-notes of Demosthenes' appeals to the people. Let us first examine the war tax. It is a highly technical and controversial subject, and I hope that you will excuse me if I am somewhat dogmatic. The questions which I wish to answer are: Was it, as is generally believed, a progressive tax? How many people paid it, and what was the limit of exemption? How much money was actually raised?

The *eisphora* was a war tax, raised by decree of the people as occasion demanded, and took the form of a capital levy. For this purpose a census of property was held in 378/7 B.C., in which according to Polybius 'the total assessment' (*τὸ σύμπαν τίμημα*) of Attica was valued at 5750 talents;[1] Demosthenes speaks of 'the assessment of the country' (*τὸ τίμημα . . . τῆς χώρας*) as being in his day 6,000 talents, and reckons levies as percentages of this sum —1 per cent. will bring in 60 talents, 2 per cent. 120 talents and so forth.[2] Now Polybius clearly thought that the 'assessment' represented the total capital (land, houses and other property) of the country—he ignores the fact that it excludes properties below the exemption limit—and represented its real value. Demosthenes, however, in one passage of his first speech against Aphobus[3] uses 'assessment' in another sense: 'three talents is the assessment of fifteen talents', he says (*πεντεκαίδεκα ταλάντων γὰρ τρία τάλαντα τίμημα*), and he implies that for smaller fortunes the proportion was less than one-fifth. On this passage, together with an obscure citation in Pollux,[4] has been built the theory that the 'assessment' was not the real value of a man's property, but the taxable value, and that the taxable value was a higher proportion of the real value for the rich than for the poor, so that the *eisphora* was the only known progressive tax of antiquity.

This theory involves very serious difficulties. In the first place it seems very perverse that even the richest should be assessed at one-fifth of their capital; the natural course would have been to assess them at the whole, and scale down the assessment of the poorer classes only. In the second place the theory conflicts with a contemporary inscription,[5] a lease in which the tenant is to pay 54 drachmae a year rent and the *eisphorae*, if any, 'according to the assessment, viz. 7 minae' (*κατὰ τὸ τίμημα καθ' ἑπτὰ μνᾶς*); the rent works out at about 8 per cent. if 7 minae is the real value of the property, but is absurd if the real value is five or more times that sum. It also makes the 'total assessment' of Attica absurd. Six thousand talents is perhaps rather a low sum, but it excludes, we must remember, thousands of small properties below the exemption limit, and, as frequent allusions in the orators show,[6] concealment of wealth and under-assessment were the rule rather than the exception. On the other hand it is quite impossible that the value of Athenian property assessable for tax can have been not merely five times 6,000 talents, but much more. 'Assessment' is then used in two senses—to denote the real value in the inscription and in the phrase 'the assessment of the country' and as Demosthenes uses it in the first speech against Aphobus. And moreover the tax was levied on the assessment in the first sense of real value, or Demosthenes' calculation that a 1 per cent. levy will yield 60 talents is nonsense. Demosthenes must be using the word in an untechnical way in the passage in which he states that the 'assessment' of 15 talents is 3 talents for the largest fortunes.

Now Demosthenes alludes several times to this 1:5 ratio, but in all the other passages[7] he uses different phraseology: 'they expected me to pay this tax' (*ταύτην ἠξίουν εἰσφέρειν τὴν εἰσφοράν*), he says, or 'to pay 500 drachmae per 25 minae' (*κατὰ τὰς πέντε καὶ εἴκοσι μνᾶς πεντακοσίας δραχμὰς εἰσφέρειν*), as if his guardians put him down to pay one-fifth of his fortune as tax. Of course tax was never levied at this fantastic rate—actually during the ten years of his minority Demosthenes paid 18 minae on the 15 talents at which he was assessed.[8] What do Demosthenes' phrases mean? Mr. Meiggs[9] has recently suggested that the one-fifth is a ceiling, the highest sum which the richest class could be asked to pay as the total of all their tax payments during their lifetime; for the poorer categories of taxpayers this ceiling would be lower. *Eisphora* was then levied as a given percentage of the real value of all taxable properties, and was not a progressive tax: but if successive levies came to a total of say a twentieth (the actual figures are unknown) of their capital, men of the poorest class could claim exemption, while men of the richest class would go on paying till a fifth of their capital was exhausted.

The theory is attractive in that it gives a meaning to Demosthenes' phraseology and tallies with Greek ways of thinking: they tended to regard a man's fortune as a static sum, ignoring income, and to set off against it the total of his payments on trierarchies, liturgies and war tax.[10] But to put such a system into practice would have involved calculations of great complexity; for in fact fortunes were not static, but rose and fell by inheritances and investment of surplus income on the one hand, and payment of dowries and sales of assets on the other. I find it hard to believe

C

that so complicated a system could have worked and I submit an alternative explanation of Demosthenes' words, which was suggested to me by my former pupil, Mr. de Ste Croix.[11] In one passage Demosthenes states that his guardians made him president (ἡγεμών) of his symmory not on a small valuation but on so high a one as to pay 500 drachmae on 25 minae.[12] Now the presidents with the second and third men (δεύτεροι and τρίτοι) of the symmories later constituted the Three Hundred,[13] who advanced the tax to the State (οἱ προεισφέροντες), subsequently recovering it from the other members of their symmories. May it not be that this system existed from the beginning of the symmories, and that it was liability for this prepayment of tax (προεισφορά) which was scaled up to one-fifth of the payer's fortune according to his wealth?

There are difficulties in this view also. There were in 357 arrears amounting to about 14 talents on the 300-odd talents which had been demanded in the previous twenty years.[14] Some of these arrears may have been due from members of the Three Hundred: it is perhaps significant that of the individual debtors mentioned by Demosthenes two are known to have been trierarchs,[15] and must therefore have been fairly wealthy men, who might have been enrolled in the Three Hundred. But at any rate half of the total arrears was made up out of quite small sums, scarcely any according to Demosthenes over 1 mina;[16] which implies 400 or 500 debtors. How did all these taxpayers still owe money to the treasury if their tax had been advanced by the Three Hundred? They might still owe money to members of the Three Hundred, but not to the State.

Two answers are possible. It may be that the 'prepayment' was a device designed for use in emergencies only, and was rarely or not at all employed in the twenty years in question. Or again the original function of the Three Hundred may have been not to prepay but to guarantee or underwrite the tax of their symmories; this is perhaps suggested by the use of 'pay' (εἰσφέρειν) and not 'prepay' (προεισφέρειν) in connection with the Three

Hundred in the earliest reference to them.[17] In that case the guarantee may well never have been enforced, for there was little enthusiasm to collect the tax when once the emergency which had demanded it was past.[18]

The second difficulty is that when in 362 an emergency levy was raised to finance a naval expedition, the people decreed that the members of the council should nominate on behalf of their demes persons who were members of the deme or owned land in it to advance the levy to the State.[19] Here the Three Hundred are entirely ignored, and it has generally been assumed that they did not yet exist. It was, on the usual view, the emergency of 362 which first called for a 'prepayment' and the procedure described above was a first experiment, which led to the establishment of the standing body of Three Hundred.

One objection to this view is that, in a speech delivered a few years before, Isaeus[20] alludes to the Three Hundred as an established institution connected with the *eisphora*. A second is that about 376 (that is directly after the establishment of the symmory system) Demosthenes was made president of his symmory, though a child of 7, because of his wealth: the post of president, that is, was not executive but carried financial responsibility from the first. It seems a necessary inference that the Three Hundred comprising the presidents, second and third men of the 100 symmories were from the beginning financially responsible for the tax due from their groups, either by prepaying or by underwriting it. Indeed this would seem to be the whole point of the symmory system.

It was not then because the Three Hundred did not yet exist that the people in 362 decreed that persons be nominated *ad hoc* in each deme to prepay the tax. It may be that a 'prepayment' had been levied very recently, and that the Three Hundred had claimed that their hands were already full; if there had been a levy in the previous year they could, since the 'prepayment' was a liturgy, have legally claimed exemption.[21] Or alternatively it may be that the symmory system through long disuse had become so disorganised that when a sudden emergency arose it had to be abandoned and *ad hoc* measures adopted. In favour of this view it may be noted that the emergency legislation ignores not only the Three Hundred but, it would seem, the whole symmory system: for it is implied that the collection was made not by symmories but by demes.[22] It may even be that this levy was not a normal *eisphora*, but a special tax on some other basis, substituted for it either because the capacity of the war taxpayers was temporarily exhausted or because the machinery for assessing and collecting a war tax was seriously out of gear. The speaker uses the words *προεισφέρειν* and *προεισφορά*, but these may not be technical terms but mean merely 'to prepay a levy'. On the other hand he alludes to the magistrates who were in charge of the levy as 'the collectors of the military fund' (*οἱ τὰ στρατιωτικὰ εἰσπράττοντες*),[23] which suggests a special military levy rather than a regular war tax.

The object of this long argument has been to prove that the *eisphora* was not a progressive tax, that is, that all liable to it paid the same proportion of their capital, whether they were rich or poor. Now for my second question, How many citizens paid? That the number was large is implied by Demosthenes' language in several passages; he speaks for instance of the mass of the people (*τῷ πλήθει τῷ ὑμετέρῳ*) as being exhausted by payment of war tax.[24] A rather more precise answer is, I think, possible. There were, it is generally agreed, 100 war tax symmories as against 20 trierarchic symmories.[25] The 20 trierarchic symmories, which were modelled on those of the *eisphora* , comprised 1,200 persons, at 60 per symmory.[26] The 100 war tax symmories on the same basis will have included 6,000 persons. What was the exemption limit? Demosthenes several times alludes to 25 minae as a basic assessment unit—'to pay 500 drachmae per 25 minae' (*κατὰ τὰς πέντε καὶ εἴκοσι μνᾶς πεντακοσίας δραχμὰς εἰσφέρειν*)[27] and, on one occasion, even more significantly assumes it as such —'you assessed me to pay 5 minae' (*πέντε μνᾶς συνετάξατ' εἰσφέρειν*), meaning to pay one-fifth.[28] This suggests that 25 minae was the minimum taxable capital. This would accord with what other figures we have. In 322 B.C. Antipater, limiting the franchise to citizens owing over 2,000 drachmae (or 20 minae), found that there were 9,000 who qualified.[29] If there were 9,000 persons who owned more than 20 minae each, there might well be about 6,000 who owned more than 25 minae.

Finally, how much war tax was actually levied? In his speech against Androtion Demosthenes tells us that the levies between 377 and 357 totalled perhaps 300 talents or a little more;[30] this works out at 0.25 per cent. per annum on the assessment of 6,000 talents. Demosthenes during his ten years' minority (376-366) paid 18 minae on his assessment of 15 talents,[31] which works out at about 0.2 per cent. per annum. This is on capital, of course, but reckoning income as 10 per cent. of capital, which is about right taking land and money together, levies during this period, which was full of wars, represented only a 2 to 2½ per cent. income tax, or in modern terms 5d. to 6d. in the pound. We may therefore with some justification be amused when Xenophon speaks of the Athenians during this very time as 'worn out by levies of war tax' (ἀποκναιόμενοι χρημάτων εἰσφοραῖς).[32] But taxation is a matter of habit—our great-grandfathers were outraged by an extra penny in the pound—and the Athenians never could form the habit of paying war tax since it was an occasional payment and, when it came, relatively heavy—Demosthenes speaks of 1 per cent. and even 2 per cent. as normal,[33] and these are equivalent to an income tax of 2s. and 4s. in the pound. And before we blame the Athenians too loudly we should remember that there was no personal allowance, wife's allowance or children's allowance to soften the blow to the poor man with a large family. Demosthenes is probably justified in invoking the jurors' sympathy for 'the farmers who pinch and scrape, but owing to the cost of bringing up their children and domestic expenses and other public demands have fallen into arrears of war tax.'[34] It must have meant much pinching to bring up a family on a farm worth 25 minae. One litigant, indeed, states that 'my father left me and my brother property of only 45 minae each, and it is not easy to live on that'.[35] On the basis of the single fourth-century figure that we possess for the price of land,[36] a farm worth 25 minae would have comprised about 7 acres—without stock, implements, house or furniture. If let at the rate of 8 per cent. which seems to have been normal,[37] it would have brought in a rent of 200 drachmae a year; and bare food for a single man, without counting clothes, shoes or any extras, cost 180 drachmae.[38] The proprietor of such a holding normally of course worked it himself with the aid of his family, and would make a larger income than the rental value, but even so little enough to feed a family.

An ill-adjusted system of war tax meant then that while the rich got off relatively very lightly, the mass of poor taxpayers were really embarrassed by even an occasional small levy, and were very reluctant to vote one. Actually very little was raised. How then did Athens pay for her wars? For the answer one may turn to Isocrates' panegyric on Timotheus.[39] Timotheus' great merit, it appears, was that he was a very cheap general. He received only 13 talents from the treasury for his great campaign round the Peloponnese in which he won Corcyra in 375. Apollodorus gives a vivid picture of his financial straits two years later, when he had to mortgage his estates and borrow right and left to keep his sixty ships together,[40] and Iphicrates, his successor, had to hire out his rowers as agricultural labourers in the intervals between operations.[41] For the campaign which resulted in the capture of Samos in 365 Timotheus received no public funds, and he financed the capture of Potidaea and other Thraceward cities in the following year from the contributions of the local allies.

These facts affect Demosthenes' second slogan, hoplite service. The Athenians cannot be accused of cowardice. They turned out for campaigns in the good old fifth-century style in Boeotia, Euboea, the Peloponnese and even as far afield as Thessaly. In 369 they raised a levy *en masse* in support of Sparta against Thebes;

6,000 fought at Mantinea in 362; 5,000 foot and 400 horse at Thermopylae in 352. For Chaeronea there was a levy *en masse*, and 5,000 foot and 500 horse fought in the Lamian war.[42] The Athenians did not object to fighting. What they were afraid of may be deduced from the scheme for a small standing army which Demosthenes put forward in the *First Philippic*. The Athenian element is to serve for a fixed period, not a long one at that, by a regular system of reliefs;[43] and the State, he insists, must make financial provision for paying them a ration allowance at the meagre rate of 2 obols a day[44]—by way of comparison ephebes (young men doing their military training in Attica) were allowed 4 obols a day for their food under Lycurgus' régime,[45] and even public slaves got 3 obols a day.[46] They will make up the balance, Demosthenes euphemistically hopes, 'from the war'.

In two other passages Demosthenes implies that hoplites were normally expected to keep themselves. In the *de Falsa Legatione*[47] he estimates the cost of the expedition to Thermopylae at 200 talents, 'if you count the private expenditure of those who served', and in the *First Olynthiac*[48] he asserts that 'if you had to serve abroad yourselves for only thirty days, and take what you would need on service from the produce of the country—while no enemy was in the country, I mean—those of you who are farmers would I think suffer a heavier loss than all you have spent on the war up to date'.

What the Athenian hoplite dreaded, then, was being shipped off to Macedonia and left there to starve for an indefinite period, while the farm or the business at home went to rack and ruin. Things were very different from the good old days of the fifth century, when a hoplite got 2 drachmae a day.[49] And it must be remembered that many hoplites were quite poor men; the qualification is generally, and probably correctly, believed to have been property to the value of 2,000 drachmae[50]—roughly 5 acres and a cow. Demosthenes in the *Meidias* is quite apologetic for introducing to the jury a poor hoplite witness—'he is poor may be, but not a rascal' (πένης μὲν ἴσως ἐστίν, οὐ πονηρὸς δέ γε)—a curious remark in a speech devoted to abuse of the rich man Meidias.[51] Lysias' client Mantitheus, when his deme assembled for the muster, found that many of his poorer fellow hoplites could not raise their journey money and organized a subscription to supply each with 30 drachmae.[52]

The same considerations applied a *fortiori* to naval service, which Demosthenes also frequently urged on the citizens, since it was thetes who served in the fleet. It may be noted that at this period Athens could not rely on volunteers to row her triremes, but conscription was regularly employed.[53] If one reads Apollodorus' speech against Polycles one realises why. Gone were the days of a drachma a day;[54] for two months only did the men get any pay, for the remaining year and five months only rations, and even the ration money was often short, and failed altogether for the return voyage.[55] For a man with a wife and family to keep this meant disaster, and it is little wonder if, as Apollodorus says, whenever a trireme put back to Athens in the middle of the year, large numbers deserted and the rest refused to sail again unless they were given something to provide for their families (εἰς διοίκησιν τῶν οἰκείων).[56]

Lack of public funds naturally increased the expenses of trierarchs also. In 373 Timotheus made his sixty trierarchs each advance 7 minae to feed their crews[57]: he being a rich man was able to cover this advance by mortgages on his estates, but other trierarchs were less fortunate; Apollodorus had to borrow freely from his father's correspondents overseas.[58] The main vice of the trierarchy, however, was the faulty working of the symmory system. Trierarchic symmories were introduced in 357 B.C.[59] because the trierarchy or syntrierarchy, whereby one or two men were responsible for the upkeep of a trireme for one year, was found too heavy a burden on some of the persons liable. But no rules seem to have been laid down for sharing the expenses within the symmory and the general practice was that all members paid an equal share. This resulted, as Demosthenes explains in the *Meidias* and the *de Corona*, in the richest members, who could well afford to be sole trierarchs two or three times over, paying one-sixteenth of a trierarchy, while the same amount was paid by the poorer members of the 1,200 who could ill afford it.[60] Demosthenes' first scheme of reform, set out in the speech on the symmories, was ill conceived; he proposed, it is true, to make payments proportional to property, but he also suggested spreading the burden yet wider over the whole body of war taxpayers.[61] The result would have been to make the trierarchy a supplementary war tax, with all its unfairness. Later Demosthenes grasped the real point, and threw the whole burden of the trierarchy on the 300 richest citizens in proportion to their means, so that some performed two trierarchies.[62]

You have no doubt been long waiting for me to mention the *theoricon*, which occupies a larger space in Demosthenes' commentators than in his speeches, and was of greater political than financial importance—as Demosthenes himself says, 'The sum of money about which you are debating is small, but the habit of mind which goes with it is important'.[63] The fund consisted of the annual surplus of regular revenue over peace-time expenses (*τὰ περιόντα χρήματα τῆς διοικήσεως*)—in war time the surplus went by law to the war fund (*τὰ στρατιωτικά*)[64]—and was used for making distributions to the citizens at the rate of 2 obols a head on some festival days.[65] According to Demosthenes even the well-to-do drew it;[66] let us then suppose that of the 21,000 citizens[67] as many as 18,000 actually took the money. The cost would then be 1 talent per day.

The number of distributions varied according to the state of the fund. One lexicographer mentions a drachma as the total in 395—394 B.C.;[68] that is three distributions were made, probably for the three days of the Dionysia. Another lexicographer speaks of payments for the Dionysia and the Panathenaea[69]—six days in all. Hypereides[70] mentions a man who impersonated his son who was abroad, and was fined a talent for the sake of 5 drachmae; this sum he may well have drawn over several years. But assuming that 5 drachmae represents a year's takings, that is that distributions were made on as many as fifteen days, the annual expenditure would be 15 talents, or one-quarter of a 1 per cent. *eisphora*.

The only evidence that large sums were involved is an anecdote in Plutarch,[71] that when the Athenians were eager to launch a fleet to assist the rebels against Alexander, Demades quenched their ardour by stating that the money would have to come from a sum which he had reserved for a distribution at the rate of 50 drachmae a head for the feast of the Choes. If this anecdote has any historical basis, I am inclined to link it with another, according to which Lycurgus (very uncharacteristically) distributed the confiscated estate of one Diphilus to the people at the rate of 50 drachmae (or some say 1 mina) a head.[72] The incident will presumably have taken place in 331, when King Agis was taking the field, and Demades and Lycurgus seem to have been working together to keep Athens out of the war. This payment of 50 drachmae was then not a normal theoric distribution, but a special bonus, arising from a windfall to the treasury.

Be that as it may, all the evidence shows that in the middle of the fourth century the *theoricon* must have been financially very small beer, and Demosthenes was rather foolish to make himself and his policy unpopular by trying to transfer it to the war fund even in peace time. When the revenue was as low as 130 talents a year, it was no doubt irritating to see even half a dozen talents squandered, and Demosthenes fell into Eubulus' trap. Later, when the revenue had risen to 400 talents, he changed his mind, and in the *Fourth Philippic* he argues—somewhat sophistically—in favour of the *theoricon*.[73] Politically the *theoricon* was, as Demades put it, 'the glue of the democracy' (*ἡ κόλλα τῆς δημοκρατίας*),[74] because all classes found it useful. The poor, which would include not only the thetes but a substantial proportion of the hoplites, naturally found even so tiny a dole very acceptable, since it enabled them to enjoy their festivals with a clear conscience. To the rich it was a valuable political weapon for the policy of peace or appeasement which they favoured. Eubulus could threaten not only *eisphorae*, which affected only 6,000 voters, but the transfer of the *theoricon* to the war fund, which affected all the citizens, if the assembly would not vote for the Peace of Philocrates.[75] Meidias could say, 'Do you expect me to pay war tax for you while you receive distributions?'[76] A large part of the *Fourth Philippic* is devoted to combating the argument of the well-to-do citizens that they cannot be expected to pay war tax and perform trierarchies if the poor draw their dole.[77]

It is somewhat paradoxical that the leaders of the peace party should have been a group of the very wealthy men who, owing to the inefficiency of the Athenian financial machine, contributed least in proportion to their means to war expenses. But, this being so, this very inefficiency played into their hands, for war inflicted disproportionate hardship on every other class. Even the well-to-do, the less wealthy of the 1,200 members of the trierarchic symmories, bore an unfair proportion of naval expenses. The more modest war taxpayers were hard pressed to pay their share of the levy. The humble hoplites and the thetes looked forward with dread to being called up for prolonged unpaid foreign service in the army and the fleet, and moreover had to sacrifice their theoric doles. It was these last who really suffered the most by war, yet it was they who, if roused to action, voted for war. On Alexander's death, Diodorus[78] tells us, the men of property (*οἱ κτηματικοί*) urged that Athens stay quiet, and it was the masses (*τὰ πλήθη*) who responded to the appeals of the orators of the war party, and declared the Lamian war, in which Athens played so prominent and so creditable a part.

It is understandable that the masses should have required some rousing to vote for war, when it meant such hardship for them. What is less easy to understand is why, once involved in war, they did not vote levies of tax which would have provided them with adequate pay for hoplite and naval service. The war taxpayers numbered only about 6,000, well under a third of the total citizen body of 21,000, and one might have expected the majority of the assembly to vote eagerly for a tax which they would not have to pay. In this connection it is worth noting the language that Demosthenes uses. He never urges the poor to soak the rich; on the contrary he appeals to the assembly to pay tax themselves. In every passage save one the war taxpayers are alluded to in the second person,[79] and the one exception is significant. It is in the speech on the symmories, where Demosthenes is curbing a warlike assembly and deprecating a levy; here he says, 'Suppose *you* want *us* to pay an $8\frac{1}{3}$ per cent. tax?'[80] The inference seems to be that, contrary to general belief, the average assembly was attended mainly by the relatively well-to-do citizens, so that the war taxpayers were, if not in a majority, a substantial part of the audience, and that it was only at moments of crisis—the speech on the symmories was delivered to combat a war scare that the Persian king was about to attack Athens—that the poorer classes came in force and might outvote those who would have to pay the tax.

If this was so in the assembly, it was even more markedly so in the law courts, where so many political issues were ultimately decided by way of the indictment for illegal proceedings (*γραφὴ παρανόμων*). We generally picture the law courts as manned by the very poor, eager to earn their 3 obols, but the language of Demosthenes and his contemporaries is hardly consistent with this view. The *Meidias*, with its constant appeal to prejudice against wealth, might seem at first sight to support it. But Meidias is represented as very rich, and moreover ostentatious, a bully and a shirker of his public obligations, and it is noteworthy that Demosthenes finds it necessary to apologise for introducing a really poor witness, the arbitrator Strato, who is a hoplite.[81] The speech might well have been delivered to an audience of well-to-do propertied persons (*οἱ εὔποροι* or *οἱ τὰς οὐσίας ἔχοντες* are phrases of commendation in other speeches), who would probably dislike an insolent rich man (*πλούσιος* is consistently a term of abuse) more than would the very poor. In the *Androtion* and the *Timocrates* Demosthenes depicts the woes of the humbler payers of war tax in a way which he evidently expects to excite the sympathy of his audience—a really poor audience would not have felt very indignant at Androtion's distraining his victims' single maidservants when they had none themselves.[82] The *Leptines* is a very strange speech to deliver to a poor audience. Not a word is said about the effect of the law on the masses, in their capacity of either audiences to the spectacles produced by the choregi or of dancers in the choruses.[83] Leptines' plea was that his law would relieve the (comparatively) poor from the burden of liturgies by abolishing the exemptions of the rich, and Demosthenes tries to prove that the quashing of the law will not adversely affect the class who had to undertake liturgies:[84] his speech must have been addressed to a jury drawn mainly from that class. Even more revealing is a remark in Deinarchus' speech against Demosthenes,[85] where he appeals to any jurors who were members of the Three Hundred when Demosthenes passed his trierarchic law to tell their neighbours how he was bribed to amend it. Such an appeal would have been ridiculous unless members of the Three Hundred, the richest men in Athens, frequently sat on juries.

Upon reflection this is not unnatural. The greatest political issues and the fate of statesmen were decided in the courts. Would it not be prudent for leading politicians to get their supporters to enrol in the 6,000 jurors? They were not obliged to empanel themselves every day for minor cases, but could turn out in force when a *cause célèbre* was to be tried. And there was probably little competition for enrolment as a juror; a working man could not keep a family on 3 obols a day—he could only just feed himself—and he could earn three times as much even by casual unskilled labour.[86] Why the poor did not attend assemblies, where the pay was better—a drachma or even 9 obols—is more difficult to explain. They perhaps found the intricacies of politics as run by the professionals (*οἱ πολιτευόμενοι*) baffling, and were frustrated by finding every decree they passed taken to the courts and quashed under the indictment for illegal proceedings.

This analysis has, I hope, helped to explain against what heavy odds Demosthenes was battling in his great struggle for Athenian democracy, and at the same time given you a more sympathetic understanding of the Athenian people to whom he spoke.

III

THE ATHENIAN DEMOCRACY AND ITS CRITICS

The Athenian Democracy and its Critics[1]

IT IS curious that in the abundant literature produced in the greatest democracy of Greece there survives no statement of democratic political theory. All the Athenian political philosophers and publicists whose works we possess were in various degrees oligarchic in sympathy. The author of the pamphlet on the 'Constitution of the Athenians' preserved among Xenophon's works is bitterly hostile to democracy. Socrates, so far as we can trace his views from the works of Xenophon and Plato, was at least highly critical of democracy. Plato's views on the subject are too well known to need stating. Isocrates in his earlier years wrote panegyrics of Athens, but in his old age, when he wrote his more philosophical works, became increasingly embittered against the political régime of his native city. Aristotle is the most judicial in his attitude, and states the pros and cons, but his ideal was a widely based oligarchy. With the historians of Athens, the same bias is evident. Only Herodotus is a democrat, but his views have not carried much weight, partly because of his reputation for naïveté, and partly because his explicit evidence refers to a period before the full democracy had evolved. Thucydides is hostile: in one of the very few passages in which he reveals his personal views he expresses approval of a régime which disfranchised about two-thirds of the citizens, those who manned the fleet on which the survival of Athens depended. Xenophon was an ardent admirer of the Spartan régime. Aristotle, in the historical part of his monograph on the Constitution of Athens, followed—rather uncritically—a source with a marked oligarchic bias. Only the fourth-century orators were democrats; and their speeches, being concerned with practical political issues—mostly of foreign policy—or with private litigation, have little to say on the basic principles of democracy, which they take for granted.[2]

The surviving literature is certainly not representative of Athenian public opinion. The majority of Athenians were proud of their constitution and deeply attached to it. The few counter-revolutions—in 411, 404, 322 and 317—were carried out by small extremist cliques, in 411 after a carefully planned campaign of deception and terror, in the other three cases with the aid of a foreign conqueror, and all were short-lived, being rapidly overwhelmed by the mass of the citizens. Nor was it only the poor majority, who most obviously benefited from the system, that were its supporters. Most of the great statesmen and generals of Athens came from wealthy families, and a substantial number from the nobility of birth; the leaders of the popular risings which unseated the oligarchic governments of 411 and 403 were men of substance.

Since, however, the majority were mute—in the literature which has survived—it is not an easy task to discern what they considered the merits of democracy to be, or, indeed, on what principles they thought that a good constitution should be based. Democratic political theory can only be tentatively reconstructed from scattered allusions. For the basic ideals of democracy the best source is the series of panegyrics on Athens. The most famous of these, Pericles' Funeral Speech, as recorded by Thucydides, is also the most instructive; its peculiarities of diction and its general tone, which is in conflict with Thucydides' own outlook, suggest that it is a fairly faithful reproduction of what Pericles really said. There is an early fourth-century Funeral Speech attributed to Lysias, which contains some useful material. Little for our purposes can be drawn from Isocrates' *Panegyricus* and *Panathenaicus*. A curious document of this class is the skit on a Funeral Speech contained in Plato's *Menexenus*, which seems close enough to type to be used—with reservations—as a statement of democratic principles. To these documents, which too often only repeat banal generalities, may be added *obiter dicta* in the political and forensic speeches of the orators, when they appeal to some general principle. Among these may be included some political speeches in Thucydides, which, though placed in a Sicilian setting, doubtless are modelled on Athenian prototypes. Another important source is the actual constitution of Athens, from whose rules general principles can sometimes be deduced. But our most valuable evidence comes from the criticisms of adversaries, which are so much more fully reported than anything from the democratic side. This evidence, though copious, is tricky to evaluate and must be used with caution. We must distinguish criticism on points of principle, where a democrat would have accepted his opponent's statement of the democratic point of view as correct, and would have argued that the principle or institution criticised was in fact a good one; and criticism on points of practice, which a democrat would have endeavoured to rebut, arguing that the accusations were untrue, or alternatively that the abuses alleged were regrettable but accidental and remediable defects of democracy.

It is the object of this paper to reconstruct from these sources democratic political theory and then to determine how far in practice the Athenian people lived up to its principles. The procedure will be to take up the various lines of criticism advanced by oligarchic critics, and to work out on what lines democrats would have answered them, using for this purpose the scattered evidence outlined above. The criticisms of the philosophical writers will be analysed first, and then those of the historians—or rather of Thucydides, who alone demands discussion. This distinction in the source of the criticism corresponds with a division in subject-matter, for the philosophers confine their attacks almost entirely to the internal working of democracy, while Thucydides is primarily interested in Athenian foreign and imperial policy.

The first and most basic charge brought by the philosophers against democracy is best expressed by Aristotle in his characteristic terse direct style: 'in such democracies each person lives as he likes; or in the words of Euripides "according to his fancy". This is a bad thing.'[3] This is no isolated text. Aristotle returns to the point elsewhere.[4] Isocrates in the *Areopagiticus*[5] declares that in the good old days it was not the case that the citizens 'had many supervisors in their education but as soon as they reached man's estate were allowed to do what they liked', and urges that the Areopagus should recover its alleged pristine power of controlling the private lives of all the citizens. Plato in the *Republic*[6] complains that under a democracy 'the city is full of liberty and free speech and everyone in it is allowed to do what he likes. . . each man in it could plan his own life as he pleases'. He then enlarges on the deplorable results of this, that the citizens are various, instead of conforming to one type, and that foreigners and even women and slaves are as free as the citizens.[7]

An Athenian democrat would no doubt have demurred at the last charge, though admitting with some pride that foreigners and slaves were exceptionally well treated at Athens,[8] but he certainly gloried in the accusation of liberty. Freedom of action and of speech were the proudest slogans of Athens, and not only political but personal freedom; as Pericles says in the Funeral Speech,[9] 'we live as free citizens both in our public life and in our attitude to one another in the affairs of daily life; we are not angry with our neighbour if he behaves as he pleases, we do not cast sour looks at him, which, if they can do no harm, cause pain'. Freedom of speech was particularly prized.[10] As Demosthenes[11] says, 'in Sparta you are not allowed to praise the laws of Athens or of this state or that, far from it, you have to praise what agrees with their constitution', whereas in Athens criticism of the democracy was freely permitted. One only has to read the works of Isocrates, Plato and Aristotle to see that this is true. The condemnation of Socrates is an apparent exception to the rule, but as Xenophon's[12] account of the matter shows, the real gravamen of the charge against Socrates was that, of his pupils, Alcibiades had done more than any other one man to ruin Athens in the recent war, and Critias had been the ruthless ringleader of the

Thirty, who had massacred thousands of Athenians a few years before.

The second main charge against democracy is most neatly stated by Plato:[13] that 'it distributes a kind of equality to the equal and the unequal alike'. The same point is made by Isocrates,[14] who distinguishes 'two equalities; one allots the same to every one and the other what is appropriate to each'. and alleges that in the good old days the Athenians 'rejected as unjust the equality which considers the good and the bad worthy of the same rights, and chose that which honours each according to his worth'. Aristotle[15] argues similarly, though he is justifiably sceptical about the criterion according to which rights are to be scaled; in democracy freedom is the criterion, that is, all free men are equal, and this is in Aristotle's view unjust, but so in his opinion are the only practical alternative criteria, wealth or birth.

Democrats in general approved of the egalitarian principle.[16] Demosthenes in one passage[17] argues that what makes all citizens public spirited and generous is 'that in a democracy each man considers that he himself has a share in equality and justice'. and in another[18] praises a law forbidding legislation directed against individuals as being good democratic doctrine, 'for as everyone has an equal share in the rest of the constitution, so everyone is entitled to an equal share in the laws'. The Athenians were not, however, either in theory or in practice, absolute egalitarians, but drew a distinction between different political functions. On one point they admitted no compromise—equality before the law; as Pericles[19] says, 'in their private disputes all share equality according to the laws'. This to us elementary principle needed emphasis, for Plato's friends in the Thirty, when they drew up a new constitution, ordained that only the 3,000 full citizens were entitled to a legal trial and that all others might be summarily executed by order of the government.[20] It was secured in the Athenian constitution not only by the right of every citizen to seek redress in the courts, but by the character of the courts, which consisted of large juries drawn by lot from the whole body of the citizens.

The Athenians also attached great importance to the equality of all citizens in formulating and deciding public policy. This was secured by the right of every citizen to speak and vote in the assembly, and by the composition of the council of Five Hundred, which prepared the agenda of the assembly; this body was annually chosen by lot from all the demes of Attica. Here democratic principle came into conflict with the oligarchic view, developed at length by Plato, that government was an art, demanding the highest skill, and should therefore be entrusted to a select few. On this question Aristotle, whose ideal was a broadly based oligarchy, whose members would not all be experts, took issue with Plato, and the arguments which he uses are applicable to a fully democratic régime, and probably drawn from democratic theory. In the first place[21] he argues that, though each individual in a large assembly may be of poor quality, the sum of their virtue and wisdom taken together may exceed the virtue and wisdom of a select few, just as dinners provided by joint contributions may be better than those provided by one rich host. His second argument[22] is rather more cogent. Politics, he suggests, is one of those arts in which the best judge is not the artist himself but the user of the product. The householder is a better judge of a house than the architect, the steersman of a rudder rather than the carpenter, the eater of a meal rather than the cook. A third justification for democratic practice is put into the mouth of Protagoras by Plato[23] in a passage which so well illustrates the tone of the Athenian assembly that it is worth quoting in full. Socrates is expressing his doubts as to whether political wisdom is teachable.

> I, like the other Greeks (he says), think that the Athenians are wise. Well, I see that when we gather for the assembly, when the city has to do something about buildings, they call for the builders as advisers and when it is about ship construction, the shipwrights, and so on with everything else that can be taught and learned. And if anyone else tries to advise them, whom they do not

think an expert, even if he be quite a gentleman, rich and aristocratic, they none the less refuse to listen, but jeer and boo, until either the speaker himself is shouted down and gives up, or the sergeants at arms, on the order of the presidents, drag him off or remove him. That is how they behave on technical questions. But when the debate is on the general government of the city, anyone gets up and advises them, whether he be a carpenter or a smith or a leather worker, a merchant or a sea-captain, rich or poor, noble or humble, and no one blames them like the others for trying to give advice, when they have not learned from any source and have had no teacher.

Protagoras' reply is in mythological form. Zeus when he created men gave various talents to each, but to all he gave a sense of decency and fair play, since without them any society would be impossible.

So, Socrates, (he concludes) that is why the Athenians and the others, when the debate is about architecture or any other technical question, think that few should take part in the discussion, and if anyone outside the few joins in, do not tolerate it, as you say—rightly in my opinion. But when they come to discuss political questions, which must be determined by justice and moderation, they properly listen to everyone, thinking that everyone shares in these qualities—or cities wouldn't exist.

The Athenians went yet further in their egalitarian principles in that they entrusted the routine administration of the city to boards of magistrates chosen by lot. This aroused the irony of Socrates,[24] who declared that 'it was silly that the rulers of the city should be appointed by lot, when no one would be willing to employ a pilot or a carpenter or a flautist chosen by lot'. It is a proof of the poverty of our information on democratic theory that no reasoned defence of this cardinal institution, the lot, has survived. The nearest thing to it is a comic passage in a private speech of Demosthenes[25] where Mantitheus, pleading against the assumption of his name by his half-brother, raises the hypothetical case that both might put in their names for the ballot for an office or the council, and that the name Mantitheus might be drawn. There would have to be a lawsuit 'and we shall be deprived of our common equality, that the man who wins the ballot holds office: we shall abuse one another and the cleverer speaker will hold the office'. It is implied that the lot was employed to give every citizen an equal chance, without regard to wealth, birth or even popularity or eloquence. This may seem to be carrying principle to extremes, but Socrates' comment is not altogether fair. It was not 'the rulers of the city' who were chosen by lot, but officials charged with limited routine duties, for which little more than 'a sense of decency and fair play' was required. Furthermore, it must be remembered that a magistrate had to pass a preliminary examination, which was, it is true, usually formal, but gave his enemies an opportunity for raking up his past;[26] was liable to be deposed by a vote of the assembly taken ten times a year;[27] and after his year was subject to a scrutiny in which his accounts were audited and any citizen could charge him with inefficiency or abuse of authority.[28] It is unlikely that many rogues or nincompoops would expose themselves to these risks.

Athenian democrats did not believe that all should share alike in the important offices, whose holders to some extent controlled policy. Pericles,[29] after affirming the equality before the law of all citizens, goes on: 'but in public esteem, when a man is distinguished in any way, he is more highly honoured in public life, not as a matter of privilege but in recognition of merit; on the other hand any one who can benefit the city is not debarred by poverty or by the obscurity of his position.' This point is even more strongly put in the mock panegyric in the *Menexenus*:[30]

> For in the main the same constitution existed then as now, an aristocracy, under which we now live and have always lived since then. A man may call it democracy, and another what he will. But in truth it is an aristocracy with the approval of the majority. We have always had kings: sometimes they were hereditary, sometimes elective. In most things the majority is in control of the city, and bestows office and power on those whom it thinks to be the best. No one is rejected for weakness or poverty or humble birth, nor honoured for their opposites, as in other cities. There is one criterion: the man who is thought to be wise and good holds power and rule.

These principles were embodied in the Athenian constitution, whereby all the important magistrates—the ten generals, who not only commanded the army and the fleet but exercised a general control over defence and foreign policy, the other military commanders, and in the fourth century the principal financial magistrates—were elected by the people; a procedure which could be regarded as aristocratic.[31] In fact, the Athenian people were rather snobbish in their choice of leaders.[32] The 'Old Oligarch'[33] sneeringly remarks, 'they do not think that they ought to share by lot in the offices of general or commander of the horse, for the people knows that it gains more by not holding these offices itself but allowing the leading citizens to hold them'. Xenophon[34] records the complaints of Nicomachides, an experienced soldier, that he has been beaten in the elections for the generalship by a rich man who knows nothing about military affairs. Demosthenes, a strong democrat, rakes up Aeschines' humble origins in a fashion which we should hardly consider in good taste, but apparently did not offend an Athenian jury. 'We have judged you, a painter of alabaster boxes and drums, and these junior clerks and nobodies (and there is no harm in such occupations, but on the other hand they are not deserving of a generalship) worthy of ambassadorships, generalships and the highest honours'.[35]

Besides the lot the other instrument whereby the Athenians secured the effective political equality of the citizens was pay. The 6,000 jurors, the council of 500 and the 350 odd magistrates were all paid for their services at various rates; it may be noted that elective magistrates—the military commanders and ambassadors—were paid, and at higher rates than the ordinary magistrates chosen by lot,[36] so that the claim that poverty was no barrier to political power was justified. During the fourth century citizens who attended the assembly—or at least a quorum who arrived first—were also paid. The philosophers objected to this practice. Aristotle[37] criticises it precisely because it fulfilled its purpose of enabling the poor to exercise their political rights. It may, however, be doubted if by his day it was fully effective.

The assembly and the juries seem, from the tone in which the orators address them, to have consisted predominantly of middle-class citizens rather than of the poor,[38] and there is evidence that the council also was mainly filled by the well-to-do.[39] The real value of the State pay had, owing to the progressive rise of prices, sunk considerably by the latter part of the fourth century, and the poor probably preferred more profitable employment. Plato[40] also objects to State pay: 'I am told', he says, 'that Pericles made the Athenians idle and lazy and garrulous and avaricious by first putting them on State pay.' This is an oft-repeated accusation but has very little substance. In a population which never sank below 20,000 adult males and probably reached twice that figure at its peak, the council and the magistracies did not provide employment except on rare occasions; a man might not hold any magistracy more than once, or sit on the council more than twice in his life.[41] Assemblies were held only on forty days in the year.[42] It was only as a juror that a citizen could obtain more or less continuous employment, and here the rate of remuneration was so low—half a labourer's wage in the fifth century and a third in the late fourth, in fact little more than bare subsistence[43]—that in the fifth century, if the picture drawn in Aristophanes' *Wasps* is true, it attracted only the elderly, past hard work, and in the early fourth century, when economic conditions were worse, according to Isocrates, the unemployed.[44]

The third main criticism of democracy comes from Aristotle,[45] that in its extreme (that is, Athenian) form 'the mass of the people (or the 'majority') is sovereign instead of the law; this happens when decrees are valid instead of the law'. It is not entirely clear what Aristotle means by this. He appears here and elsewhere to conceive of the law as an immutable code, laid down by an impartial legislator, against which the will of the citizens, assumed always to be self-interested, should not in an ideal State be allowed to prevail. He may therefore be objecting to any legislation by decision of the majority—or, for that matter, by any constitutional procedure. But this meaning seems to slide into another, that in an extreme democracy the majority in the assembly habitually overrides the existing laws, however established, by arbitrary executive action in particular cases, acting, as he puts it, like the traditional Greek tyrant.

The doctrine of the immobility of law was naturally favoured by oligarchs, who were generally conservative, or, when they wanted to alter the law, professed to be restoring an 'ancestral constitution'. Democrats, who more often wished to change things, might have been expected to work out a more progressive theory. Some thinkers in the fifth century did indeed propound the doctrine that the law was the will of the sovereign. Socrates, according to Xenophon,[46] defined law as 'what the citizens have by agreement enacted on what must be done and what avoided', and was quite prepared to admit that what the citizens enacted they could revoke, just as having declared war they could make peace. Xenophon[47] also reports a no doubt imaginary conversation between Pericles and Alcibiades, in which the former defined law as 'what the mass of the people (or "the majority"), having come together and approved it, decrees, declaring what must and what must not be done'. Led on by Alcibiades he extends this definition to oligarchies and tyrannies, declaring that what the sovereign body or person decrees is law. Asked by Alcibiades what then is violence and lawlessness, Pericles replies 'when the stronger does not persuade the weaker but compels him by force to do what he wants'. This enables Alcibiades after suitable leading questions about tyrants and oligarchies, to ask: 'Would what the whole mass of the people, overpowering the holders of property, enacts without persuading them, be violence rather than law?' Pericles at this point tells Alcibiades to go away and play, leaving the ambiguity in his theory of law unresolved. In the fourth century Demosthenes[48] enunciates a similar view in one passage, asserting that 'the laws lay down about the future (he is denouncing retrospective legislation as undemocratic) what must be done, being enacted by persuasion as they will benefit their users'. Some democrats then conceived of law as the considered will of the majority, adding the rider that the majority should persuade the minority and consider the interests of all.

In general, however, democrats tended like Aristotle to regard the laws as a code laid down once for all by a wise legislator, in their case Solon, which, immutable in principle, might occasionally require to be clarified or supplemented. These were the terms of reference given to the legislative commission set up after the restoration of the democracy in 403.[49] and the standing rules governing legislation show the same spirit. At no time was it legal to alter the law by a simple decree of the assembly. The mover of such a decree was liable to the famous 'indictment for illegal proceedings', which, if upheld by the courts, quashed the decree, and also, if brought within a year, exposed the mover to heavy penalties. In the fifth century additions to the law were prepared by special legislative commissions, and then submitted to the council and assembly,[50] but there seems to have been no constitutional means of altering the existing law.[51] After 403 an elaborate procedure was introduced for revising the law, which took the matter out of the hands of the assembly. Every year the assembly passed the laws under review, and voted on them, section by section, whether they should stand or be revised. If a revision of any section was voted, any citizen was entitled to propound alternative laws, which were given due publicity, and a court of 501 or 1,001 legislators was empanelled. The issue between the old and the proposed laws was then argued judicially (counsel for the old laws being appointed by the assembly), and the legislators, acting as a jury under oath, gave their verdict.[52]

Such was the Athenian theory on legislation. How far it was observed in practice is disputable. Both Demosthenes and Aeschines,[53] when bringing indictments for illegal proceedings, inveigh against the unscrupulous politicians (their opponents) who flout the law, and Demosthenes alleges that as a result 'there are so many contradictory laws that you have for a long while past been electing commissions to resolve the conflict, and none the less the problem can have no end. Laws are no different from decrees, and the laws, according to which decrees ought to be indicted, are more recent than the decrees themselves.' These strictures may be taken with a grain of salt. Politicians no doubt often tried to by-pass the rather cumbrous procedure for legislation—Demosthenes did so himself through Apollodorus over the allocation of the theoric fund.[54] But the indictment for illegal proceedings was a favourite political weapon, often invoked, as by Aeschines against Demosthenes on the famous issue of the Crown, on very technical grounds. And Aristophon's boast that he had been indicted (unsuccessfully) seventy-five times,[55] if it proves that some politicians often sailed near the wind, also proves that there were many jealous watchdogs of the constitution; Demosthenes' attempt to evade the law was, incidentally, foiled and Apollodorus suffered.[56]

On the other aspect of the rule of law Athenian democrats held exactly the opposite view to Aristotle's. 'Tyrannies and oligarchies', according to Aeschines,[57] 'are governed by the ways of their governments, democratic cities by the established laws.' 'No one, I think, would assert', says Demosthenes,[58] 'that there is any more important cause for the blessings which the city enjoys and for its being democratic and free, than the laws.' In another passage[59] Demosthenes contrasts law and oligarchy, declaring that in the latter any member of the government can revoke existing rules and make arbitrary enactments about the future, whereas the laws lay down what must be done for the future and are passed by persuasion in the interests of all. To Lycurgus[60] of 'the three most important factors which maintain and preserve democracy', the first is the law. Hypereides[61] declares it all-important 'that in a democracy the laws shall be sovereign'.

Both sides were naturally thinking of the worst specimens of the opposite party. Athenian democrats inevitably called to mind the arbitrary excesses of their own Four Hundred and Thirty when they spoke of oligarchies, and oligarchs could no doubt cite democracies whose acts were as brutal and illegal. On the whole the Athenian democracy seems to have lived up to its principles. Xenophon[62] has given us a vivid picture of one occasion when the assembly in a hysterical mood rode roughshod over its own rules of procedure and condemned the generals in command at Arginusae to death by one summary vote. But the emphasis given to this incident suggests that it was very exceptional. And Xenophon,[63] no favourable witness to the democracy, also testifies that after the restoration of the democracy in 403 the people religiously observed the amnesty agreed with the supporters of the Thirty. When one reads Xenophon's and Aristotle's record of the doings of the Thirty, one cannot but be amazed at the steadfast forbearance of the Athenian people.

The final and principal charge brought by the philosophers against democracy was that it meant the rule of the poor majority over the rich minority in their own interest. This is the main thesis of the 'Old Oligarch', whose treatise on the Athenian constitution takes the form of an ironical appreciation of its efficiency in promoting the interests of 'the bad' (the poor) at the expense of 'the good' (the rich); he is equally cynical in assuming that 'the good', if they got the chance, would govern in their own interest to the detriment of 'the bad'.[64] Plato in the *Republic*[65] declares that 'democracy results when the poor defeat the others and kill or expel them and share the constitution and the offices equally with the rest'. Aristotle[66] is very insistent that democracy is directed to the advantage of the indigent, going so far as to say that if, *per impossibile*, there should be more rich than poor in a city, the rule of the poor minority should be called democracy, and that of the rich majority oligarchy.

This view was naturally not accepted by democrats. Their views are doubtless reflected in the speech put into the mouth of the Syracusan democrat Athenagoras by Thucydides:[67]

> It will be said that democracy is neither wise nor fair, and that the possessors of property are best qualified to rule well. My opinion is first that the people is the name of the whole, and oligarchy of a part, and secondly that the rich are the best guardians of property, the wise the best councillors, and the masses

can best hear and judge, and that all these elements alike, jointly and severally, have an equal share in democracy.

It is more difficult to answer the question whether the Athenian democracy did or did not in fact exploit the rich for the benefit of the poor. In the distribution of political power and influence the rich seem to have fared well. In the minor offices and on the council and in the juries the poor no doubt predominated, though even here it would seem that by the fourth century the well-to-do were by no means crowded out. To the important military, diplomatic and financial offices men of birth and wealth were generally elected.[68] The orators, who, normally holding no office, guided policy by their speeches in the assembly were also mostly well-to-do, and many of them of good family.[69] It was comparatively rarely that a self-made man like Phrynichus or Aeschines achieved political influence. A rich man or an aristocrat certainly did not find that his political career was prejudiced by his wealth or birth, while poor and humbly born politicians had to face a good deal of abuse from comedians and orators.

Isocrates complains bitterly of the fiscal exploitation of the rich. In the *de Pace*[70] he rolls out a list of taxes and charges 'which cause so much vexation that property owners lead a harder life than utter paupers', and in the *Antidosis* he declares: 'when I was a boy it was thought to be such a secure and grand thing to be rich that practically everyone pretended to possess a larger property than he actually did, in his desire to acquire this reputation. But now one has to prepare a defence to prove that one is not rich, as if it were a great crime.'[71] From the meagre figures which we possess it is difficult to check these allegations. Normal peacetime expenditure (including the pay of citizens for political services) was defrayed from a variety of indirect taxes, a tax on resident aliens, royalties from the silver mines, rents of public and sacred land, court fees and fines and confiscations imposed by the courts. Certain religious festivals were financed by the system of liturgies, whereby rich men were nominated to produce plays, train teams of athletes and the like. In time of war it was often necessary to raise a property tax, which fell, it would seem, on about 6,000 persons, or a third to a quarter of the citizen body. In war time also the richest of the citizens were nominated as trierarchs, in which capacity they had to maintain a trireme in seaworthy condition for a year.

The war tax, of which great complaints were made, averaged over twenty years in the fourth century at a rate equivalent to a 5d. or 6d. in the pound income tax. We need not therefore take the laments of Isocrates and his like very seriously. The tax seems in fact to have been too widely spread, and did cause hardship to the poorest of those liable. It was, as appears from Demosthenes' speeches, very difficult to get the assembly, a substantial proportion of whom were taxpayers, to vote a levy, and hence wars were always inadequately financed.[72] Liturgies are much more difficult to calculate, as it depended greatly on the individual concerned how often he undertook them and how much he spent on each. It was useful political advertisement, almost a form of canvassing, to put up good shows,[73] and rich men were often very willing to acquire popularity by serving frequently and spending lavishly on gorgeous costumes and high salaries to stars. An evidently very rich man for whom Lysias[74] wrote a speech boasts that he undertook eleven liturgies in six years, spending in all nearly 3½ talents—a middle-class fortune. But, as he remarks, he need not have spent on them a quarter of this sum if he had confined himself to the strict requirements of the law; nor need he have performed more than a maximum of four liturgies.[75] At the other extreme another very rich man, Meidias, had, according to Demosthenes,[76] performed only one liturgy at the age of nearly fifty, and Dicaeogenes, another wealthy man, only undertook two minor ones in ten years.[77] The trierarchy was a heavier burden than the ordinary liturgies, costing from 40 to 60 minae (⅔ to 1 talent) a year,[78] and as it might fall on fortunes of 5 talents,[79] the temporary strain on a poor trierarch's resources would be severe. For this reason the burden was usually from the end of the fifth century shared between two holders,[80] and from 357 the 1,200 persons liable to trierarchic service were divided into twenty groups, whose members shared the expense:[81] thus, if a fleet of 100 ships were commissioned, twelve men would share the charge for each trierarchy. Here again the incidence of the burden varied greatly. The same man who performed eleven liturgies served seven years as trierarch during the Ionian war, spending 6 talents,[82] and a certain Aristophanes (with his father) served three trierarchies in four or five years in the Corinthian War, spending 80 minae in all.[83] Isocrates, on the other hand, who complains so bitterly of the oppression of the rich, and had made a large fortune by his rhetorical teaching, could at the age of 80 boast of only three trierarchies (including those performed by his son).[84] But it would be unfair to the Athenian upper classes to take the parsimonious orator as typical. As a public-spirited citizen we may instance the father of one of Lysias' clients, who in a career of fifty years (which included the Peloponnesian and Corinthian wars) was trierarch seven times. His son proudly displayed to the jury his father's accounts, which showed that he had altogether disbursed on trierarchies, liturgies and war tax 9 talents 20 minae,[85] an average of over 11 minae per annum. His fortune is not stated, but he certainly was a very rich man, since he entered chariots for the Isthmia and Nemea,[86] and is likely to have possessed substantially more than 15 talents, which Demosthenes implies would qualify a man to be called really rich.[87] If so, his contribution to the state would not have exceeded one-eighth of his income.

The taxation of the rich was very erratic, falling heavily in war years, and was badly distributed; before 357 all persons on the trierarchic register took their turn, though some were much richer than others, and after 357 all members of a group contributed equally.[88] This lack of system enabled some rich men to escape very lightly, and was on occasions oppressive to those with moderate fortunes. On the other hand, many rich men liked to make a splash, undertaking more trierarchies and liturgies than their legal quota, and thereby easing the burden of the others.

In general, it would seem that the average burden borne by the well-to-do in Athens was well within their means, though its erratic incidence might cause them temporary embarrassment.

The critics, however, allege that a more sinister method of soaking the rich than taxation was in vogue at Athens—that of condemning them on trumped-up charges and confiscating their property.[89] There is reason to believe that this abuse of the law courts did sometimes occur, but it is very difficult to say whether it was common.

Some general considerations need to be clarified. Athens, like all ancient States, relied for the enforcement of the law on the services of informers, and was obliged to reward them for convictions. Professional informers seem to have been a pest at Athens; but so they were everywhere—one has only to think of the reputation of *delatores* in imperial Rome. The State did not encourage frivolous accusations, subjecting to severe penalties an informer who failed to win a fifth of the jury's votes, or who abandoned a prosecution which he had instituted. Nor does it appear that informers were popular with juries. Defendants try to insinuate that their prosecutors are informers, and prosecutors, in their anxiety to prove they are not informers, sometimes go so far as to claim to be personal enemies, or even hereditary enemies, of the accused. Nevertheless, informers seem to have plied a busy trade, principally in blackmailing rich men who had guilty consciences or disliked facing the ordeal of public trial. This state of affairs naturally caused the propertied classes much anxiety, and perhaps caused them to exaggerate the real scope of the evil.[90]

Secondly, Athens, like all ancient States, lived from hand to mouth, and reckoned on the penalties inflicted by the courts as a regular source of income. It was therefore a temptation to jurors to vote in the interests of the treasury when money was short, and an informer dangled before their eyes a fat estate whose owner, he alleged, had been guilty of some serious offence. In this respect also Athens was not unique; Roman emperors short of money are alleged to have encouraged *delatores* and made good the finances by confiscation. Nor need one go so far afield as the Roman empire for a parallel. The Athenian oligarchs in the Thirty filled their treasury by condemning a number of innocuous but wealthy citizens and metics to death and seizing their property.[91] This situation also made the propertied classes nervous, and probably made them exaggerate the evil. There is no reason to believe that all large estates confiscated were confiscated because they were large. Rich Athenians were quite capable of cheating the treasury or betraying the interests of the State; and it is, for instance, very unlikely that a statesman of such severe probity as Lycurgus would have secured the confiscation of the huge estate—160 talents—of Diphilus, unless he had been guilty of a serious breach of the mining laws.[92]

There are three passages in Lysias[93] which allude to the abuse. In a speech written in 399 a litigant states that 'the council for the time being, when it has enough money for the administration, behaves correctly, but when it gets into difficulties it is obliged to receive impeachments and confiscate the property of the citizens and listen to the worst of the politicians'. In another speech, written about ten years later, another litigant says to the jury: 'You must remember that you have often heard them (his opponents) saying, when they wanted to ruin someone unjustly, that, if you would not condemn the people they tell you to condemn, your pay will fail.' And in a third speech, delivered in 387, a man accused of detaining the confiscated estate of a relative complains: 'My defence is difficult in view of the opinion some hold about Nicophemus' estate, and the present shortage of money in the city, my case being against the treasury.' These are serious allegations, and indicate an unhealthy state of affairs. But it is to be noted that they all occur in the period following the fall of Athens, when the State was almost bankrupt, and when, despite the amnesty, feeling against the rich, many of whom had backed the Thirty, was very bitter among the mass of the citizens. I have not detected any other similar suggestion in all the later speeches, forensic or political, of the orators, except one sentence in the Fourth Philippic of Demosthenes,[94] when, after appealing to the rich not to grudge to the poor their theoric payments, he turns to the poor, and says: 'But where does the difficulty arise? What is the trouble? It is when they see some people transferring to private fortunes the practice established for public moneys, and a speaker is great in your eyes at the moment, and immortal as far as security goes—but the secret vote is different from the open applause. This breeds distrust and anger.' This very guarded passage seems to mean that the rich suspected that the poor wished to increase their payments from public funds by confiscating private property, and that rich men who were applauded in the assembly were condemned by the secret ballot of the juries. Hypereides,[95] a few years later, takes pride in the disinterested justice of Athenian juries:

> There is no people or king or nation in the world more magnanimous than the people of Athens. It does not abandon to their fate those of the citizens, whether individuals or classes, who are falsely accused, but goes to their rescue. In the first place when Teisis denounced the estate of Euthycrates, which was worth more than sixty talents, as being public property, and after that again promised to denounce the estate of Philip and Nausicles, alleging that they acquired their wealth from unregistered mines, the jury, so far from welcoming such a speech or coveting other men's goods, promptly disfranchised the false accuser, not giving him a fifth of the votes. And again does not the recent action of the jurors last month deserve great praise? When Lysander denounced the mine of Epicrates as having been sunk within the boundaries—the mine he had been working for three years and pretty well all the richest men in the city were his partners—and Lysander promised to bring in 300 talents for the city—that is what he said they had got out of the mine—nevertheless the jury paid no attention to the accuser's promise but looked only to justice and declared the mine private.

Hypereides perhaps protests too much, but he does at least provide concrete instances when Athenian juries resisted very tempting baits.

If one may attempt to draw a general conclusion it would be that informers were a nuisance to the rich at Athens, and that the Athenian courts were sometimes tempted, especially in financial crises, to increase the revenue by condemning rich defendants on insufficient evidence. Neither of these abuses was, however, peculiar to a democratic régime.

These are the main criticisms brought by the philosophers against the Athenian democracy. Some are directed against abuses which democrats agreed to be such, the overriding of the law by the executive enactments of the assembly and the spoliation of the rich by the poor, but which they claimed to be alien to the principles of democracy. In these matters the Athenian people was certainly not beyond reproach, but on the whole the charges seem to have been exaggerated, and the Athenians were probably justified in claiming that arbitrary violence of this kind was more characteristic of oligarchic régimes than of their own.

Other criticisms are on points of principle and are based on an entirely different conception of the functions of the State and an entirely different estimate of human nature. The philosophers held that the State ought to mould and train the citizens in virtue, and assumed that the average man was naturally evil or at least foolish. Political power must therefore be given to a select group of wise good men, who would impose a good way of life on the rest by a rigid system of education and control. The Athenian democrats, on the other hand, took an optimistic view of human nature, and believed that every citizen should be allowed to live his own life in his own way, within the broad limits laid down by the law, and that all citizens could be trusted to take their part in the government of the city, whether by voting and speaking in the assembly, judging in the juries, carrying on the routine administration as magistrates, or selecting the men to hold high political office. On one point the Athenians were distrustful of human nature, on its ability to resist the temptations of irresponsible power;[96] hence their insistence on brief terms of office, regular review of the conduct of magistrates in office, and above all a searching scrutiny of the record of magistrates on completing their term. The philosophers are strangely blind to this danger, and are content to rely on the virtue of their usually hereditary or co-optative oligarchies of wise men.

The ideals of the Athenian democracy are perhaps best summed up in a rather florid passage of the Funeral Oration attributed to Lysias.[97] Our ancestors, he says,

> were the first and only men of that time who cast out arbitrary power and established democracy, holding that the freedom of all was the greatest concord, and sharing with one another their hopes and perils they governed themselves with free hearts, honouring the good and chastising the bad by law. They held it bestial to constrain one another by force, and the part of men to define justice by law, and to persuade by reason, and serve both by action, having law as their king and reason as their teacher.

Thucydides has very little to say on the internal government of Athens; it is with the foreign and imperial policy of the democracy that he is concerned. Here he makes only one explicit charge, that of incompetence. Under Pericles, when the régime was 'nominally a democracy but really government by the first citizen', Athens pursued a considered and consistent policy of husbanding her resources and undertaking no new commitments. By this policy she could, in Thucydides' opinion, have won the war. But when Pericles' unique authority was removed, 'his successors, being more on a level with one another and each struggling to gain the ascendancy, tended to surrender political decisions to the pleasure of the people'. The greatest mistake, he goes on, was the Sicilian expedition, not so much because it was 'an error of judgement in relation to its objective', but because 'those who sent it out did not give proper support to the expedition in their subsequent decisions, but in the course of their private cabals about the leadership of the people were slack in their conduct of the war and at home began to fall into intestine disorders'.[98]

It would be a long task to discuss whether Athens could have won the war on the purely defensive strategy which Thucydides attributes to Pericles, and whether the Sicilian expedition had a reasonable prospect of success. It may, however, be noted in passing that Thucydides' narrative does not bear out his charge that the Athenian people gave inadequate support to the expedition. It is indisputable that it was a serious blunder to risk so large a force on a distant expedition with an unconquered enemy at their gates, and that the Athenian people showed lack of judgment in succumbing to Alcibiades' eloquence. But it is hardly fair to condemn a whole régime for one blunder. Taking a longer view it cannot be said that the Athenians conducted their affairs unwisely. It took the Spartans and their Peloponnesian allies thirty years to bring to a successful conclusion a war which they had innocently hoped to win in two or three seasons, and they only won it in the end by cynically bartering 'the freedom of the Greeks', for which they were professedly fighting, to the national enemy Persia in return for subsidies. In the whole course of its history the Athenian democracy may be said to have been the most successful State in Greece. With no especial advantages except its silver mines it made itself the greatest city in the Greek world for the fifty years between the Persian and Peloponnesian wars, and after the great defeat in 404 rapidly rose again to be one of the first-class powers, a position which it held till crushed by Macedonia with the rest of Greece. Nor were strategic and political blunders a peculiarity of democracies. It would be hard to find in Athenian history any parallel to Sparta's ineptitude after her great victory over Athens. Only political incompetence of the highest order could have ranged in alliance against herself her two most faithful allies, Corinth and Thebes, and her and their two bitterest enemies, Atgos and Athens. But to break simultaneously with the Great King and launch a crusade into Asia Minor shows utter irresponsibility. The results were disastrous to Sparta in the loss of her newly won maritime empire, the rivival of Athens as a great power, and the permanent hostility of Thebes.

Thucydides' attitude is not difficult to understand. He was clearly a profound admirer of Pericles. Equally clearly he was strongly prejudiced against the type of statesman who succeeded him, notably Cleon.[99] It would be out of place here to discuss Cleon's merits, though it is worth noting that later generations did not share Thucydides' low opinion of him; a wealthy Athenian in 350 B.C. is proud to claim that his mother's first husband had been Cleomedon, 'whose father Cleon, we are told, as general of your ancestors captured a large number of Spartans alive at Pylos and was the most distinguished man in the city';[100] but no reader can fail to note Thucydides' rancour against him. As a patriotic Athenian Thucydides was deeply distressed at his city's ruin. It was natural that in his bitterness he should be unfair to the politicians whom he hated and to the régime which had given them power.

Explicitly Thucydides blames the democracy only for its incompetent conduct of the war. Implicitly he accuses it of a cynical and brutal imperialism which, he suggests, was followed by a just retribution. This result is achieved in a variety of ways; by the choice of words in describing Athenian actions, by the selection and stressing of certain incidents in the narrative, and by the speeches put into the mouths of Athenian politicians. A good example of the first method is the language used by Thucydides to describe the Athenian reduction of Naxos, the first ally which attempted to secede—the city 'was enslaved contrary to established usage' (*παρὰ τὸ καθεστηκὸς ἐδουλώθη*).[101] We are not told what precisely was done to Naxos, which later appears as a normal subject city, paying a rather low tribute but with part of its territory occupied by an Athenian cleruchy. By analogy with similar cases we may infer that the Naxians had to surrender their fleet and pay tribute instead of contributing ships to the federal fleet; that the oligarchic government, which had proved disloyal to the league, was replaced by a democracy; and that the estates of the oligarchs were confiscated, later to be partitioned among Athenian settlers. The word 'enslave' is rather a sinister word to describe this, and the vague adverbial phrase suggests, without defining, moral obliquity.[102]

The chief example of the second method is the immense stress laid on the mass execution of the Melians by means of the long debate between the Athenians and their victims, which is immediately followed by the rash decision of the assembly to undertake the Sicilian expedition, the description of the proud armada, and the long-drawn-out agony of its utter destruction. Every reader of Thucydides is left with the impression that Athens had sinned greatly, and that retribution fell upon her; and there can be no doubt that is what Thucydides felt and wished his readers to feel.

The chief speech in which Thucydides points his moral is the famous Melian dialogue,[103] where the Athenian delegates brush aside all moral considerations and openly propound the doctrine that might is right. In a similar spirit Cleon in the debate on the fate of the Mitylenaeans declares that the empire is a tyranny which must be maintained by terror,[104] and his opponent Diodotus urges clemency purely on grounds of expediency. Other speeches of importance are that of Pericles after the second invasion of Attica, when he too proclaims the empire a tyranny,[105] and the defence of the empire put up by an Athenian delegate at Sparta before the opening of the war and again at Camarina during the Sicilian expedition. In both of these the empire is frankly admitted to rest on force alone. The first speaker claims that Athens may be excused for clinging to it on the grounds of prestige, profit and fear (of what she would suffer from her subjects if she relaxed her grip), and urges in mitigation of the offence that Athens used her power with moderation.[106] The second speaker endeavours to allay Sicilian misgivings by pointing out that while it was in Athens' interest to oppress the allies at home, in Sicily she would have no motive for doing so.[107]

The speeches in Thucydides are a difficult problem. He himself says that it was 'difficult for me, when I myself heard them, and for my informants in other cases, to remember exactly what was said; I have made the various characters speak as I thought they would have spoken most appropriately about the situations which arose, keeping as closely as possible to the general tenor of what was actually said'.[108] It is possible to interpret these words in many different ways, and to evaluate the several speeches very variously according to whether Thucydides is likely to have been present himself or to have had trustworthy informants. It is virtually impossible that he can have had any information on the Melian debate, which was held behind closed doors between the Athenian commissioners and the Melian government, who were all subsequently executed, and it must be regarded as a free composition. Thucydides was not present at Sparta or at Camarina. On the other hand, he probably listened to Pericles and to the Mitylenaean debate.

If these speeches are intended to reproduce the actual tenor of Athenian public utterances, it must be admitted that the Athenians of the fifth century not only were a very remarkable, if not unique, people in openly admitting that their policy was guided purely by selfish considerations and they had no regard for political morality, but also that they underwent a complete transformation in the fourth century, when we possess genuine speeches. In these, the Funeral Speech attributed to Lysias and the *Panegyricus* and *Panathenaicus* of Isocrates, the speakers dilate not only on the glories of their former empire, but on its high purposes. By it Athens had kept Greece free from Persian rule, and had so humbled the Great King that he had formally renounced his right to enter the Aegean. Athens had given her allies not only prosperity, but freedom, everywhere liberating them from the yoke of tyrannies and oligarchies and bestowing upon them the blessings of democracy, and they had fought by her side, not for her supremacy but for their own freedom.[109] The same theme is parodied by Plato in the *Menexenus*—'we fought the Spartans at Tanagra for the freedom of the Boeotians', 'we won many victories in Sicily for the freedom of the Leontines'.[110] And in the political orations of Demosthenes in the latter part of the century an idealistic note is always struck—Athenians should everywhere champion democracy, Athens should be the leader of free Greece against the tyranny of Macedon.

It is difficult to resist the conclusion that Thucydides, in order to point his moral, put into the mouths of Athenian spokesmen what he considered to be their real sentiments, stripped of rhetorical claptrap, and that what we have in the speeches is in effect Thucydides' own opinion of the empire. His view was that Athens was universally hated by her allies or subjects, who were held down by fear or force only, and were eager to revolt on every possible opportunity—this thesis he twice states in his own person apart from the speeches[111]—and that Athens was wrong in 'enslaving' them, by her refusal to allow them to secede from the league and by her interference in their internal government. Furthermore, that the Athenians, to enforce their tyranny (as with Mitylene) or to enlarge it (as with Melos) committed or very nearly committed acts of the grossest brutality. Let us examine the validity of Thucydides' view.

His main thesis can be proved from his own narrative to be grossly oversimplified, and he himself gives the key to the truth in the statement which he attributes to Diodotus in the Mitylenaean debate. 'At present the people in all the cities is friendly to you, and either does not join in revolt with the few, or if it is compelled to do so, is immediately hostile to the rebels, and you go to war with the majority of the opposing city on your side.'[112] This analysis is borne out by almost every case where the story of a revolt is told in any detail. At Mitylene the ruling oligarchy (presumably the thousand-odd persons who were ultimately executed as being most responsible for the revolt) seceded; the people, as soon as the Spartan commandant issued arms to them, mutinied, and the city promptly surrendered.[113] Brasidas in Thrace had to lecture the Acanthians on their duty to accept the freedom which he offered them, and to clinch the argument by a threat to destroy their vintage.[114] At Torone and Mende also small cliques of conspirators admitted Brasidas, and at the latter town the people rallied to the Athenians as soon as a relieving force arrived, and were entrusted by Nicias with the punishment of their own traitors.[115] At Chios, even after the Sicilian disaster, the oligarchic government did not dare to break with

Athens for fear of the masses till a Spartan fleet arrived.[116] At Rhodes, shortly afterwards, certain prominent persons intrigued with the Spartans, and the arrival of a powerful fleet 'terrified the majority, who were unaware of what was going on'.[117] The people of Samos, having purged their oligarchs in successive revolutions, remained faithful to Athens to the bitter end.[118] There were some cities where hostility to Athens was more widespread, but in general the malcontents seem to have been limited to oligarchic groups. Thucydides' estimate of public opinion was no doubt based on his contacts with men of this type, whom he would have met before his exile as visitors to Athens and during his exile intriguing with the Spartans. His own meticulously fair and accurate narrative, however, proves that his estimate was seriously at fault.

Even if this be so, however, does it remain true that, according to the accepted canons of Greek political morality, Athens acted wrongfully in refusing to allow her allies to secede, and in interfering with their internal government? All Greeks, of course, paid lip service to the principle of autonomy, but in practice powerful States did not allow it to incommode them, and public opinion did not condemn them. To judge Athens one may compare her conduct with that of the other leading State of Greece, Sparta, whose boast that her allies were autonomous is generally admitted in our sources.

When Tegea broke with Sparta and formed an alliance with Argos in about 465 the Spartans invaded her territory and defeated her at the battle of Tegea. When shortly afterwards all the Arcadian cities except Mantinea revolted, Sparta marched against them and defeated them at Dipaea.[119] When after the Peace of Nicias Mantinea and Elis seceded from the league and Tegea began to waver, Sparta again marched and won the battle of Mantinea; next year Mantinea returned to her allegiance.[120] Elis did not participate in the battle of Mantinea and was left alone for some years. But when Sparta's hands were free after the fall of Athens, Elis was subdued and brought to obedience again.[121] Sparta, in fact, did not allow her allies to secede,[122] and no one blamed her for reducing them to obedience if they tried to do so.

When Sparta delivered her ultimatum to Athens, 'the Spartans wish the peace to continue, and this would be so if you leave the Greeks autonomous', Pericles replied that they would do so 'when the Spartans also restore to their cities the right to govern themselves not in Spartan interests, but as they themselves severally wish'.[123] In fact, both Athens and Sparta supported in their allied cities governments favourable to themselves, Athens normally favouring democracies and Sparta oligarchies. Neither usually intervened arbitrarily, but when opportunity offered—when there was a conflict in an allied city and the defeated party appealed to the leading city, or when a hostile government had revolted and been subdued—they took advantage of it.[124] There were a few democracies among Sparta's allies—Elis and Mantinea, for instance—and a few oligarchies among Athens, Mitylene, Chios and Samos. It is noticeable that all these cities had been consistently loyal, and had thus given their suzerains no opportunity for intervention.

Thucydides also implies that the Athenians violated the rights of the allies by suppressing the federal congress of the Delian League. 'At first', he writes, 'the allies were independent under their leadership and determined policy as the result of federal congresses.'[125] By contrast with Athens Pericles emphasises the divided councils of the Peloponnesians, who all have an equal vote.[126] From the speech of the Mitylenaeans at the Olympia of 428, however, it would appear that as recently as 440 a Delian Congress had been held to decide what was to be done about Samos, and that the Mitylenaeans had voted for war; allusion is also made to the equal voting power of cities and to the large number of cities voting.[127] It would seem in fact that the constitution of the Delian League was exactly modelled on that of the Peloponnesian, where every city, great or small, had one vote,[128] and that the constitution was formally observed as late as 440 B.C.

No Delian Congress is reported by Thucydides before the Peloponnesian war, and doubtless none was held; for no declaration of war was required from the League, since Athens was attacked by the Peloponnesians in violation of the Thirty Years' Peace.[129]

De facto the position of Athens and Sparta in their respective leagues was very different. Sparta had no overwhelming military predominance over her allies and had therefore to take some account of their sentiments and interests, particularly as there was in Corinth a potential leader of the opposition, which could, and sometimes did, sway the majority of the congress against her,[130] Athens from the beginning enjoyed naval predominance because many of the allies subscribed not ships but money, which in effect subsidised the Athenian fleet, and as more and more allies either commuted to money for their own convenience, or were compelled to do so after revolt, Athenian ascendancy became overwhelming. The Delian Congress therefore tended to ratify Athenian decisions automatically, particularly as the naval allies did not show the independent spirit of Corinth; even as late as 440 B.C., if Chios and the Lesbian cities had stood up for Samos, they could, with about 200 ships between them, have given Athens pause.[131]

Athens in this position undoubtedly kept a tighter rein on her allies, notably in concentrating criminal jurisdiction in her own hands and thus making sure that her friends in the allied cities were protected and her enemies suffered.[132] She also exploited her allies more openly, especially in using a part of the federal reserve fund to rebuild her own temples and in apportioning to her own citizens land forfeited by rebellious allied communities or individuals. Sparta had no temptation or opportunity to do the like, but she used her allies for her own purposes, above all to protect her against Helot revolts.[133] Both Sparta and Athens, despite their rival protestations that they stood for the autonomy of the Hellenes or liberty and democracy, in fact used their leagues to secure their own political supremacy. The Peloponnesian

League was on the whole satisfactory to the oligarchic governments of its member States, the Delian to the people in the allied cities.

On the score of brutality no one will wish to defend the decision —happily reversed the next day—to massacre the whole adult population of Mitylene, nor the execution of the Melians, or of the Scionaeans (which Thucydides dismisses without comment). It must, however, be said that in neither of the two cases which he treats in detail is Thucydides quite fair. In the speeches which he reports he represents the repeal of the Mitylenaean decision as a prudential measure only; whereas he records that the second debate was held because 'on the next day they immediately had a change of heart and reflected that this decision, to destroy a whole city instead of the guilty parties, was a great barbarity'.[134] In the Melian dialogue Thucydides implies that Melos was an unoffending neutral, which Athens found it convenient to subdue. In point of fact Melos had been a non-belligerent ally of Sparta since the beginning of the war, subscribing to her war fund and sheltering her fleet in 427,[135] and Athens had, not unnaturally, been at war with the Melians since 426.[136]

Here also Athens was not exceptional, nor did she lead the way. The Spartans set the example by the even more gratuitous massacre of the Plataeans. The Mitylenaeans and Scionaeans were at least in Athenian eyes traitors, allies who had broken their oaths, and the Melians had assisted their enemies. The Plataeans had been guilty of defending their own city when treacherously attacked by Thebes in time of peace. The only question which the Spartan judges put to them was 'whether they had done any good to the Spartans and their allies during the war'; they were in fact condemned simply for being on the other side.[137]

The Athenians, in fact, can only be condemned, if they are judged by much more lofty standards than were normally applied to international relations. Why did Thucydides take so uncharitable a view of his native city? His attitude was partly due to a misconception of public feeling natural to a man of his class, particularly when he had for many years lived in exile in oligarchic circles. He appears to have really believed that the Athenians were hated by their allies, whereas the Peloponnesian League was a free association of cities. But his attitude was also probably due to a deep-seated and perhaps unconscious desire to find a moral justification for the fall of Athens. It was not enough to say that it was due to the folly of the democratic politicians whom he so much disliked. It must have been deserved. Athens had suffered grievously; this could not have been so if she had not sinned greatly.

The opinions of Thucydides, Plato and Aristotle have naturally carried great weight, and so, curiously enough, have those of Isocrates. In the absence of any coherent statement of the democratic case, most modern historians have rather uncritically accepted the oligarchic view of Athens, and condemned what Aristotle calls the 'extreme democracy'.[138] In this article I have endeavoured to reconstruct the theory of government in which democrats believed and to assess the merits and defects of the Athenian democracy in the conduct of home affairs and of foreign and imperial policy. My readers can judge whether the 'extreme democracy', in which the people was sovereign, and vulgar persons who worked with their hands enjoyed full political rights, including access to all offices, and owing to their greater numbers preponderated in the assembly, was indeed so pernicious a form of government as Athenian philosophers and historians represent.

IV

THE SOCIAL STRUCTURE OF ATHENS IN THE FOURTH CENTURY B.C.

The Social Structure of Athens in the Fourth Century B.C.

THE political history of Athens and its literature, philosophy and art have not unnaturally received far more attention than its economic life. The achievements of the Athenian people in the former spheres were outstanding, and we possess an abundance of material for their study. In the economic field on the other hand the record of Athens is less striking, and the evidence is very scrappy and incomplete. Nevertheless, the subject perhaps deserves more intensive study than it has received. Inadequate though the evidence is for Athens it is far richer than for any other ancient city, and if the economic history of the ancient world is a feasible subject of study, it should start with the economic history of Athens. And for a full understanding of the achievements of the Athenian people in other spheres some knowledge of the material background is desirable if not essential. It adds something to our appreciation of Attic drama to know how the audience for which it was written lived, even more to our appreciation of the Attic orators to know what kind of men attended the assembly and sat on the juries. To understand the political philosophy of Plato and Aristotle it is essential to know something of the society in which they lived. Above all it is impossible fully to understand and appreciate the great political achievement of Athens, the democracy, unless we know what kind of men were the citizens who debated and voted in the assembly and the council, administered the State as magistrates and decided legal and political issues as jurors in the popular courts. Ancient critics, Plato, Isocrates, and Aristotle, denounced the democracy as a tyranny of the poor over the rich. Modern critics have declared that the democracy was a fraud, and the citizens were a leisured minority living on the labour of slaves. It is of some moment to discover which, if either, of these views is true.

In what follows I have attempted a factual analysis of Athenian society in the fourth century B.C. I have tried to determine how many free persons, citizens or foreigners, lived in Attica; how many were rich, well-to-do or poor; what proportion lived on unearned incomes, or worked on the land, or were craftsmen or labourers; how many slaves of various kinds—domestic servants, farm labourers, miners or craftsmen—Athenians and foreigners of various classes owned. I have perforce confined myself to the fourth century, and for the most part to the middle and later decades of that century, because it is only for that period that we possess even the rudimentary statistical information necessary for such an analysis, and also, thanks mainly to the private speeches of the orators, a relative abundance of intimate detail on some aspects of the Athenian economy.

The first question we have to ask is how many Athenian citizens there were: by this I mean how many adult males (from 20 upwards), and in all that follows I shall mean (unless I specify otherwise) adult males, because we do not know how many women and children there were. Demetrius of Phalerum (317-307 B.C.) took a census, in which 21,000 were counted.[1] An orator contemporary with Demosthenes says rather casually 20,000.[2] And when at the bidding of Antipater in 322 the constitution was altered, so that only owners of property assessed at 20 minae or more remained citizens, 9,000 were registered as citizens, and according to the text of Plutarch, 12,000 were disfranchised, according to that of Diodorus, 22,000. The first figure, which yields a grand total of 21,000, seems to me more likely.[3]

Besides citizens there were resident aliens or metics: we have only one figure—Demetrius of Phalerum's census gave 10,000. There were, of course, also slaves owned by citizens and metics. For these we have two very extraordinary figures. According to Athenaeus (our sole source) 400,000 were counted at the census of Demetrius of Phalerum, that is an average of thirteen per head for every citizen or metic, rich or poor. The Lexicon of Suidas[4] cites half a sentence from Hypereides, 'more than 150,000 from the silver mines and over the rest of the country', which probably comes from the speech which Hypereides delivered in defence of his proposal to free the slaves after Chaeronea. This yields an average of five slaves per free man. I would not discuss these fantastic figures, if some scholars did not still take them seriously. The best test is the amount of wheat the population of Athens consumed, because we know more or less how much was consumed, and how much the normal person ate, and even slaves had to eat.

An Athenian inscription, recording the first-fruits offered to Demeter in 329 B.C., shows, on the likely hypothesis that the first-fruits were 1/600 of barley and 1/1200 of wheat, that in that year the crop of Attica was 28,500 medimni of wheat and 340,350 medimni of barley.[5] It may have been a bad year; we have no means of telling. I have no doubt that Athenian farmers all under-estimated their crops; so that the real crop was considerably larger. On the other hand we must deduct a proportion of the crop—about a sixth—for seed corn. The wheat was all used for human consumption, barley was not much eaten, and was reckoned at half the nutritive value;[6] much if not most of the barley must have been fed to animals.[7] However, these figures do not matter much, as they were chicken-feed in comparison with imports.

On these Demosthenes gives some apparently reliable figures in the *Leptines*, though he presents them in a rather curious way.[8] He first says that the wheat imported from the Pontus was about half the total imports; I do not know how he could have known this, and I do not think he did. He then says that the annual imports from the Pontus were about 400,000 medimni, and that this could be verified from the records by the sitophylakes, the magistrates charged with regulating the price of corn on the

Athenian market. The sitophylakes are likely to have kept a record of the total imports of wheat, but it would seem to be unnecessary and difficult for them to have kept a record of the country of origin of each cargo. I infer that Demosthenes looked up the figure of the imports, and found it to be 800,000 medimni, and on the quite unverified assertion that half came from the Pontus, told the jury that 400,000 came from the Pontus—which was what he wanted to prove. A total annual import of 800,000 medimni seems to be a genuine figure, in which case the total available for consumption was, say, 830,000 medimni of wheat (allowing for a considerable underestimate of the home crop in the Eleusis inscription), and such home-grown barley as was not fed to animals.

Now a man was generally reckoned to eat $7\frac{1}{2}$ and a woman or child about 5 medimni p.a.[9] Thirty-one thousand adult male citizens and metics would at this rate have eaten 232,000 medimni p.a. We do not, as I have said, know the average size of an Athenian family, but certain vital statistics which I shall come to later suggest that the population had a high birth-rate and a high death-rate, and that children would be, by modern British standards, a large element in the population. If therefore we assume that to every man there were three women and children (as in modern England) we shall be underestimating. Ninety-three thousand women and children (at three each to 31,000 adult males) each eating 5 medimni of wheat a year would consume 465,000 medimni p.a. The free population ought thus to have consumed a minimum of about 700,000 medimni p.a. out of a total of 830,000.

There was therefore a maximum of 130,000 medimni of wheat, plus an unknown quantity of barley, to feed slaves. We do not know how many of the slaves were women—most domestic servants were—and how many men—miners, agricultural labourers, craftsmen. Assuming the proportion was 50:50, and the average consumption of wheat by a slave therefore about 6 medimni, the slave population, male and female, was at a maximum about 20,000 as against approximately 62,000 free adults, male and female, or 124,000 free persons, including children.

All these figures have a very large margin of error, but are, I believe, of the right order of magnitude. They are at any rate of the same order of magnitude as two reputable figures that we possess for the slave population of Athens. Thucydides says that in the Decelean war more than 20,000 slaves, mainly skilled men, escaped;[10] but in 413 Athens was a much richer place than in the fourth century, and the free population much larger. Xenophon in his *Vectigalia* states that, if fully exploited, the Laurium mines could have provided employment for more than 10,000 slaves, and in confirmation of this statement declares that those, if any, who remembered what the slave tax used to bring in before the Decelean war (sixty years ago) would bear him out.[11] He clearly implies that in his own day the number of miners was very much smaller.

To return to the citizens: we are informed, as I have said before, that in 322 there were 12,000 citizens who owned less than 20 minae or 2,000 drachmae. There is reason to believe that these citizens were the Solonian class of thetes, who were not liable to military service as hoplites, but had to serve when occasion demanded as rowers in the fleet.[12] There is only one check on this figure of 12,000, that in 351 B.C. the assembly, presumably guided by the generals, resolved to commission forty triremes, to man which 8,000 men would be required, and for this purpose resolved to call up the age classes from 20 to 45.[13] Allowing for the probable age distribution of the population, to which I shall allude later, this would leave a fair margin.

Twenty minae is difficult to express in modern terms. According to the one contemporary figure we possess for the price of land, it would correspond to 5-6 acres of land, perhaps a holding of 5 acres with house and stock.[14] The 12,000 thetes owned less than this, but there is one fact which suggests that a large number of citizens owned land in minimal quantities. After the restoration of the democracy in 403 it was proposed that only Athenians holding land should be citizens, and fragments of a speech against this proposal survive. Dionysius of Halicarnassus, who had read the whole speech, says that the orator asserted that 5,000 persons would have been disfranchised under the proposal:[15] and he had every reason to overestimate the number. Conditions had no doubt changed since 403, but I know of no evidence which would disprove that about half the 12,000 thetes were landowners on a very small scale. This would be the natural result of the Athenian law of inheritance, whereby sons inherited equally, so that peasant holdings were more and more subdivided. Brothers often held their deceased father's holding in common. Many Athenian thetes may have earned money seasonally at Athens, and spent part of the year on the family farm.[16]

But some 5,000 Athenians owned no vestige of land. Some of them may have been quite comfortably off. Twenty minae was, according to Demosthenes, the equivalent of about six or seven skilled industrial slaves.[17] At the upper limit of the thetic class a man might own a house, incorporating a workshop, and say five skilled slaves. Below him were craftsmen who owned four, three, two or one slave, or who worked alone assisted by their children. At the bottom of the scale were, as today, casual labourers (*μισθωτοί*), who in the latter part of the fourth century, as the Eleusis accounts show, could earn 1½ drachmae a day when in work.[18]

Did many thetes live on state pay? There was the council of 500, on which a citizen could serve two years in his lifetime, receiving 5 obols (about half a labourer's rate) per day: on the evidence it was mostly persons of independent means who served on the council. There were about 350 magistrates, paid on slightly varying but similar scales; in these quite humble persons, poor hoplites and even thetes, seem to have served. Finally, there was a register of 6,000 persons, from whom the jurors were selected on court days. Those who actually served on a jury received 3 obols for the day's work.[19] Now this was what the Athenian people, humane but not overgenerous employers, allocated as their daily ration allowances to low-grade public slaves—labourers at the Eleusinium; these slaves received free lodging and clothes in addition.[20] In other words an Athenian juror could buy himself enough food to eat on the day that he sat in court, and no more. The out-of-work may have earned an odd day's keep in this way; but once again the tone of the speeches delivered to Athenian juries suggests that most of the jurors were men of some substance.[21] All Athenian citizens could, of course, earn 1 drachma by attending the assembly on thirty days in the year, and on ten more $1\frac{1}{2}$ drachmae (a labourer's daily wage).[22] They could also draw 2 obols as theoricon on probably about six public holidays in the year.[23]

My conclusion, which is not very surprising, but does not accord with some popular misconceptions, is that out of a total population of 21,000 citizens, about 12,000, say 60 per cent., earned their living by working on very small holdings of 5 acres downwards, or as skilled craftsmen or shopkeepers, with from five slave assistants downwards, or as casual labourers.

We may now turn to the 9,000 persons (say 40 per cent. of the population) who owned over 20 minae, and were liable, if between the ages of 20 and 60, to serve as hoplites (the 1,000 richest as cavalry). This figure of 9,000, I would remind you, is attested for the year 322. Curiously enough 'the Five Thousand' in 411 B.C., when interpreted as meaning those who provided their own suits of armour, turned out to be 9,000 in number.[24] It may be a coincidence that there were 9,000 hoplites in 411 and again in 322, but it looks as if the general distribution of wealth was fairly stable throughout the fourth century. The few figures we possess for armies put into the field by Athens at intervals throughout the fourth century do not disagree, that is they are comfortably under 9,000,[25] and in the Lamian war in 323 the figures recorded by Diodorus, which yield 7,850 for the 20 to 40 age groups,[26] are according to my calculations compatible with a grand total of 9,000 citizens of hoplite census of all ages, on the assumption—which we know from Xenophon to be true—that metics of the appropriate property qualification and age groups had to serve.[27]

This depends on the age distribution of the population, for which we have slight but sure evidence from the inscriptions. Three inscriptions show that round about 330 B.C. an ephebe class, i.e. the young men of hoplite census aged 18 or 19, numbered about 500.[28] Another inscription shows that in 325/4 B.C. the arbitrators, that is citizens of hoplite class aged 60, numbered exactly 103.[29] These are startling figures, if compared with the census records of modern England, but Mr. A. R. Burn has recently demonstrated that the vital statistics of Roman Africa and Roman Carthage and sundry other areas under the Principate were not analogous to modern English figures, but to those of

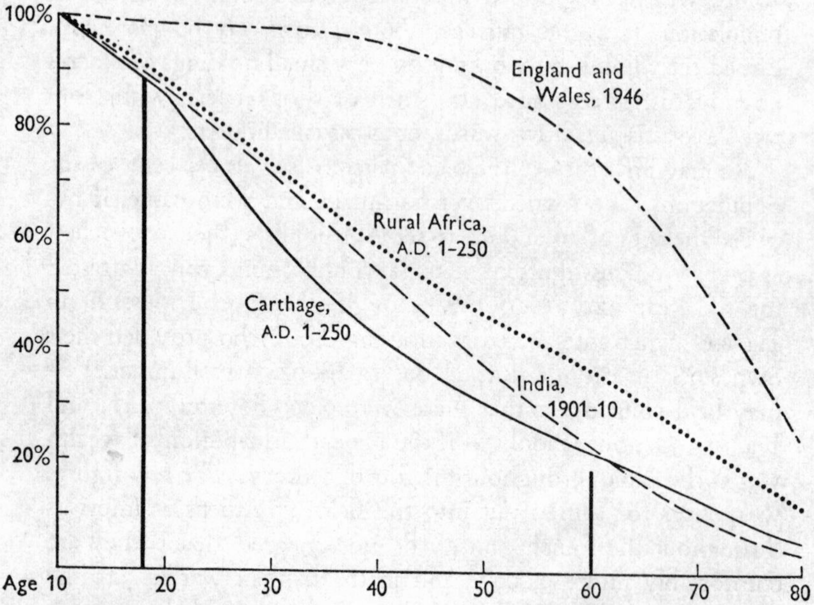

These graphs illustrate the percentages of males alive at the age of ten who reached successive ages up to eighty in Carthage (A.D. 1-250), rural Africa (A.D. 1-250), India (1901-10) and England and Wales (1946). The vertical lines show the proportion of ephebes (18) to arbitrators (60), in Athens in the fourth century B.C.

India at the beginning of this century.[30] There is no reason to believe that conditions in the fourth century B.C. in Athens and Attica were strikingly better than those in Carthage and Africa under the Principate, and in point of fact Mr. Burn's graphs, if applied to recorded Athenian figures, fit curiously well.[31] The main conclusion from his statistics, applied to Athenian figures, is that the Athenians suffered a uniformly high death rate from the age of 20 to 60 so that of 500 young men of 20 not many more than 100 survived to be 60 forty years later. Having reached about 60 a man was, it appears, so tough that he might easily live another ten or fifteen years. There are no ancient statistics of the child death rate, but it was probably at least as high as that of adults. The population would therefore have been very young, with a high percentage of children.

The line dividing hoplites from thetes was of course an arbitrary one, and there must have been many hoplites just over the line, who were relatively poor men. Demosthenes in the Meidias twice apologises for introducing to the jury a hoplite, Strato of Phalerum, who had served on all the expeditions for which his age group had been called up, and had finally been arbitrator—'a poor man no doubt, but not a knave'.[32] Mantitheus, when his deme assembled for the muster, found that many of his poorer fellow hoplites could not even raise their journey money, and organised a subscription to provide them with 30 drachmae each.[33]

Here again we have some statistical data to guide us. The citizens liable to the eisphora, the war tax on property, were in 378-7 B.C. organised in 100 groups or symmories.[34] In 357-6 the symmory system was applied to the trierarchy, the duty of maintaining a warship for one year, and the 1,200 persons liable to serve were grouped in twenty symmories.[35] The business of the eisphora and of the trierarchy symmories was similar—to collect money from the members—and it is a plausible hypothesis that it was decided to group the 1,200 potential trierarchs in symmories of sixty persons each, because sixty had been found a convenient number in the eisphora symmories. If so, there will have been about 6,000 persons liable to the eisphora. There is evidence that 25 minae was a standard unit of assessment for the eisphora,[36] and it has been inferred that citizens who owned property assessed at less than this sum were exempt from eisphora. If so, an interesting conclusion emerges, that there were 3,000 citizens who owned between 20 and 25 minae—a farm with house and stock of from 5 to 6 acres.

We now come to the 6,000-odd citizens, assessed at 25 minae upwards, who paid eisphora. We have the evidence—for what it is worth—of Demosthenes that many of these were relatively poor. Castigating the harshness of Androtion and Timocrates when collecting the arrears of eisphora, he invokes the sympathy of the jury for their victims, 'farmers who pinch and scrape, but who owing to the cost of bringing up their children, and domestic expenses and other public demands, have fallen into arrears of eisphora'.[37] He depicts Androtion and Timocrates 'removing doors, and seizing blankets, and distraining on a servant girl, if any of them employed one'.[38] If Demosthenes is speaking the truth, some of the 6,000 eisphora payers could not even afford to buy a single slave girl to help in the house.

There is statistical evidence which corroborates Demosthenes. According to Polybius the total assessment of Attica was 5,750 talents, according to Philochorus and Demosthenes 6,000 talents: for convenience' sake I will adopt the latter figure. I have argued elsewhere what 'the total assessment' or 'the assessment of the country' means, and I shall only repeat my conclusion that theoretically it represented the gross total value of the property, in all forms, whether land, houses, personal effects, slaves, cash or investments, owned by the 6,000-odd persons who were assessed above 25 minae and paid eisphora.[39] Some economic historians have thought the figure unduly small, but it must, I think, be accepted for what it purports to be. It is likely to be an underestimate, for to judge by many allusions in the orators, it was the exception rather than the rule that an Athenian taxpayer declared the whole of his property. Land and houses were however difficult to conceal, and these were probably the main items. Slaves might be underestimated both in numbers and value. Cash and loans could be concealed altogether. But there were sycophants, and one of the reasons for the reign of terror which they are alleged to have exercised over the wealthy may well have been that most wealthy men knew that their eisphora assessments would not bear investigation.

Now, if 6,000 persons were assessed at 6,000 talents, their average property would be one talent. But, as we shall see, there were among the Three Hundred, who were responsible for the collection of the eisphora, men who owned upwards of 15 talents, and among the 1,200 on the trierarchic register quite a number who owned about 5 talents. It must follow that in the lower half or two-thirds of the 6,000 the average fortune must have been well below 1 talent; a large group must have owned between 25 and 30 minae ($\frac{1}{2}$ a talent) each, and these are probably the poor farmers whom Demosthenes describes.

Now we come to the Athenian upper class, which roughly corresponded with the 1,200 persons on the trierarchic register: there was no property qualification for trierarchic service, and the list was supposed to include the 1,200 richest Athenians. We know a great deal about many individuals in this class, because in their mutual litigation about inheritances, trierarchies, liturgies, dowries, etc., they could afford to employ eminent speech writers like Lysias, Isaeus and Demosthenes. And though many of the 'facts' presented to the jury were no doubt false, they must have been plausible, and therefore typical.

Isaeus in one of his speeches states that Dicaeogenes received an inheritance which brought in 80 minae a year as rent, but that he was never trierarch, though others served who owned less property (capital), than he received in rent (income).[40] Isaeus implies that a man might be a trierarch if he owned less than $1\frac{1}{3}$ talents, but one wonders whether if pressed he could have cited examples. In another speech Isaeus speaks of a '5 talent trierarchic fortune' as something worth having.[41] Five talents must have been well above the average trierarchic estate, for if it had been the average, the 1,200 men on the trierarchic register would between them have owned 1,200 x 5 =6,000 talents, 'the whole assessment of Attica', leaving nothing at all for the other 4,800 eisphora payers. If the average trierarchic estate was only 3 talents, the total assessment of the 1,200 would have been 3,600 talents, leaving only 2,400 for the other eisphora payers, or only an average of ½ talent or 30 minae each. And an average of 3 talents means that the majority must have owned less than this amount, since a few are known to have owned considerably more. Isaeus' clients, who own fortunes ranging from 5½ or 5 talents, through 4, 3½, 3, 2½, down to 1½, seem to be a fairly representative cross-section of the richer members of the trierarchic register.[42] Demosthenes, when he complains that other estates of one or two talents, by being leased during a minority, have been doubled or trebled, and so have become liable to liturgies, appears to be talking in a rather exaggerated vein, to impress upon the jury the magnitude of his own lost fortune.[43] Actually it would seem, an estate of 2 talents or less might well be on the trierarchic register.

There were of course richer men than this, who would be found among the Three Hundred, the leaders and second and third men (*ἡγεμόνες, δεύτεροι, τρίτοι*) of the 100 eisphora symmories. Here again no property qualification was required. The Three Hundred were the 300 richest men in Athens; they were enrolled by the generals, against whose choice an appeal lay to the courts by the process of *antidosis*.[44] Demosthenes in the speeches against Aphobus implies that an assessment of 15 talents brought a man within the highest schedule of eisphora payers, and that only a very few very rich men like Timotheus, the son of Conon, came within this class. His guardians, he alleged, had assessed him in this class, and had made him leader (*ἡγεμών*) of his symmory 'on no small assessments, but on such large ones that I paid 500 drachmae on 25 minae'. Whatever these much-disputed words mean, it is plain that Demosthenes implies that by no means all the 100 leaders of the symmories, much less the second and third members, who comprised the rest of the Three Hundred, had fortunes of 15 talents.[45]

In view of this it is wise to be sceptical about the very large figures quoted for some Athenian fortunes. Lysias in an interesting speech warns the jury against believing hearsay figures. The famous Nicias was reputed to possess 100 talents, but his son Niceratus only inherited 14. Ischomachus, the improving landlord who is the hero of Xenophon's *Oeconomicus*, was thought to be worth 70 talents, but cut up for only 20.[46] Some big fortunes were occasionally made. Conon did very well in the Great King's service and left 40 talents.[47] A lucky strike in the silver mines might yield fabulous wealth. The estate of Diphilus, a fortunate concessionnaire of Laurium, when confiscated by Lycurgus for breaches of the mining law, brought 160 talents into the treasury.[48] A certain Epicrates, who was lucky enough to sink a productive shaft outside the scheduled area at Laurium, was stated by an informer to have made (with his partners, 'pretty well all the richest men in the city') 300 talents in three years from this private mine, on which he paid no lease or royalty:[49] he was reputed by hearsay to have been later worth 600 talents.[50] But the largest fortune of which we have any authentic information is that of the banker Pasion, who left a shield factory with a net annual profit of 1 talent, 50 talents invested in loans, and land to the value of 20 talents—75 to 80 talents in all.[51]

Although fortunes such as these were quite exceptional, it does nevertheless seem to have been true that there was a heavy concentration of wealth at the extreme top of Athenian society, in a small group of approximately 300 families. Demosthenes at any rate thought so in the latter part of his career. He noted that under the existing trierarchic system the rich got off with a small expenditure, whereas citizens of moderate or small fortunes were being ruined. This was partly due to the unfair system (or lack of system), whereby everyone on the trierarchic register contributed equally, and not according to his means. But Demosthenes in his reform of the trierarchy did not merely make contributions vary according to property, with the result, as he says, that a rich man, who had hitherto got off with one-sixteenth of a trierarchy, was sometimes responsible for two entire ships.[52] He seems to have thrown the whole burden of the trierarchy on the Three Hundred, who were divided into twenty symmories of fifteen members.[53] This implies that he thought that three-quarters of the men on the trierarchic register were too poor to make, without undue hardship, a significant contribution to the fleet. Whereas he claims that the remaining quarter carried the burden easily, with the result that the efficiency of the navy was greatly improved.

Whence did the great families derive their wealth? The men whom I have already mentioned are not altogether typical. There were of course other Athenians besides Conon who made great fortunes as condottieri in the service of the Great King or his satraps, or of the rebel kings of Egypt, or the Thracian chieftains. There were other entrepreneurs besides Epicrates and Diphilus who made fortunes in the Laurium silver mines. Pasion is an exceptional case, for he was a slave by orign and a metic most of his life. He made his fortune in two ways typical of metics, by banking and by running a large-scale slave factory,[54] as Cephalus of Syracuse had done in an earlier generation:[55] he must have bought his land late in life when made a citizen. Demosthenes senior is also, to all appearances, rather peculiar in possessing a fortune consisting exclusively of two slave factories, and cash and investments, without a single acre of land.[56] One may suspect that he was a self-made man, for Demosthenes never alludes to his ancestors.

Timotheus, Conon's son, appears in Demosthenes' speeches as a considerable landlord, owning, besides an estate in the Plain, other properties which he could mortgage for 7 talents.[57] He possessed no great reserves of cash, for he was obliged to borrow from the banker Pasion, having already pledged his land. Pasion began late in life to move into land, and Apollodorus, his extravagant elder son, appears later as a considerable landlord, owning property in three demes,[58] but like Timotheus short of liquid assets. If these great fortunes had in the second generation been converted into land, it seems likely that the majority of the 300 families were in land. Xenophon's friend, Ischomachus, was certainly a diligent gentleman-farmer; and he left 20 talents.[59] Phaenippus, who ought to have been one of the Three Hundred by rights (according to a Demosthenic speech), owned one estate, which was by Athenian standards vast, over 40 stades (nearly 5 miles) in circumference. Only about a quarter can have been arable, for he did not raise much more than 1,000 medimni of barley: there were also vineyards which produced over 800 metretae of wine; but most of the estate seems to have been scrub, for Phaenippus employed six donkeys carrying firewood, and reckoned to make 12 drachmae a day by sales.[60] These facts may serve to remind us that even the richest Athenians were relatively modest men.

In the speeches of Isaeus half a dozen middle-class fortunes, ranging from just over 5 to just under 2 talents, are analysed in detail; Timarchus' estate, described by Aeschines, seems to fall into the same class. The pattern is very uniform. The main item is always a farm, or two small farms, sometimes with stock (that is, presumably worked by the owner), sometimes without stock (presumably let to a tenant). There is usually also house property, in Athens or in the demes; the urban property is sometimes a bath, or a brothel or a bar. Occasionally there is a little money invested, and sometimes a few industrial slaves: Euctemon had some craftsmen, Ciron some slaves who earned wages, Timarchus nine or ten leather workers who brought him in 2 obols a day each, and two other craftsmen.[61] There were no doubt Athenians in this class whose fortunes were differently balanced, who were mainly in loans or slaves. But we do not hear much of them. Socrates, as reported by Xenophon, cited five Athenians who lived mainly on industrial slaves, but of them he only claims that one performed liturgies—the others merely lived in a comfortable style.[62] One may suspect that the owners of industrial slaves were in general rather humble people, mainly no doubt successful craftsmen.

The large slave owner like Nicias does not appear in the fourth century, even in the mines.[63] The Laurium mines after the Decelean war were but little exploited for two generations, as we learn from Xenophon's *Vectigalia* and the fragmentary accounts of the *poletai*.[64] We hear during this time of some Athenian citizens working in the mines with their own hands. Among the prospective hirers of his projected public slaves, Xenophon distinguishes 'those who are themselves in the mines and are growing old', and 'others, who would not or could not work with their hands, but would gladly make their living as supervisors'.[65] A client of Demosthenes boasts: 'In earlier times I made a lot of money from the silver mines, working and toiling myself with my own hands.'[66] More often the Athenian who leased a mine worked it by slave labour; a high proportion of the recorded lessees are otherwise known as men of property. The numbers employed were not, however, necessarily large. We know of one lessee, Pantaenetus, who owned thirty slaves; these, with a workshop, were apparently his sole assets, for he raised money on this security to buy a concession.[67] The very wealthy mine-owner Epicrates, who is said to have been worth 600 talents, had 'pretty well all the richest men in the city' in partnership with him early in his career, presumably because he needed their aid to buy and maintain enough slaves to exploit his mine.[68]

I have depicted a society in which, except for a small group of relatively very rich men at the top, and a larger group of casual labourers at the bottom, wealth was evenly distributed, and the graduation from the affluent to the needy very gentle. I have also depicted a society in which the great majority, from rich landowners down to peasants working a tiny allotment, derived most of their wealth from the land. This latter point cannot be fully substantiated, but apart from the evidence which I have given above, it is favoured by a legal point. The ownership of land (and house property) was a jealously guarded privilege of citizens, very rarely granted to foreigners.[69] And there were a large number of foreigners permanently domiciled in Attica—according to the census of Demetrius of Phalerum nearly half as many as there were citizens—who were debarred from ownership of land and houses, and had to make their living from industry and commerce.

I do not of course suggest that there was an absolute dichotomy between the activities of citizens and metics. Among the metics enfranchised in 401 were a number of land workers (*γεωργοί*), not to speak of a gardener (*κηπουρός*); these were presumably tenant farmers or agricultural labourers.[70] On the other hand we know of one banker, Aristolochus, who was an Athenian—he is recorded to have owned land;[71] of the other bankers known to us a high proportion were certainly metics, mostly freedmen.[72] We also know of two Athenian brothers, Diodotus and Diogeiton, who were merchants: the former left a fortune unlike any other recorded for an Athenian—5 talents cash on deposit, and $7\frac{2}{3}$ talents invested in nautical loans.[73] Then there is Andocides, a gentleman who went into trade during his exile,[74] and two or three obscurer figures.[75] The other merchants and sea captains whom we meet are, so far as we can trace their origin, foreigners,[76] and so are nearly all those who financed them with nautical loans: one of the exceptions here is Demosthenes senior, who had 70 minae—about a twelfth of his fortune—invested in these rather speculative securities.[77] In industry metics do not seem to have had so decisive a superiority, but the two largest factories known both belonged to men of alien origin, one of over 100 hands to Cephalus, a Syracusan, and another, which yielded a net annual profit of a talent to Pasion, a freedman.[78]

The economic structure of Athenian society helps to explain why the democracy, by contrast with other contemporary democracies, was at once so conservative and so stable. No suggestion was ever put forward for the redistribution of the land (*γῆς* ἀναδασμός) or for the cancellation of debts (χρεῶν ἀποκοπή), which more revolutionary democracies conducted. This is readily understandable in a society where property, and particularly land, was so widely distributed. Nor did 'the liberation of the slaves with revolutionary intent' (δούλων ἀπελευθέρωσις ἐπὶ νεωτερισμῷ), the third of the revolutionary perils against which Philip and Alexander guaranteed the cities of Greece under the League of Corinth,[79] ever occur at Athens. At times of national emergency the assembly was willing to free the slaves. To help man the fleet which won the battle of Arginusae all slaves of military age were called up with the promise (which was honoured) of freedom.[80] After the defeat of Chaeronea, Hyperides proposed and carried a motion to free the slaves for the defence of Athens, but when the crisis passed over, it was quashed and its author—unsuccessfully—prosecuted.[81] It is understandable that a full assembly, in which relatively few would be slave owners, might in a national emergency vote for the freeing of slaves; but normally respect for the rights of property prevailed.

The conservative tone of the Athenian democracy in its turn helps to account for its stability. In most contemporary states there was continuous class war, and counter-revolution alternated with revolution. In Athens from the establishment of the full democracy in 461 to its suppression by the Macedonian regent Antipater in 322 there were only two counter-revolutions, in 411 and 404; both were very short-lived, and the latter imposed by the victorious Spartan army and supported by a Spartan garrison. There was at all times a small group of wealthy intellectuals who hated the democracy, but in normal circumstances they found no support among the middle class of hoplites, or even in the upper trierarchic class. In 411, when the prestige of the democracy was deeply shaken by the Sicilian disaster, they did rally the middle and upper classes, resentful of the continued levies of eisphora and trierarchies which the long war was demanding, to the programme of the Five Thousand, a widely based oligarchy. But this constitutional experiment, which Thucydides praised highly, had a short life. In 404 again, when the war was lost, the Thirty at first enjoyed the support of the upper and middle classes, but they rapidly alienated it by their violent and arbitrary conduct. The result was that the bulk of the hoplite class fought on the democratic side in the civil war which followed, and that their leaders played a prominent part in the restoration of the democracy. Not even now were there reprisals or confiscations, and henceforth the democracy was unchallenged. In Athenian eyes democracy stood for the rule of law and the protection of property, as was natural when so many citizens were owners of property, and this fact reconciled to it the wealthier classes.

With an economy such as I have described, it may well be asked how Athens maintained its balance of payments with the rest of the world. It is unfortunately impossible even to begin to calculate exports and imports in figures. One can only point out first that payments must have balanced strictly, since there was no international credit system, and transactions were on a cash basis: and secondly that the bill for imports must have been very heavy. Imported corn alone, at the rate of 800,000 medimni per annum, at 5 drachmae, the normal price,[82] would have cost about 650 talents. There were other foodstuffs imported on a large scale, such as salt fish. Then there was timber, essential for housing and above all for shipbuilding, and for the latter purpose pitch, hemp and flax as well. Iron and bronze had all to be imported, both for home use and as raw material for export industries, not to speak of luxury materials for these latter, like the ivory which Demosthenes senior used to ornament his beds. Finally, slaves were nearly all imported.

On the other side there was one important agricultural export, olive oil: not much is heard of wine. Honey and figs, though noted for their quality, can hardly have been commercially significant items. Among industrial products Attic pottery is of course famous, and has perhaps, owing to its durability, unduly overshadowed other high-grade artistic products, such as silver plate and furniture. Something must be allowed for invisible exports—such as the profits of nautical loans paid in Athens, and the expenditure of visitors, commercial and others, in the city. But much of the bill was paid in cash, in drachmae minted from the Laurium silver, as is amply attested by the vast quantities of Athenian drachmae found in Thrace, the Bosporus, Asia Minor, Syria and Egypt. During the first half of the fourth century, when the mines were not very active, this resource must have been less important, but in the *Vectigalia* Xenophon can still claim that Athens attracts merchants because they can obtain payment for their goods in sound coin.[83] From about 340 silver production rose sharply, and the export of drachmae must have been considerable.

We today, wishing to sell our exports and to buy necessary imports of foodstuffs and raw materials, are acutely anxious about the sale of our exports, but have no worries about our imports, provided we can pay for them. The Athenians, in a similar position, were apparently unconscious of any export problem, but were greatly exercised by the danger of insufficient imports, particularly of corn. There were laws imposing drastic penalties on anyone resident at Athens, citizen or metic, who imported corn to any place save the Athenian market, and on anyone who lent money to finance a voyage which did not terminate at Athens.[84] Litigants take great pains to clear themselves of the imputation of having even intended to evade these laws, but reveal without any compunction to the jury that they have lent money to a shipper for a return voyage to Bosporus, on the express condition that he sail in ballast from the Peiraeus, and load wine at Mende or Scione for sale at Bosporus.[85] The kings of Bosporus are praised for expediting the export of corn from their dominions to Athens, and particularly for waiving the export tax;[86] it never apparently occurred to the Athenians that it would profit them if the import taxes at Bosporus on Athenian goods were abolished. Xenophon declares that merchants are popular everywhere, because 'all cities welcome as friends those who import things'.[87]

This attitude is partly explained by simple ignorance of economics. Every Athenian knew the unpleasant consequences when insufficient corn was shipped into the Peiraeus, and they took such obvious legal and administrative measures as lay within their power to force shippers to bring corn there. They were also aware of the periodic gluts of various Athenian products, but they attributed them to over-production, not to lack of markets. As Xenophon remarks, when there are a large number of bronze or iron workers, the price of their products goes down, and they are ruined: similarly when there is a large quantity of corn or wine grown, the price of crops goes down, agriculture becomes unprofitable, and many leave the land.[88]

The blindness of the Athenians may have been increased by the fact that a considerable proportion of imports was paid for in coin, minted from the silver mined in Attica, so that the sight of empty ships leaving the Peiraeus caused no alarm.[89] Secondly while all Athenians were consumers, and most of them producers of agricultural or industrial goods, very few were merchants. But whatever the reasons, it is a fact that the Athenians were blind to the importance of markets for their exports.

Some modern historians have read into Athenian foreign policy commercial motives, and attributed, for instance, the hostility of Athens and Corinth to a rivalry for markets. Such a view is, I would submit, quite unhistorical, It is possible to detect in Athenian foreign policy a desire to control by war or diplomacy the principal sources from which the city drew its supplies of corn and of timber, and the sea lanes along which these supplies had to travel. To such motives may be attributed Athens' interventions in Egypt and later in Sicily, and her sustained interest in the northern shores of the Pontus, her main source of corn, and in the Hellespont and the Bosporus, through which the Pontic cornships had to sail. Her anxiety for her supply of timber accounts for her persistent attempts to recover

Amphipolis, whose loss in 424 caused alarm 'because the city was useful to them both in the despatch of shipbuilding timber and in its money revenue'.[90] Even where the ancient sources, which often unduly neglect economic motives, are silent, it is not unreasonable from what we know of the Athenian people to postulate that they may have been influenced by anxiety for their essential imports. But that they were concerned about where merchants sold the goods that they bought from them there is no evidence at all.

V

HOW DID THE ATHENIAN DEMOCRACY WORK?

How did the Athenian Democracy Work?

ALCIBIADES once described the Athenian democracy as 'acknowledged folly',[1] and prima facie this would seem to be fair enough comment on a political system which entrusted most of the administration of the State to magistrates annually chosen by lot, and all political decisions to mass meetings which any citizen might—or might not—attend. Yet the fact remains that Athens was, by ancient standards, a remarkably efficient State, and that her foreign and domestic policy was directed as well as, if not better than, that of contemporary cities with what might seem to be more sensible constitutions.

To deal with administration first, the Athenian army was only average, by no means up to Spartan standards, and from the middle of the fifth century surpassed by the Boeotian. It was ill disciplined. This was especially true of the cavalry, which consisted of wealthy and usually aristocratic youths,[2] and this though the Athenians spent a great deal of money—about 40 talents a year—on it,[3] and devoted much attention to it. There were not only the two elected commanders of the cavalry and the elected commanders of the tribal squadrons.[4] There was an elective board of ten who enrolled the troopers, and the council annually checked the list and inspected the horses.[5] Yet Xenophon's little treatise on the duties of a cavalry commander reveals how slack and indisciplined the corps was.

The 'Old Oligarch' accounted for the inefficiency of the army as being due to the fact that the Athenians, a naval people, took no pride in it.[6] Socrates explained it partly by the sense of inferiority caused by the defeats at Lebadeia and Delium; and Periclean strategy must have lowered Athenian military morale.

But curiously enough he found the main explanation in amateur generals.[7] Yet all the higher military officers were elected, and the lower grades nominated,[8] and no ancient city—not even Rome—conceived any better way of choosing a general than by popular election.

The navy was on the other hand indisputably of high efficiency, although commanded by the same generals, and although administered by other bodies even less likely to be competent. The council was responsible for building as many triremes as the people ordered each year, and delegated the task to an elective sub-committee of ten. The naval architects were elected by the people.[9] The superintendents of the dockyards, who saw to the maintenance of the ships and their tackle, were probably one of the usual boards of ten chosen by lot.[10] When a fleet was to be commissioned an *ad hoc* board of ten was elected to organise the process.[11] The trierarchs, who were, as it would seem, the key men, being responsible for training the crews, maintaining the ships in fighting efficiency and actually commanding them at sea, were merely rich citizens serving in rotation.[12] The trierarchic system had its weaknesses: there were inefficient or niggardly trierarchs, and in the fourth century some who handed over their responsibilities to contractors.[13] But on the whole trierarchs, despite grumbling at the expense, seem to have taken a pride in their ships, stimulated by prizes.[14] They personally, of course, had not the skill to train their crews or navigate their ships, but they paid bonuses to attract skilled petty officers—steersmen, boatswains and the like—and good rowers, especially the top bench men.[15] It was the existence of a large pool of such experienced seamen—and shipwrights—among the citizens which gave the Athenian navy its unique efficiency.[16]

Another department of the administration which was indisputably very efficiently run was the religious festivals, including dramatic, musical and athletic displays; an Athenian chorus was, Socrates admits, unrivalled.[17] The festivals were directed partly by magistrates or boards chosen by lot, partly by elective boards,[18] but the main responsibility fell on the choregi, who like the trierarchs were rich citizens serving in rotation.[19] As with the trierarchs, their function, which they usually performed with zealous emulation, was to furnish money. Antisthenes, a rich man who had repeatedly been choregus and won the prize every time, 'though knowing nothing about music or the training of choirs, still was able to secure the best men in these fields'.[20] The excellence of the performances depended on the existence of a pool of highly skilled trainers and dancers and singers, for whose services choregi competed.[21]

More surprisingly finance, both imperial and domestic, was tolerably efficient, though this department was run entirely by boards chosen by lot, supervised by the council, until, in the latter half of the fourth century, an elective treasurer of the military fund and elective managers of the theoric fund were created.[22] There was a great multiplicity of financial magistrates, whose functions are explained in Aristotle's Constitution of Athens. A brief description of peace-time domestic finance—the war tax is discussed in another chapter—[23] may suffice to illustrate the system.

There were ten treasurers (ταμίαι) of the sacred moneys of Athena,[24] and from 434 until the middle of the fourth century ten treasurers of the sacred moneys of the other Gods:[25] these boards were combined from 406 to 386. They were mere accountants who kept the books and received and paid out money on order from the people. These accounts were used in the fifth century as reserve funds, into which surpluses were paid, and from which money could be borrowed by the people for extraordinary expenses.[26] There were the auditors (λογισταί), thirty in the fifth century, ten with ten advocates to assist them in the fourth, who audited the accounts of all magistrates who had handled public money,[27] and in addition an audit committee of the council (chosen by lot from its own number) which checked all such accounts every prytany.[28]

The ordinary internal revenue consisted on the one hand of sundry taxes, rents of public and sacred lands, and mining royalties and concession prices, and on the other hand of fees, fines and confiscations imposed by the courts.[29] Fines were collected by a board of Exactors (πράκτορες) on the instructions of the presidents of the courts.[30] The items in the first group were all farmed by a board of ten, the Sellers (πωληταί): the auctions were held in the presence of the council, which selected the concessionaires by vote: confiscated estates were similarly sold by auction. The Sellers had to make out forms showing what payments were due from concessionaires and purchasers and at what dates, and their business was then finished.[31] Another board, the ten Receivers (ἀποδέκται), were responsible for receiving the payments due, granting receipts (by deleting the demand forms drawn up by the Sellers) in the presence of the council, and reporting defaulters to the council (which could imprison them).

The Receivers also made every prytany an allocation of the funds received to the spending departments.[32] This was, so long as funds sufficed, a purely mechanical process, as certain fixed sums were allocated by law or by decree of the people for various purposes. Thus the assembly itself had a petty cash account of 10 talents a year to pay for engraving inscriptions, presenting crowns to deserving persons, supplying journey money to ambassadors, entertaining foreign envoys and the like.[33] The council had a similar fund,[34] and so did various boards of magistrates, such as the wardens of the market (ἀγορανόμοι)[35] and the managers of the Dionysia and the repairers of the temples—the two last had fixed allocations of 100 and 30 minas a year respectively.[36] Most of these funds had their separate treasurers—the treasurer of the people, the treasurer of the council,[37] the treasurer of the board for trireme construction[38] and so forth.

The allocation by the Receivers caused trouble only when funds were inadequate. The regular receipts were rather seasonal, the great majority falling due on the ninth prytany, and receipts from fees, fines and confiscations were of course very variable.[39] Moreover at some periods, notably the early years of the fourth century, the gross receipts were barely adequate to cover statutory expenditure. In some circumstances some expenses might have to be cut; Lysias complains of Nicomachus that, by increasing the number of statutory public sacrifices, he had caused ancient sacrifices to the amount of 3 talents to be omitted,[40] and Demosthenes envisages the possibility of sessions of the council and the assembly and the courts being suspended for lack of pay[41]—during the Euboean crisis of 348 the courts were apparently suspended for this reason.[42] On the other hand, as Lysias reveals, the council was in these circumstances tempted to welcome informations laid against wealthy citizens, in the hope of large fines or confiscations.[43] From his remarks, and the account in Aristotle of the functions of the Receivers, it would seem that the council took ultimate responsibility for balancing receipts and expenditure somehow.

The system seems unnecessarily complicated, with its many boards, each dealing with one stage of the process. The object probably was to make peculation or improper expenditure of public funds or slackness in exacting State dues difficult by making the money and accounts pass through many hands. The system was also excessively rigid, allowing for very little give and take except by special decree of the people. Thus, when ships had to be built in an emergency in 407-6, the people had to decree that the generals should borrow the money required from the Receivers and pay it to the shipwrights, to be repaid in due course by the board for trireme construction, whose vote was presumably exhausted.[44] Again in 343 when the people wished to give a pension of a drachma a day to an exiled Delian, Peisitheides, they paid the amount from the petty cash fund of the assembly, but, to put the payment on a regular footing, had to give instructions that on the next meeting of the legislative assembly it be added to the authorised payments made by the treasurer of the people.[45] Similarly in 329 when new sacrifices were voted to Amphiaraus, pending the next meeting of the legislative assembly the money had to be lent by the treasurer of the people.[46]

It was, however, this minute subdivision of duties and rigid regulation that made it possible for such complicated business as finance to be conducted by annual boards chosen by lot, that is by any citizen (over 30 years of age) who had sufficient confidence in himself to face the preliminary scrutiny and the more searching examination of his record which would terminate his year's office.[47]

All the evidence, from the Old Oligarch to Demosthenes and Aristotle,[48] indicates that, perhaps with the exception of the old archonships,[49] which demanded by tradition expenditure in excess of the meagre pay, and had some rather exacting duties, like the choice of dramatists to compete at the Dionysia, the offices chosen by lot were filled by quite humble citizens. In these circumstances a permanent civil service was hardly needed. There was a public slave who assisted the Sellers and Receivers. He had custody of the payment notes made by the former (no doubt under his guidance) and produced them for the latter at the appropriate dates, and received back for custody the cancelled notes when payment had been made.[50] There were also some semi-professional secretaries or under-secretaries of boards. The important secretaries were either chosen by lot, like the secretary of the Nine Archons[51] or the secretary of the council 'over the laws,' or elected, like the secretary of the council and people 'by the prytany', who recorded decrees; but by Aristotle's day even the last was chosen by lot, and only the secretary who read documents to the council and people was—for obvious reasons—elected.[52] Secretaries of minor boards of magistrates were, however, generally hired by them, as were under-secretaries. The men who occupied these posts were humble folk, even, like Nicomachus, freedmen,[53] and generally despised. Demosthenes never let Aeschines forget that in his poverty-stricken youth he had earned his living as 'secretary and attendant of petty magistracies' and as under-secretary of the council and people.[54] Such men, no doubt, acquired a knowledge of routine which was useful to their chiefs, but lest they should acquire too much influence it was laid down that no under-secretary might serve the same board more than once.[55]

Any decisions which rose above the level of routine were made by the council, which, as Aristotle reiterates, co-operated in most of the administrative work of the magistrates.[56] The council also, as we have seen, did some important work itself, either in full session or through committees. It was in fact the co-ordinating body which held the administrative machine together. But it had a second and more important function, that of steering committee of the assembly. By a rule which was very rarely broken, no decision might be taken by the assembly except on a probouleuma, a motion voted by the council, and placed by the council on the agenda.[57] This brings us to the means by which political decisions were arrived at. But first we must consider the composition and the procedure of the council and of the assembly.

The council of 500 was chosen annually by lot, 50 from each tribe.[58] Places were allocated to each deme of Athens and Attica in rough proportion to their importance, and the allotment took place in the demes.[59] Like magistrates councillors had to be over thirty years of age,[60] to take an oath,[61] and to submit individually to preliminary scrutiny[62] and final examination:[63] it may be conjectured that technically they had, like magistrates, to be of at least zeugite census. From these features, and in particular the elaborately representative structure of the council, it has been inferred that in the original Cleisthenic constitution it was intended to be the effective governing body of the State, only referring major and contentious issues to the people.[64] If so, it very soon ceased to be so. From the fact that it was chosen by lot, with the further provision that no one might serve on it more than two years in his life,[65] it is clear that the Athenians of the fifth and fourth centuries intended that the council should have no chance of developing a corporate sense, which would enable it to take an independent line, and wished it to be merely a fair sample of the Athenian people, whose views would naturally coincide with those of the people.

There was never any difficulty in filling the council, so far as we know. Even when the population was low in the latter part of the fourth century, the ephebe classes, which comprised citizens of 18 or 19 of hoplite status, averaged about 500, which means, as the table on page 82 will make clear, that the 30-year-old class each year would number from 400 to 350; so that with some few serving twice the council could have been manned from hoplites alone.[66] There are fairly strong indications that in the fourth century the council contained many well-to-do members—though it cannot be proved that no poor men sat on it. There are moreover suggestions that a man who wanted to get on in a given year had a good chance of doing so.[67] Demosthenes served a very crucial year, and Aeschines declares 'at this point Demosthenes entered the council chamber as a councillor, without having drawn the lot as a member or as a reserve, but by scheming corruption'.[68] This is no doubt a lie, but combined with the statement of Aristotle that the allotment of other magistracies had to be removed from the demes because they sold them, it does suggest that in some poor demes at any rate there were not many applicants for the seats, and that the demesmen were not unwilling to arrange for a generous carpet-bagger to be selected.[69] All this suggests that few poor men put down their names, and that competition for places was therefore rather slack.

It is not known why the poor liked serving in magistracies rather than on the council. Perhaps a magistracy better satisfied a craving for a spell of importance and authority, which being one of 500 councillors did not. At the same time the duties of a councillor were, in theory at any rate, exacting. The council sat every day except on festivals. The tribes took the presidency (prytany) in rotation (by lot) for a tenth of the year (thirty-five or thirty-six days), known therefore as a prytany. The members of the presiding tribe had to dine every day in the city hall, and summoned the council and assembly.[70]

From their number was drawn daily by lot the foreman (ἐπιστάτης) of the presidents, who for twenty-four hours had custody of the common seal of the city and the keys of the temples where the archives and moneys were stored. He was assisted by one-third of the presiding tribe whom he selected. In the fifth century he also served as chairman of the council and assembly (if one was held on his day). In the fourth he selected by lot from the other nine tribes of the council nine chairmen (πρόεδροι), and out of them a foreman of the chairman. No citizen might be foreman of the presidents more than once (so that thirty-five or thirty-six out of the fifty had to serve), and in the fourth century no chairman might serve more than once in a prytany, and no foreman of the chairmen more than once in the year.[71]

These rules are an interesting commentary on the Athenian preference for democracy over efficiency. Rather than have a chairman who might exercise undue influence on the council or the assembly they were prepared to risk having one who could not distinguish between an amendment and a substantive motion. Such inexperienced chairmen might even be a danger. According to Aeschines 'some people easily propose illegal decrees and others put them to the vote without being allotted the chairmanship in the straightforward way, but taking the chair in an underhand fashion (he does not explain how this was done, but presumably by persuading one's colleagues to abstain from the ballot), and if one of the other councillors does genuinely ballot and is allotted to be chairman . . . they threaten to lay an information against him, bullying the ordinary members'.[72]

The high odds on being placed in this position of terrifying prominence may help to account for the reluctance of the humble to serve on the council. For a foreman was not only exposed to jeers and groans, but to penalties if he put an illegal motion to the vote, or otherwise broke standing orders. It will be remembered how Nicias, in the second debate of the Sicilian expedition, urged the foreman to break the rules by allowing the question of the expedition to be reopened although already voted upon, and encouraged him by saying that to break the rules in so good a cause could not bring down punishment.[73] The final responsibility on such points of order was however apparently shared by all the presidents (in the fifth century) or chairmen (in the fourth). Socrates happened to be one of the presidents at the debate on the ten generals and courageously protested against putting the illegal motion of the council to the vote, but was overruled;[74] so was Demosthenes when he was one of the chairmen on a less famous occasion.[75]

In practice attendance at the council seems to have been rather slack, in the fourth century at any rate. Demosthenes in one passage draws a distinction between the active minority on the council, the politicians, who make speeches and propose motions, and the ordinary members, who 'keep their mouths shut and propose no motions, and perhaps don't even enter the council chamber as a rule'.[76]

The assembly had four regular meetings every prytany, or forty in the year. The agenda for them was to some extent fixed by law. Thus on the first of the four a vote had to be taken whether to continue the magistrates in office or depose any of them: next the corn supply and the security of the country had to be discussed; next lists of confiscated property and of heiresses were read, and an opportunity was given for bringing motions of censure against informers, or laying information against traitors or denouncing those who had failed to fulfil their promises to the people. The second meeting was devoted to what may be called private members' business, when anyone might speak to the poeple on any topic of private or public interest. The other two dealt with current problems under the headings of sacred affairs, foreign policy and secular affairs, with priority for three motions (selected by lot) on each topic in that order of precedence.[77] Besides the regular assemblies there were special meetings. These might be summoned to deal with some sudden emergency—Aeschines was presumably thinking of such meetings when he declared that owing to Demosthenes' disastrous foreign policy there had of late been more special than regular assemblies.[78] They might also be arranged beforehand to allow a full debate on an important issue. Thus when it had been resolved to assist the Segestans and Leontines at one assembly, a second was called at only four days' interval to discuss the details of the expedition, and two assemblies (on successive days) were set aside to discuss the Peace of Philocrates.[79]

How large and how regular attendance at the assembly was, it is difficult to say. The oligarchs in 411, defending the constitution of the 5,000, declared to the democrats at Samos, 'that owing to military service and business overseas more than 5,000 Athenians had never yet assembled to debate any question however important.'[80] This refers to the war years, in which many Athenians were on active service, and is a tendentious statement: it suggests that normal peace-time attendance may have been well over 5,000. This conclusion is supported by the fact that a quorum of 6,000 was required not only for ostracism,[81] but for some quite unexciting issues, such as grants of citizenship,[82] or special leave to propose a motion for remission of public debts,[83] and that there is no hint that the quorum was ever not forthcoming—though it was perhaps on these occasions that the Scythian police literally roped people into the assembly.[84]

The social composition of the assembly is also difficult to gauge. Socrates speaks of the assembly as composed of fullers, shoemakers, carpenters, smiths, peasants, merchants and shopkeepers.[85] On the other hand, as I have argued in another chapter, the assemblies which Demosthenes addressed seem generally to have been predominantly middle or upper class—hoplites and payers of war tax.[86] Special meetings must have attracted a larger working-class attendance. It was no doubt to such a meeting that Demosthenes addressed the speech on the Symmories, where alone he appears to be facing an assembly of poor men, who might recklessly vote a heavy war tax.[87] The assemblies on the Peace of Philocrates must also have contained a large element of the poorer citizens, or Eubulus' intervention, that rejection of the peace would mean both war tax and transfer of the theoric money to the military fund, would not have been so effective.[88]

Demosthenes gives a moving description of the special assembly summoned when Philip occupied Elatea.[89] 'It was evening when a messenger came to the presidents with the news that Elatea was captured. They immediately got up in the middle of dinner and expelled the occupants of the stalls in the market place and burnt the hurdles, while others sent for the generals and summoned the trumpeter: and the city was full of tumult. The next day, at dawn, the presidents summoned the council to the council chamber, and you went to the assembly, and before the council had opened proceedings and voted a resolution the whole people was sitting up on the Pnyx. And then the council came in and the presidents announced the news that had been brought to them, and introduced the messenger, and he spoke. Then the herald asked: "Who wishes to speak?" And no one came forward.'

But perhaps the most vivid picture of the assembly's formal procedure is the charming skit in the Thesmophoriazusae:[90] the genuine nucleus can be readily separated from the comic additions and alterations. The session opens with a bidding prayer proclaimed by the female herald. 'Let there be silence! Let there be silence! Ye shall pray to the Thesmophorae, Demeter and the Maiden, and to Plutus and to Calligeneia, and to Earth the foster mother, and to Hermes and the Graces, that this present assembly and meeting may act for the best for the weal of the city of Athens, and for our own good: and that she who acts and speaks the best for the people of Athens, and womankind, may prevail. This ye shall pray, and for good to yourselves.' There follows a long curse. 'Ye shall pray to the Olympian and Pythian and Delian gods and goddesses, and to the other gods, that whosoever shall plot evil against the people of womankind, or shall negotiate with Euripides or the Persians to the harm of womankind, or shall plan to be a tyrant or to restore a tyrant (there follows a catalogue of sins especially offensive to womankind), may he perish miserably and all his house; and ye shall pray that the gods give good to all the rest of you.' Business now begins. 'Listen all. The council of womankind has resolved as follows. Timoclea was foreman: Lysilla was secretary: Sostrate proposed the motion: "That an assembly be held on the middle day of the Thesmophoria in the morning, when we all have most leisure, and that the first item on the agenda be: what should be done to Euripides, since it is evident that he wrongs us all." Who wishes to speak?'

For the way in which decisions were reached in the council and assembly we have three main sources, the descriptions of famous debates in the historians, Thucydides and Xenophon; the speeches of the orators, chiefly Demosthenes and Aeschines, defending their own and denouncing their adversaries' political tactics; and the inscriptions which record actual decrees. The principal questions to be asked are: What were the respective roles of the council and the assembly? Did the assembly merely rubber-stamp resolutions worked out in detail in the council, or did it make the real decisions and even in effect exercise the initiative? And secondly, within the council and the assembly respectively, how far could and did the ordinary citizen take the initiative, and how far did political leaders, official or unofficial, monopolise the tribune?

We may take the inscriptions first, as the most authentic records. Fifth and early fourth century inscriptions are relatively uninformative because they are too concisely drafted. The official record gives only what is essential. The prescript merely states: 'It was resolved by the council and people', and gives the names of the presiding tribe and its foreman (since both were in some measure responsible for putting the decree to the vote), that of the secretary (who kept the minute of the decree and was charged with having it correctly engraved) and that of the proposer (who might be prosecuted for moving an illegal decree): the name of the archon is sometimes added (for the date). There follows (in indirect speech) the text of the decree, usually with nothing to show whether it was drafted by the council or in the assembly.

The only exceptions which are informative are amendments, which, if in the form: 'So and so proposed: Otherwise as resolved by the council; but that . . .', reveal that the original motion was drafted in the council, and put forward in its name. By this test it is possible to determine that several important fifth-century decrees were drafted in detail in council, and passed with minor modifications by the people. They include the alliance with Egesta of *c.* 458, the great reassessment of the tribute in 425, the privileges granted to Neapolis for its loyalty, the honours voted to the assassins of Phrynichus in 409, and the privileges given to the loyal Samians in 405 and 403: one of the last decrees is unique in being formally moved from the chair by the whole body of presidents, presumably to emphasise the council's unanimity.[91]

Some interesting points of detail arise from these decrees. The same man who had proposed a motion in the council might amend it in the assembly.[92] The council might draft a complex resolution, leaving some contentious clause or clauses open for the people to decide. Thus the council proposed various honours for Neapolis, but resolved that the question of whether the 'first fruits' should be reserved to Athena be left for discussion in the assembly. The assembly, in the form of an amendment, voted that they should.[93] In the decree about the assassins of Phrynichus the mover of the amendment not only suggested supplementary honours but instructed the council, if the principal honorand should (at a future date) ask for further privileges, to draft a resolution and bring it before the people.[94] This is an indication of how the people, in a very small way, could circumvent the rule of the probouleuma and take the initiative.

Conversely, when an amendment opens with the words 'otherwise as moved by so and so', it may reasonably be inferred that the substantive motion was not a probouleuma, but had been moved in the assembly by the citizen named. On this assumption some important decrees had not been drafted in the council. The regulations for the colony of Brea were proposed by its official founder, Democleides; the rules for the Eleusinian first fruits by a special board of draftsmen.[95] One of the decrees dealing with the settlement of Chalcis after its revolt in 446 was moved by a certain Anticles. That he made his proposal in the assembly is further suggested by a clause 'that the people forthwith (αὐτίκα μάλα) elect five men to go to Chalcis and administer the oath'. The word 'forthwith' is more natural in the mouth of a speaker in the assembly, where the vote could be taken straight away, than in that of a speaker in the council proposing action in an assembly to be held perhaps several days hence.[96]

If this last point is valid the first decree conferring various privileges on Methone in 428 was proposed by a citizen, Diopeithes, in the assembly.[97] It opens with the clause 'that the people forthwith vote with regard to the Methonaeans whether the people wishes forthwith to assess tribute or if it is enough for them to pay only what accrued to the Goddess from the tribute which they were assessed to pay at the last Panathenaea, and to be immune from the rest'. The decree goes on to confer various favours on Methone. At the end there is a note: 'the people voted that the Methonaeans pay only what accrued to the Goddess from the tribute which they were assessed to pay at the last Panathenaea, and be immune from the rest'. The words 'forthwith', twice used, again suggest a speaker in the assembly: when the council in their probouleuma about Neapolis left a similar decision to a special vote of the people they used a different formula: 'and about the first fruits for the Parthenos, which were even then paid to the Goddess, that the matter be considered in the people with regard to them'.[98]

The reason, it may be suggested, why Diopeithes formulated his proposal in this curiously cumbersome way may have been that amendments were not taken, as in modern practice, before the motion. In that case the whole motion might be jeopardised by one contentious clause, and a prudent politician therefore reserved such a clause for a special vote to be taken immediately after the main motion had been passed.

Early in the fourth century the formula of the prescript begins to be varied. In many decrees, it is still, as in the fifth century, 'it was resolved by the council and people', but in others it is 'it was resolved by people'.[99] Usually the first formula appears to be used when the people adopted the resolution of the council, and the second when the decree was moved in the assembly, but it is doubtful if this distinction was always strictly observed. It was technically correct to use the formula 'it was resolved by the council and people' in all cases, as was done in the fifth century, since no decree could be passed unless the council had passed a resolution putting the matter on the agenda; and in some cases the old practice seems to have been maintained.[100] Moreover no great importance seems to have attached to the formula and secretaries were sometimes careless. There are one or two decrees which must have been passed by the assembly but are headed 'it was resolved by the council';[101] presumably the secretary had forgotten to alter the prescript of the council's resolution when it was adopted by the people. In other cases the formula of enactment 'it was resolved by the (council and) people', is omitted altogether:[102] it cannot have been considered of vital significance.

Towards the end of the fifth century the drafting of decrees becomes less economical, and therefore more instructive to us. What evidently happened was this. Although in the stereotyped formula of the prescript the mover or amender of a motion is always said to speak, and in the technical language of the law was called the speaker (*ῥήτωρ*), motions and amendments were actually handed in in writing to the secretary, who read them aloud. The orators normally use the verb 'to write' for to move a resolution, and Aeschines tells a story which vividly illustrates the procedure: Demosthenes, he says, at an assembly showed to one of his neighbours 'a decree written by himself, with the name Demosthenes written on it', and asked whether he should give it to the secretary for the chairmen to put it to the vote.[103] If the motion, with or without amendments, were passed, the secretary seems to have handed over the papers without revision to the engraver to inscribe. A rather comic result of this slovenly procedure is seen in a decree granting the title of proxenos and benefactor in 408-7 to one Oeniades of Palaesciathos.[104] In the council's resolution he had been described as 'of Sciathos': an amendment was passed 'to alter "of Sciathos" to read "Oeniades of Palaesciathos"'; and this is solemnly engraved, although the correction has been made in the substantive motion.

An even more flagrant case of slovenly drafting is a decree passed on the motion of Cephisophon in favour of the Samians in 403.[105] It contains the provision 'that the embassy of the Samians be introduced to the people to deal with their requirements', which is clearly a purely procedural clause of the probouleuma, which should have been deleted when it was adopted by the people. Among the other provisions are 'that all the privileges which the people of the Athenians previously voted to the people of the Samians be confirmed', and an invitation of the embassy to dinner in the prytaneum. The main decree is followed by an amendment, also proposed by Cephisophon, 'that it has been voted by the people of the Athenians that the previous decrees about the Samians be confirmed, as the council resolved in its probouleuma and introduced to the people', and a second invitation of the embassy to dinner. It is difficult to see what to make of this muddle. Did the council forget to record in its probouleuma a resolution which it had passed confirming the earlier decrees and omit to invite the embassy to dinner? And did Cephisophon in his amendment correct these errors? And were the corrections embodied in the decree, as well as being recorded as an amendment?

A more revealing form of carelessness is to leave in the text of the decree the words (in indirect speech) 'it has been resolved by the council' or 'by the people', in addition to the statement in the prescript 'it was resolved by the (council and) people'.

This is a much more useful clue than the wording of the prescript. For a man moving a resolution in the council would never begin with the words: 'it is resolved by the people,' nor a speaker in the assembly with the words 'it is resolved by the council'.

In the 370s began a yet more slovenly practice. After the standard prescript including the words 'it was resolved by the council and people,' many decrees are drafted on such lines as this: 'With regard to the statement made by the envoys from —— that it is resolved by the council that the chairmen who shall by lot preside at the next assembly shall introduce them to the people and shall communicate a resolution of the council to the people that the council resolves that, whereas, etc.'[106] What has happened is that the whole probouleuma has been copied verbatim, and in these cases it is manifest that the assembly merely rubber-stamped it.

A unique decree of 333 B.C. reveals a very different procedure.[107] After a prescript ending with the words: 'it was resolved by the council: Antidotus son of Apollodorus of Sypalettus proposed,' is a probouleuma instructing the chairmen of the next assembly to introduce the Citian delegation to the assembly and 'to communicate a resolution of the council to the people that the council resolves that the people, having heard the Citians about the foundation of the temple and any other Athenian who wishes, shall decide as it thinks best'. There follows a second prescript (in the next prytany) ending 'it was resolved by the people: Lycurgus son of Lycophron proposed', and the decree of the people (incorporating the words 'it was resolved by the people') granting the request of the Citians.

This decree is unique in preserving such a non-committal probouleuma: the reason probably is that the Citians engraved it themselves (the secretary is not instructed to do so), and thought it safest to have the whole dossier of documents inscribed as it was handed to them by the secretary. But there are many decrees identical in form with the second half of the Citian decree. Not all such decrees presuppose a purely non-committal probouleuma. A decree granting honours and privileges to one Archippus begins 'that it has been resolved by the people' but its preamble runs 'with regard to the statement of Archippus and the probouleuma which the council passed about him'.[108] Here it may be conjectured that the council had endorsed Archippus' claims and suggested in general terms that the people award him suitable honours, and that a speaker in the assembly made concrete proposals. Another decree, accepting the proffered alliance of Arcadia, Achaea, Elis and Phlius,[109] is also presented in the form of a motion in the assembly, 'that it has been resolved by the people', and opens with the proposal that the herald shall forthwith (in the assembly) pray for the blessing of the Gods on the alliance; but the preamble recites that 'the allies have introduced a resolution into the council to receive the alliance', and that 'the council have passed a probouleuma to the same effect'. Here it would seem that the council had made a firm recommendation. The speaker in the assembly may have formulated the exact terms of the alliance, or may have merely redrafted the council's motion, prefixing it with the proposal for a solemn prayer and an explanatory preamble.

As a rule, however, it would seem that if the probouleuma was adopted, it was engraved *totidem verbis*, with amendments, if any, subjoined; and it is therefore probable that decrees which open with the words 'that it has been resolved by the people' were for the most part, like that of Lycurgus on the Citians, proposed in the assembly on the basis of a purely formal probouleuma.

Using these clues it is often possible to distinguish when the initiative came from the council and when it left the assembly a free choice. The decree in favour of Clazomenae in 387 B.C. would seem to have been drafted by Poliagros in the assembly.[110] This decree, like that of Diopeithes on Methone, reserves some points for a special vote of the people: 'and about a governor and a garrison that the people decide forthwith whether they be established in Clazomenae or whether the people of Clazomenae be authorised to decide whether they wish to receive them or not'. At the end is a note: 'the people voted that they pay no other taxes (than the 5 per cent. mentioned in the decree) and receive neither garrison nor governor'.

It also appears that the alliances with Chios and Byzantium, immediately before the formation of the second Athenian League, and the foundation charter of the League itself, were drafted in the assembly.[111] On the other hand, subsequent accessions to the League were handled by the council, whose resolutions the people confirmed.[112]

The general conclusion which emerges from the inscriptions is that the council was not a policy-making body. On uncontentious matters it drafted decrees, sometimes leaving minor difficulties to be settled by the people, but on any major issue, and some minor ones, it merely put the question on the agenda of the assembly. This conclusion is borne out by the reports of debates in Thucydides. All the great issues were debated in the assembly and decided there, the Corcyraean alliance, the rejection of the Spartan ultimatum in 431, the fate of Mitylene, the Spartan overtures in 425 and again in 420, the Sicilian expedition.[113] The role of the council is rarely so much as mentioned, though of course it must have introduced the envoys. Only in 420 do we hear of the Spartan envoys going first to the council, and then to the assembly, where by a trick of Alcibiades they disowned the plenipotentiary powers which they had claimed before the council, and so enabled Alicibiades to discredit them.

In Xenophon's story of the trial of the ten generals the council plays a bigger part. The generals reported to the council, which on the motion of Timocrates imprisoned them and brought them before the assembly. After a long and rather inconclusive debate, in which the generals took part, the assembly, as it was getting too dark to count votes, decided to postpone the question and instructed the council to produce a probouleuma on how they should be tried. The enemies of the generals now took advantage of the fact that one of their number, Callixenus, was on the council. He made an attack on the generals and got a probouleuma passed that the people should vote for or against the death sentence on all without further debate, as the case had been fully discussed already. At the assembly, however, protests were raised and Euryptolemus proposed a rival motion. The people then voted between the probouleuma and Euryptolemus' motion, and after a recount adopted the former. This narrative incidentally reveals another procedural possibility. Even if the council made a definite recommendation, it could not only be amended: a quite different motion might be substituted.[114]

The orators do not add greatly to our knowledge. They confirm that vital decisions were left entirely to the assembly. In the debate on the peace of Philocrates there was apparently no substantive probouleuma before the assembly: by the procedure proposed by Demosthenes, on the first day any citizen might speak and propose a motion, on the second the motions were to be put to the vote.[115] It is clear from Demosthenes' narrative that on the capture of Elatea the council had no proposals to make, and left it to the assembly to produce them. At the same time the orators show that it might be tactically convenient to get a question raised through a friend on the council; thus Demosthenes probably used Apollodorus to move a probouleuma on the allocation of the surplus to the theoric and military funds.[116] Demosthenes also mentions a case, which by the nature of things could not be recorded on stone, where a probouleuma was rejected by the assembly. When the news of the disaster of Tamynae arrived the council passed a resolution that all the rest of the cavalry be sent to the front. At the assembly Meidias, to evade active service as a trooper, volunteered to be a trierarch 'before even the chairmen had taken their seats', but after debate it was decided not to mobilise the cavalry.[117]

Turning to the question of individual initiative, it is already plain that if, as often, the council made a noncommittal probouleuma any citizen could move a decree on the subject in the assembly, and that if they made a definite recommendation, any citizen could propose amendments, an alternative motion or outright rejection. It remains to consider however whether, and if so how, a citizen could get a question on to the agenda. The probouleuma rule did at least mean that no decree could be passed in the assembly unless the council had passed a formal resolution introducing the topic, and what evidence there is confirms the natural hypothesis that only a councillor could move a motion in council. The orators imply this by their language: 'Apollodorus, being a member of the council, moved a decree in the council and brought forward a probouleuma in the assembly',[118] or again: 'Timarchus, being a councillor, moved that . . .'.[119] The clearest evidence comes from Demosthenes' activities at the time of the negotiations which led up to the Peace of Philocrates. He was during the earlier stages on the council, and used his position to move various minor decrees—that the first Athenian envoys be crowned, that Philip's envoys be introduced to the people and that they be allocated seats in the theatre, that the second Athenian envoys sail forthwith[120]—but later, when his year was over, he cites 'the probouleuma which the council voted on my report and the testimony of its mover'.[121]

In practice no doubt a politician normally saw to it that he had some friends and allies on the council each year.[122] But failing that there were other procedures. Demosthenes tells us how Timocrates ought legally to have proceeded in order to secure the passage of his bill to allow bail to State debtors. In this particular case special leave to introduce the motion was required from the people. This done, he should have followed the usual course by making a written application (*πρόσοδον γράφεσθαι*) to the council and then (if they put the matter on the agenda) making a proposal in the assembly.[123] The right of 'application' was often granted to foreigners, and was apparently an inherent right of citizens.[124] Aeschines describes how Demosthenes used it —'he walked into the council chamber and pushing aside the ordinary members carried out a probouleuma to the assembly, exploiting the inexperience of the mover; and he got this motion put to the vote in the assembly too, and a decree of the people passed, when the assembly had already risen and I had left (or I never would have allowed it) and the majority had dispersed'.[125] How widely the right of 'application' was used we do not know. The council of course was not compelled to take the matter up,[126] and may well have killed large numbers of frivolous motions at birth; but it is unlikely that they would have refused to put on the agenda a proposal from anyone of political importance.

The inscriptions reveal the last resort of a private citizen who had some cause greatly at heart. In a number of cases a citizen moves in the assembly "that the council pass a probouleuma and bring it forward to the people that . . .". This might be done, as in the case of the ten generals, when the assembly already had the matter on its agenda, and wished to have it reintroduced at a later session.[127] But it would appear that this procedure could be used to introduce a topic *de novo*. Most cases are grants of honours,[128] but one is an important matter of public interest, Hegesippus' decree of 357-6, enacting the death penalty and confiscation of goods for anyone who molested the allies of Athens, which arose out of an attack on Eretria, but was of general application.[129] It seems likely that motions of this type might be made at the second assembly of each prytany, 'in which anyone who wishes may, having made a humble petition, speak to the people on any matter he wishes, private or public'.[130]

It would appear then that the control of the council over the assembly amounted to very little. It was no doubt the intention of the Athenians that the council, consisting of men of mature years and—in theory at any rate—of some substance, who were on oath and liable to prosecution if they betrayed their trust, should act as some check on possibly irresponsible conduct by the assembly. It was their duty to refuse to put to the vote illegal proposals, and they could refuse to give facilities to foolish ones. They no doubt saved the people's time by doing so, and by drafting uncontentious, but sometimes complicated, measures for the assembly's approval. Finally they saw to it that no motion was proposed without due notice and publicity. But policy was decided in the assembly.

What has been said above applies to decrees. For laws a more elaborate procedure was laid down in the fourth century at any rate. According to Aeschines it was the duty of the six thesmothetae, the judicial members of the college of archons, to make an annual review of the laws, and if they found any contradictions or ambiguities in the code, to post the relevant laws up. The presidents then held a special legislative session of the assembly, and the people voted which law to delete or to confirm.[131] It was presumably at this annual review that amendments could be made to the code under the procedure described by Demosthenes. On the eleventh day of the first prytany the code was submitted to a vote of the people section by section, the laws relating to the council, the general laws, those relating to the nine archons and to the other magistrates. If the people approved any section it stood. If they disapproved, the chairmen of the third assembly after this placed on its agenda the holding of a legislative meeting: meanwhile any citizen might post up new laws (with the old laws which they would supersede). The legislative assembly consisted of a limited number of citizens—in one case 1,001 plus the council of 500—from those who had taken the heliastic oath, and were therefore over 30. Having heard both the proposers of the new laws and five elected advocates for the old laws, it decided by vote.[132]

A procedure of this kind is first recorded when the laws were revised after the restoration of the democracy in 403,[133] and it probably did not exist before then. In the fifth century, at any rate, a number of enactments were passed as decrees which would have required legislation in the fourth, such as the establishment *c.* 448 of a priestess of Athena Nike and the allocation to her of a salary from public funds,[134] or the establishment in 434 of the treasurers of the other Gods, and the enactment of rules on the use of sacred funds.[135] These decrees were moved by ordinary citizens. The regulations for the cult of Eleusis were drafted *c.* 418 by a special board of draftsmen (*συγγραφεῖς*), but were presented to the council and people by the normal procedure, and amended in the assembly.[136] The appointment of a board of draftsmen was not peculiar to changes of law; such a board drafted regulations for Miletus,[137] and was no doubt appointed for difficult and technical measures of any kind. What literary evidence we have suggests that the Athenians in the fifth century were not acutely conscious of any such clear distinction between laws and decrees as the orators of the fourth century insist upon so strongly.[138] And finally, until the laws were codified between 411 and 403, it is difficult to see what mechanical test there can have been to distinguish them from decrees.[139] The fourth-century system may have had merits as ensuring the constitutional stability so much valued by the Greeks, but it made the administration unduly rigid. No change, however minute, could be made in the administrative routine except by legislation on the one annual occasion set apart for it: even Peisitheides' pension could only be put on a permanent basis by this process.[140]

A law passed by the proper procedure was still liable to be quashed by the courts by the indictment of its author for passing an inexpedient law, or one contradictory to a law still in the code.[141] Decrees which were irregularly enacted, or whose content conflicted with any law, were liable to the indictment for illegal proceedings, which goes back to before 415[142]—probably to 461[143]—though how exactly it was applied in the absence of any clear distinction between laws and decrees is obscure. This brings us to the vital part played in Athenian politics by the courts. Not only could measures and their authors be thus indicted, but many forms of indictment and impeachment were available against politicians—for treason, deceiving the people, peculation, bribery and so forth, and all were freely used. The juries, which varied in size according to the importance of the case, but in political cases normally numbered some thousands,[144] were chosen by lot from a panel, also chosen by lot, of

6,000 citizens.[145] All citizens, however poor, were eligible for this service,[146] and in the fifth century it would appear from Aristophanes' *Wasps* that the courts were mainly manned by old men of the humbler classes, who thus earned a meagre pension, or at any rate pocket money.[147] By Demosthenes' day the juries seem to have become predominantly middle or upper class. They probably acted as a conservative brake on the constitution—as for instance in quashing Hypereides' decree to free the slaves after Chaeronea.[148]

It would seem on the face of it that policy was initiated by any citizen who chose to offer his advice to the people, and was decided by the people in the assembly. Did the Athenians really guide their affairs as wisely as they did by this anarchic method, or was there some form of government, in the modern sense, official or unofficial, or were there parties, approximating to modern political parties, which provided alternative governments, or at the least supported coherent alternative policies? It is sometimes stated or implied that the ten generals formed a kind of government in the fifth century, and that they enjoyed certain constitutional prerogatives which helped them to perform this function.

The evidence for any important constitutional prerogatives is exceedingly weak. The generals were primarily executive officers in the military and naval spheres, and their duties were to mobilise armies and fleets on the instructions of the assembly, and to command such armies and fleets with a view to achieving objectives laid down, in more or less detail, by the people. They might, like other magistrates, or envoys, or the council, be given full powers, but, so far as we know, only within certain terms of reference. Thus Nicias, Alcibiades and Lamachus were given full powers 'to aid the Egestaeans against the Selinuntines, and to assist in the resettlement of Leontini, and to take such other action in Sicily as they should consider in the best interests of Athens': later they were given full power 'to act as they thought best about the size of the force and the whole expedition'.[149]

Occasionally, when secrecy was essential, as in the attempted seizure of Megara and the double attack on Boeotia in 424, the generals seem to have acted on their own initiative without consulting the people.[150]

It seems that the generals could be granted by the people, and normally were granted in wartime, priority of access to the presidents of the council and assembly, and perhaps the right of initiating business in the council and assembly. In one wartime decree the generals are instructed, with the presidents, to call an assembly,[151] and in another, it would seem, to initiate certain business.[152] In the second case a decree was as a result passed on the motion of the generals, and there is one other instance of this formula being used.[153] In another wartime decree certain business is given precedence before the council 'unless the generals require anything'.[154]

Such modest prerogatives hardly raised the generals above the level of the ordinary citizen, who could make an application to the council. In the fourth century generals seem normally to have followed this procedure; two decrees, moved in the normal way by a councillor in the council, begin 'with reference to the statement made by Timotheus the general' and 'whereas Timotheus the general states that . . .'.[155]

The idea that the board of generals acted as such as a government is manifestly false. The generals were ten individuals, who often advocated diametrically opposed policies, as did Nicias and Alcibiades over the Sicilian expedition. The utmost that can be said is that the people usually followed the advice of a general or generals, or that generals were usually political leaders and vice versa. This was partly because a general who had served many times had the necessary experience and technical knowledge to offer informed advice: thus when the Sicilian expedition had been decided upon, much against his will, an appeal was made to Nicias to estimate the forces required.[156] But it was even more due to the fact that in the fifth century the people elected as generals men whose opinion they respected, mainly on the rather irrelevant grounds of ancestry and wealth. This clearly comes out at the beginning of Alcibiades' career. 'Though still young at that date by the standard of any other city', says Thucydides, 'he was honoured for the distinction of his ancestors'. Annoyed by the Spartans having made their first unofficial approaches through two generals, Nicias and Laches, instead of through himself, though he had put himself out to look after their prisoners, he successfully persuaded the assembly to reject their pleas for a rapprochement, and was elected general (for the first time) next year.[157]

Anything like a continuous government was only achieved when one man (or a coherent group of men) succeeded in holding the confidence of the people over a long period, in which case he (or they) was usually in the fifth century regularly re-elected general. The most famous case is, of course, that of Pericles. There is no sound evidence that Pericles enjoyed any constitutional precedence over his colleagues, or indeed any special powers. This has been inferred from the fact that on two occasions, the Samian war of 440 and the first invasion of Attica in 431, Thucydides speaks of Pericles as commanding 'himself the tenth'.[158] But on the analogy of 'himself the fifth' and 'himself the third', which merely mean with four or two colleagues, this phrase was probably intended to emphasize that the importance of the operation was such that all ten generals served. And even if Thucydides did mean to convey by the phrase that Pericles was given some authority or precedence over his colleagues, he implies that such supreme authority was accorded to him specially for these particular operations, and not as a general rule.

It has also been inferred from the fact that, although normally the ten generals came each from a tribe, in several years (441, 439, 433, 432 and perhaps 431) two generals came from Pericles' tribe and none from another, that Pericles was chosen from the whole citizen body (as commander-in-chief). But in later years, when Pericles was dead, two generals were sometimes (probably in 426, and certainly in either 415 or 414) chosen from one tribe, and neither of the pair was a man on whom there was any reason to confer a supreme command.[159] The tribal rule was probably broken in order to give a chance to other able men in a tribe which possessed an outstanding general who was continually re-elected. We know too little of Athenian elections to understand how it was done. Candidates were as today nominated—usually it would seem in the assembly, though a formal probouleuma was required for elections as for any other business—and a vote taken between them, if more than one nomination was made.[160] It is possible that Aristotle's phrase 'one from each tribe' is inaccurate, and that what happened was that each tribe nominated candidates, between whom the whole people voted. In that case it would not have been impossible to arrange for a tribe which had no very distinguished candidate in its own number to select an outsider.[161]

An extraordinary constitutional position has also been inferred for Pericles from the fact that during the first invasion of Attica in 431 he 'did not hold an assembly or any meeting' of the Athenians.[162] But this refers to a state of emergency. During the actual invasion period, when all citizens were mobilised, the people may well have suspended sessions of the assembly, and have left it to the discretion of the generals (whose decisions would in fact be determined by Pericles, either in virtue of his personal prestige, or perhaps his authority as 'tenth himself') to summon an assembly or other meeting if they required it.

Pericles did not rule Athens for many years in virtue of any constitutional prerogatives. He owed his power, as Thucydides tells us, to his authority and judgment, and to his manifest incorruptibility.[163] He had to persuade the people to vote for every measure that he wished to have passed, and if they lost confidence in him they could, as they once did, depose and fine him,[164] and they could flout his advice, as again they did in trying to parley with the Spartans in 430.[165]

In the last third of the fifth century we find a new type of political leader emerging, an orator like Cleon, whom no one thought of electing general until he accidentally proved his ability. This became normal in the fourth century, when most generals carried little political weight, and the assembly was swayed by orators. The reason was no doubt the growing specialisation both in politics and in war. A gentleman of birth and wealth was no longer felt to be qualified as such both to advise the people and to take command in war. The army and navy were led by semi-professional generals like Iphicrates or Chabrias—in one case a foreign mercenary captain, Charidemus, was given the citizenship so that he might qualify—who also hired their services to other powers. They were thus much abroad and not in close touch with Athenian politics, and their loyalty was not above question. The other generals were mere lay figures. As Demosthenes complains: 'You elect from among yourselves ten regimental commanders, ten generals, ten squadron leaders and two cavalry commanders. Except for one, whom you send out to war, the rest organise processions with the managers of the festivals. You are like makers of terracotta statuettes: you make regimental commanders and squadron leaders for the market, not for war'.[166]

On the other hand politics, with the development of rhetorical technique, required special training. Many of the orators were men of family and wealth like Lycurgus, but it was possible for a poor man, like Aeschines or Demades, or indeed Demosthenes, whose inherited fortune was largely embezzled by his guardians, to achieve prominence. Being a politician must have been a full-time job, involving not only regular attendance at the assembly, but maintaining a watch on the council and keeping oneself informed on foreign affairs, finance, the navy, the corn supply and public affairs generally. Poor politicians seem generally to have maintained themselves at first by writing speeches for private litigants; Demosthenes did so, and Demades prided himself that he had not.[167] Having once gained a name they lived on politics. This did not necessarily mean, as Demosthenes alleged of his adversaries, that they were systematically bribed by foreign powers. Many no doubt did accept regular subsidies from foreign powers whose interests they supported on other grounds. More usually they seem to have accepted fees rather than bribes from interested parties, whether cities or individuals, who wished measures to be promoted in their favour.

The receipt of such payments was tolerated by public opinion. 'As I said in the assembly, members of the jury', declared Hypereides, 'you willingly allow generals and orators to make large profits—it is not the laws that allow them to do so, but your kindness and humanity—only maintaining one condition, that the money is taken for and not against your interests'. The profits were indeed large if Hypereides was correct in saying that 'Demosthenes and Demades had received more than 60 talents each just for decrees in the city and grants of honours to individuals, apart from the King's money, and Alexander's'.[168]

In the latter half of the fourth century certain important financial offices were made elective,[169] and the holders of these exercised great political influence. Thus Eubulus was one of the managers of the theoric fund,[170] into which surplus revenues flowed in peace time, and Lycurgus held an office concerned with the administration of the public revenues.[171] It is fairly certain however that these posts carried no constitutional prerogatives beyond some power of supervision over the minor financial officials: thus the Sellers farmed the taxes and mines 'with the treasurer of the military fund and those elected to manage the theoric fund'.[172] Aeschines, indeed, declares that 'owing to the confidence that you had in Eubulus, those elected to manage the theoric fund held the office of Auditor, and that of Receivers, and that of the Superintendents of the Dockyards, and built an arsenal, and acted as highway commissioners and had practically the whole administration of the city in their hands'.[173] But this is mere rhetoric. The position of the elective financial magistrates was probably similar to that of the generals in the fifth century. The people elected to these offices men whom it trusted, and by holding them they acquired experience which added to their authority. This appears clearly in the case of Lycurgus, who held office for one quadrennium only (the post being quadrennial and re-election prohibited), but *de facto* administered the finances for twelve years.[174]

There was throughout Athenian history a class of semi-professional politicians, at first consisting of the gentry, later partly of the gentry and partly of poor men of rhetorical talent. These were the people who held the elective offices, were chosen as envoys to foreign States, proposed motions in the council and in the assembly, and prosecuted (and defended) in political trials. In the fourth century orators they are clearly recognised as a class, distinct from the mass of ordinary citizens, who held the offices which went by lot and merely voted in the council, assembly and law courts. The commoner apparently regarded the politicians with some suspicion, and Demosthenes in several passages exploits this feeling. 'In the old days, when the people dared to act and fight itself it was master of the politicians, and controlled all rewards, and it was a privilege for anyone to receive honour and office and rewards from the people. But today on the contrary the politicians control rewards, and everything is done through them, and you, the people . . . have become underlings, a mere appanage, content if they give you a share of the theoric moneys, or celebrate the Boedromia.'[175] Or again: 'If you acquit, the council will be in the hands of the orators: if you condemn, in those of the ordinary members. For when the majority see that this council has been deprived of its crown owing to the misconduct of the orators, they will not leave the business to them, but will give the best advice themselves.'[176] Another speech in the Demosthenic corpus is full of abuse of politicians. 'But I do not imagine that their excuses and accusations and pretended feuds deceive you. For you have often seen them declaring that they are enemies in the courts and on the tribune and privately co-operating and sharing the profits.'[177]

There were no parties in anything like the modern sense,

either among the politicians or the general public. At the one end of the scale there were groups or cliques among the politicians. Demosthenes complains (the allusion is to the financial organisation of the war tax):[178] 'You conduct politics by symmories. An orator is the director, and there is a general under him, and the three hundred to cheer'.[179] But such alliances were probably based on personalities rather than principles, and seem to have been temporary.[180]

At the other end of scale there was a broad distinction of outlook between the propertied classes and the poor. Aristotle thought that he could discern this distinction throughout Athenian political history,[181] and he is not likely to have been entirely wrong. In domestic affairs it is difficult to trace it. There was no overt oligarchical party. Oligarchs had to confine themselves in normal times to cabals and intrigues and pamphlets, and only came into the open when they could stage a counter-revolution, as in 411, or had the armed backing of a foreign conqueror as in 404 and 322. All politicians had at any rate to pay lip service to the democracy and oligarch was not even used as a term of political abuse: in his most violent speech Demosthenes no more than hints that Meidias and his friends are secret oligarchs.[182]

The distinction can be most clearly discerned in foreign policy—which of course involved finance. On a number of occasions we are told that the propertied classes favoured peace or appeasement, while the poor were more bellicose. The Oxyrhynchus historian states that this was so in 396,[183] Diodorus on Alexander's death.[184] Aristophanes declares: 'We must launch the fleet: the poor man agrees, the rich and the farmers don't agree.'[185] But this merely means that people tended to vote according to their economic interests. The rich disliked paying war tax and serving frequently as trierarchs, farmers feared their land would be ravaged and they themselves called up for military service. The poor on the other hand had less to lose, and might hope for land allotments abroad in case of success, besides being more keenly interested in the defence of the democratic régime, which they rightly felt was threatened by the predominance of Sparta and Macedon.

The conclusion seems inevitable that Athenian policy was really determined by mass meetings of the citizens on the advice of anyone who could win the people's ear. The success of Athens is a testimony to the basic sense of the ordinary Athenian citizen. The assembly was, like all crowds, sometimes unduly swayed by mass emotion—anger as in the first debate on Mitylene, indignation as in the vote on the ten generals, or optimism as in the debates on the Sicilian expedition. In the first case it luckily recovered its judgment in time, and by a judicious breach of its standing orders reversed its decision. In the second it repented too late to save its victims. But in general the assembly seems to have kept its head, and very rarely to have broken its rules of procedure—the case of the ten generals would not have achieved such notoriety if such incidents had not been very rare.

Moreover the people demanded high standards of its advisers. Legally the proposer of a decree was responsible to the people; he could be—and frequently was—indicted if his motion was illegal or even if his policy was inexpedient. According to an ancient law cited by Deinarchus a 'speaker', in the technical sense of the proposer of a motion, had, like the generals, to own land in Attica and to have legitimate children,[186] and even if this law was a dead letter, it illustrates the serious view which the Athenians took of the responsibility attaching to political leadership.

In practice the people did not suffer fools gladly. Socrates remarks that in discussing any technical problem the people would listen only to experts, and booed and shouted down a clever speaker who wasted its time by ill-informed rhetoric.[187] Another anecdote told of Socrates illustrates the demands made by the assembly of its advisers.[188] Young Glaucon was ambitious to become a leading politician and kept making speeches, only to be howled down and make himself ridiculous. Socrates to wean him from his folly puts him through a little questionnaire. 'Tell me the sources of the revenues of the city at the present time, and their amount.' Glaucon confesses ignorance. 'Well, if you have omitted that question, tell us the expenses of the city: for obviously you are planning to cut down superfluous expenditure.' Glaucon can give no answer, and Socrates goes on. 'Then tell us first the military and naval strength of the city and secondly that of its enemies.' Glaucon again confesses ignorance. 'But I know that you have taken an interest in the security of the country, and know which garrisons are well placed and which not, and how many men are adequate or not.' Glaucon has never visited the frontier. 'I know you have not been to the silver mines, so as to know why they produce less than they used to do. But I am sure that you have not neglected the question of how long home-grown corn can feed the city, and how much extra is required annually.' It was informed advice, and not mere eloquence, that the people expected from rising politicians, and they saw to it that they got it.

NOTES

I. THE ECONOMIC BASIS OF THE ATHENIAN DEMOCRACY

[1] For the convenience of readers unfamiliar with Attic currency, the following table is given:

1 talent = 60 minae = 6,000 drachmae
1 mina = 100 drachmae
1 drachma = 6 obols

Owing to the very different standards of living and patterns of spending it is useless and even misleading to try to translate Attic into modern currency, especially now when the value of money is changing so fast. The following facts will give a rough idea of the value of money in fifth- and fourth-century Athens (fourth-century prices and wages were higher than fifth.) In the Erechtheium accounts (*IG* I.² 373-4) of 409/8-407/6 B.C. the standard wage (for citizens, metics and slaves alike) is 1 drachma per day, occasionally 1½ drachmae. In the Eleusinian accounts (*IG* II-III.² 1672-3) of 329/8 and 327/6 B.C. unskilled labourers get 1½ drachmae per day, skilled men 2 or 2½ drachmae. In 351 B.C. Demosthenes (IV. 28) reckons 2 obols a day as ration allowance for soldiers and sailors: as he is trying to prove that his projected standing force can be cheaply maintained he is probably being optimistic. In the Eleusinian accounts public slaves are allowed 3 obols a day for food, and ephebes (young men of 18 and 19 undergoing military training) in the 330's were allowed 4 obols a day for their rations (Arist. *Ath. Pol.* 42. 3). Clothing was relatively dear. Tunics bought for the Eleusinian public slaves cost over 7 drachmae each, leather jerkins 4½, 3 or 2½, and shoes 6 drachmae a pair; a cloak is priced in Aristophanes' *Plutus*, 982-3 (of 388 B.C.) at 20 drachmae, and shoes at 8 drachmae—perhaps rather high prices in the context. For the maintenance of two girls and a boy, with a male nurse and a maid, in about 400 B.C. Lysias (XXXII. 28) allows 1,000 drachmae a year and Demosthenes (XXVII. 36), speaking in 363 B.C., accepts 700 drachmae a year as a reasonable sum for the maintenance of himself and his sister and mother during his minority. These work out at about 3⅓ obols and nearly 4 obols each per day, which seems very little, but rent is not included and Greeks considered that women and children ate much less than men. Disabled citizens who could do no work and owned less than 3 minae were given public assistance at the rate of 1 obol a day in the early fourth century and 2 obols in the late fourth (Arist. *Ath. Pol.* 49. 4, Lysias, XXIV. 13), but this was merely a dole; Lysias' client did follow a trade.

[2] Aristotle (*Ath. Pol.* 7. 4) commenting on Solon's exclusion of thetes from all offices, remarks: *διὸ καὶ νῦν ἐπειδὰν ἔρηται τὸν μέλλοντα κληροῦσθαί τιν' ἀρχήν, ποῖον τέλος τελεῖ, οὐδ' ἂν εἷς εἴποι θητικόν.* This seems to imply that

the Solonian rule was still technically in force, but ignored in practice. Similarly with the higher qualification for the Treasurers of Athena: *κληροῦται δ' εἷς ἐκ τῆς φυλῆς ἐκ πεντακοσιομεδίμνων κατὰ τὸν Σόλωνος νόμον (ἔτι γὰρ ὁ νόμος κύριός ἐστιν), ἄρχει δ' ὁ λαχὼν κἂν πάνυ πένης ᾖ* (Arist. *Ath. Pol.* 47. 1). The 'Old Oligarch' declares that in his day (c. 425 B.C.) the *δῆμος* (which in his political terminology means roughly the thetes) filled the offices appointed by lot ([Xen.] *Ath. Pol.* i. 3).

[3] Actually Pericles is only recorded to have introduced pay for jurors (Arist. *Ath. Pol.* 27. 3), but this was presumably the last stage in the process. Plato (*Gorgias*, 515e) attributes pay in general to Pericles.

[4] For pay for office in general see [Xen.] *Ath. Pol.* i. 3, Thuc. VIII. 67. 3, Arist. *Ath. Pol.* 24. 3, 29. 5. Aristotle gives a few specific rates in *Ath. Pol.* 62. 2 (4 obols for the nine archons, a drachma for sundry other offices; cf. also 42. 3). Aristophanes (*Ach.* 66, 90) suggests that ambassadors received 2 drachmae (but Westermann in *Class. Phil.* 1910, pp. 203-16 infers about 1½ drachmae from inscriptions; this would include travelling expenses) and also that taxiarchs were paid, apparently 3 drachmae (*id. ib.* 595-607; cf. Larsen, *Class. Phil.* 1946, pp. 91-8), contrary to the general view (based on a misinterpretation of [Xen.] *Ath. Pol.* i. 3) that the elective military offices were unpaid.

[5] Arist. *Ath. Pol.* 62. 2. It might be inferred from 29. 5 that the fifth-century rate was 3 obols, but a decree which abolished all pay except for a few essential offices may have reduced the rates for these.

[6] Arist. *Ath. Pol.* 27. 3, 62. 2, Schol. on Aristoph. *Wasps*, 88, 300. The *τριώβολον* is first mentioned in the *Knights* (51, 255, etc.) of 424 B.C.

[7] Arist. *Ath. Pol.* 41. 3. It appears from Aristoph. *Eccl.* 183-8, 380-93 (cf. 289-310) that only a limited number who arrived first got the pay, and that it was already (393-1 B.C.) 3 obols.

[8] Arist. *Ath. Pol.* 62. 2.

[9] The number 350 is based on a count from Arist. *Ath. Pol.* 47-61, which is a fairly exhaustive list (compare Gilbert, *Greek Const. Ant.* pp. 230-65, Busolt-Swoboda, *Griechische Staatskunde*, II, pp. 1081-1150). Our information for the fifth century is very incomplete, but known cases of old offices abolished and new offices created about cancel out. Arist. *Ath. Pol.* 24. 3, *ἀρχαὶ δ' ἔνδημοι μὲν εἰς ἑπτακοσίους ἄνδρας, ὑπερόριοι δ' εἰς ἑπτακοσίους*, is certainly corrupt on linguistic grounds, apart from being statistically impossible; perhaps the author gave 350 as the total for each class, making a total of 700. For rates of pay see note 4. A drachma seems on our limited evidence fairly universal, and if some got more, others got less, and some it appears only perquisites (e.g. the *athlothetae*, according to Arist. *Ath. Pol.* 62. 2, dined at public expense during the month in which the Panathenaea was held).

[10] The council was summoned *ὅσαι ἡμέραι πλὴν ἐάν τις ἀφέσιμος ᾖ* (Arist. *Ath. Pol.* 43. 3: the excepted days would include festivals and assembly days, leaving perhaps 300). For irregular attendance see Dem. XXII. 36. Thuc. VIII. 69. 4, *ἐπέστησαν τοῖς ἀπὸ τοῦ κυάμου βουλευταῖς οὖσιν ἐν τῷ βουλευτηρίῳ καὶ εἶπον αὐτοῖς ἐξιέναι λαβοῦσι τὸν μισθόν. ἔφερον δ' αὐτοῖς*

τοῦ ὑπολοίπου χρόνου παντὸς αὐτοὶ καὶ ἐξιοῦσιν ἐδίδοσαν, has been taken to imply that councillors received a daily wage irrespective of attendance, but it is equally possible (and indeed suggested by the emphatic *παντός*) that the oligarchs gave the councillors the maximum they could have earned to get them to go quietly. Evidently members were paid day by day (since they were already paid up to date) and it is difficult to believe that in these circumstances they could claim for days when they were absent or no session was held.

11 *Wasps*, 661–3.

12 Dem. XXIV. 80.

13 [Xen.] *Ath. Pol.* iii. 7.

14 *Wasps*, 100 ff., 216 ff., etc.

15 The figure is obtained by deducting 600 talents given by Thuc. II. 13. 3 as the gross revenue from the empire, from at least 1,000 talents given by Xenophon (*Anab.* VII. 1. 27) as the combined home and imperial revenue (both refer to the beginning of the Peloponnesian war). This is roughly confirmed by Aristophanes (*Wasps*, 656–60), who gives nearly 2,000 talents as the total revenue from all sources when the imperial tribute had been raised to 1,460 talents on paper (see *Ath. Trib. Lists*, III, pp. 344 ff.).

16 Dem. X. 37.

17 For this distinction see Dem. XXIV. 96–101.

18 Lysias, XIX. 11, XXVII. 1, XXX. 22, Dem. XXIV. 96–101.

19 Dem. X. 38, Theopompus, *FGH* II. 115, fr. 166.

20 [Xen.] *Ath. Pol.* i. 16–8.

21 Thuc. II. 13. 3 gives 600 talents, but the quota lists show a yield of only about 400 talents from the tribute of the allies (see *Ath. Trib. Lists*, III, pp. 333 ff.).

22 E.g. in 446 B.C. after the suppression of the Euboean revolt all the inhabitants of Hestiaea were expelled and replaced by an Athenian colony (Thuc. I. 114. 3), while at Chalcis the aristocracy only were expropriated in favour of Athenian cleruchs (Aelian, *Var. Hist.* VI. 1, Plut. *Pericles*, 23).

23 See Appendix.

24 Plut. *Pericles*, 11.

25 Thuc. II. 13. 8.

26 Arist. *Ath. Pol.* 24. 3.

27 Thuc. III. 17. 4, VI. 8. 1, 31. 3. After the Sicilian disaster the rate had to be cut to 3 obols owing to lack of funds (Thuc. VIII. 45. 2).

28 See Tod, I. 53, and R. S. Stanier, *JHS* LXXXIII (1953), 68–76.

29 Plut. *Pericles*, 12.

30 Thuc. II. 13. 3, Tod, I. 64.

31 Herod. VIII. 44.

32 Herod. VIII. 1.

33 Herod. IX. 28.

34 Nepos, *Miltiades*, 5. Suidas, s.v. *Ἱππίας* (citing Ephorus).

35 Herod. V. 97, VIII. 65. Aristophanes (*Eccl.* 1133) also gives this figure, though by this time (393–1) it was probably no longer true; he also (*Wasps*, 709) speaks of *δύο μυριάδες τῶν δημοτικῶν* (i.e. thetes) in 422.

[36] See Appendix.

[37] Thuc. I. 121. 3, 143. 1, VII. 13. 2, 63-4.

[38] Plut. *Pericles*, 11.

[39] Arist. *Ath. Pol.* 24. 3, Thuc. II. 13. 8.

[40] Thuc. IV. 101. 2.

[41] id. V. 11. 2.

[42] id. VI. 43, VII. 16. 2, 20. 2, 42. 1.

[43] id. III. 87. 3.

[44] Lysias, XX. 13, *ὑμῶν ψηφισαμένων πεντακισχιλίοις παραδοῦναι τὰ πράγματα καταλογεὺς ὢν ἐννακισχιλίους κατέλεξεν*: cf. Thuc. VIII. 97. 1, *τοῖς πεντακισχιλίοις ἐψηφίσαντο τὰ πράγματα παραδοῦναι (εἶναι δ' αὐτῶν ὁπόσοι καὶ ὅπλα παρέχονται)*. See Appendix.

[45] See pp. 76, 79, 81–2.

[46] See Gilbert, *Greek Const. Ant.* pp. 176-83, Busolt-Swoboda, *Griech. Staatskunde*, II, pp. 984-6. The minor role played by the merchant class in Athenian politics is explained partly because so many merchants were metics, partly because merchants were mostly humble folk, owning little more than their one ship, and operating on capital borrowed on its security and that of their cargo.

[47] Xen. *Mem.* II. viii. 1-5.

[48] Isaeus, V. 39, *εἰς δὲ τοὺς μισθωτοὺς ἰόντας δι' ἔνδειαν τῶν ἐπιτηδείων*, Isocr. XIV. 48, *ἄλλους δ' ἐπὶ θητείαν ἰόντας, τοὺς δ' ὅπως ἕκαστοι δύνανται τὰ καθ' ἡμέραν ποριζομένους*.

[49] Xen. *Mem.* II. v. 2, Dem. XXXVI. 28-9, 43.

[50] Plato, *Rep.* 565a.

[51] Xen. *Mem.* III. vii. 6.

[52] Arist. *Pol.* IV. iv. 21 (1291b).

[53] Lysias, V. 5. Cf. Dem. XLV. 86.

[54] E.g. the poor citizen, Chremylus, who is the hero of the *Plutus*, has a stock comic slave, Carion. In the *Ecclesiazusae* no slaves appear in the earlier part of the play when the women steal their husbands' clothes and the husbands subsequently wake up and have to put on their wives' clothes, but at the end a slave girl of Praxagora suddenly appears to do a comic turn. Yet Praxagora's communist programme includes *μηδ' ἀνδραπόδοις τὸν μὲν χρῆσθαι πολλοῖς, τὸν δ' οὐδ' ἀκολούθῳ* and she surely belongs to the second class.

[55] Thuc. III. 17. 4.

[56] Thuc. VII. 75. 5 implies that most of the attendants of the Athenian cavalrymen and hoplites at Syracuse were slaves.

[57] Thuc. IV. 101. 2. In Isaeus, V. 11, Dicaeogenes is reproached for sending a poor relation, whom he has defrauded of his inheritance, to serve his brother *ἀντ' ἀκολούθου* at Corinth (probably in the Corinthian war).

[58] Dem. XXIV. 197, *θύρας ἀφαιρεῖν καὶ στρώμαθ' ὑποσπᾶν καὶ διάκονον, εἴ τις ἐχρῆτο, ταύτην ἐνεχυράζειν*.

[59] See pp. 28–9.

[60] See pp. 88–9.

[61] Lysias, VII. 9-10, Isaeus, XI. 42. The metics who are described as *γεωργοί*

in Tod, II. 100, are probably tenant farmers (they could not be owners of land), though they might be agricultural labourers. Cf. Xen. *Symp.* VIII. 25, on bad farming by tenants.

[62] Lysias, IV. 1, VII. 16, 34, Dem. XLVII. 53, LIII. 6. The freedmen who describe themselves as *γεωργοί* in *IG* II–III.[2] 1553-78 (see Gomme, *Population of Athens*, pp. 41-3 for an analysis) were probably former agricultural slaves, now labourers or tenants. The *ἄγροικος* in Theophrastus (*Char.* IV. 5) discusses politics with his agricultural *οἰκέται* and *μισθωτοί*. An Athenian landowner in Naxos employed a *πελάτης* (apparently full time, *ἐθήτευεν ἐκεῖ παρ' ἡμῖν)* as well as slaves (Plato, *Euthyphro*, 4c).

[63] Dem. LIII. 19–21.

[64] Dem. LVII. 45.

[65] Dem. XLVII. 52, Isaeus, VI. 33.

[66] Lysias, XX. 11.

[67] Dem. XXII. 65 = XXIV. 172, *οἱ γεωργοῦντες καὶ φειδόμενοι, διὰ παιδοτροφίας δὲ καὶ οἰκεῖα ἀναλώματα καὶ λῃτουργίας ἑτέρας ἐκλελοιπότας εἰσφοράν*. The liturgies here referred to cannot be the State liturgies, which fell on a relatively wealthy class, but those of the demes (Isaeus, II. 42, *IG* I[2]. 186–7B, II-III[2]. 1178, 1198, 1200).

[68] *Pol.* 1323a, cf. 1252b, *ὁ γὰρ βοῦς ἀντ' οἰκέτου τοῖς πένησίν ἐστιν*.

[69] See pp. 83–4.

[70] Dem. XXI. 83, 95.

[71] Lysias, XVI. 14.

[72] For the price of land see below, p. 142, note 36. Rents are reckoned at about 8 per cent. of capital value in Isaeus, XI. 42 and *IG* II-III.[2] 2496. For the cost of living see note 1. The poor farmers in Aristophanes' *Plutus* (223-4) are represented as working in the fields themselves.

[73] Xen. *Vect.* iv. 14-15. Xenophon was writing over two generations later, quoting popular report, which may well have exaggerated Nicias' wealth (cf. Lysias, XIX. 47).

[74] Dem. XXXVII. 4.

[75] Lysias, XII. 19.

[76] Dem. XXXVI. 11; Demosthenes' 32-3 knifemakers brought in half a talent a year (Dem. XXVII. 9). See Dem. XXXVI. 5, for Pasion's land.

[77] Dem. XXVII. 9-11.

[78] [Plut.] *Vit. X Or. Isocrates* (*Mor.* 836E).

[79] Xen. *Mem.* II. vii. 3-6.

[80] Xen.*Mem.* III. xi. 4.

[81] Aesch. I. 97.

[82] Lycurgus, *c. Leocr.* 23, 58; Demosthenes (XXVII. 9) reckons his skilled knifemakers at 3 minae a head at the lowest.

[83] Isaeus, VIII. 35.

[84] Isaeus, VI. 19, 20, 33-34.

[85] Xen. *Mem.* II. iii, 3, *οἰκέτας μὲν οἱ δυνάμενοι ὠνοῦνται ἵνα συνέργους ἔχωσιν*.

[86] Lysias, XXIV. 6, *τέχνην δὲ κέκτημαι βραχέα δυναμένην ὠφελεῖν, ἣν αὐτὸς μὲν ἤδη χαλεπῶς ἐργάζομαι, τὸν διαδεξόμενον δ' αὐτὴν οὔπω δύναμαι κτήσασθαι.*

[87] Suidas, s.v. ἀποψηφίσεις (453 B).

[88] Ath. VI. 272c.

[89] *Die Bevölkerung der griechisch-römischen Welt*, pp. 84-99, cf. also R. L. Sargent, *The size of the slave population at Athens during the fifth and fourth centuries* B.C., and W. L. Westermann, 'Athenaeus and the slaves of Athens,' in *Athenian Studies presented to W. S. Ferguson.*

[90] Thuc. VII. 27. 5. The figure must be an estimate, but even Thucydides' estimates are worthy of serious consideration. He implies that this loss was a very serious matter for the Athenians, i.e. that 20,000 was a substantial proportion of the total slave population.

[91] Xen. *Vect.* iv. 25.

[92] Xen. *Vect.* iv. 22, *πολλοὶ δ' εἰσὶ καὶ αὐτῶν τῶν ἐν τοῖς ἔργοις γηράσκοντες, πολλοὶ δὲ καὶ ἄλλοι καὶ Ἀθηναῖοι καὶ ξένοι οἳ τῷ σώματι μὲν οὔτε βούλοιντ' ἂν οὔτε δύναιντ' ἂν ἐργάζεσθαι, τῇ δὲ γνώμῃ ἐπιμελούμενοι ἡδέως ἂν τὰ ἐπιτήδεια πορίζοιντο.*

[93] Dem. XLII. 20, *πολλὰ ἐκ τῶν ἔργων τῶν ἀργυρειων ἐγώ, Φαίνιππε, πρότερον αὐτὸς τῷ ἐμαυτοῦ σώματι πονῶν καὶ ἐργαζόμενος συνελεξάμην.*

[94] Arist. *Ath. Pol.* 62. 3.

[95] Dem. XIII. 2, 10.

[96] Gilbert, *Greek Const. Ant.* pp. 173-4.

[97] op. cit. p. 229.

[98] Xen. *Vect.* iv. 25.

[99] The evidence is fully set out and analysed by Margaret Crosby in *Hesperia*, 1950, pp. 189 ff.

[100] Suidas, s.v. ἀγράφων μετάλλων δίκη.

[101] Xen. *Hell.* I. vi. 24, Aristoph. *Frogs*, 693-4.

[102] Arist. *Ath. Pol.* 40. 2.

[103] [Plut.] *Vit. X Or. Hypereides* (*Mor.* 849A).

[104] [Xen.] *Ath. Pol.* i. 10.

[105] Xen. *Hell.* II. iii. 48.

[106] Plato, *Rep.* 563b.

II. THE ATHENS OF DEMOSTHENES

[1] II. 62. 7.

[2] XIV. 19, 27; cf. Philochorus, *FGH* III. 328. *fr.* 46.

[3] XXVII. 9.

[4] Pollux, VIII. 130.

[5] *JG* II-III^2. 2496. Isaeus, XI. 42, assumes 8 per cent as a normal rent for land.

[6] E.g. Lysias, III. 24; Isaeus, VII. 39, XI. 47; Isocrates, VII. 35; Dem. XXVII. 8, XXVIII. 3-4, XLII. 22-3, XLV. 66; Aeschines, I. 101; cf. Plato, *Rep.* 343d.

[7] XXVII. 7, 9, XXVIII. 4, XXIX. 59.

[8] XXVII. 37.

[9] In his new edition of Bury's *History of Greece*, p. 890.

[10] E.g. Lysias, XIX. 28-30, 42-3.

[11] See now his article in *Classica et Mediaevalia*, XIV (1953), pp. 30-70.

[12] Dem. XXVIII. 4, cf. XXI. 157.

[13] See note 25.

[14] Dem. XXII. 44.

[15] Leptines *ἐκ Κοίλης* and Callicrates son of Eupherus, whom Demosthenes cites in XXII. 60, were trierarchs (*IG* II-III.[2] 1609, II, l. 72; cf. 1622C, ll. 361-3, 375-7, and 1622B, ll. 165-6).

[16] Dem. XXII. 60. I have assumed that this paragraph refers to the arrears which Androtion actually collected, seven talents according to XXII. 44. If the whole fourteen talents were in small sums the total of debtors would be about double.

[17] Isaeus, VI. 60, *καὶ τὰς εἰσφορὰς εἰσενηνόχασιν ἀμφότεροι πάσας ἐν τοῖς τριακοσίοις . . . εἰς δὲ τοὺς τριακοσίους ἐγγέγραπται καὶ εἰσφέρει τὰς εἰσφοράς*.

[18] Cf. the incident recorded in Dem. III. 4-5.

[19] Dem. L. 8.

[20] See note 17.

[21] Dem. L. 9 shows that *προεισφορά* was a liturgy subject to the normal rules.

[22] This is implied by Dem. L. 8-9, *προσεπηνέχθη μου τοὔνομα ἐν τριττοῖς δήμοις . . . τούτων ἐγὼ . . . ἔθηκα τὰς προεισφορὰς πρῶτος*.

[23] Dem. L. 10.

[24] XXIV. 111; cf. I. 20, II. 31, where, addressing the assembly, he speaks loosely of everyone paying *εἰσφορά*.

[25] The evidence is Cleidemus (*FGH* III. 323, fr. 8) quoted by Photius, s.v. *ναυκραρία*: he speaks of 100 symmories, and these must be those of the *εἰσφορά*, since the trierarchic symmories numbered only 20 (Dem. XIV. 17). The figure is confirmed by the Three Hundred *προεισφέροντες* (Dem. XLII. 25); for the Three Hundred seem to be identical with *τοὺς ἡγεμόνας τῶν συμμοριῶν ἢ τοὺς δευτέρους καὶ τρίτους* (Dem. XVIII. 103; cf. Aesch. III. 222). We know from Dem. XXVIII. 4, XXI. 157 that the *εἰσφορά* symmories had *ἡγεμόνες* whereas the trierarchic had *ἐπιμεληταί* (Dem. XLVII. 21, 22, 24).

[26] Dem. XIV. 16-7.

[27] XXVII. 7, XXVIII. 4.

[28] XXIX. 59.

[29] Diod. XVIII. 18. 4-5.

[30] XXII. 44.

[31] XXVII. 37.

[32] Xen. *Hell.* VI. ii. 1.

[33] XIV. 27; cf. III. 4 for a war tax of 60 talents (1 per cent.) actually voted if not collected.

[34] XXII. 65 (=XXIV. 172), *οἱ γεωργοῦντες καὶ φειδόμενοι διὰ παιδοτροφίας δὲ καὶ οἰκεῖα ἀναλώματα καὶ λειτουργίας ἑτέρας ἐκλελοιπότες εἰσφοράς*. This is not to say that all who owed arrears of *εἰσφορά* were poor men. Cf. note 15.

[35] Dem. XLII. 22.

[36] Lysias, XIX. 29, 42. Aristophanes bought more than 300 *plethra* of land and a house (of the value of 50 minae) for rather more than 5 talents. The price works out at about 85 drachmae the *plethron*, or about 360 drachmae the acre.

[37] Cf. note 5.

[38] Cf. note 86.

[39] XV. 107-13.

[40] Dem. XLIX. 6-21.

[41] Xen. *Hell.* VI. ii. 37.

[42] *Ib.* VI. v. 49; Diod. XV. 84. 2, XVI. 37. 3, 85. 2, XVIII. 10. 2, 11. 3.

[43] IV. 21.

[44] IV. 28-9.

[45] Arist. *Ath. Pol.* 42. 3.

[46] The Eleusis accounts of 329 B.C. (*IG* II-III². 1672, ll. 4-5, 42-3, 117-18 141-2).

[47] XIX. 84, *ἡ πρότερον βοήθει᾿ εἰς Πύλας . . . ἣν μετὰ πλειόνων ἢ διακοσίων ταλάντων ἐποιήσασθε, ἂν λογίσησθε τὰς ἰδίας δαπάνας τάς τῶν στρατευσαμένων.*

[48] I. 27, *εἰ γὰρ ὑμᾶς δεήσειεν αὐτοὺς τριάκονθ᾿ ἡμέρας μόνας ἔξω γενέσθαι, καὶ ὅσ᾿ ἀνάγκη στρατοπέδῳ χρωμένους τῶν ἐκ τῆς χώρας λαμβάνειν, μηδενὸς ὄντος ἐν αὐτῇ πολεμίου λέγω, πλείον᾿ ἂν οἶμαι ζημιωθῆναι τοὺς γεωργοῦντας ὑμῶν ἢ ὅσ᾿ εἰς ἅπαντα τὸν πρὸ τοῦ πόλεμον δεδαπάνησθε.*

[49] Thuc. III. 17. 4.

[50] It appears from Harpocration, s.v. *θῆτες* (citing Aristophanes), that *θῆτες* did not serve as hoplites; cf. Thuc. III. 16. 1, VI. 43, VIII. 24. 2. The Solonian classes were by the fourth century based on property, not income (Isaeus, VII. 39). The figure of 2,000 drachmae for zeugites is an inference from Diod. XVIII. 18. 4-5, on the assumption that Antipater set up a hoplite franchise. The figure was probably reached by multiplying by ten the Solonian income of 200 *μέτρα* (Arist. *Ath. Pol.* 7. 4), converted on the Solonian scale of values (Plut. *Solon*, 23) into 200 drachmae; this figure is slightly confirmed by the value of the Lesbian *κλῆροι* (Thuc. III. 50. 2) which were probably intended to raise thetic occupants to zeugite status.

[51] XXI. 83, 95.

[52] Lysias, XVI. 14.

[53] Isocr. VIII. 48; Dem. XXI. 154-5 (cf. L. 6-7, 16, III. 4, IV. 36).

[54] That this was the rate till the Sicilian disaster (when it was halved, Thuc. VIII. 45. 3) is shown by Thuc. III. 17. 4, VI. 31. 3; cf. VI. 8. 1 (a trireme costs a talent a month).

55 Dem. L. 10, 12, 14, 23, 53.

56 *Ib.* 11-12.

57 XLIX. 11-12.

58 L. 17, 56.

59 XLVII. 21, 44.

60 XXI. 154-5, XVIII. 102-4.

61 XIV. 16-20. It should be observed that the trierarchic symmories are under this scheme to provide *σώματα* (persons to act as trierarchs), but that the expense is to fall on the whole *τίμημα τῆς χώρας* of 6,000 talents.

62 Dem. XVIII. 102-4; Aesch. III. 222; Harpocration, *s.v.* *συμμορία*, (citing Hypereides).

63 Dem. XIII. 2, *τἀργύριον μέν ἐστι τοῦθ', ὑπὲρ οὗ βουλεύεσθε, μικρόν, τὸ δ' ἔθος μέγα, ὃ γίγνεται μετὰ τούτου.*

64 LIX. 4-5; for the meaning of *διοίκησις* see XXIV. 96-101.

65 I. 19-20, XIII. 2, 10; cf. III. 10-13, 19, 31, Harpocration, *s.v.* *θεωρικά*, Suidas, *s.v.* *θεωρικά, θεωρικόν*, Libanius, *Hypoth. in Olynth.* I. 4.

66 X. 38.

67 See p. 76.

68 Hesychius, *s.v.* *δραχμὴ χαλαζῶσα;* cf. Harpocration, *s.v.* *θεωρικά.*

69 Hesychius, *s.v.* *θεωρικὰ χρήματα.*

70 I. 26.

71 *Mor.* 818E F.

72 [Plut.] *Vit. X Or. Lycurgus* (*Mor.* 843D).

73 Dem. X. 35-43.

74 Plut. *Mor.* 1011B.

75 Dem. XIX. 291.

76 Dem. XXI. 203.

77 X. 35 ff., esp. 39.

78 XVIII. 10, cf. *Hell. Oxy.* i. 2-3, and Aristophanes, *Eccl.* 197-8, for a similar situation in the early fourth century.

79 E.g. I. 6, 20, II. 24, 27, 31, III. 33, IV. 7, VIII. 23, X. 19.

80 XIV. 27.

81 XXI. 83, 95. Cf. the very apologetic and humble tone taken to the jury by a really poor litigant in LVII. esp. 25, 31, 35, 45.

82 XXII. 47 ff., XXIV. 160 ff., esp. 197.

83 He merely says airily that there will always be enough men to perform the liturgies (XX. 22), a statement refuted by XXI. 13. [Xen.] *Ath. Pol.* i. 13, emphasises how the *δῆμος* draws money from the choregi and gymnasiarchs *ᾄδων καὶ τρέχων καὶ ὀρχούμενος.*

84 Leptines' law opened with the preamble *ὅπως ἂν οἱ πλουσιώτατοι λῃτουργῶσιν* (XX. 127), and his argument, which Demosthenes tries to refute, was *ὡς αἱ λειτουργίαι νῦν μὲν εἰς πένητας ἀνθρώπους ἔρχονται, ἐκ δὲ τοῦ νόμου τούτου λῃτουργήσουσιν οἱ πλουσιώτατοι* (XX. 18).

85 Deinarchus, *in Dem.* 42.

86 In the Eleusinian accounts (*IG* II-III.[2] 1672) of 329 B.C., 3 obols is allowed

for *τροφή* for the public slaves (ll. 4-5, 42-3, 117-18, 141-2); casual labourers (*μισθωτοί*) doing unskilled work get 1½ drachmae (ll. 28-30, 32-4, 45-6, 60-2); skilled men get 2 drachmae (ll. 110-11, carpenters, 177-8, stone polishers) or 2½ drachmae (26-8, bricklayers, 31-2, stone masons).

III. THE ATHENIAN DEMOCRACY AND ITS CRITICS

[1] The latter part of this paper, dealing with Thucydides, owes much to, and is indeed in parts a summary of, an article by my former pupil, Mr. G. E. M. de Ste Croix, entitled 'The character of the Athenian Empire', since published in *Historia* III (1954-5), pp. 1-41. I owe Mr. de Ste Croix a deep debt of gratitude for having allowed me to anticipate his article (where the questions at issue are more fully discussed and documented), and also for many comments, criticisms and references in the earlier part of my paper, which he read in MS. I also wish to express my gratitude to Mr. A. G. Woodhead, who read this paper in MS. and offered a number of useful comments.

[2] I have not, save for occasional references, included Aristophanes—or, for that matter, the tragedians—in my survey, because with Gomme (*Class. Rev.* LII (1938), pp. 97-107) I hold that Aristophanes wrote comedies and not political tracts. While he makes it fairly obvious that he strongly disliked certain features of the democracy, such as vulgar politicians like Cleon, he does not—and did not intend to—preach political doctrine, and his jokes cannot necessarily be taken for criticism.

[3] *Pol.* V. ix. 15 (1310a).

[4] *Pol.* VI. ii. 3 (1317b); iv. 20 (1319b).

[5] VII. 37; cf. VII. 20, XII. 131.

[6] VIII. 557b.

[7] *Ib.* 563b. The same complaint about metics and slaves is made in [Xen.] *Ath. Pol.* i. 10-12.

[8] See Dem. XXI. 46-50 and IX. 3 on slaves.

[9] Thuc. II. 37. 2. Cf. Nicias' words, *τῆς ἐν αὐτῇ ἀνεπιτάκτου πᾶσιν ἐς τὴν δίαιταν ἐξουσίας* (*id.* VII. 69. 2).

[10] Cf. Eurip. *Hippolytus*, 421-3; *Ion*, 670-2.

[11] XX. 106.

[12] *Mem.* I. ii. 12 ff.; cf. Aesch. I. 173.

[13] *Republic*, VIII. 558c; cf. *Laws*, VI. 757.

[14] VII. 21; cf. III. 14.

[15] *Pol.* II. ix. 1-5 (1280a); V. i. 2-7 (1301a); VI. ii. 2 (1317b). In VI. iii (1318a) Aristotle makes an ingenious attempt to combine democratic and oligarchic equality.

[16] For praise of *ἰσότης* see Eurip. *Supplices*, 404-8, 433-41; *Phoenissae*, 535ff.

[17] XXI. 67.

[18] XXIV. 59.

[19] Thuc. II. 37. 1.

[20] Xen. *Hell.* II. iii. 51.

[21] *Pol.* III. xi. 1-2 (1281b); in §5 he limits this argument to certain bodies of men only, excluding those in which the majority are 'brutes'.

[22] *Pol.* III. xi. 14 (1282a); here again he limits the argument to cases where the majority are not 'too slavish'.

[23] *Protagoras*, 319b–323a.

[24] Xen. *Mem.* I. ii. 9.

[25] XXXIX. 10–11.

[26] Arist. *Ath. Pol.* 55. 2; cf. Lysias, XVI and XXXI, for hostile speeches at a *δοκιμασία*.

[27] *Ib.* 43. 4.

[28] *Ib.* 48. 3–5, 54. 2.

[29] Thuc. II. 37. 1.

[30] Plato, *Menex.* 238cd.

[31] Arist. *Pol.* II. xii. 2 (1273b).

[32] For the fourth century see J. Sundwall, 'Epigraphische Beiträge', *Klio*, Beiheft IV (1906), §§2, 5, 8.

[33] [Xen.] *Ath. Pol.* i. 3.

[34] *Mem.* III. iv. 1.

[35] XIX. 237. In 282 Demosthenes states what he thinks are the proper qualifications for high office—trierarchies, liturgies, etc. Cf. the vulgar abuse of Cleon and other politicians as being low persons engaged in trade by Aristophanes in the *Knights*.

[36] Aristophanes jibes at ambassadors with their 2 drachmae a day (*Acharnians*, 66, 90) and military officers with 3 drachmae (*ib.* 595-607).

[37] *Pol.* IV. vi. 5-6 (1293a); elsewhere Aristotle is prepared to accept political pay, provided that precautions are taken to prevent the poor outnumbering the rich (IV. xiii. 6 (1297a), xiv. 13 (1298b)).

[38] See above, pp. 35–7.

[39] Lysias, XIII. 20. Rich men like Demosthenes and Apollodorus apparently found no difficulty in securing a seat on the council when convenient (Dem. XXI. 111; XIX. 154, 286; LIX. 3-4). See also J. Sundwall, *op. cit.* §1 (pp. 1-18).

[40] *Gorgias*, 515e.

[41] Arist. *Ath. Pol.* 62. 3.

[42] *Ib.* 43. 3.

[43] See above, p. 143, note 86.

[44] VII. 54; VIII. 130. But see n. 38.

[45] *Pol.* IV. iv. 25 (1292a); vi. 2–6 (1292b–93a).

[46] *Mem.* IV. iv. 13-14.

[47] *Mem.* I. ii. 40–6.

[48] XXIV. 76.

[49] Andoc. I. 81–5.

[50] As in Tod, I. 74; Arist. *Ath. Pol.* 29. 2.

[51] This appears from the fact that the commissioners of 411 thought it necessary to repeal the γραφὴ παρανόμων (and other similar constitutional safeguards) before any substantive change of the law was proposed (Arist. *Ath. Pol.* 29. 4; Thuc. VIII. 67. 2).

[52] Dem. XX. 88 ff.; XXIV. 18 ff.; Aesch. III. 38 ff.

[53] Dem. XX. 91; Aesch. III. 3.

[54] Dem. LIX. 4.

[55] Aesch. III. 194.

[56] Dem. LIX. 5.

[57] I. 4, repeated verbatim in III. 6.

[58] XXIV. 5.

[59] XXIV. 75-6.

[60] *C. Leocr.* 4.

[61] III. 5.

[62] *Hell.* I. vii.

[63] *Ib.* II. iv. 43. Cf. Plato, *Menex.* 243e, *Epist.* vii, 325b, and Isocr. XVIII. 31-2, 44, 46, 68.

[64] [Xen.] *Ath. Pol.* i. 4-9.

[65] VIII. 557a.

[66] *Pol.* III. vii. 5 (1279b); viii. 2-7 (1279b-80a); IV. iv. 1-3, 6 (1290ab).

[67] VI. 39. 1.

[68] Cf. [Xen.] *Ath. Pol.* i. 3; Dem. XXIV. 112; Arist. *Ath. Pol.* 21. 1; Eupolis, fr. 117. Cf. note 32.

[69] J. Sundwall, *op. cit.* §8 (pp. 59-84).

[70] VIII. 128.

[71] XV. 159-60.

[72] See above, pp. 29–32.

[73] Cf. Xen. *Mem.* III. iv. 3; Dem. XIX. 282.

[74] XXI. 1-5.

[75] Dem. XX. 8 shows that a man could claim a year's exemption after a liturgy: if there were, as Demosthenes says (XXI. 21), only about sixty liturgies to fill per annum, they cannot have fallen very often on the individual rich citizen.

[76] XXI. 156 (cf. 154).

[77] Isaeus, V. 35-6.

[78] Lysias' client reckons 6 talents for seven years (XXI. 2); Demosthenes states that a contractor would take over a trierarchy for 1 talent (XXI. 155), but himself paid only 20 minae (a third of a talent) in lieu of performing a (half?) trierarchy (XXI. 80). In Lysias, XIX. 29 and 42, the speaker claims to have spent 80 minae ($1\frac{1}{3}$ talents) on three (half?) trierarchies.

[79] Isaeus, VII. 32, 42.

[80] Isocr. XVIII. 59-60; Lysias, XXXII. 24; Dem. L. 39, 68.

[81] Dem. XLVII. 21, 44; cf. XIV. 16-17.

[82] Lysias, XXI. 2. He could have claimed two years' exemption after each year of service (Isaeus, VII. 38).

[83] Lysias, XIX. 29, 42-3.

[84] Isocr. XV. 145.

[85] Lysias, XIX. 57-9.

[86] *Ib.* 63.

[87] Dem. XXVII. 7-9; cf. XXVIII. 11; XXIX. 59.

[88] Dem. XVIII. 102-4; XXI. 154-5.

[89] Isocr. XV. 160; cf. Plato, *Rep.* VIII. 565a; Arist. *Pol.* V. v. 1, 5 (1304b-1305a); VI. v. 3, 5 (1320a).

[90] Sycophants are fully dealt with in R. J. Bonner and G. Smith, *The Administration of Justice from Homer to Aristotle*, II, Chapter iii, and J. O. Lofberg, *Sycophancy in Athens* (Chicago, 1917).

[91] Arist. *Ath. Pol.* 35. 4; Xen. *Hell.* II. iii. 21; Lysias, XII. 5 ff.

[92] Plut. *Mor.* 843 D.

[93] XXX. 22; XXVII. 1; XIX. 11. There is a similar suggestion in Aristophanes, *Knights*, 1358-61.

[94] X. 44-5.

[95] III. 33-6.

[96] Ἀρχὴ ἄνδρα δείξει seems to be a democratic proverb; it is attributed to Bias of Priene by Aristotle (*Ethica Nicomachea*, V. i. 16) and quoted by Demosthenes (*proem* 48).

[97] II. 18-19.

[98] II. 65. 7-11.

[99] Apart from the unfavourable notices in III. 36. 6 and IV. 21. 3 there is a note of spite in IV. 28. 5 and 39. 3 and especially in V. 16. 1.

[100] Dem. XL. 25.

[101] I. 98. 4.

[102] Thucydides' use of the word δουλόω is discussed in *The Athenian Tribute Lists*, III. pp. 155-7.

[103] V. 85-113.

[104] III. 37-40 (esp. 37. 2).

[105] II. 63.

[106] I. 75-7.

[107] VI. 82-7 (esp. 85. 1).

[108] I. 22. 1.

[109] [Lysias], II. 55-7; Isocr. IV. 100-9, 117-20; XII. 54, 59-61, 68.

[110] 242a-243a.

[111] II. 8. 4-5; VIII. 2. 1-2.

[112] III. 47. 2.

[113] III. 27.

[114] IV. 84-8.

[115] IV. 110-13, 123. 1-2, 130. 2-7.

[116] VIII. 9. 2-3, 14. 1-2.

[117] VIII. 44. 1-2.

[118] VIII. 21, 72; Xen. *Hell.* II. ii. 6; iii. 6; Tod, I. 96; II. 97.

[119] Herod. IX. 35. 2; cf. Andrewes in *Phoenix*, VI (1952), 1-5, for the chronology.

[120] Thuc. V. 81. 1. It is worth noting that the Mantineans before the battle speak of their anticipated position if they lost it (and became allies of Sparta again) as *δουλεία* (Thuc. V. 69. 1).

[121] Xen. *Hell.* III. ii. 21ff.

[122] Incidentally Sparta took hostages from her Arcadian allies to ensure their loyalty (Thuc. V. 61. 5).

[123] Thuc. I. 139. 3, 144. 2.

[124] For Athens the evidence is collected in G. F. Hill, *Sources for Greek History* (edd. Meiggs and Andrewes, 1951), p. 355, and in *The Athenian Tribute Lists*, III. pp. 149–54. Sparta sometimes installed or tightened oligarchies without any pretext, as at Argos and Sicyon (Thuc. V. 81. 2).

[125] I. 97. 1.

[126] I. 141. 6–7.

[127] III. 10–12, esp. 10. 4–5 and 11. 3–4. The chronology is studiously vague, but the Mitylenaeans are referring to a period after 449 (when Athens had 'relaxed her hostility to the Persians') and indeed to a time when the only allies on the congress still supplying ships were Chios and Lesbos, that is 440 at the earliest. The Mitylenaeans would scarcely be at such pains to excuse their submissiveness to Athens in voting for war against rebel allies unless they had done so recently in a famous case.

[128] I. 121. 1.

[129] The Spartans later had a guilty conscience about this (Thuc. VII. 18. 2).

[130] As in 440, when Corinth persuaded the Peloponnesian congress not to make war on Athens (Thuc. I. 40. 5). The initiative in this earlier proposal to violate the Thirty Years' Peace must have come from Sparta, since she alone could summon a league congress, and naturally only did so when she approved the proposal to be debated.

[131] Samos herself had seventy ships in 440 (Thuc. I. 116. 1), and Lesbos and Chios provided forty-five to assist Athens against her (I. 116. 2, 117. 2). This was far from their full strength, for Chios in 411, after losses in the Sicilian expedition (VI. 43; VII. 20. 2), had sixty ships left (VIII. 6. 4).

[132] As the 'Old Oligarch' explains ([Xen.] *Ath. Pol.* i. 14–16). For an Athenian defence of the system see Thuc. I. 77; Isocrates, IV. 113; XII. 60.

[133] The clause in the alliance between Sparta and Athens, *ἢν δὲ ἡ δουλεία ἐπανιστῆται ἐπικουρεῖν Ἀθηναίους Λακεδαιμονίοις*, appears to have been standard, seeing that Sparta was able to call up all her allies in the great revolt of 464 (Thuc. I. 102. 1; cf. II. 27. 2 for Aegina, III. 54. 5 for Plataea and Xen. *Hell.* V. ii. 3 for Mantinea.

[134] III 36. 4.

[135] This emerges from Tod, I. 62. The subscriptions were evidently collected by the Spartan admiral Alcidas (see F. E. Adcock, 'Alcidas *ἀργυρολόγος*' in *Mélanges Glotz*, I. 1–6) who seems to have called twice at Melos, on his way out and on his way back—hence the two Melian subscriptions recorded.

[136] Thuc. III. 91. 1–2.

[137] Thuc. III. 52. 4, 68. 1–2.

[138] The phrase is used in *Pol.* III. iv. 12 (1277b); IV. xii. 3 (1296b); IV. xiv. 7 (1298a); V. x. 30, 35 (1312b); V. xi. 11 (1313b); VI. v. 5 (1320a). From the first three passages it appears that Aristotle considered a democracy 'extreme' when working people are in a majority and can hold office, and the people is sovereign.

IV. THE SOCIAL STRUCTURE OF ATHENS IN THE FOURTH CENTURY B.C.

[1] Athenaeus, VI. 272C.

[2] Dem. XXV. 51.

[3] Plut. *Phocion*, 28. 7; Diod. XVIII. 18. 5. One may add that according to [Plut.] *Vit. X Or. Lycurgus* (*Mor.* 843 D) the confiscated property of Diphilus, worth 160 talents, was distributed between the citizens at 50, or as others say, 100 drachmae each—yielding the result of 19,000 + on the 50 drachmae basis. I do not understand Gomme's argument (*The Population of Athens*, p. 18) that 'it is the latter (Diodorus') figure only which is consistent with the statistics of the Lamian war discussed above'. Diodorus' figures for the Lamian war (see below, notes 26–7) refer to hoplites only.

[4] 453B, s.v. *ἀποψηφίσεις*.

[5] *IG* II–III.[2] 1672, discussed by Gomme, op. cit. pp. 28 ff. and A. Jardé, *Les céréales dans l'antiquité grecque*, pp. 36 ff.

[6] Jardé, op. cit. pp. 123–4, 130–1.

[7] In the absence of any census of animals certainty is impossible, but on Jardé's very conservative estimates (op. cit. pp. 124–7) more than the whole crop would be required for animal feed.

[8] Dem. XX. 31–2.

[9] Jardé, op. cit. pp. 128 ff.

[10] Thuc. VII. 27. 5.

[11] Xen. *Vect.* iv. 25.

[12] See above, p. 142, note 50.

[13] Dem. III. 4.

[14] See above, p. 142, note 6.

[15] Lysias, XXXIV, *hypothesis*.

[16] Rather similar conditions prevail in some countries today. If I may quote from personal experience, my domestic servant Abdu in Cairo owned (jointly with a brother, I believe) a very small holding including some shares in some date palms in Abu Simbel, where he kept his wife and children. Abdu earned most of his income in wages in Cairo, but spent a third of the year at home.

[17] Dem. XXVII. 9, reckons his knife-makers as worth 5 or 6 or at a minimum 3 minae.

[18] Isaeus, V. 39 and Isocr. XIV. 48, speak of *μισθωτοί* or those who go *ἐπὶ θήτειαν* as being the lowest of the low. For wages see above, p. 143, note 86.

[19] For details on State pay see above, p. 136, notes 4-14; for the social standing of *βουλευταί*, p. 145, note 39.

[20] *IG* II-III.[2] 1672, lines 4-5, 42-3, 117-18, 141-2 (rations) 102-5, 190, 230, (clothes and shoes).

[21] See above, pp. 36–7.

[22] Arist. *Ath. Pol.* 62. 2.

[23] See above, pp. 33–5.

[24] Lysias, XX. 13; cf. Thuc. VIII. 97. 1.

[25] The Athenians put 6,600 men into the field in 394 (Xen. *Hell.* IV. ii. 17), 6,000 in 362 (Diod. XV. 84), 5,400 in 352 (Diod. XVI. 37).

[26] Diod. XVIII. 10. 2, 11. 3, gives 5,000 hoplites and 500 cavalry from seven out of the ten tribes.

[27] Xen. *Vect.* ii. 2-5, is explicit that metics normally served on expeditions and were not reserved as they were in 431 (Thuc. II. 13. 7) for garrison duty. Diodorus (loc. cit.) distinguishes *πολιτικοί* from *μισθόφοροι* in the Athenian forces in the Lamian War; metics would clearly fall in the former category.

[28] *IG* II-III.[2] 1156, gives 43-5 ephebes for Cecropis in 334-3; *Hesperia, Suppl.* VIII, 273, gives 53-5 for Oeneis *c.* 330, *Ephemeris Archaiologike*, 1918, 73 gives 63 for Leontis in 327–6. There is also a later figure (*IG* II-III.[2] 478) of about 33 ephebes for Erechtheis in 305-4, which must be multiplied by twelve, as there were by then twelve tribes. See Gomme, *op. cit.* pp. 67-70 for these figures.

[29] *IG* II-III.[2] 1926. Mr. D. M. Lewis has reconstructed part of another list of arbitrators (*BSA* L (1955), 27-36). This gives not less than fifty-four names for the first five tribes.

[30] *Past and Present*, IV (1953), pp. 1-31.

[31] See diagram.

[32] Dem. XXI. 83, 95.

[33] Lysias, XVI. 14.

[34] See above, p. 141, note 25.

[35] Dem. XIV. 16-17.

[36] Dem. XXVII. 7; XXVIII. 4; cf. XXIX. 59.

[37] Dem. XXII. 65 (=XXIV. 172).

[38] Dem. XXIV. 197.

[39] See above, pp. 23ff.

[40] Isaeus, V. 35-6.

[41] Isaeus, VII. 32, 42.

[42] Isaeus, XI. 42 (5½ tal.); VII. 32, 42 (5 tal.); X. 23 (4 tal.+); XI. 44 (3 tal. 4000 dr.); VI. 33 (*c.* 3½ tal.); III. 2 (3 tal.); XI. 41 (2½ tal.); VIII. 35 (over 90 minae).

[43] Dem. XXVII. 64.

[44] Dem. XLII. 1-5, 25; see above, p. 141, note 25.

[45] Dem. XXVII. 7, 9; XXVIII. 4; XXIX. 59.

[46] Lysias, XIX. 45 ff.

[47] Lysias, XIX. 40.

[48] [Plut.] *Mor.* 843D.

[49] Hypereides, III. 35.

[50] Harpocration and Suidas, s.v. Ἐπικράτης.

[51] Dem. XXXVI. 5 ff.

[52] Dem. XVIII. 102–4; cf. XXI. 154–5.

[53] This is implied by Dem. XVIII. 103 (the opposition of the *ἡγεμόνες, δεύτεροι* and *τρίτοι* to the law; cf. Deinarchus, *in Dem.* 43) and Aesch. III. 223 (the number of trierarchs reduced to 300), and confirmed by Harpocration, s.v. *συμμορία* (citing Hypereides for 300 trierarchs divided into symmories of 15).

[54] Dem. XXXVI. 11.

[55] Lysias, XII. 19.

[56] Dem. XXVII. 9 ff.

[57] Dem. XLIX. 11.

[58] Dem. L. 8.

[59] Xen. *Oec. passim*, esp. xx. 22–9; for his fortune Lysias, XIX. 46.

[60] Dem. XLII. 5 (40 stades round), 7 (wood), 20 (barley and wine).

[61] The following table sets out the facts:

Reference	*Land (and stock)*	*House property*	*Industrial slaves*	*Money*
Isaeus, V. 22	60 *πλέθρα* in the Plain	2 *οἰκίδια* and 1 *βαλανεῖον*	—	—
Isaeus, VI. 33	*ἄγρος* at Athmonia (75 minae), goats, goatherd and two teams (26½ minae)	*οἰκία* at Athens (mortgaged for 44 minae), *βαλανεῖον* in Serangium (30 minae). Also (ch. 19–20) a brothel in Peiraeus and a wine shop in Cerameicus.	*δημιοῦργοι*	—
Isaeus, VIII. 35	*ἄγρος* at Phlya (1 tal.)	2 houses at Athens (20 and 13 minae)	*ἀνδράποδα μισθοφοροῦντα* (with 3 female slaves and furniture worth 13 minae)	—
Isaeus, XI. 41	*ἄγρος* at Eleusis (2 tal.). 60 sheep, 100 goats, 1 horse	—	—	—
Isaeus, XI. 42–3	*ἄγρος* at Thria (2½ tal.). Sheep, stock and crops (49 minae)	houses at Melite (30 minae) and Eleusis (5 minae)	—	loans (40 minae) *ἔρανοι* (10 minae) cash (9 minae)

Isaeus, XI. 44	χωρία at Oenoe and Prospalta (50 and 30 minae)	house at Athens (20 minae)	—	—
Aesch. I. 97 ff.	ἐσχατιᾳ at Sphettos, χωρίον at Alopece (20 minae). His father had sold a χωρίον at Cephisia and an ἄγρος at Amphitropae (ch. 101)	house at Athens (20 minae). His father had sold two ἐργαστήρια in the mines (ch. 101).	9 or 10 σκυτοτόμοι, 1 ποικιλτής, and a woman weaver	loans

[62] Xen. *Mem.* II. vii. 3-6.

[63] Xen. *Vect.* iv. 14-15 has to go back to the fifth century for examples.

[64] Xen. *Vect.* iv. and *Hesperia*, 1950, pp. 189 ff.; cf. Hopper, *BSA*, XLVIII (1953), pp. 200 ff.

[65] Xen. *Vect.* iv. 22.

[66] Dem. XLII. 20.

[67] Dem. XXXVII. 4.

[68] Hypereides, III. 36.

[69] This point is rightly emphasised by M. I. Finley, *Studies in Land and Credit in Ancient Athens* 500-200 B.C., pp. 74 ff.

[70] Tod, II. 100.

[71] Dem. XLV. 63; XXXVI. 50.

[72] Besides Pasion and Phormio, Demosthenes mentions Socrates, Satyrus and Timodemus as freedmen bankers (XXXVI. 28-9) and Socles who bequeathed his widow to Timodemus cannot have been an Athenian. Eumathes (Isaeus *frag.* xii) and Epigenes and Conon (Deinarchus, I. 43) were metics. Nothing is known of Pylades (Dem. XXVII. 11), Heracleides (XXXIII. 6), Blepaeus (XL. 52) or Theocles (LIII. 9).

[73] Lysias, XXXII. 4, 6, 15, 25.

[74] Andoc. II. 11.

[75] In Dem. LII. 20 two brothers, Megacleides and Thrasyllus, of Eleusis, borrow for a voyage to Ace.

[76] Lampis was a metic (Dem. XXXIV. 37, *οἰκῶν Ἀθήνησι*), Hegestratus a Massaliot (XXXII. 5, 8), Apaturius a Byzantine (XXXIII. 6), Artemon a Phaselite (XXXV. 1-3, 15) Lycon a Heracleot (LII. 3) and his partner Cephisiades a metic (LII. 3, 9). Cf. *IG* II-III.^{2} 360, 408.

[77] Dem. XXVII. 11. Other Athenian investors in bottomry are Diodotus (Lysias, XXXII. 6) and Androcles; but his partner Nausicrates is a Carystian (Dem. XXXV. 10). Foreign lenders include Theodore the Phoenician (XXXIV. 6), Lycon the Heracleot (LII. 20), and Chrysippus (as appears from XXXIV. 38, 50). Many of the lenders are themselves merchants or retired merchants (Lysias, XXXII. 4, 6; Dem. XXXIII. 4; XXXIV. 38; LII. 20).

[78] Besides Cephalus (Lysias, XII. 19) and Pasion (Dem. XXXVI. 11) another metic industrialist is Leocrates (Lycurgus, *c. Leocr.* 23. 58). Athenians include

Demosthenes' father (Dem. XXVII. 9 ff.), Isocrates' father (Plut. *Mor.* 836E), Comon (Dem. XLVIII. 12), Timarchus, Euctemon and Ciron (see note 61), and the three men mentioned in Xen. *Mem.* II. vii. 3-6. These are slave owners. Many humble Athenians worked as craftsmen themselves, as is shown by Xen. *Mem.* III. vii. 6 and Aristophanes, *Plutus*, 510 ff.

79 [Dem.] XVII. 15.

80 Xen. *Hell.* I. vi. 24; cf. Aristophanes, *Frogs*, 190, 693.

81 [Plut.] *Mor.* 849A; cf. Lycurgus, *c. Leocr.* 41.

82 Dem. XXXIV. 39.

83 Xen. *Vect.* iii. 2.

84 Dem. XXXIV. 37; XXXV. 50-1; cf. LVI. 5-6, 11, 13.

85 Dem. XXXV. 10.

86 Dem. XXXIV. 36; cf. XX. 29 ff. and Tod, II. 167.

87 Xen. *Hipparchicus*, iv. 7.

88 Xen. *Vect.* iv. 6.

89 Xen. *Vect.* iii. 2.

90 Thuc. IV. 108. 1.

V. HOW DID THE ATHENIAN DEMOCRACY WORK?

1 Thuc. VI. 89. 6.

2 Xen. *Mem.* III. iii. 8 ff., v. 16-21, *Hipparchicus*, i. 7 *et passim.*

3 Xen. *Hipparchicus*, i. 19.

4 Arist. *Ath. Pol.* 61. 4, 5.

5 *Ib.* 49. Cf. Xen. op. cit. i. 8.

6 [Xen.] *Ath. Pol.*, ii. 1 ff.

7 Xen. *Mem.* III. v. esp. 21 ff.

8 The taxiarchs appointed the *λοχαγοί*, Arist. *Ath. Pol.* 61. 3.

9 Arist. *Ath. Pol.* 46. 1.

10 Tod, I. 96, line 30 (*νεωροί*), II. 200, line 179 (*ἐπιμεληταὶ τῶν νεωρίων*); cf. Dem. XXII. 63, XLVII. 21, 26, Aesch. III. 25. Their accounts are published in *IG* II-III.[2] 1604-32; nos. 1607 and 1623 show that they were ten, one from each tribe.

11 Tod, II. 200, lines 250-5, cf. Dem. XVIII. 107, XLVII. 26, L. 10.

12 Gilbert, *Gr. Const. Ant.* 370-6, Busolt-Swoboda, *Gr. Staatskunde*, II. 1199 ff., *P.W.K.* VIIA, 106 ff.

13 Dem. XXI. 80, 155, LI. 7 ff.

14 Dem. LI. 1, Tod, II. 200, lines 189 ff.

15 Thuc. VI. 31. 3, Dem. L. 7.

16 Thuc. I. 143. 1, [Xen.] *Ath. Pol.* i. 2.

17 Xen. *Mem.* III. iii. 12.

18 The three principal archons managed the major festivals (Arist. *Ath. Pol.*

56. 3-5, 57. 1, 58. 1), assisted by boards of ἀθλοθέται, (chosen by lot) for the Panathenaea (op. cit. 60. 1), of ἐπιμεληταί (at first elected, later chosen by lot) for the Dionysia (op. cit. 56. 4, cf. Dem. XXI. 15, IV. 35) and of ἐπιμεληταί (elected) for the Mysteries (Arist. *Ath. Pol.* 57. 1, Dem. XXI. 171). There were also two boards of ἱεροποιοί, chosen by lot (Arist. *Ath. Pol.* 54. 6, 7).

[19] Gilbert, *Gr. Const. Ant.*, 359-63, Busolt-Swoboda, *Gr. Staatskunde*, II, 1086 ff.

[20] Xen. *Mem.* III. iv. 4.

[21] Dem. XXI. 15, 17, 58-60, cf. [Xen.] *Ath. Pol.* i. 13.

[22] See p. 129.

[23] See above, pp. 23 ff.

[24] Arist. *Ath. Pol.* 47. 1.

[25] Tod, I. 51; for the suppression of the office see Busolt-Swoboda, *Gr. Staatskunde*, II. 1139.

[26] For specimens of their accounts see Tod, I. 50, 55, 64, 69-70, 75, 78, 81, 83, 92.

[27] Tod, I. 30, 51A, Arist. *Ath. Pol.* 54.

[28] Op. cit., 48. 3.

[29] This appears to be the distinction drawn in Dem. XXIV. 96 ff. between τὰ ἐκ τῶν τελῶν χρήματα and τὰ προσκαταβλήματα: cf. Aristoph. *Wasps*, 658-9.

[30] Dem. XLIII. 71, LVIII. 48, Andoc. I. 77, 79. Aesch. I. 35, *Lex. Seguer.* 190. 26. There is incidentally no justification for the statement often made on the strength of Aristoph. *Knights*, 1358-61 and Lysias, XXVII. 1, that fines went directly to pay the jurors. It is clear from Dem. XXIV. 97-9 that the pay of jurors, as of the council and the assembly, came out of the same pool as the expenditure on the cavalry and the sacrifices.

[31] Arist. *Ath. Pol.* 47. 2-3.

[32] Op. cit., 47. 5, 48. 1-2, cf. Tod, II. 116, μερίσαι δὲ τὸ ἀργύριον τὸ εἰρημένον (in the decree) τοὺς ἀποδέκτας ἐκ τῶν καταβαλλομένων χρημάτων, ἐπειδὰν τὰ ἐκ τῶν νόμων μερ[ίσωσι].

[33] Called τὰ κατὰ τὰ ψηφίσματα ἀναλισκόμενα or μεριζόμενα τῷ δήμῳ (e.g. Tod, II. 135, 142, 153, 167, 173, 178, 198) or τὰ δέκα τάλαντα (ib. 123, 139).

[34] *IG* II-III^2. 120, lines 21-2.

[35] *Syll.* ^{3} 313.

[36] Arist. *Ath. Pol.* 50. 1, 56. 4.

[37] See notes 33 and 34.

[38] Dem. XXII. 17: cf. the elected treasurers of the two sacred triremes, who had an annual allocation of 12 talents each (Arist. *Ath. Pol.* 61. 7, Dem. XXI. 171, 174).

[39] Arist. *Ath. Pol.* 47. 3-4, Dem. XXIV. 98-9.

[40] Lysias, XXX. 19-22.

[41] Dem. XXIV. 99.

[42] Dem. XXXIX. 17; cf. XLV. 4.

[43] Lysias, XXX. 22.

[44] Tod, I. 91 (=*SEG* X. 138): cf. II. 167, where the treasurer of the people is instructed to supply money for crowns from the assembly's fund, but for the present (presumably because the ten talents were exhausted) the Receivers are to pay it from the military fund.

[45] *Syll.*³ 226.

[46] *Syll.*³ 298.

[47] See above, p. 48.

[48] [Xen.] *Ath. Pol.* i. 3, Dem. XXIV. 112, cf. LVII. 25, Arist. *Ath. Pol.*, 7. 4, 47. 1.

[49] Dem. LIX. 72 (Theogenes, a man of good family but poor, only enters for the office of basileus when a wealthy friend promises to help with his expenses on entering office and to serve as his assessor).

[50] Arist. *Ath. Pol.* 47. 5, 48. 1: the same man had custody of the archives (Dem. XIX. 129).

[51] Arist. *Ath. Pol.* 55. 1-2.

[52] *Ib.* 54. 3-5.

[53] Lysias, XXX. 2, 27-8.

[54] Dem. XVIII. 261, XIX. 70, 200, 249; also merely abusive references in XVIII. 127, 265, XIX. 95, 314.

[55] Lysias, XXX. 29.

[56] Arist. *Ath. Pol.* 47. 1.

[57] Arist. *Ath. Pol.* 45. 4, cf. Dem. XIX. 185, XXII. 5.

[58] Arist. *Ath. Pol.* 43. 2.

[59] Op. cit., 62. 1. For an analysis of deme representation see A.W. Gomme, *The Population of Athens*, Note A (pp. 49-66), J. A. O. Larsen, *Representative Government in Greek and Roman History*, 5-9.

[60] Xen. *Mem.* I. ii. 35.

[61] Arist. *Ath. Pol.* 22. 2, cf. Xen. *Mem.* I. i. 18, Lysias, XXXI. 1, 2, Dem. XXIV. 147-8, LIX. 4.

[62] Arist. *Ath. Pol.* 45. 3, cf. Dem. XXI. 111; Lysias XVI and XXXI were delivered at the *dokimasia* of a *bouleutes*.

[63] Aesch. III. 20, Dem. XXII. 38-9.

[64] Larsen, *op. cit.*, 15-18.

[65] Arist. *Ath. Pol.* 62. 3.

[66] See above, p. 150, note 28.

[67] See above, p. 145, note 39.

[68] Aesch. III. 62, cf. 73.

[69] Arist. *Ath. Pol.* 62. 1. This practice of letting a carpet-bagger stand accounts for the slight variations in the number of councillors from each deme which the inscriptions show, see Larsen, op. cit., 7-8.

[70] Arist. *Ath. Pol.* 43. 2-3.

[71] Op. cit., 44. 1-3: for the earlier system see besides the inscriptions the passages cited in notes 73-4 and the comic account of a council meeting in Aristoph. *Knights*, 624-82 (esp. 665, 674) and of an assembly in *Acharnians*, 19 ff. (esp. 23, 40).

[72] Aesch. III. 3.

[73] Thuc. VI. 14.

[74] Xen. *Hell.* I. vii. 14–5, Plato, *Apol.* 32b. In Xen. *Mem.* I. i. 18, IV. iv. 2, Plato, *Gorg.* 473e Socrates is represented as being actually ἐπιστάτης, but the less dramatic version of the story is preferable.

[75] Aesch. II. 84.

[76] Dem. XXII. 36–7, cf. XXIV. 147 and Xen. *Hipparchicus*, i. 8 and Aesch. III. 9 for ῥήτορες in the council.

[77] Arist. *Ath. Pol.* 43. 4–6, cf. 30. 5 for the use of the lot in selecting agenda: the same rules on agenda applied in the council (Dem. XIX. 185).

[78] Aesch. II. 72.

[79] Thuc. VI. 8, Aesch. II. 65–67.

[80] Thuc. VIII. 72. 1.

[81] Plut. *Arist.* 7, Philochorus, *FGH* III. 328. fr. 30.

[82] Dem. LIX. 89.

[83] Dem. XXIV. 45–6.

[84] Aristoph. *Acharnians*, 21–2, *Eccles.* 378–9, and the scholiasts and lexicographers. It may be noted that in the Acharnians this device is employed for a κυρία ἐκκλησία (the first of the prytany), when the business was dull and formal; later extra pay was given for κυρίαι ἐκκλησίαι (Arist. *Ath. Pol.* 62. 2).

[85] Xen. *Mem.* III. vii. 6.

[86] See above, pp. 35–6.

[87] Dem. XIV, esp. 24 ff.

[88] Dem. XIX. 291.

[89] Dem. XVIII. 169–70.

[90] Lines 295–310, 331–51, 372–9. For other allusions to the prayer and curse see Dem. XVIII. 282, XIX. 70–1, XXIII. 97, Deinarchus I. 47–8, II. 17, and for the herald's invitation to speak Aesch. I. 23.

[91] Tod, I. 31, 66, 84B, 86, 96, II. 97.

[92] As in I. 96 and II. 97.

[93] *Ib.* I. 84B; cf. *BSA* XLVI (1951), p. 200 for a revised text and interpretation.

[94] *Ib.* I. 86.

[95] *Ib.* I. 44, 74.

[96] *Ib.* I. 42. The words αὐτίκα μάλα also occur in *SEG* X. 14, Tod, I. 61, 77, II, 114, 123, 142, 144, 146, *Syll.*[3] 198, 204. In all these immediate action by or in the assembly is proposed, presumably in the assembly. When the words occur in a decree of the council they refer to action to be taken forthwith in or by council, as in Tod, II. 103 and *Syll.*[3] 227, lines 18 and 30, and also Tod. II. 97 and 137, which appear to be probouleumata adopted *en bloc* by the assembly.

[97] *Ib.* I. 61.

[98] *Ib.* I. 84B.

[99] E.g. in Tod. II. 114, 136, 174–5, 178, etc.

[100] In Tod. II. 123, 142, 144, 146, 147, 168, *IG* II–III.[2] 70, 134, although the prescript is ἔδοξε τῇ βουλῇ καὶ τῷ δήμῳ, the decree itself incorporates the words δεδόχθαι or ἐψηφίσθαι τῷ δήμῳ, which shows that (in the form in which it

was engraved) it was moved in the assembly. Furthermore 123 contains the clause *ἑλέσθαι τὸν δῆμον πρέσβεις τρεῖς αὐτίκα μάλα:* 142 has similarly *ἀναγράψαι δὲ αὐτῶν τὰ ὀνόματα αὐτίκα μάλα ἐνάντιον τοῦ δήμου*; and 144 and 146 open *εὐξάσθαι μὲν τὸν κήρυκα αὐτίκα μάλα.*

[101] Tod. II. 103 (alliance with Eretria) must have been confirmed by the people, and would not have been engraved until it was confirmed; yet it is headed *ἔδοξε τῇ βουλῇ*. It seems unlikely too that the honours voted by the council to Dionysius of Syracuse (*ib.* II. 108) were not ratified by the people. In *IG* II-III.[2] 32 a decree headed *ἔδοξε τῇ βουλῇ* is followed by an amendment *τὰ μὲν ἄλλα κάθαπερ τῇ βουλῇ,* and must therefore have been passed by the people.

[102] Tod, II. 134, 167, 181.

[103] Aesch. II. 64, 68.

[104] Tod, I. 90.

[105] *Ib.* II. 97A.

[106] E.g. in Tod, II. 124, 126, 131, 133, 135, 143, 157, 159, 170.

[107] *Ib.* II. 189.

[108] *IG* II-III.[2] 336.

[109] Tod, II. 144.

[110] *Ib.* II. 114.

[111] *Ib.* II. 118, 121, 123.

[112] *Ib.* II. 124, 126.

[113] Thuc. I. 31-44, 139-45, III. 36-49, IV. 17-22, V. 44-6, VI. 8-26. Cf. the debate on Pylos, in which Nicias resigned the generalship in favour of Cleon, in IV. 27-8.

[114] Xen. *Hell.* I. vii.

[115] Aesch. II. 65-68.

[116] Dem. LIX. 4. Cf. XXIII. 9, 14, for the tactical convenience of having a probouleuma ready for a snap vote.

[117] Dem. XXI. 162.

[118] Dem. LIX. 4.

[119] Dem. XIX. 286.

[120] Dem. XIX. 234 (cf. Aesch. II. 45-6), XVIII. 28 (cf. Aesch. II. 55), XVIII. 25, XIX. 154. Cf. also Aesch. II. 19.

[121] Dem. XIX. 31.

[122] Cf. Xenophon's advice to a hipparch *ἐν τῇ βουλῇ ἔχειν ῥήτορας ἐπιτηδείους* (*Hipparchicus* i. 8).

[123] Dem. XXIV. 48.

[124] E.g. Tod, II. 131, 133, 173 for foreigners. The clause in the decree of Tisamenus (Andoc. I. 84), *ἐξεῖναι δὲ καὶ ἰδιώτῃ τῷ βουλομένῳ εἰσιόντι εἰς τὴν βουλὴν συμβουλεύειν ὅτι ἂν ἀγαθὸν ἔχῃ περὶ τῶν νόμων* should, I think, be taken to mean that private citizens were on this occasion officially encouraged to use their rights. Cf. Andoc. I. 111, Dem. XIX. 10, 17, XXIV. 11, for *προσιέναι τῇ βουλῇ*. Decrees passed as a result of a *πρόσοδος* normally in the fourth century begin with some such words as *περὶ ὧν λέγουσι . . . .* In

most cases the persons alluded to are foreign envoys (e.g. Tod, II. 122, 124, 126, 131, 133-5, 146-7, 159, 167-8, 175, 178, 189) but sometimes citizens (*IG* II-III.[2] 70, 243 and probably Tod. II. 108), including priests (*IG* II-III[2]. 47, 410) and other functionaries (*ib.* 403).

[125] Aesch. III. 125-6.

[126] This appears from the last clause of Tod. I. 74, *ἡ δὲ βουλὴ ἐς τὸν δῆμον ἐχσενενκέτω ἐπάναγκες* (the report of Lampon on the Eleusinian first-fruits of oil).

[127] Xen. *Hell.* I. vii. 7.

[128] *Syll.*[3] 281 (a decree of the people beginning *περὶ ὧν ὁ δῆμος προσέταξεν τῇ βουλῇ προβουλεύσασαν ἐξενειγκε͂ν περὶ Πυθέου καθ' ὅτι τιμηθήσεται ὑπὸ τοῦ δήμου*), 304 (which gives the whole procedure, IA the original motion in the people by Telemachus of Acharnae, IB the probouleuma moved by his fellow demesman Cephisodotus, and IC the final decree of the people moved by Telemachus: IIA is a second and later probouleuma, resulting in IIB a second decree).

[129] Tod. II. 154 (here only the original motion in the people is recorded, and it is apparently assumed that the council and people duly confirmed it).

[130] Arist. *Ath. Pol.* 43. 6.

[131] Aesch. III. 38-40.

[132] Dem. XXIV. 17 ff. cf. XX. 81 ff. For the number of the *νομοθέται* see Dem. XXIV. 27 (whence Pollux, VIII. 101): in Andoc. I. 84 they number 500 only (again plus the council), and are elected by the demes. Despite the heliastic oath (Dem. XXIV. 21) the *νομοθέται* followed the procedure of the assembly, and were presided over by *πρόεδροι* and an *ἐπιστάτης* (*Syll.*[3] 200, 226, and *Hesperia* XXI (1952), p. 355).

[133] Andoc. I. 81 ff. discussed by Harrison in *JHS* 1955, pp. 22 ff.

[134] Tod. I. 40. Contrast the *νομοθεσία* required in the fourth century for an annual payment of 30 drachmae for a sacrifice to Amphiaraus (*Syll.*[3] 298).

[135] Tod. I. 51. Contrast the *νομοθεσία* required for altering the rules about the surplus (Dem. III. 10-11).

[136] Tod. I. 74. Contrast legislation on the same topic in 353/2 (*Syll.*[3] 200).

[137] *SEG.* X. 14. The most famous board of *συγγραφεῖς* is of course that of 411 (Thuc. VIII. 67. 1, Arist. *Ath. Pol.* 29. 2).

[138] See above, p. 51.

[139] See Harrison, *JHS*, 1955, pp. 22 ff.

[140] *Syll.*[3] 226.

[141] Dem. XXIV. 33.

[142] Andoc. I. 17: it was evidently regarded as a bulwark of the constitution in 411, Thuc. VIII. 67. 2, Arist. *Ath. Pol.* 29. 4.

[143] It was presumably one of the safeguards substituted in 461 for *ἡ τῆς πολιτείας φυλακή* of the Areopagus (Arist. *Ath. Pol.* 25. 2).

[144] Dem. XXIV. 9 (1000), Deinarchus, *in Dem.* 109 (1,500), Lysias XIII. 35 (2,000), Deinarchus *in Dem.* 52 (2500). In Andoc. I. 17 the whole body of 6,000 jurors formed the jury, it would seem.

145 Arist. *Ath. Pol.* 24. 3, Aristoph. *Wasps*, 661 (6,000); Arist. *Ath. Pol.* 27. 4 (the lot).

146 Arist. *Ath. Pol.* 63. 3, cf. 7. 3.

147 Aristoph. *Wasps*, 605 ff. for the fee: the jurors are represented as old men (*χόρος γερόντων σφηκῶν,* cf. *Knights* 255, *ὦ γέροντες ἡλιάσται)*, and former rowers in the fleet (cf. *Wasps*, 231). The Old Oligarch regards the jurors as men of the people ([Xen.] *Ath. Pol.* i. 16-18), and Aristotle comments that the introduction of pay meant that ordinary people put in to be jurors rather than the respectable classes (*Ath. Pol.* 27. 4).

148 See above, pp. 19, 36–7.

149 Thuc. VI. 8. 2, 26. 1. For other magistrates see Tod, I. 44 (the founder of a colony); for envoys, Andoc. III. 33, *αὐτοκράτορας γὰρ πεμφθῆναι εἰς Λακεδαίμονα διὰ ταῦθ' ἵνα μὴ πάλιν ἐπαναφέρωμεν*; for the council, Tod, I. 51, *SEG* X. 64a, 84, cf. Dem. XIX. 154, Andoc. I. 15.

150 Thuc. IV. 66, 76.

151 Thuc. IV. 118. 14. Cf. *SEG* X. 84.

152 *SEG* X. 86.

153 *Syll.*³ 132.

154 Tod, I. 61, line 55, cf. Arist. *Ath. Pol.* 30. 5.

155 *IG* II–III.² 108, Tod, II. 143.

156 Thuc. VI. 25. 1.

157 Thuc. VI. 43. 2, 44. 3–45, 52. 2.

158 Thuc. I. 116. 1, II. 13. 1.

159 The evidence is fully set out in C. Hignett, *A History of the Athenian Constitution*, Appendix XI, pp. 347–56. I am indebted to Mr. D. M. Lewis for the probable addition of 426 to the list.

160 Dem. XVIII. 149, *προβληθεὶς πυλάγορος οὗτος καὶ τριῶν ἢ τεττάρων χειροτονησάντων αὐτὸν ἀνερρήθη*, 285, *ὁ δῆμος. . . οὐ σὲ ἐχειροτόνησε προβληθέντα*, Aesch. II. 18, *ψήφισμα ἔγραψεν ὁ Φιλοκράτης ἑλέσθαι πρέσβεις πρὸς Φίλιππον ἄνδρας δέκα . . . χειροτονουμένων δὲ τῶν δέκα πρεσβευτῶν ἐγὼ μὲν προεβλήθην ὑπὸ Ναυσικλέους, Δημοσθένης δ' ὑπ' αὐτοῦ Φιλοκράτους*, cf. Dem. XXI. 15,200. See Arist. *Ath. Pol.* 44. 4 for the probouleuma for elections.

161 Arist. *Ath. Pol.* 22. 2, 61. 1. Nomination by tribes would be analogous with the procedure for appointing choregi (Arist. *Ath. Pol.* 56. 3, Dem. XXI. 13). Demes were sometimes represented in the council by members of other demes (see above, note 69) by a similar arrangement.

162 Thuc. II. 22. 1.

163 Thuc. II. 65. 8.

164 Thuc. II. 65. 3–4.

165 Thuc. II. 59. 2.

166 Dem. IV. 26.

167 Demades, 9.

168 Hypereides, I. 24–25. Cf. Dem. LVIII. 35.

169 Arist. *Ath. Pol.* 43. 1.

[170] Aesch. III. 25.

[171] His precise title is unknown. Hypereides says that he was *ταχθεὶς ἐπὶ τῇ διοικήσει τῶν χρημάτων* (fr. 118) and that the people elected him *ἐπὶ τὴν διοίκησιν τῶν αὐτοῦ ἅπασαν ταμίαν* (I.28). Demosthenes says that he *αὐτὸν ἐν τῷ περὶ τὴν διοίκησιν μέρει τάξας τῆς πολιτείας* (*Ep*. iii. 2). In the garbled decree in [Plut.] *Vit. X. Or.* (*Mor.* 852 A) he is styled *τῆς κοινῆς προσόδου ταμίας.*

[172] Arist. *Ath. Pol.* 47. 2, cf. 49. 3.

[173] Aesch. III. 25.

[174] Diodorus (XVI. 88) speaks of him as *τὰς προσόδους τῆς πόλεως διοικήσας* for twelve years, and the decree cited in note 171 says that he was *τῆς κοινῆς προσόδου ταμίας τῇ πόλει ἐπὶ τρεῖς πενταετηρίδας,* but in the Life of Lycurgus ([Plut.] *Mor.* 841 B) it is explained that he actually held office for one quadrennium only.

[175] Dem. III. 30.

[176] *Ib.* XXII. 37.

[177] *Ib.* LVIII. 39-40.

[178] See above, pp. 23 ff.

[179] Dem. II. 29, XIII. 20. Cf. Aesch. III. 7.

[180] See R. Sealey in *JHS* 1955, 74-81.

[181] Arist. *Ath. Pol.* 28.

[182] Dem. XXI. 208 ff.

[183] *Hell. Oxy.* i 2-3.

[184] Diod. XVIII. 10.

[185] Aristoph. *Eccl.* 197-8.

[186] Deinarchus, *in Dem.* 72.

[187] Plato, *Protagoras*, 319b-323a cited on pp. 46 7 above.

[188] Xen. *Mem.* III. vi.

APPENDIX

The Citizen Population of Athens during the Peloponnesian War

IN THE first quarter of the fifth century the adult male citizen population of Athens would seem from the meagre and imprecise data available to have numbered about 30,000, of whom about 10,000 were hoplites; under which term I include, unless otherwise stated or implied, the cavalry (see above, p.8). During the period between the Persian and Peloponnesian wars we have one figure only, and that not a very useful one. For the battle of Tanagra (458 or 457) the Athenians raised a hoplite army of 14,000: they themselves served in full force (*πανδημεί*) and they had with them 1,000 Argives and other allies (Thuc. I. 107. 5). There were at this date some Athenian hoplites, but probably not many, engaged elsewhere, at Aegina and in Egypt. These figures imply that the Athenian hoplite force had risen somewhat, perhaps by 25 per cent., above 10,000.

For the year 431 Thucydides (II. 13. 6–8) gives us full hoplite statistics. Pericles reminded the people 'that there were 13,000 hoplites apart from the 16,000 in the forts and on the walls. For as many as that at first kept guard whenever the enemy invaded, from the oldest and the youngest, and all the metic hoplites. For there were 35 stades of the Phaleric wall . . .' Thucydides proceeds to give a detailed description, showing that there were in all 148 stades (over 16 miles) of wall to patrol. He then mentions the 1,200 cavalry, including the mounted archers; 1,000 of them will have been the real cavalry, drawn from the highest census classes and to be added to the hoplite total.

These are startling figures, and many attempts have been made to get round them. Some have misinterpreted Thucydides' words, by making the 16,000 include the thetes (Delbrück,

Geschichte der Kriegskunst, I. 15-24). Others have amended the text, either reducing the 16,000 to 6,000 (Beloch, *Klio* V (1905), 356-74, Busolt, *Griechische Geschichte*, III. ii. 878-88, *Griechische Staatskunde*, II. 764-6), or adding colonists to the metics to fill out the 16,000 (Beloch, *Die Bevölkerung der griechisch-römischen Welt*, 60-66). But Thucydides' language is explicit, and the figures cannot be rejected as textual errors. That of 13,000 for the field army is confirmed by Thucydides himself in a later passage (II. 31. 2), where he records that 10,000 Athenian hoplites took part in the invasion of the Megarid, while 3,000 were at Potidaea. Diodorus (that is, Ephorus), moreover, gives the same gross total, divided into '12,000 hoplites and more than 17,000 garrison troops and metics' (Diod. XII. 40. 4).

The figures raise two main difficulties: first the apparent disproportion between the field army, comprising the active service age groups, and the defence army, consisting of the oldest and youngest and metics; and secondly the very large gross total, as compared with earlier and later figures. There is also a third minor difficulty, the proportion between the number of deaths from the plague among the cavalry and the hoplites.

Only one explanation of the first difficulty has been offered, that of Professor Gomme in *CQ.* XXI (1927), 142-151, repeated in his *Population of Athens*, pp. 4-5. Gomme suggests that there were many men in the active service age groups (which he takes to have been 20-49) who were unfit for the field army but capable of garrison duty, and that these men were classed with the youngest (18-19) and oldest (50-59).

There are serious objections to this theory. It is in the first place not what Thucydides says. Secondly it is a pure speculation, unsupported by any evidence. The Athenians recognised the unfit (ἀδύνατοι), who were presumably totally exempt, but these were men obviously incapable of fighting at all, lame like Lysias' client in Oration XXIV or blind like Timarchus' uncle (Aesch. I. 102-4). A man might also presumably be excused on a particular occasion if he were ill at the time, like the two Spartans who were sent back to base from Thermopylae because of an attack of ophthalmia (Herod. VII. 229). We know of no case at Athens, but we may conjecture that in such circumstances a man would, like Aeschines when he wished to evade an embassy, send in an affidavit (ἐξωμοσία) backed by a doctor's certificate (Dem. XIX. 124). The Athenians also recognised that service in the cavalry demanded an exceptional standard of physical fitness, and members of the corps or those designated to serve could, by an affidavit that they were physically unfit for cavalry service, get themselves removed from the list (Arist. *Ath. Pol.* 49.2, cf. Xen. *Hipparch.* ix. 5), presumably becoming hoplites unless totally incapacitated. But there was only one hoplite register (κατάλογος). In this sense the word is always used in the singular, as in Thuc. VI. 43, VII. 16. 1, 20. 2, VIII. 24. 2, cf. Xen. *Mem.* III. iv. 1 and Dem. XIII. 4, ὑπὲρ τὸν κατάλογον, explained by Pollux, II. 11, as over 60; the plural κατάλογοι in Thuc. VI. 26. 2, 31. 3, bears a different meaning—selective call-up within this single register. The men were listed in year groups, 42 in all from 18 to 59 (Arist. *Ath. Pol.* 53. 4), and the call-up, unless it was selective (ἐν τοῖς μέρεσιν), was by year groups (ἐν τοῖς ἐπωνύμοις, Arist. *Ath. Pol.* 53. 7 and Aesch. II. 168, cf. Lysias, XIV. 6). Neither at Athens nor anywhere else in the ancient world is it recorded that liability for active or defence service was regulated by any other criterion but age.

Let us then set aside this theory and examine the facts afresh. Thucydides' language implies that because of the exceptionally heavy demands of defence, the number of men allocated to it was increased during these years. This again implies that the rules governing the employment of the oldest and youngest and of the metics were not rigid but might vary according to circumstances.

As to the youngest there can be no dispute. What is meant is the 18- and 19-year-old classes, the ephebes. About the oldest there is room for doubt. It is usually stated on the strength of a statement by Lycurgus (*c. Leocratem*, 39-40) that they were the

50–59 classes. But this passage merely proves that for the battle of Chaeroneia, an extreme emergency, all men up to 50 were called up, so that the defence of the city was left to the over 50 classes. For the expedition to Thermopylae in 347, on the other hand, it was decided to mobilise men up to 40 only (Aesch. II. 133; some MSS. give 30), and so too for the Lamian war (Diod. XVIII. 10). An anecdote in Plutarch's *Phocion* (ch. 24) implies that theoretically all men up to 60 might be called up for active service. Our evidence in fact suggests that there was no fixed age limit for active service, and that the call-up was adjusted according to the needs of the situation. In 431 the 20–39s may have been allocated (as in the Lamian war) to the field army, and the 40–59s (with the 18–19s) to home defence.

It is also generally stated that the metics were normally called up for home defence only. This doctrine, however, rests on the present passage only. Metics were certainly employed regularly on foreign service in the fourth century, as appears from Xenophon's proposal for their exemption from hoplite service (*de Vect.* ii. 2–5). In the fifth century they were called up for Delium (Thuc. IV. 90. 1), and 3,000 were employed in this very year for the invasion of the Megarid (Thuc. II. 31. 2). It would seem that in principle and in practice metics were liable to service abroad, and that it was exceptional to reserve them for home defence, as in 431.

On the number of metic hoplites we have no evidence. There is, as Gomme has pointed out, no justification for assuming that the 3,000 who served in the Megarid represent the whole number of metic hoplites, or even all those in the active service age groups. It is hardly a coincidence that 3,000 metics were called up at a time when 3,000 Athenians were detained at Potidaea (Thuc. II. 31. 2): only so many metics were levied for the Megarid campaign as would bring the invading army up to full strength. On general grounds of probability it may be conjectured that the number of metic hoplites was far in excess of 3,000. A century later, under Demetrius of Phaleron, the metics numbered 10,000, nearly half the contemporary citizen total of 21,000 (Athenaeus, VI. 272c). In 431, when Athens was far more prosperous, the number is likely to have been considerably greater, with a high proportion of hoplites.

It has been argued above (see pp. 82–3) that there is reason to believe that the age distribution of the Athenian population was similar to that worked out by Mr. A. R. Burn for various areas of the Roman Empire. On this assumption, if 14,000 (the hoplite field army and the cavalry) represent the 20–39 age groups, the 40–59s will have amounted to slightly under half that figure, rather less than 7,000. The two very large ephebic classes would have totalled rather over 2,000. There will then have been 9,000 citizens in the garrison army, and we are left with 7,000 metic hoplites, which seems not unreasonable. The total number of citizens of military age and hoplite census will then have been 23,000, or not counting the ephebes, 21,000.

It will be convenient to deal at this stage with the third difficulty. Under the year 427 Thucydides (III. 87. 3) states that 'no fewer than 4,400 hoplites from the regiments (*ἐκ τῶν τάξεων*) and 300 cavalry died (of the plague from 430 to 427) and an incalculable number of the remainder of the population'. It has been argued that if the hoplites were as numerous as Thucydides' figures imply (22,000 including the ephebes by my calculations), the proportion of deaths among them (20 per cent.) is too low as compared with the proportion among the cavalry (30 per cent.), especially as the latter, being all young men, might have been expected to suffer less. Gomme endeavours to solve this difficulty by postulating that the phrase 'hoplites from the regiments' means the field army of 13,000 (giving a proportion of 34 per cent. deaths), but this is illegitimate. It is certain that all hoplites (with the possible exception of the ephebes) were entered in the tribal regiments (*τάξεις*), and the contrast between the exact numbers given for the hoplites and cavalry and the 'incalculable number' for the rest of the population shows that Thucydides is dealing on the one hand with the classes of the citizens of whom a register was kept (that is the cavalry and all the hoplites), and the thetes, who were at this period not entered on any unified list, and among whom therefore the number of deaths was not recorded. The phrase 'from the regiments' is presumably added either to exclude the ephebes, or more probably thetes equipped as hoplites for service in the fleet as marines. The proportion of 20 per cent. deaths among the hoplites must then stand.

But the whole argument is very flimsy. We do not know in the first place whether mortality was more severe among the old or the young. And in the second place the 1,000 cavalry are a very small sample on which to base an average. The corps may well for accidental reasons have suffered abnormally. Hagnon's hoplite army at Potidaea, Thucydides tells us (II. 58. 3), lost 1,050 men out of 4,000 (26 per cent.) in forty days. The corps of cavalry, which was constantly mobilised during this period, may well have suffered such an acute epidemic.

To turn to the second difficulty, the number of hoplites will, if my interpretation of Thucydides' figures is correct, have approximately doubled in the fifty years since the Persian wars. This is a striking but not impossible increase. Since hoplite status depended on the assessed value of a man's property (see p. 142, note 50), it implies primarily an evenly distributed increase in wealth as assessed in money. This is *a priori* probable in mid-fifth-century Athens. The thetes were earning good money in State service (primarily as rowers) and in industry, which was thriving, and in particular in the great programme of public works. Some will have been able to invest in enough slaves or house property to qualify as hoplites.

Besides the real increase in wealth there was probably a fictitious increase due to an inflationary trend. From 483 the Laurium mines were producing large quantities of silver, and from the foundation of the Delian League, and especially from 449, when the reserve fund began to be spent on public works, considerable sums of tribute money were pumped into the Athenian economy. Prices must have risen, and our tenuous evidence suggests that they did. In a Solonian law a drachma was equated with a medimnus (Plut. *Solon*, 23. 3), and there seems no reason why prices should have risen in the next century. By the beginning of the fourth century, if we may take seriously an allusion in Aristophanes (*Eccl.* 547-8), wheat stood at 3 drachmae the medimnus. Assessments no doubt lagged behind prices, but the revaluation of property must have brought some thetes into the hoplite class, in the way that Aristotle (*Pol.* 1306b) remarks was liable to happen in times of prosperity.

These two factors, the real increase of personal and of house property and the apparent increase in the value of all property, including land, must have increased the number of hoplites, but it is difficult to believe that they alone can have doubled it. Many thetes must also have acquired land. Redistribution of land in Attica would not, of course, affect the issue unless large estates were broken up, for which there is not a scrap of evidence. Land must have been acquired abroad. There are two ways in which this could have happened, by private acquisition and by state action.

The first possibility has been strangely ignored. In the charter of the Second Athenian League (Tod. II. 123) there is a clause which has been generally interpreted as a guarantee against Athenian cleruchies. But if so it is very strangely phrased: 'And that from the archonship of Nausinicus it be not lawful for any Athenian to acquire a house or land in the territories of the allies either privately or publicly either by purchase or mortgage or in any other way'. Cleruchies would no doubt be covered by the word 'publicly', but what the potential allies of Athens evidently feared more was private purchase or mortgage. This implies that many Athenians had in the days of the Delian League exploited their predominant position to claim the right of land ownership (*γῆς ἔγκτησις*) in the territories of the allies.

It may however be doubted whether the private acquisition of land abroad by Athenian citizens greatly affected the total of hoplites; for the majority of the purchasers or mortgagees would probably have been well-to-do men already in the hoplite class. This brings us to the question of cleruchies and colonies. This problem is fully discussed in *The Athenian Tribute Lists*, III, 282–297, a passage to which I owe much.

In both the inscriptions (e.g. *IG* I^2. 140) and the literary authorities a distinction is drawn (though in the latter, especially the late secondary sources, it is often blurred) between colonies (*ἀποικίαι*) and colonists (*ἄποικοι*, sometimes called, when the reference is to their initial despatch, *ἔποικοι*) on the one hand, and cleruchies (*κληρουχίαι*) and cleruchs (*κληροῦχοι*) on the other. There is scarcely any fifth-century evidence on the significance of the distinction, but on the analogy of general Greek practice it may be assumed that a colony was, technically at any rate, an independent State, and that the colonists ceased to be Athenian citizens and became citizens of the colony. Cleruchs, on the other hand, in the fourth century certainly remained Athenian citizens, and may be presumed to have done so in the fifth.

The effect of planting a colony was therefore to diminish the number of Athenian citizens, but not necessarily the number of Athenian hoplites. For the majority of the settlers were probably thetes. The amendment to the decree relating to the foundation of the colony of Brea, 'that the colonists for Brea be from the thetes and zeugites' (Tod. I. 44), is probably to be interpreted, as Mr. de Ste Croix has suggested to me, as making the zeugites eligible in addition to the thetes (who had been specified in the lost opening paragraphs of the decree), rather than as restricting participation in the colony to the two lowest classes; for it is hardly likely that many rich Athenians would have wished to leave Athens (and abandon their citizenship) to settle in the wilds of Thrace. A cleruchy, on the other hand, would leave the number of citizens unchanged but would raise some from thetic to zeugite rank. For once again the majority of cleruchs were probably by origin thetes, and in the one case in which we know the value of the allotments, at Lesbos (Thuc. III. 50. 2), they brought in a rent of 200 drachmae a year, which was probably equivalent to the minimum zeugite qualification (see above, p. 142, note 50).

Not only were thetes thus converted into zeugites, but zeugites were prevented from sinking to thetic status. When a poor zeugite left more than one son, the sons would, according to general practice, divide the property equally, and thus both or all become thetes. But if the father or one or more of the sons acquired allotments, there would be property enough for two or more sons all to maintain their zeugite qualification. Colonies would have had a similar effect: if the second son of a poor zeugite joined a colony, his brother would succeed to the whole of his father's farm. In a period when, as I shall argue later, the population was expanding rapidly, the number of hoplites might, but for this, have sunk by the splitting up of small farms.

It is not in all cases possible to distinguish which settlements were colonies and which cleruchies. Besides Thurii (443) and Amphipolis (437), in which Athenian settlers were in a minority. the following very probably were colonies:

Histiaea (446). Thuc. VII. 57. 2. In another passage (VIII. 95. 7) he alludes to the population as Athenians, but he is presumably thinking not of their legal status but of their origins. Diodorus (XII. 22) also calls it a colony, and adds *τήν τε πόλιν καὶ τὴν χώραν κατεκληρούχησαν*, but this is not inconsistent, for in a colony the houses and land had to be divided into lots for the settlers: Diodorus uses the same phrase in describing the foundation of Amphipolis (XI. 70. 5). He gives the number of settlers as 1,000. Theopompus (fr. 387 in *F. Gr. Hist.*) gives 2,000 settlers.

Brea (*c.* 445). Tod. I. 44. Plutarch (*Pericles*, 11) gives the number of settlers as 1,000.

Aegina (431). Thuc. II. 27. 1, VIII. 69. 3 and perhaps VII. 57. 2. Numbers not recorded.

Potidaea (430). Thuc. II. 70. 4, Tod, I. 60. Diodorus (XII. 46) uses the same phrase as with Histiaea and gives the number as 1,000.

Melos (416). Thuc. V. 116. 4. 500 settlers.

The 600 Athenian settlers at Sinope (Plut. *Pericles*, 20) presumably became Sinopians, and the settlers at Amisus (Theopompus, fr. 389, cf. Plut. *Lucullus*, 19, Appian, *Mithr.* 83) also presumably became citizens of the town, refounded as Peiraeus. Astacus (Memnon, fr. 12, Diod, XII. 34, Strabo, 563) was also refounded with additional settlers. An inscription (*Syll.*³ 65) records τῆς ἀποι[κίας] τῆς ἐς 'Ερ. . . . This has been restored as Eretria, Eresos or Erythrae. The last is perhaps the most probable: it may be doubted whether the 'colony' was more than a reinforcement of the population of Erythrae, which may have been officially refounded. Another inscription (*SEG*. X. 17) mentions οἰκισταί in connection with Colophon. This again probably only means that Colophon was officially refounded with additional settlers. It might also mean that cleruchs were sent to Colophon: in the fourth century οἰκισταί were sent to the Chersonese (*IG*. II-III². 1613, 297-8), which was then certainly a cleruchy (Dem. VIII. 6, cf. XXIII. 103 and Aesch. II. 72).

The following were fairly certainly cleruchies:

Naxos, Andros and a place in Euboea (Carystus?) (449). Plutarch (*Pericles*, 11) states that Pericles planted 500 cleruchs in Naxos and 250 in Andros: as his list includes undoubted colonies the passage is dubious evidence for the legal status of the settlers. Diodorus (XI. 88) states that Tolmides went to Euboea and distributed the land of the Naxians to 1,000 citizens. A lacuna is suspected in the text; the 1,000 settlers were probably distributed between Naxos (500), Andros (250) and a place (or places) in Euboea (250). As in 449 the tribute of Carystus was reduced from 7½ to 5 talents, and that of Andros from 12 to 6 (the earliest figure for Naxos is 6⅔ in 447, which is low for an island of this size, and implies a similar reduction), it is inferred that land was taken from these cities (and perhaps others in Euboea for which figures are lacking) for the Athenian settlers. Diodorus' words imply cleruchies. The settlers certainly did not become Naxians, Andrians and Carystians(?), for in that case there would have been no reason to reduce the tribute of these cities; and 250 is surely too small for an independent colony.

Chalcis (446). Aelian, *Var. Hist.* VI. 1, *'Αθηναῖοι κρατήσαντες Χαλκιδέων κατεκληρούχησαν αὐτῶν τὴν γῆν εἰς δισχιλίους κλήρους, τὴν Ἱπποβοτῶν καλουμένην χώραν* (cf. Plut. *Pericles*, 23, for the expulsion of the Hippobotae in 446). Probably 1,800 cleruchs, allowing for the share (presumably a tenth as at Lesbos: Thuc. III. 50. 2) dedicated according to Aelian to Athena.

Lesbos (427). Thuc. III. 50. 2, Tod. I, 63. 3,000 lots and 2,7000 cleruchs (300 lots to the gods).

The Chersonese is a doubtful case. Plutarch in one passage (*Pericles*, 11) speaks of 1,000 cleruchs, and in another (op. cit. 19) of 1,000 colonists. Diodorus (XI. 88) says *χιλίοις τῶν πολιτῶν κατεκληρούχησε τὴν χώραν*; this in view of the parallel passages about Naxos, Histiaea and Potidaea is of doubtful value. The tribute of the Chersonesite cities was reduced from 18 talents in 451 to 13 talents 4,840 drachmae in 449 (perhaps owing to the Thracian devastations), and later (the change is first traceable in 442) to only 1 talent. This does not affect the question of cleruchy or colony, as land must have been surrendered for either.

Finally there are Lemnos, Imbros and Scyros. These three islands were regarded in the fourth century as virtually appanages of Attica. Made independent on the fall of Athens (Andoc. III. 12), they were within a decade in Athenian hands again (Xen. *Hell.* IV. viii. 15) and were recognised as Athenian possessions by the King's Peace (ib. V. i. 31). They were at this period cleruchies, the communities being styled *ὁ δῆμος ὁ 'Αθηναίων ὁ ἐν Ἴμβρῳ οἰκῶν* and the like for Scyros and the two Lemnian cities, Hephaestia and Myrina (*IG*. XII. 8. 3 ff., 26, 46, 668). This proves nothing about their status in the fifth century, for in the fourth all Athenian outsettlements (except for a colony sent to the Adriatic, Tod. II. 200) were cleruchies (e.g. Aesch. I. 53,

*Syll.*³. 276 for Samos: Dem. VIII. 6, XXIII. 103, Aesch. II. 72 for the Chersonese; Tod. II. 146 for Potidaea). The fourth-century evidence does however suggest that the whole population of the islands was Athenian by descent.

Scyros. Cimon expelled the natives and settled it with Athenians c. 473 (Thuc. I. 98. 2, Plut. *Cimon*, 8, Diod. XI. 60). Both Thucydides and Plutarch use the neutral word *οἰκίζειν*. Diodorus says *κτιστὴν Ἀθηναῖον καταστήσας κατεκληρούχησε τὴν γῆν*. The use of the verb *κατακληρουχεῖν* is, as noted above, indecisive. A founder (*κτιστής*) might imply a colony, but, as we have seen, *οἰκισταί* were in the fourth century sent to establish a cleruchy.

Lemnos and Imbros. The Pelasgian inhabitants of Hephaestia and Myrina were expelled by Miltiades before the Persian wars, and Athenian settlers substituted (Herod. VI. 136, 140), and the same was probably done at Imbros (this is implied by Herod. V. 26, cf. VI. 41 and 104). An inscription from Hephaestia which must be dated before the Persian wars (*BCH*, XXXVI (1912), 330–38) gives a list of names arranged in the Athenian tribes. This might equally well mean that the city was inhabited by cleruchs, still in their Athenian tribes, or that Hephaestia, as a colony of Athens, had tribes of the same names as the Athenian. The two Lemnian cities and Imbros paid tribute in the Delian League. The cities which paid tribute can hardly be, as had been suggested, the Pelasgians, for all the evidence indicates that they were completely expelled or exterminated. They must then be Athenian colonies, for cleruchs, being Athenian citizens, could not pay separately. Other Athenian colonies, founded after the inception of the Delian League, did not, it is true, pay tribute either. But these old colonies may have been assessed by Aristeides, correctly from the constitutional point of view, and the rule changed later.

In 449 the Lemnians, who in 451 had paid 9 talents, were (probably) assessed at 3 for Hephaestia and 1 for Myrina (from 443 certainly 3 and 1½). This has been taken to mean that they surrendered land to Athenian cleruchs; but it would be very odd for the Athenians to have planted cleruchs in the islands instead of reinforcing the colonists, and other explanations are possible for the reduction in tribute. Members of this supposed second batch of settlers have also been seen in two mid-fifth-century lists from Athens (*IG* I², 947–8), where 'Lemnians' or 'Lemnians from Myrina' are recorded under Athenian tribes. But it is also possible that lists of Lemnian colonists in their own (identical) tribes, probably those who died fighting for Athens, may have been set up in the mother city.

This list suggests that colonies were sent either (*a*) as at Amisus and Sinope (and Thurii), to reinforce existing cities (and to strengthen the pro-Athenian party in them), or (*b*) as at Histiaea, Potidaea, Aegina and Melos, to occupy the sites of enemy cities destroyed, or (*c*) as at Brea (and Amphipolis) to occupy strategic points on barbarian soil. On these principles Scyros was probably a colony of type (*b*). Cleruchies were planted in the territory of an existing city. The land was obtained at Chalcis by the confiscation of the estates of the anti-Athenian oligarchy. It may be conjectured that the land at Naxos and Carystus (?) had been confiscated after the reduction of those two cities, and was now utilised for allotment.

In the Chersonese Plutarch (*Pericles*, 19) suggests that the Athenian settlers occupied waste lands in the cities, which had suffered greatly from Thracian raids. Since the settlers were not enrolled in the cities (as the reductions of tribute show), they were probably cleruchs.

To return to the population of Athens, on this reckoning several thousands of Athenians were despatched as colonists during the Pentecontaetia, and ceased thereby to be citizens: the number cannot be calculated, as no figures have survived except the 600 at Sinope and 1,000 at Brea and 1,000 or 2,000 at Histiaea. Several thousand Athenian citizens were also given allotments in cleruchies and thereby raised to or maintained in zeugite status. If the Chersonese be reckoned a cleruchy the minimum figure is

3,800. Are these 4,000 (or, if the Chersonese was a colony, 3,000) odd hoplites to be included in Thucydides' figures or not?

It is the generally accepted doctrine that cleruchies were regarded as garrisons, and that cleruchs were therefore not liable to military service outside the territory in which they were planted. On this assumption Gomme very properly excludes cleruchs altogether from the hoplite strength given by Thucydides as available for field service and for the defence of the walls of Athens and the forts of Attica.

The accepted doctrine is, however, based on very tenuous evidence. It rests in fact on two passages, one in Plutarch's Life of Pericles (11. 7) and the other in Isocrates' *Panegyricus* (IV. 107). Plutarch states that the objects of the policy of colonies and cleruchies (which he does not distinguish) was two-fold, on the one hand to drain Athens of its unemployed and relieve the poverty of the people, and on the other to provide a deterrent and a garrison to prevent allied revolts. Plutarch's opinions on Athenian policy are not of great value in any case, and his failure to distinguish cleruchies and colonies, the latter of which might be regarded as strategical strongpoints, makes his evidence on the particular point at issue of even less value. Isocrates is concerned to prove that the Athenians did not act from self-interested motives in planting cleruchies, 'which we sent out to those cities which were depopulated to protect the places, not from greed'. Isocrates' argument is highly tendentious. He had to find a disinterested motive for cleruchies, and he finds it in rather vague strategical needs—for it is not clear against whom the places required to be protected in his view; as the allies were according to him perfectly contented, presumably against external enemies.

This is apparently the sole evidence that the cleruchies were intended to serve as garrisons, and that the cleruchs were therefore reserved for the defence of these settlements and not liable to general military service. If that was the intention of the cleruchies they do not seem to have fulfilled it very efficiently. After the fall of Mitylene in 427, 2,700 cleruchs were 'sent out' to Lesbos, but three years later, in 424, Mitylenaean exiles were able to seize Rhoeteum and Antandrus and raid Lesbos (Thuc. IV. 52); Thucydides records no opposition by the cleruch garrison. In 411 the Chians brought about the revolt of Methymna and Mitylene, and again no opposition is recorded (VIII. 22). In Euboea 2,000 cleruchs had been planted in Chalcidian territory in 446, but in 411 the Peloponnesians after the battle of Eretria brought about the revolt of the whole island except Oreus, and the explanation of the exception is that the Athenians themselves (that is, the Athenian colonists of Histiaea) held it (VIII. 95. 7). The implication is clear that there were no Athenians holding Chalcis.

These two instances prove either that the cleruchs of military age were away on active service or garrison duty elsewhere, or that they did not reside on their lots at all. The latter is perhaps the likelier alternative, seeing that no cleruch families are mentioned as suffering when Euboea and Lesbos revolted in 411. In the old days before the Persian wars the 4,000 cleruchs who were allotted the lands of the Chalcidian hippobotae certainly did settle in Euboea, as Herodotus' narrative of the events of 490 proves (Herod. V. 77, VI. 100-01). Thucydides says that the Athenians 'sent out' (*ἀπέπεμψαν*) cleruchs to Lesbos, but one may wonder whether 'to send out' was not by now a term of art.

A very mutilated inscription (Tod, I. 63) has been taken to prove that Athenian cleruchs actually went to Lesbos, but the fragments actually demonstrate nothing more than that the Mitylenaeans had some dealings with cleruchs, which would have been the case whether the latter were resident or not. Gomme (*A Historical Commentary on Thucydides*, II, 328-32) has, on the basis of a (necessarily) very hypothetical reconstruction of this inscription, proposed a theory that the cleruchs, having gone out in 427, were withdrawn, and the land restored to the Mitylenaeans, before 424. But Thucydides would hardly have omitted so striking and sudden a reversal of policy. It seems more likely that the cleruchs stayed at home and that the Lesbians (presumably the old tenants of the oligarchic landlords) worked the land and paid them their fixed rent. Why should they not draw their rents at Athens, instead of living in an alien land (and where were the houses for them to live in?). The same conditions probably applied in Chalcis. In Naxos we hear of an Athenian family residing (Plato, *Euthyphro*, 4*c*), but it is not stated that they were cleruchs. They were evidently well off, employing slaves and hired labour on their farm, and may have been private owners of a large estate which they had bought. Eutherus had also resided abroad until the fall of Athens, and had then been reduced to poverty, 'since we were deprived of our lands overseas, and my father left me nothing in Attica' (Xen. *Mem*. II. viii. 1). But he too is not stated to have been a cleruch, and seems to have come from a well-off family, owning land both in Attica and several places abroad. There is in fact no clear evidence of an Athenian cleruch residing on his lot overseas during the Pentecontaetia and the Peloponnesian war. I would suggest that they were not obliged or expected to do so, and that the allotments were regarded as endowments which qualified them for hoplite service: they might prefer to cultivate them themselves, but they seem normally to have been absentee landlords.

A priori it would seem natural that the Athenians, when they sent out some citizens as colonists and some as cleruchs, deleting the former from the citizen roll and maintaining the latter on it, intended that the latter should continue to perform their civic duties, one of the most important of which was military service. It would have been a fantastic waste of man power to sterilise 2,700 able-bodied citizens as a permanent garrison of Lesbos, and almost as fantastic to allocate 1,800 to hold Chalcis, to which the Athenian army could cross any day, while Naxos and Andros do not appear to have needed garrisons at all.

There is unfortunately no clear and explicit evidence whether in fact cleruchs served or no. Thucydides mentions that in Sicily besides the Athenians themselves there were 'still using the same language and customs as they, Lemnians and Imbrians, and Aeginetans (who then occupied Aegina), and moreover Histiaeans who inhabited Histiaea in Euboea, colonists' (VII. 57. 2). It is a matter of taste how this sentence is punctuated, but all four communities were colonies, the Lemnians and Imbrians being clearly the old colonists, who had been so long separated from Athens that it was noteworthy that they still kept up Athenian speech and manners, and not the putative cleruchs of later date. Thucydides elsewhere (V. 74. 3, VIII. 69. 3) twice mentions Aeginetan colonists serving, and on several occasions Lemnians and Imbrians. These, 'with some few of the other allies', assisted Athens in the revolt of Mitylene (III. 5. 1). Cleon said that he would take with him to Pylos no one from Athens, but 'the Lemnians and Imbrians who were there' (IV. 28. 4), and 'the best troops of the Lemnians and Imbrians' served under him in the Amphipolis campaign (V. 8. 2). Thucydides does not record the presence of cleruchs in the Athenian forces, either because they did not serve, or more probably because they served in the normal course as citizens. I would therefore argue that the 3,000 or 4,000 cleruchs were called up for service in the appropriate age groups, and either fought in the field army or helped to man the walls and forts. If this thesis is accepted the very high hoplite total given by Thucydides for 431 becomes more plausible.

Besides the increase in wealth during the Pentecontaetia, which so greatly increased the hoplite class, there must also have been a very considerable increase in population. We have no figures for the thetic class, but on general grounds (see above p. 9) it is to be inferred that despite the promotion of some thousands to the hoplite class and the drafting of several thousands to colonies, it maintained its numbers at about 20,000 if it did not increase them. This is not impossible or indeed surprising. Modern populations of the same pattern as the Athenian—those of Egypt and India, for instance—respond very rapidly to economic prosperity. The birth rate is high, and the population is only kept down by high mortality. If there is more food available, more survive and the population leaps up rapidly.

It is somewhat surprising, in view of these figures, that at Delium in 424 the Athenians were able to muster a hoplite force of only 7,000, although they held a levy in full force (*πανδημεί*), including not only metics but non-resident foreigners (Thuc. IV. 90. 1, 93. 3, 94. 1). We do not know what precisely 'in full force' means in this context, but the phrase probably refers to all classes rather than all age groups (IV. 94. 1, *πανστρατιᾶς ξένων τῶν παρόντων και ἀστῶν γενομένης*; similarly the invasion of the Megarid in 431 is stated in II. 31 to have been *πανστρατιᾷ* although less than half the hoplites, with many light-armed, took part): for a large number of thetes were mustered to build the fortified post at Delium (IV. 90. 4, 94. 1, 101. 2). But hoplites were certainly mustered up to 45 at least, since Socrates served (Plut. *Alcibiades*, 7). The plague had, of course, intervened, carrying off 4,400 hoplites and 300 cavalry, and no doubt maiming many more—Thucydides records that many who recovered lost their hands or feet or their eyesight (II. 49. 8). The low number mustered at Delium is however probably to be explained chiefly by the fact that secrecy was of the essence of the operation, and that no previous notice of the call-up can have been given, so that many hoplites in outlying demes may not have received their summons in time.

The next figure which we possess is the 9,000 who were enrolled in 411 in the register of the "Five Thousand" (Ps.-Lysias, XX, 13). This again is a surprisingly low figure. The figure would presumably include those over 60, who can hardly have been deprived of political rights. It has been argued (by Ferguson in *C.A.H.* V. 338, supported by Gomme, *Population of Athens*, 7) that it included only those over thirty. There is however no justification for this view. Neither in Thucydides nor in Aristotle (*Ath. Pol.* 29. 5 and 30) is any age qualification suggested for the "Five Thousand"; it is only the councillors drawn from this body who are to be over 30. One must assume that all over 20 were eligible. About 800 out of 9,000 would be over 60, leaving 8,200 from 20 to 59. There had, it is true, been heavy casualties since 424; 1,000 hoplites fell in that year at Delium (Thuc. IV. 101. 2), 600 more at Amphipolis (V. 11. 2), and 2,700 sailed for Sicily (VI. 43, VII. 20. 2), very few of whom ever returned. The effects of the plague, which recurred seriously in the winter of 427-6 (III. 87. 1-2), will moreover still have been felt, if children were affected as much as adults. Nevertheless the drop is startling from 21,000 in 431, if 8,200 represents all Athenians of zeugite status between 20 and 59. It is, however, noteworthy that the simple criterion of zeugite census is never mentioned in the story of the revolution. In the early stages it was proposed that the "Five Thousand" were to comprise 'those best able to serve with their money and their persons' (*Ath. Pol.* 29. 5, Thuc. VIII, 65. 3), and after the fall of the Four Hundred this phrase is clarified as 'those who provide arms' (Thuc. VIII. 97. 1). It would appear that the "Five Thousand" were originally intended to be a much more select body than the zeugites, and that even later the term was not widened to include all of them, but only such as actually possessed hoplite equipment. By this stage of the war many zeugites must have been greatly impoverished and unable to replace their armour.

To summarise the above argument, I would maintain that the figures given by Thucydides and the other ancient authorities are credible. They indicate that during the Pentecontaetia, and especially in its latter half, the numbers of the hoplite class rose rapidly, increasing from about 10,000 at the time of the Persian war to well over 20,000 at the beginning of the Peloponnesian war. They also indicate that the population as a whole must have grown at a prodigious rate. Here no precise figures can be given, but despite the emigration of many thousands of Athenians to colonies, the number of citizens seems to have increased very substantially. Both these movements were the result of a great increase in the national income of the Athenian people, due in part to the expansion of trade and industry, in part to the intensive exploitation of the silver mines, but mainly to the income, distributed in wages, from the Empire, and the acquisition of land in the Empire, privately by purchase or mortgage, and publicly in colonies and cleruchies. This increase in wealth meant both that larger families survived and the population thus expanded, and that a larger proportion of citizens qualified as hoplites; the second movement was probably accentuated by the drop in the real value of the hoplite census caused by rising prices.

During the thirty years of the Peloponnesian war there seems to have been as sharp a fall both in the hoplite class and, though here again no figures are available, in the population generally. This was due to some extent to heavy war casualties, but more to the Plague: for the former would in normal circumstances have had little permanent effect, but the latter, through the presumably heavy mortality among children, would have brought about a lasting decrease. Probably as important as, if not more important than, these factors, however, was the fall in prosperity, due to the devastation of Attica, the decline of productive industry and trade, and in the later stages of the war, the closing of the silver mines, and the loss of imperial revenue and of landed property overseas. These factors would have both reduced many hoplites to thetic status, and have checked the recovery of the population in general. The full effect of the closing of the silver mines and the loss of the imperial revenue and overseas possessions would not have been felt till after the end of the war, when the population seems to have sunk to a figure below what it had reached in the early fifth century.

INDEX OF PASSAGES CITED

LITERARY AUTHORITIES

N

INSCRIPTIONS

GENERAL INDEX